Sign up for our newsletter to hear
about new and upcoming releases.

www.ylva-publishing.com

Other Books by Jae

BACHELORETTE Number Twelve

Jae

Acknowledgments

Every writer knows it takes a village to write a book, and that's certainly true for my novels. I work with more beta readers than most writers, and I wouldn't want to write a book without a single one of them!

A big thank-you to my amazing team of alpha and beta readers: Trish and Melanie for the overnight delivery service and for being amazing friends; Chris Zett, Mae, Ashley, and Kathy for keeping an eye on the medical details; Pat for being the Kansas City native who helped with the setting; Andi, Nate, Declan, MJ, and Cam for beta reading the Riley scenes; Julie for proofreading; and Anne-France for enthusiastically declaring *Bachelorette Number Twelve* her new favorite early on.

I'm also grateful to my editor, Claire Jarrett, for taking on this project despite her busy schedule.

Chapter 1

ELLIE STOOD ON HER TIPTOES on top of the ugliest orange plastic chair she'd ever laid eyes on, stretching to the right as far as she could, when a pair of sneakers squeaked to an abrupt stop behind her.

"That better be a workplace safety demonstration on what *not* to do," a cool voice cut through the background noise in the emergency department. It drowned out the steady beep of cardiac monitors, a ringing phone, and loud coughing from one of the treatment cubicles.

Ellie dropped to her heels and glanced over her shoulder.

Dr. Regina Novak loomed in front of her, athletic arms folded across her blue scrub top and her full lips compressed into a disapproving line. "This"—she jerked her chin in the direction of Ellie's feet on the chair—"is exactly how many of our patients end up in the ED."

She was right. Of course Ellie knew that. But the doctor's superior tone grated on her nerves. One of the reasons she enjoyed being an ED nurse was that emergency physicians tended to be more laid-back, not as abrasive and arrogant as some of the surgeons.

Clearly, Dr. Regina Novak was the exception. She was all the stereotypes about doctors with God complexes rolled into one five-foot-ten package—an admittedly gorgeous package, but that was beside the point. She had rubbed Ellie the wrong way ever since Dr. Novak's first day as a new attending at Campbell Medical Center, and every interaction in the seven months since had only cemented that first impression.

"I'll be right down. I just need to…" Ellie stretched to her right again and pinned the end of the string to the wall. "There. All done."

Dr. Novak squinted at the string of paper hearts as if Ellie had fixed alien artifacts to the wall. "What is that?"

Ellie gazed down at her from on top of the chair. Was it childish that she enjoyed being able to look down at the tall doctor for once? Reluctantly, she jumped down. "Paper hearts," she said with what she hoped to be a disarming smile.

"I can see that." Dr. Novak gripped the lanyard that held her hospital ID as if she wanted to strangle Ellie with it. "I mean, why are you putting that up here?"

Wasn't it obvious? "Because February is the month of love, and tomorrow is Valentine's Day. I thought putting up some decorations would cheer up our patients and create an uplifting atmosphere."

"This is an emergency department. The least uplifting and romantic place on earth," Dr. Novak replied coolly. "People come here because they are sick or injured and need help. I doubt they feel like celebrating anything, least of all this commercialized nonsense holiday."

Ah. Ellie should have known Dr. Novak didn't have a romantic bone in her body. "It's not just for the patients," she said quietly. "The staff could use a boost of morale too. We have several couples who'll spend Valentine's Day working. What's wrong with celebrating their love by putting up some paper hearts here and a few balloons in the break room?"

At the mention of balloons, Dr. Novak's jaw tightened even more. "We need to focus on functionality. This stuff will get in the way."

"Up there?" She couldn't be serious.

"It's inappropriate."

Ellie had a feeling Dr. Novak could keep up this silent stare-down until their shift ended. Time to play her trump card. "Not according to the charge nurse and the director of nursing. I cleared it with them."

Dr. Novak sent her a look that could have saved all the glaciers in Antarctica from melting, but since the director of nursing had okayed the Valentine's Day decorations, there was nothing she could do about them. "At least tie it in with American Heart Month. Hang up a poster to raise awareness about cardiovascular diseases or something."

Did this woman ever think of anything but medicine? "Sure," Ellie said. "I can do that."

After one last glare up at the offending paper hearts, Dr. Novak strode away. "And get a step stool before you break your neck," she called back over her shoulder. "We can't afford to be short-staffed this week."

Ellie playfully clutched her chest behind Dr. Novak's back. *Wow, such heartfelt concern. Thanks, Doc.* She seriously doubted Dr. Novak had a date for Valentine's Day, but if she did, Ellie pitied the poor person.

"You're not still glaring at the poor paper hearts, are you?"

Regina lowered her gaze from where she'd been staring at the wall.

Dr. Kayla Vaughn, the night shift attending who would relieve her, leaned against the counter at the workstation. She had her braids tied back into a bun and was already equipped with three of the most important tools of their trade: a tablet computer, the stethoscope in her pocket, and a large cup of coffee.

"What? No, of course not." Regina had managed to ignore the paper hearts since Ellie had put them up the day before. "Just relaxing my eyes while I'm thinking about how to phrase 'accidentally swallowed the engagement ring her boyfriend hid in the chocolate mousse' on the discharge sheet."

Kayla laughed. "Sounds like an interesting shift."

Regina gave a noncommittal grunt. "The usual."

"Candle burns, lacerations from cutting flowers, and allergic reactions to chocolate candy hearts?"

"Check, check, and check." Regina drew three check marks in the air. "Crossed off every square on the Valentine's Day ED bingo card. February 14 should be considered a health hazard."

"Oh, so it's not just the paper hearts you hate; it's Valentine's Day in general."

"Nonsense," Regina said. "I couldn't care less if other people want to waste their hard-earned money on cheesy cards and overpriced chocolate."

The charge nurse looked over and raised one eyebrow.

"Aww, come on," Kayla said. "It's the celebration of love."

"Oh yeah," Regina muttered. "I'm sure Hallmark, florists, and jewelry stores love and celebrate all the extra cash they're making."

Kayla shook her head at Regina. "You might change your mind and stop hating Valentine's Day once you meet that special someone."

"Doubtful." The supreme silliness of Valentine's Day wouldn't change, even if her relationship status did. Besides, who said she was looking for a special someone? She was perfectly happy on her own, thank you very much. "And I told you I don't hate it. I just hate distractions while I'm working." Regina flicked her gaze up toward the damn string of paper hearts. "In our job, distractions can cost lives."

Kayla chuckled into her coffee. "Don't you think you're being overly dramatic? I don't think anyone will die because Ellie put up a few Valentine's Day decorations."

Okay, maybe not. But it was still annoying as hell. They were a hospital, not a preschool that put up badly done paper cut-outs for every holiday that came along. What was next? Ellie wanting to organize an Easter egg hunt in the ED?

Besides, it wasn't only the decorations that annoyed her. It was that Ellie had—once again—gone straight to the higher-ups in the hospital hierarchy instead of asking her and the other attending physicians.

Apparently, that was becoming a habit with Ellie. In their first week of working together, she had gone above Regina's head and complained to the chief of the emergency department because she was convinced Regina had delayed the treatment of a patient with an abscess on his arm because he was a drug user and didn't have health insurance.

Ridiculous. Regina remembered that patient well—she remembered every drug-using patient with an abscess—and the last thing she would ever do was to unnecessarily delay the kind of treatment that could have saved her brother's life.

She slashed her hand through the air, ending that line of thought. Enough about abscesses, Ellie, and that cheesy holiday. She finished writing the discharge order, closed the digital chart, and pointed at the intake board up on the wall. "I've worked some serious magic clearing the board before the end of my shift. Only two patients left for you to take care of."

Kayla gave a low whistle. "Just when I thought you weren't into giving gifts on Valentine's Day! What have we got?"

"The patient in exam one presented with pain in his jaw. No chest pain or shortness of breath, but a BP of 170/115 with no prior history of hypertension." Regina gave her colleague a meaningful look.

"Smoker?" Kayla asked.

Regina nodded. "Two packs a day. The EKG is inconclusive, and we're still waiting for the cardiac enzyme labs. In exam two, we've got one of the Valentine's Day victims. She and her boyfriend were trying to spice things up in the bedroom by using a sex swing, and somehow, her head went through the drywall."

Kayla whistled quietly. "And you thought romance was dead."

Regina ignored the comment. "Anyway, she lost consciousness for a minute, and she's got a headache, but no neck stiffness, nausea, or blurry vision. Her GCS is fourteen. She's waiting for a CT scan to rule out something more serious than a concussion."

"Great. I'll take over, then, so you can leave," Kayla said. "Any plans for your days off?"

Regina shrugged. "Sleep." She wasn't one for small talk or sharing details about her private life with co-workers.

"Are you going to the Heart-to-Heart Auction on Friday?"

"Heart-to-Heart Auction?" Regina repeated. Her colleague made no sense at all.

"You haven't heard about it? How's that even possible? The nurses, techs, and residents have talked about nothing else all week!"

Regina gave another shrug. She was there to work, not to chat about everyone's social calendar.

"It's our annual charity event," Kayla continued. "Twelve of Kansas City's most eligible singles, many of them CMC staff, will be auctioned off for a good cause. It's always great fun, plus all the money raised goes to our pediatric cardiac care program."

"Sounds, um, nice." Well, at least the part about the proceeds going to sick children. Watching desperate singles bid on the people gullible enough to volunteer was about as nice as getting puked on by a patient with food poisoning. "But I wasn't planning on going. See you next shift."

When she got up and headed toward the locker room, Kayla quickly put down her coffee mug and jogged after her. "Um, wait. I'm actually helping organize the auction, and I'm not just filling you in on the details to make small talk. Marissa was supposed to be one of the bachelorettes, but she bailed at the last minute, and now I'm wondering if you might consider covering for her."

"You mean…covering her shift?"

"I mean climbing up on the auction block and," Kayla stepped closer, waggled her eyebrows, and lowered her voice, "selling your body to the highest bidder."

Regina gave her the kind of look she normally reserved for fresh-out-of-med-school residents who were about to do something that would get a patient killed.

Kayla gulped audibly. "I'm kidding. It's not like that. The bachelors and bachelorettes are only auctioned off for a few dates—just dinner and some other fun activities. You don't even need to kiss your date. All you have to do is strut down the catwalk and smile while they bid on you."

That mental image did nothing to convince Regina otherwise. Letting herself be auctioned off like a slab of meat? No, thanks. "Hard pass."

"Oh, come on! It's for the children!"

"I'd be happy to make a donation," Regina said.

Kayla shook her head. "We don't need you to write a check. We need a replacement for Bachelorette Number Twelve."

"Ask someone else." Anyone else. Regina looked around, and her gaze landed on Ellie, who was sitting out of earshot at the nurses' station, charting. With her long, brunette hair that shone beneath the fluorescent lights and her warm smile that soothed even their youngest patients, she would surely be popular with bidders. "What about her? She clearly enjoys all that romantic stuff." She unobtrusively nodded in Ellie's direction.

Of course, Ellie chose that moment to glance up from the digital chart. She gave Regina a questioning look, but not even a hint of her typical smile dimpled her cheeks.

Regina was used to it. Ellie had taken a dislike to her from day one. Well, the feeling was mutual.

She gave Ellie a quick never-mind wave.

"Ellie was a bachelorette a few years ago, and she did great, but you know people. Everyone dreams of nabbing a doctor, not a nurse. I bet you'd raise a chunk of money for the children."

"Why don't you do it, then?" Regina shot back. "Last I checked, you were a doctor too."

"Sorry, I can't." Kayla pointed at her wedding ring, which she wore on a chain around her neck. "Being single is a requirement."

Regina folded her arms across her scrub top. "What makes you think I'm single?"

"Oh, I don't know… Maybe your cynical attitude toward Valentine's Day," Kayla muttered.

Regina pierced her with a glare that made Kayla gulp again.

"Okay, okay. You didn't correct me earlier when I said you'd appreciate Valentine's Day once you found your special someone. Plus emergency medicine is a small world. I know people who know people who did their residency at Cedars-Sinai too."

"Then your spy network probably also told you that I'm gay. I'm sure that disqualifies me as a bachelorette." Regina didn't usually find it necessary to out herself to her colleagues, but she wasn't ashamed of her sexual orientation and wasn't above using it to get out of this silly auction.

"Why would it?" Kayla asked. "You can keep it strictly platonic. Besides, who said only men would bid on you? The women-loving ladies in the audience deserve to have a hottie to bid on too."

Regina tilted her head in vague acknowledgment. "True, but—"

"Great!" Kayla clapped her hands. "So I can add you to the lineup?"

"I really don't—"

"Please say yes. It'll be fun. Plus it'll do wonders for your reputation."

"My *reputation*?" Regina drew out the word. Her reputation as an emergency physician was stellar. She had graduated at the top of her class from Harvard Medical School and had been the chief resident of her residency program. Her reputation didn't need any help, least of all from an absurd event where she would be auctioned off like livestock.

"Yeah," Kayla said. "Doing the charity auction will go a long way to convince the nurses you're not a stuck-up snob who believes she's better than everyone else."

Regina huffed. "No one thinks that."

Kayla gave her a look.

Well, even if they did, Regina didn't give a rat's ass. She was here to do her job, not to win a popularity contest with the nursing staff.

"Then prove it. Prove you're a team player by becoming our twelfth bachelorette." Kayla nudged her. "Come on. You know I wouldn't be asking you for this favor if I weren't desperate."

Regina made a face. "Thanks a lot. Maybe it's a good thing you aren't allowed to be a bachelorette—your compliments are seriously lacking."

"You know what I mean. Pleeeease! You don't want me to be distracted at work because I'm worried about having to find a replacement, do you?"

Before Regina could answer, Ellie rushed over from the nurses' station. "EMS just called in. They're en route with a thirty-five-year-old female in acute respiratory distress due to anaphylaxis. She's got a history of nut allergies, and the husband thinks she might have accidentally eaten some chocolate that contained almonds."

Ugh. Another Valentine's Day victim. Adrenaline flooded Regina, and she opened her mouth to ask for their ETA. Then she remembered that her shift was over and she had handed off the baton to Kayla.

"They're two minutes out," Ellie said as if anticipating her question anyway.

Kayla rattled off orders, then turned back toward Regina. "I'll add you to the lineup, okay?"

Regina took a deep breath to tell her she'd let herself be auctioned off when hell froze over.

But Ellie's gaze went back and forth between them, then came to rest on Regina. She cocked her head, probably waiting to see who would take charge of the incoming patient.

Or maybe she knew what Kayla had asked Regina to do and was curious to find out if Regina had the guts to step onto the auction block.

The wail of a siren started up in the distance, then quickly grew louder.

Regina gritted her teeth. This wasn't the time for silly arguments. *Ah, to hell with it.* No way would she let Ellie think she was scared to get up on stage when Ellie had already done it. Besides, it was for the children. "All right. I'll do it. But you owe me big-time!"

Kayla jogged toward the trauma bay. "Thanks," she called back over her shoulder.

As Regina headed toward the locker room to change into her street clothes, a heavy weight seemed to settle on her shoulders. Why did she have a feeling she would end up regretting this?

Chapter 2

THE FRIDAY AFTER VALENTINE'S DAY, Ellie entered the lobby of the historic Muehlebach Hotel, careful not to get her coat or her best dress caught in the revolving doors. The heels of her pumps echoed across the intricate tile floor.

"Wow." Two steps into the lobby, she stopped to take it all in.

Beth bumped into her from behind. "Hey, careful! You can't just—!"

She paused next to Ellie, and now both stood and stared.

The Muehlebach, once *the* place to stay in Kansas City, wasn't used as an active hotel anymore, just for special events like the Heart-to-Heart Auction. Clearly, whoever had decorated the lobby for the auction loved Valentine's Day as much as Ellie did.

Red, heart-shaped helium balloons crowded around the crystal chandeliers on the high ceiling. Two bouquets of red roses flanked the mantel of the giant marble fireplace. Pink ribbons twisted around the square mahogany columns, and swathes of blood-red cloth were draped above the ornamented brass elevators to the left and right. Cupid figurines perched in the key slots behind the marble-topped front desk, each one holding a tiny bow with a golden, heart-tipped arrow. A romantic love ballad played in the background.

"Hey, you two!" Jasmine stuck her head out of the elevator door she held open for them. "Are you coming? The ballroom is up there."

More dressed-up people entered through the revolving door behind them, so Ellie hurried forward as fast as her unfamiliar footwear allowed and squeezed into the tiny elevator with her friends and colleagues.

The ballroom upstairs was as elegant as the lobby. Red and white balloons formed two huge, intertwined hearts on one of the walls. Crystal chandeliers hung from the ornamented ceiling, throwing their soft light on an elevated stage and a connected catwalk that extended into the room. Countless round tables, all draped with white linen, took up every bit of space. Ornate chairs with crimson velvet covers were arranged around each one.

This was huge! No comparison to the much smaller ballroom and stage they had started out with their first year, when Ellie had been talked into letting herself be auctioned off. She hadn't been able to attend the past two years because she'd worked the night shift. While she had heard the event had grown and attracted more philanthropists and donors, seeing the impressive changes still took her by surprise.

The auction attendees looked more polished too. All around them, people in tuxedos, sequined ball gowns, and cocktail dresses mingled, chatting over canapés and champagne. She caught sight of purses that probably cost more than she made in a month.

"Why do I suddenly feel like Cinderella at the ball?" Ellie whispered to Beth and Jasmine. This so wasn't her crowd. If the hospital hadn't given them tickets, security might have kicked them out.

Beth nodded, wide-eyed. "Yeah, Cinderella *after* the stroke of midnight!"

"Well, Cinderella found her prince at the ball, so…" Jasmine dragged them with her toward the open bar.

Apparently, the event organizers thought people would bid higher after they'd had some liquid encouragement—and they were probably right.

"You know I'm not interested in princes," Ellie said.

Jasmine waved her hand. "Fine, a princess for you, then. Have you thought about who you'll bid on?"

Ellie firmly shook her head. "I'm not going to bid."

"Why not? It's an auction, Ellie. That's why we're here. To bid on the hotties."

"I'm here to support our colleagues and a good cause," Ellie answered.

"Me too—with my wallet. I think at least one of us should walk out of here with one of KC's most eligible bachelors…or bachelorettes. Preferably one of us who hasn't been on a date in forever." Jasmine gave her a meaningful look, which Ellie promptly ignored.

"I doubt we'll be able to outbid the Gucci and Prada folks," Ellie said.

"We will if we do it strategically," Jasmine said. "Just wait until the last couple of bachelors, when everyone else has run out of steam or money."

"The best strategy doesn't change the fact that all the bachelorettes are probably as straight as an arrow."

"Maybe," Jasmine said with a grin. "Maybe not."

What was that supposed to mean? As far as Ellie knew, none of the doctors and paramedics up for auction were gay or bi.

"You could still bid," Beth threw in before Ellie could ask. "Remember that you're not just bidding on the guy or gal but on the entire package."

"No, thanks," Ellie muttered. "I'm not interested in anyone's package."

Jasmine and Beth burst out laughing.

Ellie's cheeks heated despite the cool temperatures in the ballroom. "I didn't mean it like that! I was talking about the date packages, like dinner at a posh restaurant, a private suite at a Chiefs game, and stuff like that!"

"Sure you were!"

Her friends were still chuckling as they reached the front of the line at the bar.

Ellie took a moment to read the list of Valentine's Day cocktails behind the bar, then decided on one called Love Potion Number Nine.

Once they had their drinks, Jasmine insisted they register for auction paddles before they headed to their table, which was toward the back.

"I won't use mine," Ellie said as she put her numbered paddle down on the table next to the roses centerpiece. "Unless it's to give you a swat if you don't stop trying to convince me otherwise."

Jasmine giggled. "Ooh! I had no idea you're into spanking."

Ellie picked up the paddle and lightly swatted Jasmine's shoulder. "Why are we friends with her again?" she asked Beth.

Beth held up both hands, palms out, in a leave-me-out-of-this gesture. "I'm actually with her on this. You need a date, my friend. You haven't been out with anyone in at least six months, not even on Valentine's Day."

"Hey, it's not that I'm not open to dating." In fact, she would love to meet someone special. She just wasn't desperate enough to buy herself the company of a woman. "But I'm not forcing it. My soulmate will come into my life when the time is right. I doubt it'll happen tonight, though. In fact, my bank account says it *definitely* won't happen tonight. The auction is strictly a spectator sport for me."

"How can you be such a romantic yet so pragmatic at the same time?" Jasmine studied her with a shake of her head.

Ellie grinned. "It's called multitasking. I can even walk and chew gum at the same time."

"Oh yeah?" Jasmine poked her with the auction program. "I remember a certain nurse who sent an emesis basin flying because she couldn't walk and stare at a certain doctor at the same time."

Ellie resisted the urge to fan herself with the paddle. "I wasn't staring at her." Okay, maybe she had been. Dr. Novak was an attractive woman—objectively speaking. But the initial *wow* had turned into *ugh* within a minute of meeting her. "I was merely pausing to introduce myself. Unlike her, I have manners."

Jasmine chuckled. "Yeah, you introduced yourself by throwing the basin at her feet."

Ellie's cheeks burned. "It was an accident. No reason to ignore me and not even introduce herself."

"She didn't introduce herself to me either," Beth said, "so don't take it personally. We've all worked with doctors like that. If you don't have an MD behind your name, they think you're not worth talking to."

"Yeah, a few are arrogant assholes, but some just come across as cold and snobbish, while they're really sizzling hot." Jasmine turned around the auction program and showed them the picture of a bachelor, his shirt half unbuttoned and a red rose clenched between his toothpaste-commercial-white teeth.

Beth took a look. "Nope, not him. He might be hot, but he's an ass too. My friend who works in the OR says he's got only one volume: shouting."

"Oh." Jasmine folded the corner of the dog-eared page back up.

While her friends leafed through the program, Ellie leaned back to people-watch. She hummed appreciatively as she sipped her Love Potion Number Nine. *Yum.* The pomegranate juice, strawberry vodka, and black raspberry liqueur blended together into the perfect mix of sweet and tart. Heart-shaped strawberries were skewered on a Cupid's arrow that rested on the glass.

Jasmine held her champagne flute with one hand while flipping through the program with the other, studying the bios and photos of the bachelors with the kind of attention some of Ellie's married lesbian friends gave picking out a sperm donor. Every now and then, she folded back one of the pages.

Ellie couldn't help grinning as she watched her. "You're really serious about this, aren't you?"

Jasmine nodded without looking up from the program. "You bet your sweet ass I am," she said with a determination she usually reserved for saving lives as an ED nurse. "I—"

"Shh, it's starting!" Beth pointed toward the stage.

Ellie turned so she was facing the front of the room.

A blond guy walked up to the podium and leaned in to the microphone. "Welcome to the fourth annual Heart-to-Heart Auction! I'm Noah Hanson from *Soundbites* on KRCX radio, and I'll be your emcee for the night!"

Someone in the front of the room let out a wolf whistle, giving Ellie a good idea of how rowdy the evening might get, despite how refined this crowd looked.

The emcee laughed. "Sorry, I'm not up for grabs tonight, but if you've had a chance to leaf through our program, you'll have noticed that we have an amazing lineup of twelve of KC's most eligible singles braving the catwalk. All proceeds will go to the pediatric cardiac care program at Campbell Medical Center, so don't be shy—bid high and often." He made a dramatic pause. "So, without further ado… Here's your first bachelor!"

Jasmine leaned forward as if preparing herself for a sprint. "Get ready, girls! One of us is getting herself an eligible hottie!"

Ellie pulled one of the strawberries off the arrow-shaped skewer and popped it into her mouth. Even if Jasmine's prediction came true, one thing was for sure: it wouldn't be her.

"Do it for the children, she said. It'll be fun, she said," Regina muttered as she waited in the wings of the stage.

Nearby, two of the bachelors—both surgeons—were betting on which of them would go for more money.

Regina bit her lip so she wouldn't tell them to shut up. Her feet ached in those damn three-inch heels, and her patience was wearing thin.

Why, oh why had she let Kayla rope her into this? And why couldn't she be among the first to be auctioned off instead of the last one?

She wasn't nervous. Of course not. She handled cardiac arrests, strokes, and subdural hematomas for a living, bringing people back from the brink of death on a regular basis. A silly auction wouldn't make her sweat.

Standing around, waiting, had just never been her thing. She was a woman of action.

But as much as she hoped for a last-minute miracle that would get her out of this, she knew it wouldn't happen. The only way out was through.

She took a step forward and peeked through a tiny gap in the burgundy velvet curtain.

On the catwalk, one of the respiratory therapists took off his shirt and waved it over his head like a lasso. Apparently, the two surgeons had successfully convinced him that a striptease was expected of each bachelor, even though Kayla had told them it was fine to keep it PG-rated. He turned, gyrated, and flexed his butt in the direction of the audience.

Regina groaned. *Ugh.* She would have to work with him again during her next shift and so didn't need this mental image. Quickly, she looked away and scanned the crowd instead.

The audience seemed to be having a great time. Everyone was laughing, clapping, whistling, catcalling, and tossing back champagne as fast as the waiters could serve it.

Well, everyone except for one woman.

Regina's gaze paused on a familiar face in the crowd.

Ellie sat at a table toward the back, sipping a cherry-red drink that looked like one of those disgustingly sweet cocktails. She smiled politely but seemed unimpressed by the RT's on-stage antics.

Would that smile waver when she saw Regina walk out onto the stage? Would she lose respect for her as a professional when Regina had to strut around and show some leg to drive up the bidding?

What do you care? It wasn't as if Ellie seemed to have much respect for her anyway.

But truth be told, Regina did care. Not really about Ellie's opinion, of course. She had always kept up a professional demeanor at work, though. Only once had her colleagues gotten a glimpse of the woman behind the white lab coat, and afterward, nothing had been the same.

Well, this isn't work. Besides, according to Kayla, Ellie had been a bachelorette in the past, so she wasn't in a position to judge.

For a second, Regina wondered what Ellie had worn up on stage. Had she danced, twirled, or flashed a bit of cleavage to drive up the bidding?

No, no, no, no. Don't think about it. She's someone you work with. Someone you don't even like. She doesn't have cleavage.

But even at this distance, her eyes told her otherwise. Ellie actually looked fantastic in a simple but flattering red dress.

Not that Regina cared about that either. She just wasn't used to seeing Ellie in anything but scrubs.

"Are you ready?" the stage manager asked from behind her.

Regina turned and gave her a questioning glance.

"You're up after him." The stage manager waved her clipboard at one of the surgeons.

The other one had stepped out onto the stage without Regina noticing.

Regina braced her shoulders and gave a stiff nod. "Ready."

It didn't take long before the emcee's voice filtered through the buzz of the crowd as he called out, "Please welcome our last bachelorette of the night, Dr. Regina Novak!"

He drew out her name as if she were a boxer about to step into the ring—and Regina felt like that too.

It's for the children, was her last thought before she pushed the curtain aside, plastered a confident grin onto her face, and walked out onto the stage.

Ellie clutched her paddle with both hands. Had she misheard over the clapping and hooting, or had the emcee just announced Regina Novak as Bachelorette Number Twelve?

Quickly, she flipped through the program. Bachelorette Number Twelve was supposed to be one of their fourth-year residents. Dr. Novak's picture was nowhere to be found, but there was no mistaking the woman now stepping out into the spotlight.

She strode across the stage with the same confidence Ellie had watched in the ED a hundred times before. But unlike those times, Dr. Novak wasn't wearing scrubs now.

Her black, formfitting halter-neck dress showed off her slim figure and left her toned arms and shoulders bare. Its broad strap crisscrossed above her breasts and framed her elegant neck. The hemline ended several inches above the knees, revealing her long legs as she strutted down the catwalk in a pair of high heels that could have been classified as lethal weapons.

Jesus, she had gorgeous legs! Okay, gorgeous *everything*, but she was still an arrogant ass.

Dr. Novak paused in the middle of the catwalk and took up a confident, almost challenging stance. Unlike some of the other bachelors and bachelorettes, she didn't dance or strip.

Not that she needed to—she commandeered everyone's attention without any showy moves. Even the people who had lost interest in the auction and hung out at the bar now turned their heads.

The slightest hint of a smile played on Dr. Novak's lips. It seemed to dare the crowd to bid on her. Her chin-length, black hair, tucked behind one ear, shone like a raven's feathers under the bright stage lights.

Ellie's mouth had gone dry, and she'd finished her cocktail earlier, so she grabbed a champagne flute from the tray of a passing waiter and took a big gulp.

All right, Dr. Novak cleaned up unexpectedly well. So what? That didn't make up for her snobbish personality.

A loud whistle from Jasmine nearly pierced Ellie's eardrum.

"Jazzy!" Ellie clutched her ear. "Cut it out!"

"What? She's *hot* with a capital H!" Jasmine gave her a meaningful look. "And according to one of the EMTs who used to work with her in California, she also happens to be gay."

She is? Ellie hadn't known. She'd learned very little about Dr. Novak from the usually effective hospital rumor mill. Not that she had tried to find out anything about her, of course. "Oh? Um, I mean, so? Even if it's true, that doesn't mean I'll bid on her, if that's what you think. I can't stand her, so why would I pay for her company? Having to work with her is bad enough."

"Can't stand her. Mm-hmm. Right. That's why your eyes nearly bounced across the room when she walked out from behind the curtain."

Ellie tried to cross her arms over her chest but realized she was white-knuckling the auction paddle. "They did not. I just took a closer look to make sure it's really her. She looks very different in scrubs."

Jasmine chuckled. "She sure—"

"Shhh." Beth glared at them both. "You're missing her introduction!"

Ellie turned her attention back to what the emcee was saying.

"…has graciously agreed to step in for a colleague who couldn't make it."

Ah, so that was why she wasn't in the program. Ellie wondered who had talked Dr. Novak into stepping in and what they'd had to offer her in exchange. Surely she hadn't volunteered out of the kindness of her heart.

"Dr. Novak is an emergency physician by day and an avid piano player and disc golf athlete by night, so I think her date can safely assume she's good with her hands." The emcee gave an exaggerated wink.

Ellie cringed. She might not have liked the hospital's newest attending, but she appreciated comments like that even less.

Dr. Novak's annoyingly beautiful face remained impassive, however.

Despite her dislike, Ellie couldn't help admiring her composure.

"The three words that describe her best are calm, efficient, and inventive," the emcee said, reading from his notes.

Ellie suppressed a snort. *More like cold, arrogant, and dismissive.*

"The highest bidder won't just win a chance to experience Dr. Novak's renowned bedside manner; the package also involves a romantic ice-skating date at Crown Center, dinner at The Meadow, a surprise activity planned by our bachelorette, and a hands-on baking class for two, taught by Sasha Peterson, the baker who made Jenna Blake's wedding cake."

That sounded like fun! Too bad Ellie wouldn't get to do any of that.

"Let's start the bidding at one hundred dollars for that awesome date package with Dr. Novak." The emcee scanned the audience. "Do we have one hundred?"

"One hundred," someone shouted a few tables to Ellie's left.

She craned her neck to see who it was.

A guy with a comb-over and an expensive-looking tuxedo had stuck his paddle into the air.

"We have one hundred over here. Do I hear one-fifty?"

The bidding rapidly went up, then stalled at eight hundred.

Eight hundred for a date package! Ellie couldn't believe it. She'd paid less for her first car. Granted, it had been a piece of junk, but it had been hers.

"Come on, folks! Don't be shy! Getting to spend several dates with Dr. Novak will be worth every cent!" The emcee circled his finger at the doctor, encouraging her to strut her stuff to drive up the bidding.

Dr. Novak sent him a look that made him duck behind the podium. Then she sauntered down the catwalk with her head held high.

Now she was closer than before so Ellie could see the play of her lithe muscles with every confident stride. God, those legs! Ellie tried to take another sip of champagne, but not a drop of liquid hit her lips. She must have emptied the glass without realizing.

When Dr. Novak reached the end of the catwalk, she paused and gave the audience a sexy grin.

"Eight-fifty," the guy with the comb-over yelled.

For a second, Dr. Novak's gaze seemed to connect with Ellie's, and something flashed in her eyes. Irritation? Uneasiness? A cry for help?

Ellie shook her head at herself. *Ridiculous.* She had seen Dr. Novak talk down a drunk patient who had hurled bedpans at the nurses; she could handle going on a few dates with Mr. Comb-Over.

Then Dr. Novak did a slow turn and strode back down the catwalk.

"We've got eight-fifty from the gentleman with paddle number forty-seven," the emcee's voice boomed through the hotel's sound system. "Who'll give me nine?"

Jasmine nudged her. "Come on. Do it."

Ellie refused to answer. Sure, she had some money saved, but that was for emergencies. She would gladly donate half of it to the children's cardiac care program, but she wouldn't bid on a woman who had never said even one word to her that wasn't work-related.

Besides, Dr. Novak didn't need Ellie to rescue her. Someone else would bid in a second. Probably several someones because now the audience could see the back of the black dress—or rather, the lack thereof—for the first time.

The dress dipped low in the back, revealing an intriguing amount of bare skin…and the fact that she couldn't possibly be wearing a bra.

Ellie's mouth went as dry as the sandwiches in the hospital cafeteria. Where was a waiter when she needed a drink? She fanned herself.

"Great!" The emcee nodded approvingly at someone in Ellie's vicinity. "We've got nine hundred from the lady with paddle number thirty-three."

Ellie looked around to see who'd been bidding.

No one at the table to her right had paddle number thirty-three.

Neither did anyone at the table to her left.

And why were they all staring back at her or someone at her table?

With a sinking feeling, Ellie peered at Jasmine. "You didn't…? You wouldn't…!"

But Jasmine had put her paddle down next to the auction program, and it didn't have the right number either. She was smirking at Ellie.

"What?" Ellie mouthed.

Still smirking, Jasmine pointed.

It took Ellie's overheated brain a second to figure out what she was gesturing at.

The number thirty-three.

On the paddle she was using to fan herself.

"Wait, what?" Ellie stared at her traitorous hand and quickly lowered it to the table. "No, no, no, no, I didn't mean to bid! I just—"

"Anyone want to take it to nine-fifty?" the emcee asked. "Or a whopping thousand?"

Ellie shot Comb-Over Guy a pleading look, but he was talking to the man next to him and seemed to have given up on bidding.

"Nine hundred going once…"

Sweat broke out on Ellie's brow. She clutched the edge of the linen-draped table so she wouldn't fan herself and make the emcee think she was bidding again.

"Going twice…"

Come on. Someone. Anyone! Ellie's gaze bounced from table to table.

"And…sold to the lady in red with paddle number thirty-three." The thump of the gavel coming down on the podium echoed through the ballroom. "Let's give the highest bidder a round of applause for her generosity."

Loud clapping from the crowd around her reverberated in Ellie's ears. Or maybe it was her own thundering heartbeat.

Oh God. Ellie barely resisted the urge to bury her burning cheeks in her hands. She had accidentally bought herself several dates with a woman she couldn't stand.

Chapter 3

Finally, it was over! If the emcee had made one more unoriginal comment about her "hands-on" skills or a date with her being "just what the doctor ordered," Regina would have stripped off her heels and stabbed him with one.

She paused in the middle of the catwalk and squinted against the bright stage lights following her every step as she tried to make out who the highest bidder was. According to the emcee, it seemed to be a woman, so at least she wouldn't have to put up with a guy thinking he could take liberties because he'd paid for her company.

A spotlight moved through the ballroom in search of the "lady in red" who'd paid nine hundred dollars to go on a date with her.

Regina snorted quietly. What a complete waste of money! It had been quite some time since she had last been on a date. Most of them were as boring as dry toast.

And now she was about to find out how much worse it would be on a paid-for date.

The spotlight stopped on a table toward the back.

Regina lifted one hand to block out the glare of the stage light that made it impossible to see the crowd clearly from where she was standing now.

What the fuck?

The vision in red looked a lot like…

No, that couldn't be right. She lifted her other hand too and shaded her eyes. But another glance confirmed what she had thought she'd seen.

The highest bidder wasn't some mysterious stranger.

It was Ellie Fisher.

They stared at each other as if the crowd between them didn't exist.

What the hell was Ellie planning? She wasn't really after a date with her, was she? Was Ellie even interested in women?

Regina had no idea since she'd always made it a point to stay away from the emergency department rumor mill.

But even if Ellie was queer, she had never shown any kind of interest in Regina—certainly not enough interest to spend nine hundred of her hard-earned dollars on a date with her!

Ellie didn't exactly look ecstatic to have won the highest bid. The expression on her face resembled the one Regina had seen on patients when she told them they'd have to have surgery. Her cheeks had taken on the scarlet color of her dress, and she had slid lower in her seat as if she considered ducking beneath the table to hide from the beam of light.

Was she embarrassed that now everyone knew she had bid on Regina?

But then why had she done it? Was this some kind of power play? Revenge for Regina protesting the Valentine's Day decorations? Or an attempt to reverse their roles and be the one to call the shots during their dates?

If that was why Ellie had bid on her, she would be in for a surprise. Regina had no intention of turning into a meek damsel just because Ellie had shelled out a lot of money.

She cursed herself for ever agreeing to this silly auction as she tore her gaze away from Ellie and slipped behind the curtain.

But before she could change back into more comfortable clothes, the stage manager stopped her. "We've set up a short reception next door for our bachelors and bachelorettes to meet their winning bidders. If you'd follow me..."

Maybe it was for the best. They could sort this out right now, so they wouldn't have to talk about it at work and could keep their interaction in the ED strictly professional.

Regina marched down the hall and pushed open the door the stage manager indicated.

Her fellow bachelorettes and bachelors had already found their winners. Laughter and the clinking of champagne flutes echoed throughout the reception room as they toasted their upcoming dates.

Regina seemed to be the only one who didn't feel like celebrating. She looked around, searching for Ellie, but couldn't find her anywhere.

Probably still in the ballroom, writing a check for me. She grimaced—and, of course, that was the moment the door opened again and Ellie walked in.

"No, you don't understand," she said to the auction volunteer who'd walked her in. "I didn't mean to—" She stopped abruptly. Her big, brown eyes went deer-in-headlights-wide as she came face-to-face with Regina.

Avoiding awkward situations like this was why Regina had never dated anyone she worked with. But then again, she wasn't the one who had bought a date. Ellie had—and it was time to find out why.

Regina marched over to her.

"Dr. Novak, meet Ellie Fisher." The volunteer gestured back and forth between them. "Ms. Fisher, meet—"

Regina interrupted him with an impatient swipe of her hand. "Thanks. We know each other."

"Oh. Great. I mean… I'll leave you two alone, then." He scurried away, probably sensing the tense atmosphere.

Ellie looked as if she would have loved to rush after him. "Um, hi." She shuffled her feet in a way that was kind of cute.

No, Regina firmly told herself. Ellie wasn't cute. She was up to something. And Regina would find out what. Now. She pierced her with a stare she normally reserved for parents she suspected of abusing their kids. "Why did you bid on me?"

"I…I didn't mean to," Ellie blurted out.

Ouch. Despite some people accusing Regina of having a big ego, that kind of hurt.

"I was just…"

"What?" Regina snapped.

"Um, swatting at a fly with the paddle?" It sounded like a tentative question more than an explanation.

Regina squinted at her. "A fly?"

Ellie nodded while staring down at her pumps. "Yeah. A really big one."

"Remember the patient from last week? The one who came in with a flashlight stuck up his rectum and told us he slipped in the shower and fell on it?"

Head still down, Ellie nodded again.

"I'm getting the same feeling of being lied to right now."

Ellie peered up at her through a few strands of hair that had escaped the low bun at the nape of her neck. "I'm sorry. I really didn't mean to bid on you or embarrass you in any way."

It was easy to recognize that as the truth, but that made things even worse. "Embarrass me?" Regina repeated slowly. "I'm not embarrassed to be seen going out with a woman. But maybe you are."

Ellie swiped the loose hair back from her face with both hands and now fully looked at Regina for the first time. "Me? Why would I be embarrassed? Even the cleaning staff at CMC knows I'm gay."

"So...you do date women." Regina mentally kicked herself. There was no reason for her to take any interest in this new information. It didn't matter. "But you don't want to go on a date with me."

"Um, no." Quickly, she waved at Regina's dress but again glanced away as if trying not to stare. "I mean, no offense, you're beautiful and all, but..."

"But you don't like me."

Ellie looked up as if startled by Regina's bluntness. A light pink dusted her cheeks. But then she met her gaze. "Not overly, to be honest."

That took guts. Regina frowned at herself. Guts? What the hell was wrong with her? Ellie had openly insulted her, and yet she couldn't help admiring her. She set her jaw. "Well, the feeling is mutual, so it's clearly better to keep our interaction strictly professional. Let me go talk to one of the organizers. I'm sure I can get you your money back." She whirled around to march off.

"Wait!" Warm fingers wrapped around her bare arm.

Regina turned back around and glowered at Ellie's hand.

Ellie snatched it away. "Sorry. I... I don't think that's a good idea. The money goes to sick children, and it wouldn't feel right for them to pay for my mistake."

Mistake. Regina ground her teeth. "Right. We'll just tell them we went on our date, then. We don't actually have to go."

Ellie fiddled with the red satin bow at the waist of her dress. "Actually...we do."

"What?" Regina put her hands on her hips. For once, her three-inch heels were good for something, giving her even more of a height advantage. "What's that supposed to mean?"

"I was a bachelorette a few years back."

"Yes, I heard."

Ellie blinked. "You did?"

"People constantly think they have to catch me up on hospital lore. So?" Regina gave her an impatient wave. "What does you having been a bachelorette have to do with anything?"

"That's how I know we're expected to be seen together, having fun. The auction organizers are sending someone along to take photos, which they'll use to promote next year's auction. Plus the sponsors might post a few pictures on their social media too."

Great. Regina rubbed her eyes, not caring that she was probably messing up her makeup. "So we can't get out of it."

Ellie nibbled her full bottom lip. "No. Not unless we want to be complete a-holes who don't care about children with heart conditions."

Was it just her imagination, or was there a faint note of challenge in Ellie's tone? She didn't really think Regina would walk out now, sick kids be damned, did she? Of course she wouldn't! Regina squared her shoulders. She had made it through med school and eighty-hour work weeks as a resident. She could make it through one measly date. "Well, it's just a date. Not like we have to get married or anything."

Ellie fiddled with the bow at her waist again. "Actually, it's at least two."

Regina squinted at her. "Two what?"

"Dates." A twinkle entered Ellie's brown eyes. "Didn't you listen to what the emcee announced or read the fine print before you signed on the dotted line? The highest bidder wins an entire date package with four activities that we can stretch out over as many days as we want. We could do two activities over two days or each one separately over four days."

Two or four days? Kayla hadn't offered that information—probably because she'd been afraid Regina would back out if she knew. *Hell, yeah! I would have.* She rarely spent that much time with anyone, even the last woman she'd dated. She'd better pack her first aid kit because they'd surely kill each other before the first date was over.

The slight grin on Ellie's face faded. "You really didn't know? You thought all the activities the emcee mentioned would be squeezed into one date?"

Truth be told, Regina had barely listened to the emcee's silly babbling. Something about ice-skating was all she could remember. "Why not? If we plan it efficiently, we could get it all done within a few hours."

Ellie's grin reappeared. "Plan it efficiently? It's a date, not getting a polytrauma ready for the OR."

Too bad. Regina would have preferred handling a polytrauma. At least it wouldn't involve spending two days making awkward small talk with a co-worker she couldn't stand.

"Oh, come on," Ellie said as if reading her thoughts. "It won't be so bad. We can totally do this." She sounded as if she was giving herself a pep talk.

"Yeah."

"For the children," they both said at the same time.

They nodded at each other, then stood in silence for a moment.

The easy chatter of the other singles and their highest bidders drifted over.

"All right," Regina finally said. "Let's get this over with in as few days as possible."

"Two is probably doable," Ellie answered. "We could start with going ice-skating in the morning, then attend Ms. Peterson's baking class in the afternoon, if that's okay with her. Then we could knock out the last two activities on another day."

Regina suppressed a sigh and nodded.

"Do you want to give me your number?" Ellie asked, then added, "So we can compare shift schedules and agree on a day and time for our first, um, date."

That was probably a good idea. Getting Ellie's number from hospital admin would send rumors flying. She took the phone Ellie handed her and added her name and number.

"Thanks." Ellie took her phone back and glanced at the screen, then up at Regina. "Um, Dr. Novak?"

"Yes?"

"No, I mean, you put your name as Dr. Novak."

"Because it *is* my name."

Ellie's lips twitched, but Regina couldn't tell if she was suppressing a grimace or a smile. "It's your name at work. Do you seriously want me to call you 'Dr. Novak' while we're on a date?"

"A just-for-publicity's-sake date," Regina said.

"Still. It's not work-related, so we should be on equal footing." Ellie held her gaze. "If I kept calling you 'Doctor' over a candlelight dinner, I'd feel like I have a medical fetish."

Regina sighed. This was exactly why she didn't date co-workers. Mixing business with pleasure was never a good idea. Not that she expected there to be any pleasure on their dates. "Fine."

A smile dimpled Ellie's cheeks. "I can call you by your first name?"

"If you must."

"Well, I could call you Bachelorette Number Twelve if you prefer."

Regina fixed her with a glare as piercing as a scalpel. "Only if you want me to call you Paddle Number Thirty-Three."

"Okay, okay. First name it is."

Regina lifted one finger in warning. "Just while we're on a… while we're not at work."

"Of course." Ellie tapped a message into her phone, then slid it into her purse. "I just sent you a text, so you now have my number too."

Regina gave her a nod.

Another awkward silence descended on them.

"I guess I'll see you at the ice-skating rink," Regina finally said.

"Actually," Ellie said, "you'll see me at work before that."

A dull pounding crept up the back of Regina's neck. She pinched the bridge of her nose. "There's probably no chance of keeping this between the two of us, is there?"

Ellie's laughter sounded amused, not sarcastic. She gestured in the direction of the ballroom. "Have you forgotten how many nurses, doctors, paramedics, and RTs were in the audience?"

"So what will we tell them when they ask about our dates?"

"I guess that depends."

"On?"

An impish twinkle lit up Ellie's dark eyes. "How good or boring our dates are."

Regina raised both brows at her and put a growl into her voice. "Are you challenging me?"

"Well," Ellie said, again with that charming little smile, "I did pay nine hundred dollars, so…"

Regina was stunned into silence for a moment, not sure if she wanted to yell at her or kiss that damn grin off her lips.

Where had that thought come from? Of course there wouldn't be any kissing. None whatsoever. "Don't you worry," she finally replied. "I'll make sure you have the best dates ever. Um, strictly for publicity purposes, of course. Can't have you looking bored in the promo photos."

"Right. Can you even ice-skate? I hear you're from California."

So the hospital gossips were talking about her behind her back. *Great.* Regina flashed her teeth, not caring if it looked like a grin or a threatening growl meant to put Ellie in her place. "Guess you'll have to wait and find out."

Then, ensuring she had the last word, she pivoted on her heel and marched from the reception room.

I didn't just say that, did I? Ellie stared at Regina's retreating back—her nearly naked back. Why had she challenged Regina to provide a great date experience?

Any second, she would wake up and laugh about the ridiculous dream she'd had.

She pinched herself hard. Pain flared up her arm, but the bustling reception didn't turn into her cozy bedroom.

This was really happening. She had accidentally bought several dates with Dr. Novak.

With Regina, her mind helpfully supplied.

She couldn't believe she had insisted on calling the doctor by her first name. "It was that damn Love Potion Number Nine," she muttered. The cocktail had been stronger than she'd realized, loosening her tongue. The glass of champagne she had chugged down at the sight of all that smooth skin hadn't helped either.

"Love?" a voice said next to her. "Wow, you really got your money's worth if you're already talking about love!"

Ellie turned her head and groaned.

Of course. Just what she needed. Her sister Vickie stood there in her navy-blue dress EMT uniform and with a big grin on her face.

"Haha. Very funny." Ellie gave her a gentle swat on the shoulder. "What are you doing here? I thought you weren't planning on coming to the auction?"

"I wasn't. My friend Brandon talked me into it at the last minute." Vickie nodded toward one of the EMTs across the room.

"Wasn't he one of the bachelors?" Ellie asked.

"Yeah. He panicked and made me promise to bid on him in case no one else would." Vickie studied her. "Was that why you bid on the doc? Because she asked you to?"

Ellie snorted. "As if. She's got an ego the size of the western hemisphere. It would never cross her mind that no one would be bidding on her."

"So she's not paying you back the nine hundred dollars?"

Ellie shook her head.

"Shit, Ellie! That's a lot of money!"

"I know, I know." Ellie scrubbed both hands across her face, then remembered that she was wearing a bit of makeup and stopped. "At least it's going to a good cause."

"Yeah, but why did you bid on her?" her sister asked. "Just a few days ago, you couldn't stop complaining about Doctor McIcy, and all it took to change your mind was for her to flash some skin up on stage?"

"No. That's not—"

"You bid on her, didn't you?"

"Well, okay, yes, but... It's complicated."

Vickie laughed. "Oh, now I see what's going on! That's what you said when Mom and Dad found out you had faked being bad at math because you had a crush on the girl who tutored you."

Heat stung Ellie's cheeks. She vehemently shook her head. "This isn't like that. I didn't mean to bid. It was—"

"A Freudian slip of the paddle?"

Ellie ignored the comment. "I was just fanning myself with the paddle because…um, I got a little overheated."

Her sister gave her a knowing look. "Right."

"No, really. The only thing I'll be faking this time is having fun on a date with Regina."

"Ooh, it's *Regina* now?" Vickie drew out the name in a singsong tone.

Ellie sent a pleading-for-heavenly-intervention gaze up at the chandeliers. "It's hard to believe you're the older one. What am I supposed to do? Call her 'Doctor' while we bake heart-shaped cupcakes?"

Vickie grinned. "Could be fun."

"Like I said, no fun involved. I'm just doing this for the children."

"Yours and Regina's?"

Ellie tried to channel Regina by letting out an intimidating growl but ended up sounding like a cat with a hair ball. "The children in the cardiac care program."

"Right. You're doing this for charity. Going out with an attractive woman is going to be a big sacrifice on your part."

"Yep," Ellie said with an exaggeratedly destitute expression. "I'm going to suffer through every second of it. Now go see what Brandon wants. He's waving at you."

After one last amused grin, her sister finally strolled away.

Ellie watched her go with a shake of her head. She loved her family. But this time, Vickie's teasing was totally off. There wouldn't be any hand-in-hand skating—Regina would rip her arm out of its socket if she tried—and they definitely wouldn't feed each other cupcakes.

More likely, Regina would give her a lecture on the health hazards of eating too much sugar.

A sound somewhere between a sigh and a chuckle escaped Ellie. Yes, she would suffer through every single second of their dates, no matter how—objectively speaking—attractive Regina was. She couldn't even make up an emergency at work, as she had done a time or two in the past to get out of an awful date, since Regina worked in the same hospital and would instantly know she was lying.

Despite her usual optimism, she knew one thing for sure: February wouldn't be the month of love for her.

Chapter 4

AFTER THREE BUSY TWELVE-HOUR SHIFTS in a row, all that kept Ellie going was coffee, adrenaline, and the donuts from the break room.

Finally, an hour before her shift ended, the flow of incoming patients eased.

With a groan, she dropped onto a chair at the nurses' station to catch up on her charting.

Jasmine looked up from the lab report she was studying. "So? Any news?"

"About the boy who fell from the second-story window? We stabilized him and sent him upstairs to the ICU. I think he'll make it."

"That's great, but I meant…" Jasmine rolled her chair closer to Ellie's and lowered her voice. "Did you talk to Dr. Novak about your first date?"

"Um, no, not yet. She's on nights this week, covering for Dr. Vaughn, and I've been busy on days. You know how it is. All I did for the past three days was work and sleep." It was the truth, but not the whole truth. She hadn't known what to say, so she had waited, hoping Regina would contact her instead.

She hadn't.

Jasmine nudged her. "Ooh, speaking of the devil! There she is!"

Ellie glanced up.

Regina left the locker room down the hall, dressed in a clean pair of scrubs, her hair tied back into a stubby ponytail so it wouldn't get in the way. Instead of heading toward the nurses' station, she ducked into the break room, probably to get some coffee before her shift started.

Jasmine drilled her elbow into Ellie's ribs again. "Go talk to her!"

"Now?"

"Why not? It's qu—"

This time, Ellie was the one to nudge her before she could say *quiet* and then all hell would break loose. But maybe Jasmine was right. She should get this over with. The auction organizers and sponsors were waiting for them to confirm the dates. "Okay. I'll..." She waved in the direction of the break room.

Jasmine gave her a thumbs-up.

Ellie tried to appear entirely relaxed as she walked toward the break room and paused in the doorway.

The room was empty except for Regina. The wall-mounted TV showed a news program with the sound muted. Regina stood at the kitchenette, shoved a mug beneath the coffee machine, and pressed a button. Then, as if sensing Ellie's presence, she turned.

Their gazes met, but Regina didn't smile; she gave her a businesslike nod.

"Um, hi." Ellie hesitated, then entered the break room. "You're in early."

Another short nod.

Regina wasn't the chatty kind. Ellie wondered what they would talk about on their dates. Would they have anything to say to each other?

"Do you need me to take a look at a patient?" Regina asked.

"Oh. No. Dr. Silva already checked out all of mine. I was wondering..." Ellie took a step closer. "How is Thursday for you?"

Regina stared at her as if she had requested a unit of green blood.

"For our first date," Ellie added. "Didn't you see the email the auction organizers sent us? They want to know if Thursday would work for our first two date activities. I haven't replied yet, but I think we're both off on Thursday, right?"

Regina crossed the remaining space between them with one long stride. Her gray eyes sparked like a flintstone someone had struck against a piece of steel to make a fire. "This isn't the place to talk about it. But if you insist, at least don't call it a"—she lowered her voice to a sharp hiss—"date. The only thing that travels faster than an incoming ambulance is hospital gossip; you know that."

Ellie steeled herself against the stab of hurt piercing her chest. Would it really be so bad if people thought they were dating? It wasn't as if there was anything wrong with her. But apparently, she didn't measure up to

Regina's impossibly high standards. She shouldn't care, yet she did. "Half of the staff attended the auction, and the other half knew within two minutes of their first shift afterward. But fine, if you insist… How is Thursday for our first two not-a-date activities?"

She knew it was like waving a red flag at a bull, but she couldn't help it. Regina's abrasive attitude just rubbed her the wrong way.

Regina's full lips compressed into a thin line. After glowering at Ellie for a few more seconds, she unclenched her jaw. "Fine. When and where?"

"We'll have to confirm it with the auction organizers, but how about eleven o'clock at the Crown Center Ice Terrace? Ms. Peterson would like to start the baking class at one, if that works for us, so that would give us two hours for the ice-skating."

Regina nodded as if confirming a dentist appointment, then turned back toward the coffee machine, clearly dismissing her.

Ellie stared at her back. *Wow.* These dates were going to be the tensest in the history of womankind.

Regina kept her head held high as she left the break room and crossed the ED.

A nurse and a respiratory therapist stuck their heads together and whispered to each other.

Her skin crawled as she passed them. This hit too close to home. It reminded her of those weeks after Riley's death, when her colleagues had looked at her with a mixture of pity and curiosity, as if they wondered when she might fall apart or fail at her job—the way she had failed to save her brother.

Gritting her teeth, she slammed the door shut on that memory and triple-locked it.

The feeling of being watched didn't stop as she snatched an electronic chart tablet from the charging rack.

It had been like this all week. Ever since the auction, she felt the gazes of her colleagues following her around. As soon as she turned toward them, they all hastily looked elsewhere and pretended to be busy.

No one dared to say anything, but she knew they were talking about her. Her and Ellie.

Not that there was a *her and Ellie.*

Ellie openly calling it a date in the middle of the emergency department didn't help. Calling them *not-a-date activities* wasn't any better. In fact, it was worse.

Regina grimaced. It sounded as if they were arranging to meet up for no-strings-attached sex. She shoved the thought aside before any mental image had a chance to form.

She really should have texted Ellie to arrange their first…meetup while they weren't at work. Usually, she dealt with things by confronting them head-on, but this sudden collision of work and her private life had thrown her off-balance.

Or maybe Ellie herself had.

The way she refused to be intimidated, sometimes even challenging her… Regina wasn't used to that.

Truth be told, she had jumped at the chance to cover the night shift for Kayla, so she didn't have to work with Ellie for a few days.

But she couldn't avoid her forever. On Thursday, she would have to spend the entire day with her, ice-skating and baking.

So? It didn't mean she and Ellie had to get all chummy with each other. She would get their dates over and done with and go back to business as usual.

With a determined nod, she went in search of the day shift attending to relieve him.

Chapter 5

ELLIE PEERED ACROSS THE RED-PAVED Crown Center Square, past the fountain and several closed red, blue, and yellow umbrellas to the shopping center across the street.

She had no idea which direction Regina would be coming from—if she was coming at all.

It was ten minutes after eleven, and the first skaters were gliding over the ice of the outdoor rink beneath the billowing white canopy behind her.

The square was bustling, even on a weekday morning—families headed to LEGOLAND Discovery Center or the SEA LIFE Kansas City Aquarium, and tourists checked out the Hallmark headquarters—but so far, she hadn't spotted Regina anywhere.

Mitch, the photographer the auction organizers had sent, shuffled his feet next to her. "Looks like your date stood you up."

"Maybe she's just running late," Ellie said despite the sinking feeling spiraling through her stomach. She couldn't even identify what it was. Surely she should be relieved that she didn't have to spend the day with Regina. But despite her dislike for the prickly doctor, part of her had been curious to find out if there was a softer, less businesslike side to Regina away from the hospital.

She pulled her phone from her coat pocket to text Regina.

Oh! She had a message from her!

Had Regina texted to say she wasn't coming? Ellie swallowed as she tapped the screen.

ETA three minutes, Regina had texted.

That had been three minutes ago.

Regina was coming.

Ellie's shoulders sagged—just because it would have looked bad for the hospital and the auction if Regina hadn't shown. "She's on her way," she told Mitch.

Movement to her left drew her eye.

Regina was crossing the square toward them. She wasn't running. She was moving with the same determined but controlled strides Ellie had seen hundreds of times in the ED. But unlike at work, Regina's cheeks were flushed, either from exertion or from the winter temperatures. She wasn't wearing a hat or a scarf, and her hands were shoved into the pockets of her long, black wool coat.

Ellie shook her head as she watched her approach. Apparently, the rumor about Regina being from California was true. She clearly had no clue how to dress for Midwestern winters.

Regina took the stairs to the Ice Terrace two at a time. Her gaze brushed Mitch, then dismissed him to focus on Ellie.

Jesus, those gray eyes were intense and impenetrable like a thick wall of stone. Ellie refused to look away. "Hi."

Regina gave her a nod. "Hi."

No apology for being late? Regina might be a brilliant physician, but she had clearly failed Manners 101.

"What?" Regina said when Ellie continued to look at her.

"I wasn't sure you'd show."

A shadow darted across Regina's impassive face. For a moment, she appeared almost insulted that Ellie would think that. "I told you I'd be here. It's for the kids, after all. I merely miscalculated how bad traffic would be."

Mitch cleared his throat. "Well, this promises to be a lovely date."

Ellie bit back the giggle that rose up her chest. Okay, so this probably wouldn't be the most heartwarming date ever, but maybe she could at least use their time together to build up an immunity so she wouldn't find Regina so annoyingly attractive anymore. "Shall we go rent our skates?"

She had half expected Regina to bring her own instead of renting skates like a mere mortal, but then again, Regina was from California, so why would she own skates?

Regina just nodded and gestured for her to lead the way.

The entrance to the rental area was at the parking garage, so Ellie led them over to it. They walked past a colorful mural of people ice-skating.

A penguin on skates, wearing a red scarf and a fluffy hat, was grinning down at them from the wall to their right.

Ellie grinned back and pointed at it. "This one's new."

"So you've been here before?" Regina asked.

"Oh yeah. Skating at the Ice Terrace was an annual family tradition when I was a kid. I can remember coming here when I was barely tall enough to peer across the counter." Ellie nodded toward the high, pock-marked counter, where several people were lined up.

Regina didn't comment, but a lift of her perfectly shaped eyebrows communicated "you're barely tall enough now" as clearly as if she'd said it out loud.

They joined the people at the counter and waited their turn. The line moved slowly, giving them plenty of time to talk.

Regina didn't seem inclined to hold up her end of the conversation, so Ellie finally added, "I don't know if they still do it, but the first few hours of skating were always free on opening day. Plus there was free hot chocolate. Money was tight when I was growing up, so…"

She cut herself off. Why had she told Regina that? They weren't on a real date, trying to get to know each other.

"Ah," was all Regina said.

Was she judging Ellie's family for their financial struggles? Ellie couldn't tell.

"So you've got home-court advantage," Regina added.

Home-court advantage? What a weird way to phrase that. Ellie eyed her. "Um, you do know this is supposed to be a date, right? We're not trying to win a speed-skating competition."

"Right," Regina said, but there was a glint in her eyes.

Ellie gave her a warning look. "Seriously, Regina. No competitive stunts, please. I'm not in the mood to end up in our own emergency department on my day off."

Regina blinked at her.

"Did I say something wrong?"

"No. You just called me Regina."

"We agreed that I could call you that. Or do you prefer Gina?" Ellie asked. "I have a cousin who—"

"No," Regina said sharply.

"Reggie, then?" Ellie couldn't resist teasing her.

A low growl came from Regina.

"No? How about Ginny?" Ellie asked in her most innocent tone.

"Regina. Not Reggie. Not Gina. Not Ginny. Re-gi-na." She emphasized each syllable.

"Regina." Ellie repeated the name and found that she liked it. "It fits you." Crap, she hadn't meant to say that part out loud.

"How so?"

"Well, it means *queen*."

A muffled sound came from Mitch, as if he was trying to suppress a laugh.

The family in front of them moved to the side, making space at the counter, and Ellie quickly stepped forward before Regina could answer.

A minute later, they took a seat on a nearby bench to put on their gray rental skates.

Ellie laced them up tightly. She had a feeling she'd need the ankle support while skating with Regina.

Regina didn't feel like a queen at all as she hobbled over the blue rubber floor on the narrow blades, following Ellie and the photographer to the ice rink.

The scuffed skates felt stiff and heavy on her feet, and she hoped she wouldn't embarrass herself on the ice. She hated being less than competent at anything. Always had, but she hated it even more fiercely on their first date.

Just-for-publicity's-sake date, she reminded herself. It wasn't as if she was truly trying to impress Ellie.

But Mike—or whatever his name was—was taking up position next to the gate, camera at the ready to take photos of them while they skated.

Great. Every second of her embarrassing not-a-date activity would be well-documented.

The ice rink's overhead speakers were blaring some cheesy love song, which didn't improve her mood at all.

What on earth was supposed to be romantic about skating in circles, doing lap after lap like a hamster in a wheel?

Ellie passed through the gate without hesitation. Within seconds, she had found her balance on the ice and took two strokes to push away, gliding effortlessly. Then she twirled around in a circle. "Come on," she called back to Regina. "It's like riding a bike."

Regina scowled at her. Why did people say things like that? If this were like riding a bike, she would have brakes and a helmet. She hesitated. Should she tell Ellie she had never been ice-skating before?

Nah. Maybe she could fake her way through it. She was a pretty good athlete after all and usually took to new sports like disc golf immediately. Perhaps this would be the same.

Determined, she rolled her shoulders back and stepped onto the ice.

She didn't fall and counted that as a win. But she wasn't gliding smoothly. More like taking stutter steps. She probably looked like a newborn giraffe trying to walk for the first time, especially compared to Ellie's graceful form.

Regina imitated her stance, knees slightly bent, and set off. No way would she cling to the railing like a scared kid.

Okay. Left. Right. Left. Hey, this wasn't so b—

Her left foot slid too much to the side. She tried to compensate, lurched to the other side, and fell. Her butt collided with the hard ice, and her bare hands stung where she tried to break her fall.

Riley had always told her that her pride would be her downfall one day. He probably hadn't meant it literally, though.

Ellie skated back and slid to a stop in front of her. "Did you hurt yourself?"

"No. Probably just bruised my ass." *And my ego.*

"I can take a look at that later." Ellie snapped her mouth shut. A bright pink stained her cheeks. "I mean…"

Regina waved her off and tried not to picture Ellie taking a close look at her bare butt. "Thanks. I'm fine." She lifted up on one knee, then managed to get to her feet.

"It's been a while for you, huh?"

"Excuse me?"

The pink color of Ellie's cheeks turned into a dark crimson. "Since you ice-skated," she added quickly.

Oh. Regina really needed to get her mind off bare butts and anything else that involved naked skin. "Actually…never."

Ellie stared at her. "This is your first time?"

Christ, could she stop making everything sound so sexual? Regina glowered at her. "Like you said, I'm from California."

"Yeah, but there's ice-skating in California…right?"

"Of course there is. I just didn't have time for it."

"Ah." Ellie gave her a knowing look. "All work and no play?"

Regina had been accused of being a workaholic before. In fact, each and every woman she'd dated had told her so. But, of course, she had no intention of dating Ellie, so she didn't care what she thought. "I have my priorities. Ice-skating was never one of them."

"Why didn't you tell me you don't know how to skate?" Ellie shook her head, then held out her gloved hand for Regina to take. "Here, hold on to me until you get your sea legs."

"Ice legs," Regina said. "And I'm fine. I'll get the hang of it in a second."

Ellie put her free hand on her hip. "God, you're stubborn."

"And you aren't?" Regina nodded down at the hand Ellie was still holding out to her.

They stood staring each other down for several moments.

"Ooh, great idea," Mike called from the side of the rink. "Skating hand in hand makes for a very romantic picture. Let's try that."

Regina gave him a lethal glare. Maybe she should tell him she was a doctor and knew ways to kill him without leaving any evidence.

Ellie was still waiting, hand outstretched, head cocked to the side as if she wondered what the big deal was.

It wasn't, right? All she needed to do was hold Ellie's hand until the photographer had snapped a few pictures. It wasn't as if she'd been asked to get down on one knee and confess her undying love.

Reluctantly, she took Ellie's hand, which was encased in a screamingly pink wool glove. She made sure her own was on top.

Ellie chuckled. "Has anyone ever told you that you have control issues?"

"No one who lived to tell the tale," Regina answered.

"I didn't know death threats were part of the amazing date package I was promised." Ellie seemed far from intimidated, though. Her large, dark eyes sparkled with humor, as if poking fun at her.

Regina usually hated that, but she grudgingly respected Ellie for giving as good as she got. "Well, you did challenge me to provide a date that wasn't boring."

"Right. Come on, then." Ellie pushed off, pulling Regina with her. Despite her challenging tone, she skated slowly, her grip on Regina's hand gentle but steady.

The first lap was awkward. They made their way around the rink at the pace of two waddling penguins and probably looked about as elegant.

Well, at least she did. Ellie, however, clearly felt at home on the ice. She wasn't exactly an Olympic skater. There was nothing flashy about her skating; she didn't try to glide backward or attempt a pirouette, but each movement had a quiet, unassuming grace.

"Relax." Ellie squeezed her hand. "I won't let you fall."

Regina huffed. Her fingers felt stiff in Ellie's. "I'm not afraid to fall. But I doubt you could hold me up."

"Hey, I'm stronger than I look. And if not, I'll at least provide a soft landing." Grinning, Ellie indicated her ample curves.

Thanks for pointing them out. Regina really didn't need that encouragement. Instead, she focused on her goal: looking as proficient at skating as Ellie did by the time they passed Mike with his annoying camera again.

As they approached him, she tugged her hand back. "You can let go now."

"Are you sure?" Ellie asked.

"Of course. In fact, I'll race you. Last one to make it over there"—Regina pulled her hand free and pointed to the other side of the rink, at a banner that was left over from a Valentine's Day couples skate night—"buys dinner on our second date."

"Um, dinner is covered by our sponsor."

Regina shrugged. "Drinks, then."

"Okay," Ellie said and took off, whizzing down the ice.

"Hey!" Regina raced after her. Despite her longer legs, she knew she had no chance to reach the other side first if she followed Ellie along the edge of the rink, so she cut through the middle.

"Cheater!" Ellie shouted as Regina caught up with her.

"Ha! Look who's talking!" Regina shouted back.

For a few yards, they soared across the ice side by side, skating in sync.

The flow of air whipped Regina's hair back, but she didn't feel cold, just refreshed.

The sound of Ellie's laughter echoed around the rink, and Regina found herself grinning wildly.

A strange feeling washed over her—something lighthearted, almost giddy. Something she hadn't felt in so long, it took her a few seconds to identify it: she was having *fun*—with Ellie Fisher, of all people!

Ellie gave a burst of speed and shot ahead of Regina. She was mere yards from the couples skate night banner now.

Regina wasn't about to give up, though. She dug the edge of one blade into the ice and pushed off.

In her eagerness to win, she miscalculated how fast she was going and how hard she had pushed. Plus she had forgotten that she hadn't yet learned how to stop. She catapulted forward and slammed into Ellie from behind, just as she was about to reach the banner.

Somehow, they managed to stay on their feet. They sailed across the ice with Regina's front pressed against Ellie's back and her arms wrapped tightly around Ellie.

Maybe ice-skating wasn't as unromantic as she'd thought.

Then they slammed against the railing, and she shot out her hands to catch them both and stop them from somersaulting over the wall.

Ellie wasn't sure if she was living through her personal nightmare or a secret fantasy. She was pressed against the hip-high wall, with Regina's long hands grabbing on to the railing on either side of her, keeping her trapped between the wall and Regina's very warm body.

Regina had unbuttoned her coat, and her front pressed against Ellie's back from pelvis to chest.

"You okay?" Regina's voice rumbled through her, sounding as breathless as Ellie felt.

Her ragged panting, inches from Ellie's ear, sent puffs of hot air over the back of her head, stirring her hair.

A shiver went through Ellie, and it took her a moment to focus on other areas of her body. Pain flared through her knees and one hip, where she had hit the wall, and her hands smarted from catching herself against the railing. By tomorrow, she would probably have a few bruises, but it didn't feel as if anything was seriously injured. She nodded, then cleared her throat. "Yeah. I'm fine." She sounded raspy—just because she had slammed against the railing and the air had been pressed from her lungs, of course.

Mitch came running to their side of the rink, camera still raised to chest level. "Wow, that was ho— Um, I mean, that was something. I've never seen a newbie skate like that."

Ellie hadn't either. She should have known Regina wouldn't stumble around like an uncoordinated beginner for long. The woman would probably master whatever she set her mind on within a single hour.

Regina moved away, interrupting the contact between their bodies.

Cold crept up Ellie's back. As the adrenaline drained from her body, her legs felt a little jittery. Carefully, she turned away from the railing.

Regina ran her gaze over her.

Ellie knew that analytical look. She had seen it before in the ED, but never directed at her. Regina was checking her for signs of an injury—a limp, swelling, unequally dilated pupils. The intensity of that gaze made her squirm. "I'm fine," she said again. This time, her voice sounded more convincing. "I bumped my knees and hip, but it doesn't hurt anymore."

Regina studied her for a moment longer. Then she nodded. "Good. I'd hate to miss out on that drink you owe me."

Ellie's jaw gaped open. "What? I won. *You* owe *me* a drink!"

"Nonsense. I caught myself against the railing about zero point two seconds before you slammed into it."

"Before you shoved me into it, you mean—from behind, which means I reached the other side first."

"Please don't kill each other, ladies," Mitch called over to them. "It'll reflect badly on me and the auction if one of you has to be carried off the ice in a body bag." He raised his camera. "Come on. Smile. We want everyone to see how much fun you're having."

Right. They needed to pretend to have a good time. And for a few seconds, that had actually been true. Ellie should have known it wouldn't last.

Mitch waved at them. "You're too far apart. Scoot closer, or I'll have to Photoshop you together."

They looked at each other, then shuffled closer until their shoulders brushed.

Heat emanated from Regina, engulfing Ellie's side. "Wow. You're really hot."

"Thanks," Regina said with a matter-of-fact expression.

The heat crept from Ellie's shoulder into her cheeks. She eyed Regina. Did she have that huge an ego, or had she just made a joke? Ellie could have sworn Regina had no sense of humor at all. "No, I mean, you run hot. Your body temperature. No wonder you're not wearing a hat or scarf."

One corner of Regina's mouth twisted upward. "I didn't know you paid attention to what I'm wearing."

"What? No, I'm not." If Regina didn't stop, the heat from Ellie's cheeks would make the surface of the ice melt. She paused as the sensual undertone of Regina's reply caught up with her. "Hey, wait a minute! Were you…flirting?"

"Please," Regina said, her tone a vocal eye roll. "This is just for the kids, remember?"

"Right."

They glanced at each other out of the corner of their eyes.

"Um, ladies, you look about as cozy as two boxers right before the bell." Mitch pointed at Regina. "Can you put one arm around her?"

Regina lifted her arm at a glacial pace and draped it along Ellie's shoulders with obvious reluctance.

You would think Mitch asked her to stick it into a lion's cage!

The arm across her shoulders felt as stiff as a plank…a very warm, deliciously smelling plank. Ellie found herself inhaling through her nose as she tried to identify the scent—something crisp and bold that made her think of deep oceans and dense mountain forests. It might have been too overpowering on anyone else, yet it also had a faint sweeter note that was even harder to describe. For a moment, it reminded her of the blueberry jam her grandma used to make.

When the heat along her side increased, Ellie realized she had leaned closer to that complex scent—to Regina.

"Very nice," Mitch called. The shutter clicked several times. "Now put your arm around her too, Eleanor."

Ellie groaned. Hadn't she told Mitch to call her Ellie? He must have gotten her full name from the auction organizers. "Ellie, please. No one has called me Eleanor since my parents grounded me for biting my sister when I was six."

"Eleanor," Regina repeated. "Interesting." Her tone indicated that she was filing it away to use as future ammunition.

Great. Ellie rubbed her forehead and sighed. "I'll make you a deal. You don't call me *Eleanor*, and I don't—"

"Bite me?" Regina threw in.

Ellie ignored the image of her nibbling Regina's neck that flashed through her mind. "Call you *Reggie*."

Regina snatched her arm away from Ellie's shoulders and took off.

Wha—? It hadn't been that bad of a deal, had it? The woman really had no sense of humor at all.

But Regina wasn't whizzing around the rink to get away from her. She was rushing toward a small group of people gathering in a half circle around a woman and a preteen who were sitting on the ice. The woman was cradling her arm against her chest, her face scrunched up in agony, and the girl was clutching her mouth.

They needed help.

Without thinking twice, Ellie took off after Regina.

"Hey!" Mitch shouted after them. "Where are you going?"

Neither of them answered.

As Ellie slid to a stop next to her, Regina pulled a pair of disposable gloves from the inside pocket of her coat and snapped them on.

She hadn't thought to bring a scarf or a hat to their ice-skating date but had nitrile gloves on her? Typical Regina!

Regina seemed to sense Ellie next to her. She gave her the tiniest nod before facing the crowd again. "Back off, people! I'm a doctor!" Regina's voice boomed through the rink. "Make some space for me and my colleague!"

The people around them immediately backed away.

"Can you check her out?" Regina pointed at the woman. "I'll take care of the kid."

That made sense because blood was dripping down the girl's chin, forming a pattern on the ice, and Regina was the one with the gloves. "Got it."

The girl looked up at them. Ellie guessed her to be the same age as her cousin's oldest daughter, about twelve. Her face was pale, but something defiant sparked in her eyes. She said something, but since her hand was pressed to her mouth, Ellie didn't catch what it was.

The rink attendant squeezed past the onlookers. He seemed to be barely out of his teens, and a visible tremor ran through his lanky frame as he stared at the blood dripping from the girl's chin. "Oh my God!"

"Calm down," Regina said before he could faint. "We've got this. Go get us a first aid kit."

The rink attendant hurried off, slipping and sliding on the ice.

We've got this. The words echoed through Ellie's mind, warming her from the inside out as she knelt next to the woman. It felt good to have Regina treat her like an equal part of their two-woman team. Or maybe part of the warmth was from Regina's arm brushing hers as she knelt next to her and spoke to the girl.

Ellie forced her attention to her own patient, ignoring Regina's body heat against her side. "Hi," she said softly. "I'm Ellie. I'm a nurse. What's your name?"

"Caitlin." The woman—a blonde in her mid-thirties—tried to get up. "Can you help my kid first? They slammed into me, and I think they cut their lip on their braces."

Ellie gently pressed her back down and flicked her gaze over to the patient Regina was treating. *They? Oh.* So Caitlin's child was nonbinary? "Don't worry. They're in good hands with Dr. Novak."

Caitlin sank back with a relieved sigh—either at the mention of Regina's profession or because Ellie had readily switched to gender-neutral pronouns.

"Where does it hurt?" Ellie asked.

"My arm." Caitlin cradled it protectively against her chest.

"Do you hurt anywhere else?"

Caitlin shook her head.

Ellie studied her eyes. Both pupils were wide with a mix of pain and worry, but they didn't seem unequal. "You didn't hit your head?"

"No," Caitlin said. "Just stuck my hand out to break the fall."

The cold crept through the fabric of her jeans as Ellie crawled closer on her knees so she could examine her.

Everything was quiet. The onlookers seemed to be holding their breaths while they watched Ellie and Regina work side by side.

Only a rapid click-click-click interrupted the silence.

Ellie glanced up.

Mitch had followed them to this side of the rink. He held his camera at eye level as he snapped pictures of them. "Don't mind me. This is just too perfect to—"

Regina was on her feet in a second, towering over their patients so Mitch's view was blocked. "Stop!"

"Okay, okay." Mitch raised one hand and lowered the camera.

"No, not okay," Regina snarled. "You're going to delete the photos you took of them."

"But it's great publici—"

"Now, or I'll ram your camera so far up your ass, you'll need a five-hour surgical procedure to remove it."

A muffled giggle came from Caitlin's child.

Mitch pressed a few buttons on his camera. "Done."

Regina sent one last icy stare in his direction before she knelt in front of her patient again.

The fine hairs on Ellie's forearms prickled at the intensity still emanating from Regina. For once, she appreciated the cold, bossy attitude, though. She hated to admit it, but Regina in protective mode was kind of hot.

"Sorry," Regina said to her patient. "You'd better not repeat the word I just said, or you'll get me in trouble with your mom."

Caitlin laughed. "Don't worry. They've heard worse. I was cursing up a storm when I fell."

"Let's take a look." Ellie slid up the sleeve of Caitlin's coat and the sweatshirt she wore underneath.

Her wrist was already starting to swell, but Ellie couldn't make out any open wounds or deformities. "Can you move your fingers?"

Caitlin wiggled her fingers and groaned. "Yeah, but it hurts. I think I sprained it."

Ellie's money was on a fracture of the distal radius, but maybe that wasn't the moment to tell her that. "We should get you to an ER to take some X-rays, just in case."

Caitlin sighed. She pulled the injured limb back against her chest and wrapped her good arm around her child's shoulders. "How's your lip?"

Ellie glanced over too.

Regina knelt in front of the tween, the first aid kit open next to her. A wrapper from a piece of gauze and a pair of scissors littered the ice. "No talking," she said sternly, but her fingers were gentle as she applied pressure to the injured bottom lip, pressing it against the kid's teeth to get the bleeding stopped.

It seemed to work. No more red droplets were dripping onto the ice.

"I don't think it needs stitches," Regina said. "Cuts inside the mouth bleed a lot, but they look scarier than they are. How are you?"

Caitlin sighed again. "In need of X-rays, apparently. Can I drive myself? Calling an ambulance would cost an arm and a leg." She made a face at her choice of words.

"Not necessary," Regina said. "We'll take you."

"We will?" Ellie asked. Not that she was against Regina's suggestion. She just hadn't expected Regina to offer. Maybe Dr. McIcy did have a softer side.

"Um, I meant, *I* will take them. I know you said you weren't in the mood to end up in our emergency department on your day off. We can cancel the rest of our date, and you can go home."

Oh, was that why Regina had offered? So she could get out of their date? Good thing Ellie didn't have romantic intentions, because that was just…ouch. But she wasn't about to let Regina off the hook so easily. They had an obligation to the kids and to their sponsors to fulfill after all. "And miss all the fun?" Ellie shook her head. "I'll come with you."

Caitlin's gaze darted back and forth between them. "Oh, you two are…? Our little mishap is interrupting a date?"

"Not really," Regina said.

"Well," Ellie added, "technically, it is."

Caitlin gave them a quizzical look.

They glanced at each other. "It's complicated," they said in unison.

A knowing smile darted across Caitlin's tense face. "Ah. I get it. One of my best friends is gay. She says sometimes it's hard to figure out if it's a date or two friends hanging out."

"No, that's not… We're not…" Ellie sent Regina a please-help look.

"It's not hard to figure out at all," Regina said fiercely. "We're colleagues." She waved at the rink attendant and tossed him the token she had received at the skate rental counter. "Send someone to get our shoes. Let's get them off the ice."

Several of the onlookers started to applaud as they finally escorted their patients toward the gate.

Ellie shook her head. What a surreal not-a-date date!

"What?" Regina asked as she paused at the gate and steadied first Caitlin, then the tween as they stepped off the ice.

"Nothing. Just… This wasn't exactly what I expected." Ellie pointed back toward the rink, where a Zamboni machine was cleaning up the mess. The image that flashed through her mind wasn't of the blood-splattered ice, though. It was one of Regina, cheeks flushed and grinning wildly as they raced side by side.

"Well, this might not have been in the auction program, but you challenged me to provide a date that wasn't boring—and I think I delivered that." Regina strode off the ice with a confident toss of her head.

Ellie stared after her. Then she burst out laughing. "Yes," she murmured. "I think you did." She had no idea what to say if anyone asked how their date had gone, but *boring* wasn't on the list of words she would use to describe it.

Ellie eyed the gray Mazda SUV Regina led them to. She wasn't an expert on cars, but this one looked brand-new and pristine. No vehicle she'd owned had ever been this clean.

"Um, you know what?" Mitch said when they reached the SUV. "I think you don't need me anymore, do you? I got some great pics of the two of you ice-skating; that should be enough."

"What about baking class?" Ellie asked. "Don't you need to take pictures of that too?"

Mitch shook his head. "I had a feeling you wouldn't just hand over your patients to someone else, so I called Ms. Peterson while you were, um, playing doctor. She said she only has the kitchen at the culinary center until four. Depending on how long your visit to the ER takes, that might not be enough time."

"So baking class is canceled?" Regina asked.

Ellie nudged her with an elbow, making Regina raise her eyebrows and stare at the offending appendage. "Jeez, don't sound so happy about it!"

"Does this"—Regina pointed at her unsmiling expression—"look like my happy face? I'm merely asking, okay?" She fixed her gaze back on Mitch. "What else did Ms. Peterson say?"

"She suggested you come to her bakery on your next day off instead, and you can do your second date activity there," Mitch said. "Let me know when. Bye."

Before anyone could answer, he hastened toward his own car.

Regina narrowed her eyes at his rapidly retreating back. "What was that?"

"I think your threat to ram his camera up his…um, rectum might have made him a little leery of you," Ellie said with a grin.

"Men," Regina muttered. "They scare so easily."

When Caitlin was about to climb into the backseat next to her kid, Regina stopped her. "Why don't you sit up front? It'll be easier to get in and out without bumping your arm. Ellie can ride in the back and keep an eye on the lip to make sure it doesn't start bleeding again."

Caitlin hesitated and glanced at her kid, who rolled their eyes and mumbled something—probably "I'm fine, Mom." Finally, Caitlin nodded.

As Regina held open the passenger-side door for Caitlin to get in, Ellie climbed into the backseat next to her patient.

New-car smell engulfed her, and she slid her hand over the soft, light-gray leather. Clearly, Regina didn't have a dog or any nieces or nephews, or she wouldn't have picked a car like this.

"What?" Regina asked as she got behind the wheel.

"Nothing, nothing," Ellie said quickly. She turned toward the tween. "I'm sorry; I didn't catch your name earlier."

"Ri'eh," the kid mumbled from behind the ice pack the rink attendant had gotten them.

"Ryan?" Ellie asked.

Caitlin turned in the passenger seat. "Their name is Riley."

Regina froze with the seat belt pulled down halfway across her chest. Then, belatedly, she clicked it in place with more force than necessary.

Ellie looked at the rearview mirror to catch a glimpse of her face, but, as usual, it didn't give anything away. Her hands on the wheel were steady as she started the car and smoothly maneuvered out of the parking garage.

"You okay?" Ellie brushed her fingertips over Regina's shoulder to let her know she was talking to her, not Caitlin or Riley.

Regina flinched beneath her touch. "Yes, of course. Why wouldn't I be okay? I'm not the one who got injured." She glanced into the rearview mirror. "How's the lip, kiddo?"

Kiddo, Ellie mentally repeated. *Not Riley.* Why hadn't she used the kid's name? Was this an attempt to keep her distance and not get attached to any of her patients? Or did Regina have a problem with Riley being nonbinary?

The thought made Ellie stiffen. Many of her friends were queer, and her family had been supportive from the start, so she sometimes forgot that people outside of her bubble—even LGBT people—weren't always so accepting of identities they didn't understand. She prayed that Regina wasn't one of them.

Riley dropped the ice pack onto the seat between them and pulled out their lip to present the injury.

"Oh, no, no, no." Ellie grabbed the ice pack and placed it back against the spot beneath the injured bottom lip. "Keep pressure on it for a while longer. We don't want it to start bleeding again, messing up this nice leather, right?"

"R't," Riley said.

Silence fell, and the engine sounded overly loud as Regina accelerated down Grand Boulevard.

Chapter 6

REGINA MARCHED AHEAD OF THE others, leading the way toward the emergency department. As the sliding glass doors swished open, she filled her lungs with the comforting smells of disinfectants, floor cleaner, and coffee.

The tension in her shoulders eased. Finally, she was back on familiar ground. Ice-skating with Ellie had thrown her off-balance, and it wasn't just because she'd never done that before.

Then the kid being named Riley…

Of all the names in the world, why did it have to be that one?

It had taken her by surprise, but she wouldn't let it happen a second time. Not around Ellie.

Somehow, she had seemed to notice Regina's single second of vulnerability.

Regina could still feel that light touch to her shoulder. She struggled not to reach up and rub away the tingling sensation.

She led the way through the admissions area, past the registration desk, and gave the triage nurse a curt nod without breaking her stride.

Kayla looked up from the set of lab results she was studying. "Uh, hi. What are you doing here? I thought you're on your date? Don't tell me you stood up poor Ellie!"

Regina gritted her teeth. The last thing she needed was her colleague starting rumors. She stepped aside so Kayla could see Ellie, Caitlin, and Riley following behind her.

"You're both here?" Kayla chuckled. "If this is your idea of a date, it's no wonder you two are single!"

"I'm single because I choose to be, thank you very much," Regina muttered. "Not that it's any of your business." She looked around.

"Which exam room is free? I have a patient who needs a standard wrist X-ray series to—"

"You mean *I* have a patient," Kayla said. "It's your day off. This is my show."

"Oh, come on. I'm here; I'm—"

"On a date," Kayla said. "Which you should get back to. I've got this."

Ridiculous. Since she was already familiar with what had happened, it would have been way more efficient for her to treat Caitlin and Riley. But she didn't want to get into a pissing contest in front of the kid. "Fine. But make sure you get AP, lateral, and oblique views, and don't forget to include the carpal bones. And have someone take a second look at the kid's lip. I placed a piece of gauze on the laceration, and—"

"I've got this," Kayla said again.

A light tug came on Regina's coat sleeve. When she turned her head, she met Ellie's gaze.

"Come on," Ellie said. "We can keep Riley and Caitlin company while she waits for someone from radiology to come down and get her."

This time, Regina managed not to flinch at the name—or Ellie's touch to her arm.

"You don't have to wait," Caitlin said. "I texted my mother-in-law, and she'll be here to pick us up as soon as she can."

"Still," Ellie said. "I don't mind waiting with you. I can stay with Riley while you get your wrist X-rayed."

Regina nodded. "I'm staying too. I want to see those X-rays."

A smile crinkled the corners of Ellie's dark eyes. "Right. That's why you're staying. Because you never get a chance to see a set of X-rays in your job."

Regina shrugged, using the movement to pull her arm free of Ellie's gentle grasp. "You can never see too many X-rays. Plus two sets of eyes are always better than one." If Ellie thought she was staying because she had developed a soft spot for Riley and Caitlin, she was completely wrong.

Okay, mostly wrong. She was staying because she wanted to make sure they couldn't go back to their date. Here, in the hospital, their roles were clear, and she was the one calling the shots. Out there, on the ice and probably during baking class too, she didn't have a professional script to follow and had no idea how to interact with Ellie.

"Get the kid a fresh ice pack, will you?" she said gruffly, just to get Ellie to stop looking at her with that little grin.

Instead, Ellie's grin broadened. "One ice pack, coming right up."

Apparently, radiology was having a busy day. Dr. Vaughn had already examined Riley's lip and confirmed that no stitches were necessary, but Caitlin was still waiting for her X-rays.

Regina had claimed the seat in the corner and sat with her head held high. She looked like the queen of the waiting room. Her gaze went from person to person, and Ellie had a feeling she was mentally listing a diagnosis and treatment for every patient around them. Once she was done, she pulled out her phone and started reading something that appeared to be a medical journal.

Did she ever just shut off her brain and relax?

The waiting room was surprisingly busy for this early on a Thursday afternoon. Across the room, someone was coughing every few seconds, and several people were cradling an arm or had shoved their swollen foot into an unlaced boot—they had probably slipped on patches of snow remaining on the sidewalks.

Only a few open seats remained, yet everyone was giving Regina a wide berth.

Well, everyone but Riley. The tween had plopped down on the orange plastic chair next to Regina and stared morosely down at the phone on their lap. Its screen was badly cracked and wouldn't turn on, no matter how often they tried.

"Do you want my phone to play a game while we wait?" Caitlin offered.

Riley made a face, then flinched as the grimace tugged on their lip. "No, thanks, Mom. Candy Crush is so basic."

"Nothing like having kids to make you feel old and boring," Caitlin muttered but was smiling.

Riley craned their neck to get a glimpse of Regina's phone. "Do you have any games?"

Regina didn't answer.

For a few seconds, Ellie thought that maybe Regina hadn't understood the question. Riley had spoken while trying not to move their lip, muffling the words.

But Regina remained focused on her phone, and one long finger slowly scrolled down the tiny screen.

Ellie extended her leg to the left and nudged one of Regina's shiny ankle boots. "Riley's talking to you."

Regina looked up. "Me?"

Ellie struggled not to laugh at the baffled expression on her face. "Yeah, you." She gave Riley a smile, encouraging them to ask again.

"Are you doing anything fun?" Riley pointed at her phone.

Regina nodded. "I'm reading an article on recurrent nocturnal syncope."

Now it was Riley's turn to sport a baffled look. "Uh, I meant *real* fun. Do you have TikTok or any games?"

Ellie was about to offer up her phone for some *Minecraft* when Regina nodded.

Regina had games on her phone? Ellie hadn't expected that.

"I have *Cell to Singularity.*"

"What's that?" Riley asked.

By now, the entire waiting room seemed to listen in on their conversation, and Ellie found herself leaning slightly to her left so she wouldn't miss it.

"It's an evolution game. You start as an amino acid, then upgrade to single cells."

She's such a geek. Ellie dug her teeth into her bottom lip so she wouldn't laugh, but she wasn't very successful as a soft chuckle escaped her.

"What?" Regina glared at her. "It's really soothing. Helps me slow down my brain after a busy shift."

Okay, Ellie could understand that. For her, it was relaxing with an audiobook, a glass of wine, and a jigsaw puzzle.

"Sounds, um, great," Riley said in a tone that indicated they found it about as interesting as watching grass grow.

Regina gave a regal nod. "It is. I'm about to unlock dinosaurs."

Riley looked back up. "What kind?"

"No idea. I haven't unlocked them yet."

"Can I see? I was really into dinosaurs when I was a kid and can probably tell you what they are."

The way Riley made it sound—as if they were a mature adult now—made everyone laugh.

Even Regina's lips twitched up, and Ellie couldn't help staring. Had she ever seen Regina smile? Well, Regina had worn a broad grin as they had raced each other across the ice earlier, but during a typical shift in the ED, Regina rotated through only two facial expressions: practiced impassiveness and disapproval. The genuine smile seemed to transform her entire face.

"Um, Riley, not everyone is comfortable handing their phone over to a stranger," Caitlin said.

"It's okay." Regina tapped a few times to open the game app, then handed over her phone.

Within seconds, they were both immersed in the game, with Riley leaning close to Regina so she could see the screen and give instructions.

Interesting. Ellie would have bet an entire month's paycheck that Regina was bad with kids, but she actually wasn't. A little awkward maybe, as if it was a skill that had gone rusty, yet she didn't try to reach over and tap the screen to show Riley how it was done. She let them figure it out on their own, only giving some verbal guidance.

Caitlin cleared her throat, startling Ellie's attention away from Regina and to her other side.

"So," Caitlin said, her voice pitched low, "please forgive me if I'm being too intrusive, but if the two of you going ice-skating wasn't a date, why was the guy with the camera talking about there being a second date? Why was there even a guy following you around with a camera?"

Ellie peered at Regina, but she seemed to be focused entirely on the game. "Because I, um, bought a date package with her at a singles auction."

A sharp hiss came from Regina. She had looked up from the phone to shoot her a glare.

"What?" Ellie said.

"Do you have to tell everyone?" Regina glanced around the waiting room with a grim expression as if afraid one of the nurses would hear.

"All of our colleagues already know."

"Bad enough," Regina mumbled.

Did she have to keep acting as if being associated with Ellie in any way other than professional was a stain on her reputation?

"Why wouldn't you want anyone to know?" Caitlin clutched her chest with her good hand. "It's so romantic!"

"No, it's not. I wasn't trying to bid on her. I just—"

"Swatted at a fly," Regina said. "A really big one."

Damn. Of course Regina would remember every word she'd said, including that silly excuse she had come up with.

Caitlin looked back and forth between them, squinting. Then her expression cleared, and a big grin spread over her face.

"Oh no!" Riley hectically tapped at the phone. "I think I caused a meteor and made them all extinct! Sorry." They handed back the device with a sheepish expression.

"Don't worry about it. It's all part of the game." Regina slid the phone into her coat pocket and stood. "I'm going to get us some coffee."

Riley jumped up. "Can I come and get a Coke?"

"Sure." Caitlin dug through her purse with one hand. "Here, let me give you some cash."

Regina waved her off. "I've got this."

"Are you sure?" Caitlin asked. "You've already gone out of your way to help us. You shouldn't have to pay for our drinks too."

"I'm not," Regina said. "It's on her." She pointed at Ellie.

"Me?" Ellie touched her fingertips to her chest in faux protest. "I'm a nurse. Since you're a doctor making the big bucks, shouldn't you pay?"

"Big bucks? Please! The only thing big is my medical school debt. Besides, you're the one who lost our little ice-skating race, which means drinks are on you." Regina marched out of the waiting room with Riley at her heels before Ellie could think of a reply.

"I didn't lose!" Ellie called after her. "You did!"

But Regina was already gone.

Ellie huffed and turned toward Caitlin. "Can you believe that woman?"

"Let me pay. It's the least I can do." Caitlin held out a twenty-dollar bill.

Ellie gently pushed her hand away. She hadn't meant to make Caitlin feel guilty; she just hadn't been able to resist verbally sparring with Regina. "No, it's okay. We weren't really arguing about money. It's not like we can't afford a cup of coffee. We just…" She tugged on the end of her scarf, not sure how to explain.

"Ah." The corners of Caitlin's lips tilted up into an amused smile, and she shoved the twenty-dollar bill back into her purse. "So the two of you work together in this ER?"

"Yeah."

"And you bid on her in a singles auction?"

"By accident."

"So it wasn't because you have the biggest crush on her?"

"Me? On her? Please!" Ellie popped her P for emphasis. "Are you sure you didn't hit your head when you fell?"

Caitlin kept looking at her with that knowing grin. "There was no fly, was there?"

A burning heat spread through Ellie's cheeks. "Okay, no. But it really was an accident. I never in a million years would have bid on her."

"So tall, gorgeous, and smart isn't your type?"

Ellie willed her blush to fade. "Cold, rude, and arrogant isn't."

"Cold, rude, and arrogant?" Caitlin repeated the words as if they were in a language she didn't speak. "Are we talking about the same woman?"

Were they? Ellie considered it. She tried to disregard all the interactions she'd had with Regina at work—from that very first meeting, when Regina hadn't even introduced herself—and see only the woman she had been ice-skating with.

Regina hadn't been exactly warm and fuzzy that day either. But cold, rude, and arrogant… No, that description didn't fit her. Closed-off, competitive, and confident, sure.

But there were also other traits lurking beneath that reserved surface. Ellie had caught glimpses of them throughout the day—just enough to know they were there, but not enough to grasp what they were, other than *complex*.

The mystery that was Regina Novak called to her like a jigsaw puzzle that was starting to form but was far from being done.

No, no, no. Not a good idea. This wasn't an episode of *Grey's Anatomy* or something. This was real life, and she would only get frostbite if she tried to get close to Dr. McIcy.

"Ms. Hart?"

Ellie had never been so grateful to see her friend Jasmine, who stood in the doorway with an empty wheelchair.

Caitlin lifted her good hand. "That's me."

"I'll take you to get your wrist X-rayed." Jasmine glanced over at Ellie. "Well, well, well, look what the cat dragged in. Dr. Vaughn told me you were here. Beth and I had a bet going that your date wouldn't go well, but we didn't think the two of you would end up in the emergency department."

Ellie gave her a sheepish grin. "Hey, it's not because we tried to bash each other's head in. We were just at the wrong place at the wrong time." She put a hand on Caitlin's uninjured arm. "Or maybe the right place at the right time."

Jasmine helped Caitlin settle into the wheelchair, as was hospital policy. "So, how are things going?"

"Let's just say our first date has been quite the adventure," Ellie said.

"Sure looks like it." Behind Caitlin's back, Jasmine made the sign for "call me" at Ellie and waggled her brows as if she expected her to report back with the most salacious details.

Ellie shook her head. There was nothing to tell.

Jasmine and Caitlin hadn't been gone long when Regina returned, carrying two paper cups. She was alone, with Riley nowhere to be seen.

"Where's Riley?"

"I traded the kid for these." Regina nodded down at the paper cups with a deadpan expression.

Maybe she did have a sense of humor after all, even if it was a weird one. "Where's Riley really?"

"I lost them when we ran into Jasmine and Caitlin. Apparently, getting to see how X-rays are taken is more interesting to a twelve-year-old than killing off dinosaurs." Regina gracefully lowered herself onto the corner seat next to Ellie without spilling a single drop, then held out one cup. "Here."

Their fingers grazed as Ellie reached for the paper cup. Warmth shot up her arm, but she told herself it was only from the hot beverage. "Thanks." She had expected coffee from the vending machine, but the color and the heavenly scent wafting up were all wrong for that. "Hot chocolate?"

"That's what you said your annual tradition was—ice-skating and hot chocolate, right?"

Ellie struggled not to let her mouth gape open. So Regina had actually listened when she'd talked about her childhood, even though she'd seemed completely uninterested. "Right." She blew across the surface of the dark brown liquid, then took a careful sip.

The sweet, creamy taste of hot chocolate hit her taste buds—and it wasn't the watery stuff from the vending machine. Someone had used milk to make this.

"Yum. Where did you get this?" She went back for a bigger sip, then licked a bit of chocolate milk off her upper lip.

Regina's gaze seemed to follow the path of her tongue for a second. Or maybe Ellie had just imagined it, because Regina's face remained entirely impassive as she shrugged and blew on her own beverage. "Cafeteria."

"There's hot chocolate like this in the cafeteria?"

Another shrug. "Apparently."

Ellie searched for her wallet with her free hand. "What do I owe you?"

Regina waved her off. "It's fine."

Ellie sent her a teasing grin across the rim of the paper cup. "Oh, does that mean you admit to having lost our little race?"

"Ha!" Regina snorted into her coffee. "Never. Hot chocolate does not constitute a real drink. You still owe me one."

"Well…" Ellie paused to enjoy another sip. "We still have three date activities to cross off our list. I'm sure we can squeeze in that drink *you* owe *me* somewhere."

For some reason, the thought of spending all that time with Regina no longer seemed as daunting.

By the time they left the hospital, it was nearly three, and Regina was grateful they had postponed the baking class.

She'd had enough social interaction for one day. While she worked with people all day, this was different. In the ED, no one expected small talk and other niceties from her.

Or maybe what was so exhausting was that Ellie didn't seem to be happy with small talk. She kept looking at Regina as if she wanted to dig deeper and ask questions Regina wasn't willing to answer.

She checked her wristwatch. They had been standing in the parking lot for longer than it had taken to get Caitlin's wrist X-rayed—or at least it felt that way to Regina. Caitlin had introduced them to her mother-in-law, who'd come to pick them up, and now the hug that Ellie and Caitlin exchanged seemed to last forever.

Christ, they had just met a few hours before. What was there to say except for *bye* and *get better soon*?

"I don't know how to thank you," Caitlin said, her arms still wrapped around Ellie. She glanced at Regina over Ellie's shoulder. "Both of you."

Regina held up her hand to stop her should Caitlin get the idea to hug her too. "We were happy to help. Keep that arm elevated, and don't forget to go back to the hospital for your cast once the swelling has gone down."

"Will do, Doc. Thank you." Caitlin finally let go of Ellie and put the hand that wasn't resting in a sling on Riley's shoulder instead. "I hope your dating arrangement works out for the two of you, but if not..." She dug through her purse and finally produced a card, which she pressed into Ellie's hand. "Give me a call, and I'll set you up with my friend. You're exactly her type."

Regina's car keys clattered to the asphalt. Scowling, she bent to pick them up.

She didn't care if Ellie went out with Caitlin's friend. Why would she? She was just here to fulfill her obligation to the pediatric cardiac care program, not because she actually wanted to date Ellie.

Maybe it would even be a good thing if Ellie went out with someone else. It would stop the hospital rumor mill about the two of them.

But it had to be timed with her reputation in mind. Yes. That was what didn't sit right with her. There were social rules to be followed for things like this—like how long to wait until you started going out with someone else. If their colleagues got wind of Ellie letting herself be set up with someone else so soon, they would think Regina had been an awful date or at least totally forgettable.

No way. She couldn't have that. She had a reputation to uphold after all.

The scraping of shoes over the asphalt next to her wrenched her from her thoughts.

Riley shuffled their feet. "Um, thanks for taking care of my lip and for the Coke and for letting me use your phone."

"You're welcome," Regina said. "Next time, try not to kill off the dinosaurs before we unlock the stegosaurus."

Riley laughed. "Okay."

Her own words echoed through Regina's mind. What was she saying? There wouldn't be a next time. Maybe Ellie would hang out with them and Caitlin's friend, but she wouldn't join them. Once she and Ellie had done the baking class and the two other date activities, they would never see each other outside of work again, and her social life would go back to consisting of weekly practices with her disc golf team.

God, she couldn't wait.

She lifted her hand for a quick wave, then fixed her gaze on Ellie and jerked her head toward where she'd parked her car. "Let's go."

Chapter 7

REGINA CLICKED THE SEAT BELT into place and looked at Ellie in the passenger seat. "So, where to?"

"I don't know," Ellie answered. "Are we going back to the ice-skating rink since we were interrupted in the middle of our not-a-date date?"

It hadn't even occurred to Regina that they would do that. Truth be told, her ankles were killing her after being stuck in the unfamiliar rental skates and crouching down on the ice to take care of their patients. Not that she would ever admit that. "No point. Mike is gone."

"Mike?"

"Photographer guy."

"Um, his name is Mitch."

Regina shrugged. "Whatever. He's gone, and the sponsors have their pictures, so we can go our separate ways for today."

"You know, you really could give me an inferiority complex with the way you can't wait to get rid of me."

Regina studied her—the challenging tilt of Ellie's head, the glint in her dark eyes, the slight twitch of her lips as if she didn't know whether to frown or grin in amusement. "You don't look as if you're about to descend into an existential crisis."

"I'm not," Ellie said. "I learned not to base my self-worth on what others think of me."

Ellie's voice was pitched lower than usual, with an undertone Regina couldn't quite identify. Very likely, a painful experience had taught Ellie that lesson.

Regina bit her lip so she wouldn't ask. None of her business. "So…" She cleared her throat. "I should probably just drive you home. Or did you leave your car at the Ice Terrace?"

"No, I took the MAX."

"Then I'll take you home. Where do you live?"

"In Brookside," Ellie said. "Just a few miles from here. Head to the Plaza, then turn onto Brookside Boulevard. I'll tell you where to go from there."

Regina hadn't explored KC much since moving here seven months ago—she'd been too busy settling into her first attending position—but she'd been to Brookside. It wasn't far from her apartment, so she regularly went grocery shopping there.

She made a U-turn in front of the ED and steered her SUV south toward the Plaza.

When they had met up at the Ice Terrace this morning, she had assumed they would say goodbye and go their separate ways as soon as the baking class ended. She hadn't expected to drive Ellie home. It made the entire day feel too much like an actual date, not just a show they had put on for the photographer and their sponsors.

Yet at the same time, she couldn't help being curious to see where Ellie lived.

At the public library, Ellie had her turn right, then take Oak Street. As they headed south and away from the UMKC campus, the scenery changed and became more residential. Regina caught glimpses of an interesting mix of architectural styles—first impressive mansions, brick or stone Tudors, and colonial revivals on big lots, then single-family bungalows with wide porches and immaculately trimmed lawns.

As architects, her parents would have loved it, but Regina had barely talked to them in almost a year.

Ellie, however, didn't look at the homes.

Regina could feel her gaze rest on her as she drove. "What?"

Ellie shifted in the passenger seat to face Regina more fully. "I didn't want to say something earlier, when we were still with them, but you were kind of weird with Riley."

Every muscle in Regina's body went taut. She had sensed that Ellie had noticed, but she hadn't expected to be called out on it. She should have known better. "I have no idea what you're talking about."

"It wasn't because they're nonbinary, was it?" Ellie asked as if Regina hadn't spoken.

"What? No!"

"I know it can be confusing because we're so used to putting people into boxes. Man or woman, girl or—"

"I'm not confused," Regina said sharply. "I never fit into any of the boxes people wanted to put me in, so I get it. I don't have a problem with Riley being nonbinary." This time, she forced herself to say the name, even though it scraped along her vocal cords like the coarsest sandpaper and made her throat burn.

Ellie studied her intently. "This is the first time you said their name. You haven't used it all afternoon. Not once. And if someone else did, you flinched like you'd been electrocuted." Her voice was soft, yet also unyielding—she wouldn't back away from this topic.

"Not because they're nonbinary."

"No?"

"No! It's because—" She stopped herself. What on earth was wrong with her? She had nearly spilled her guts to Ellie, when Ellie was the last person she should tell. She was a co-worker. Someone who could start the rumors, the pitiful glances again with a few words to her friends at the hospital. Regina had moved to Kansas City to escape all of that, not to repeat it.

Ellie watched her without saying a word. She didn't pressure Regina to finish her sentence. But her gaze remained on Regina.

She could feel it on the side of her face, like a laser beam that would give her a sunburn.

In a couple of minutes, they would be at Ellie's place. She could just stay silent, then drop her off with a quick "see you at work."

There was nothing Ellie could do to make her talk if she didn't want to.

But as much as she hated talking about it, she also didn't want Ellie to think she held hateful prejudices against nonbinary people.

Oh, get over it. Why should I care what she thinks?

But dammit, she did.

She hit the steering wheel with her tightly clenched fist. "My brother's name is Riley, okay?" *Was.* She couldn't make herself say it, though.

That laser beam on her right cheek was back, drilling into her. "Why would that make it awkward to call Riley—Caitlin's kid—by their name? I have a cousin named Regina, yet I don't have a problem calling you—"

"He's dead!" The words burst out of Regina in a rough shout. *I let him die.*

A loud gasp from Ellie echoed through the car.

Then silence fell, so all-encompassing that Regina's overly fast heart-beat thumped through her ears. *Shit, shit, shit.*

"Regina..." Ellie's voice was gentle but alarmed. "Um, do you want to pull over for a minute?"

Regina kept her foot on the gas. "No. I'll—"

"Please. You're shaking all over."

"Bullshit." Regina glanced at her hands. They weren't— What the hell? They *were* shaking. She had always had the steadiest hands in her med school class. This had never happened to her before. Okay, maybe once, when she'd had to call her parents to tell them Riley had died.

But here...now, with Ellie... She wasn't supposed to let her guard down like that. Regina gripped the steering wheel with both hands to stop the trembling.

Thankfully, her knees got the message too.

"Regina..." Ellie reached across the middle console and put her hand on Regina's right forearm.

That sunburned feeling, as if Ellie had focused on her too closely, spread over every inch of Regina's skin. "I'm fine." She hurled out the words as if they would ward off Ellie's touch, but they didn't. That gentle hand remained where it was. "And I don't have a problem with Riley being nonbinary." There, she had said the name again. She was fine.

"I'm sorry."

For her brother's death or for accusing her of discriminating against nonbinary people? Maybe both, but Regina didn't ask. If she talked about this for even a second longer, that burning sensation would fry her to a crisp from the inside out.

"You don't have to talk about it if you don't want to." Ellie's voice was as soft as her touch. "But if you ever—"

"I don't."

"If you ever do, you know where to find me."

At the hospital—the place where Regina didn't even want to think about her brother, much less have everyone know about him.

"Um, turn left here."

For a second, Regina's brain didn't grasp what Ellie had said. Then she hit the brake and abruptly turned the wheel, using the motion to pull her arm away from Ellie's touch.

Ellie said nothing. She placed her hand on her own lap. "At the next street, turn left, and we're there."

Regina was grateful for the distraction. She focused hard on her surroundings, as if there would be a quiz afterward.

A quiet street lay in front of her, lined by tall, mature trees on both sides. All the houses seemed to be single-family, mostly bungalows with one or two stories. Patches of snow still remained on the small lawns, but Regina could easily imagine how neatly trimmed the grass would be in summer.

"It's the third house on the right." Ellie pointed at a charming little two-story home. Its red front door and shutters stood out against the light-gray exterior with a white trim that looked as if it had been recently painted. A path led from the sidewalk to a covered porch, where a patio swing hung from the eaves on the right.

Somehow, it fit Ellie.

The narrow driveway was apparently shared with the neighbor to the right, and a big SUV was parked there, so Regina stopped the car along the curb. She hesitated. The urge to get out of here and floor it down the street gripped her, but she didn't want Ellie to complain again about Regina wanting to quickly get rid of her, so she shut off the engine.

Ellie unbuckled her seat belt and turned toward her. "Do you want to come in for a drink?"

"No, thanks." There wasn't a drink strong enough to make Regina answer the questions she could see in Ellie's eyes. All she wanted was to get this over with so she could be alone.

"Are you okay to drive home?" Ellie asked.

"I'm fine."

Ellie worried her bottom lip, apparently far from convinced.

That sunburned feeling on Regina's skin started again. She undid her seat belt and reached out to open the driver's side door.

Ellie gave her a curious look. "Did you change your mind about not coming in, or are you going to walk me to the door?"

Damn. Regina froze with her hand still extended. She had acted on instinct, probably because she was exhausted and overheated after that moment of weakness and needed to get some fresh air. "No, of course not. Why would I do that? This isn't a date date."

"Then why are you getting out?"

"I just want to stretch my legs after all that sitting around in the waiting room." Regina shoved the door open and climbed out.

A neighbor walking his dog waved as Ellie followed suit. "Hey, Ellie."

"Hi, Frank." Ellie raised her hand in greeting.

Apparently, this was one of those neighborhoods where people actually knew each other. *Ugh.* That was why Regina was leasing an apartment in one of the historic high-rises at the Plaza, where she was close to the hospital and everything else she needed but could maintain some anonymity.

As she followed Ellie along the short path to the front door, a rustling sound came from the tree to her left.

Before Regina could even glance up, a big chunk of snow dropped down and plopped onto her head. The cold mass slid down her neck and slithered beneath the collar of her coat and into her sweater. "Ew." She hunched her shoulders and bent at the hip to stop its trek down her back. Cursing, she stretched her arm back and tried to dig it out. But no matter how much she contorted herself, she couldn't reach that spot between her shoulder blades where a big lump was melting against her skin.

Ellie scrambled to her side. A giggle burst from her at Regina's contortionist maneuvers. "That should teach you to wear a scarf, California Girl. Here. Hold still."

Regina was too stunned to move. She froze, still bent over, as Ellie gently swiped her hair aside and reached beneath the layers of Regina's coat and sweater. Ellie had taken off her gloves earlier, and now her warm fingers trailed down Regina's skin, causing more goose bumps than the snow.

Regina forgot to breathe as the icy nip of the snow was replaced by the heat of Ellie's touch.

"Wow," a woman's voice came from the porch. "This date seems to have gone well. You haven't even made it inside, and you've already got your hand down her shirt."

With a startled squeak, Ellie snatched her hand out from beneath Regina's sweater, and Regina nearly bumped her head against Ellie's chin as she quickly straightened.

The remainder of the snow slid down to the small of her back, where it melted and drenched her shirt. Regina shivered but ignored it to glare at the stranger.

"What?" Ellie whirled around to the woman on the porch. "No, no. I'm not... We're not... It's not what it looks like."

Regina grimaced at the not very believable defense.

The stranger grinned down at them. She seemed familiar, but Regina couldn't place her. Wait, was Ellie living with someone? She wouldn't have bid on her if she were in a relationship, would she? But then again, Ellie claimed it had been an accident.

A small dog of indeterminable breed tugged free of the woman's hold and ran straight for Ellie, its leash trailing behind. Its floppy ears bobbed up and down with every leap, and its tail wagged so furiously that the dog's rear end shook back and forth.

"Hey, Wally. How's my favorite borkie?" Ellie crouched down and ran her fingers through the dog's long, wiry coat, apparently not minding when Wally licked her hands.

Then, as if knowing only one speed, the dog ran over to Regina. Tail still wagging, it sniffed her pant leg, then jumped around her.

All right. Fine. She would pet the dog to stop all that jumping. She bent and patted Wally's head.

The dog's tan-and-black fur was silkier than she'd expected and longer in some places on its face, its lush texture giving Wally bushy eyebrows. She had to admit that the dog seemed like an entertaining pet.

The woman jogged down the four steps from the porch and grabbed Wally's leash. "You have to excuse Wally. He's an attention hound, and he likes PDAs as much as his second mom does." She pointed at Ellie.

Second mom? So she and Ellie did live together.

Ellie got up from her crouched position. "Shut up, Vickie," she said, but her tone was more affectionate than really scolding. She turned toward Regina. "You remember my sister, Vickie, right?"

Sister? Oh. So they weren't a couple. Good—it would have looked bad for the auction if it turned out Ellie was already involved with someone else.

But why would Regina remember Ellie's sister? She squinted at Vickie. She was a little taller than Ellie, around Regina's age—thirty-one—and had the same big, brown eyes and that fresh-faced girl-next-door look as her sister. But instead of Ellie's long, glossy hair, she wore hers in an intentionally messy pixie cut.

Ah. Regina finally remembered where she had seen her before: at the hospital. Vickie was an EMT. Now that she wasn't wearing a uniform, Regina hadn't recognized her. "Yes, of course," she said, as if she had known who Vickie was all along and hadn't mistaken her for Ellie's partner.

They nodded at each other.

Great. Now it wasn't just Ellie who would tell everyone at the hospital all about their date—and about Riley. Every EMT and paramedic in KCMO would soon know too.

"Wally and I are off to pick up tacos from Jalapeños. Want to come?" Vickie looked from her sister to Regina, clearly including her in the invitation too.

"No, thanks," Regina said before Ellie could answer. "I'd better get home. Text me what days are good for you for the baking class so I can work something out with Ms. Peterson." She was already walking backward.

Ellie watched her go but didn't try to stop her. "Will do. See you at work."

Regina nodded and turned on her heel. She felt Ellie's gaze on her all the way to her car and even as she drove down the street.

Why the hell had she told her about Riley? She hated having someone from work all mixed up in her private life. The one time it had happened before, it hadn't ended well.

But Ellie wasn't part of her private life, she told herself. Not really. She was meeting up with her to fulfill an obligation to the hospital's charity. That meant it was work.

Then why had skating side by side and ending up against the low wall surrounding the ice rink, pressed against Ellie, not felt like work at all?

As soon as Regina's SUV had disappeared down the street, Vickie whirled around and gripped Ellie's shoulders. "Spill!"

Ellie brushed off her hands and set off walking toward Jalapeños. "There's nothing to spill."

"Right." Vickie jogged after her, with Wally at her heels. "You spent most of the day with the legendary Dr. McIcy, and all you did was trade stories from the emergency department."

"Actually, that's where we spent most of the day."

"Wait, you both got called in to work?"

"No. When we were at the Ice Terrace, a woman fell and broke her wrist, and her child had a split lip that was bleeding pretty bad, so we drove them to CMC and then kept them company in the waiting room."

Vickie let out a whistle that made Wally bark. "How did you get Dr. McIcy to do that?"

Ellie turned and tugged on her sister's scarf. "Come on. Be nice. It was actually Regina who suggested we drive them and stay to make sure they're taken care of."

"Ooh." A smirk settled on Vickie's lips.

"What's that supposed to mean?"

"Nothing."

Ellie tugged harder.

"It's just interesting to hear you call her by her first name—and to see you getting all protective of her."

"I'm not. Protective of her, that is." Or was she? Okay, maybe a tiny little bit. Seeing Regina as pale as freshly fallen snow, shaking so much that the entire driver's seat had vibrated… Ellie's stomach bunched into a tightly wound ball. "Just trying to be fair."

Vickie gave her the side-eye. "What aren't you telling me?"

"Nothing." Ellie marched faster, but her sister kept up.

"Come on. It's me. What's going on?"

Ellie sighed. She and Vickie had always been close. Vickie had been the first person she'd come out to as a teen and the first person she'd told that she planned to drop out of med school. But sharing Regina's personal pain didn't feel right. "Nothing. I just… I'm a little conflicted about her. She can be an arrogant ass, but earlier, she let her guard down for a split second, and I think there's more to her than I initially thought."

"So, she's just misunderstood and actually a complete teddy bear?"

Ellie laughed. "Well, I wouldn't go that far. But she has her moments."

Vickie playfully raised her eyebrows. "Like that moment when you had your hand beneath her shirt?"

"It was perfectly innocent. I was scooping out snow!" Despite her protest, heat crept up from beneath her scarf and rushed up her neck. True, she had merely tried to help Regina get rid of the snow. Only once she'd reached beneath her sweater had she realized how intimate it was… and how soft Regina's skin felt.

"Scooping out snow?" Vickie made it sound as if she were discussing an especially kinky fetish. "Is that what they're calling it now?"

"Yep. Kinda like this." Ellie scooped up two handfuls of snow from a low wall around someone's property, formed it into a snowball, and aimed it at her sister.

Laughing and shouting, they chased each other down the street.

Chapter 8

THE NEXT DAY, A RARE miracle happened: Ellie had time to take a real lunch break instead of just wolfing down a granola bar while charting.

She and her colleague Beth headed over to the cafeteria, which was on the same level as the ED, to grab a sandwich and some coffee.

As they got in line at the coffee station, Ellie leaned against the steel rail. A dull pain flared through her bruised hip, so she quickly shifted away from the rail.

Beth glanced up from the ham and cheese sandwich on her tray. "You okay?"

"Yep. All good." Ellie pushed her tray forward.

The cafeteria worker behind the counter—a short woman with a big smile—turned toward her. "What can I get you?"

Ellie returned the smile. She opened her mouth to order coffee, then changed her mind. What she was really in the mood for was the yummy hot chocolate Regina had brought her from the cafeteria the day before. The ED often got busy on Friday afternoons, and she needed some chocolate and sugar to make it through the rest of her shift. "Could I have a hot chocolate, please?"

"Coming right up." Within a minute, the cafeteria worker slid a paper cup in front of her.

Ellie stared at the hot liquid. It was much darker than the hot chocolate Regina had brought her. "Um, is that the one made with milk?"

The cafeteria worker gave her a puzzled look. "I don't know what you're talking about. This is the only hot chocolate we have."

Huh. Apparently, the extra creamy kind of hot chocolate wasn't available for mere mortals. How had Regina managed to procure it?

Beth chuckled. "What? You thought they'd decorate it with some whipped cream and marshmallows?"

"No, of course not." How was she supposed to explain? Beth probably wouldn't believe that Regina had a nice bone in her body, so she waved it away. "Well, maybe they should. I'll put it into the suggestion box."

"You're welcome to try, but I wouldn't hold my breath," the cafeteria worker said before taking Beth's order.

Ellie paid at the register, flashing her hospital ID for the employee discount, then carried the tray with the hot chocolate and her sandwich to one of the small tables. Gingerly, she lowered herself onto the seat. *Ouch.* She felt like one big bruise.

"Seriously, what's up with you?" Beth asked as she joined her at the table. "You're acting weird and moving like my ninety-year-old grandma. Come to think of it… So is Dr. Novak." She pointed across the room.

Ellie swiveled on her chair.

Regina had just entered the cafeteria. Her light-blue scrubs were free of wrinkles and didn't have a single stain, as if she hadn't already worked half a shift. Her black hair was pulled back into its signature tight, stubby ponytail, not a strand out of place, emphasizing her amazing cheekbones that Ellie had always envied. As she stood surveying the entree station, her intense presence filled the room.

Ellie couldn't help staring. Was this really the same woman who'd shook all over at the mere mention of her brother? She couldn't reconcile it.

Regina made her way over to the salad bar.

"Hmm, you're right," Ellie murmured.

Instead of Regina's usual smooth stride, she was walking stiffly. So far, Ellie hadn't noticed. She had caught glimpses of Regina earlier, but all of her patients had been checked out by one of the residents, so they hadn't exchanged more than a quick "hi" in passing.

"Of course I'm right. You're both walking funny, like you—" Beth paused. Her eyes went wide, and she slapped the table with both hands, making their trays rattle. "Wait a second! Does that mean the two of you did the horizontal mambo all night long?"

"No!"

Several people at the surrounding tables glanced over.

Heat stung Ellie's cheeks. She leaned across the table so no one could overhear them and repeated more quietly, "No. We're just sore from—"

Someone walked up to their table. The hum of conversation and the clanking of cutlery around them seemed to dim.

Ellie looked up, already sensing whom she would see.

Of course it was Regina towering next to their table. Her hands holding a tray with a plate heaped high with salad were rock-steady and her gray eyes cool as she fixed her gaze on Ellie.

"Um, hi," Ellie said. *Great.* Why did she sound as if she had been caught prying open Regina's locker?

Regina gave her the shortest of nods. "The airway cart in trauma bay two is running low on laryngoscope blades. Could you restock it when you get a minute?"

Laryngoscope blades? That was why Regina had come over? Not even a "hi, how are you?" after everything that had happened the day before? Ellie couldn't believe it. "Sure," she said, trying to keep her face as impassive as Regina's was. "I'll do that as soon as we're done here."

Beth's chair squeaked as she pushed it back and got up. "You know what? I think this sandwich needs more mustard." She looked back and forth between Ellie and Regina. When neither said anything, she headed toward the station with the condiments, leaving them alone.

Regina stared after Beth, not even bothering to tamp down her glare. She hated gossip, especially at work and when she was the topic of it—and it was obvious that she'd been.

As soon as she'd walked up to their table, they'd stopped talking.

Narrowing her eyes, she zeroed in on Ellie. "I don't appreciate the details of my personal life being spread all over the hospital."

"I'm sorry." Ellie had the audacity to look sincere. "But there's not much I can do. The entire hospital knows, so…"

Regina's body temperature skyrocketed so fast that she thought steam would shoot out of her ears. "Not much you can do? You can stop telling everyone about"—she took a deep breath and forced her volume down to a fierce rasp instead of a shout—"my brother."

"What? No!" Ellie clutched the edge of the table. "We weren't… I didn't tell her about your brother or about…yesterday. In the car."

Regina pressed her teeth together so hard that her jaw ached. "Right. You weren't talking about me at all. That's why both of you shut up the moment you realized I was there."

"We *were* talking about you. But not about…that. What I meant was that the entire hospital knows we were out on a date, so, of course, everyone has been asking me about it." Ellie looked up at Regina with her big, brown eyes.

Either she was the best actress Regina had ever seen—and that was saying something since she'd lived in LA for a while—or she was telling the truth.

Regina's body temperature went from scalding to merely hot. "If you didn't tell them about"—she licked her lips—"Riley, what's there to gossip about? We spent most of yesterday right here, at work. I hope you told them that."

"I did, but… Well, Beth thinks we…"

Regina waved her hand in a spit-it-out gesture. Her patience was running thin.

"She noticed that we're both, um, walking a little funny today."

A huff escaped Regina. "She's imagining things. I'm not walking funny." Granted, her legs had felt as stiff as two boards when she'd gotten up this morning, but she'd been careful not to let anyone see how sore she felt. Mind over matter. She'd always been a champion at hiding her pain and had perfected that skill in the past year.

One corner of Ellie's mouth twitched as if she was struggling not to grin. "Actually, you are a little." She held out her hands, palms out, before Regina could level a heated glare at her. "And apparently, so am I."

The remainder of Regina's anger dissipated. *Damn.* Had Ellie hurt herself…or rather, had she hurt Ellie when she'd slammed into her the day before?

She scanned every inch of Ellie's body, trying to make out any injury beneath her set of blue scrubs and the white, long-sleeved top she wore beneath. Other than several strands of her hair that had escaped from her ponytail, she looked perfect, though.

Um, perfectly unharmed.

"I'll have one of the residents check you out." Mentally, Regina went over the shift schedule to pick the most qualified resident.

"No, that's not necessary," Ellie said. "I'm fine. Just a couple of bruises and some sore muscles because it's been ages since I last ice-skated. That's why Beth thought…"

"Thought what?"

Ellie caught her bottom lip between her teeth.

Why the hell did that nervous little habit look so sexy? And why was Ellie blushing? "Thought what?" Regina growled, even though now her annoyance was directed more at herself than at Ellie.

"That we're sore from something much more pleasant than crashing into a wall at the ice-skating rink."

Regina's brain wasn't usually slow to grasp the meaning of a sentence. She blamed it on a mostly sleepless night that it took her several seconds to understand what Ellie was getting at. "Sex?" She wasn't sure whether she should laugh or shout. "She thinks we had—"

"Shh!" Ellie's face had taken on the color of the ketchup packet on her tray. She glanced left and right. "Yes, that's what she thinks."

"I hope you set the record straight…so to speak."

Ellie spread her hands. "I was trying to, but she probably thinks I'm in a postcoital stupor because I ordered the extra creamy hot chocolate, and it turned out the cafeteria worker had never heard of it."

Regina shrugged. "He or she must be new."

Slowly, Beth returned to the table with about half a dozen packets of mustard.

"Make sure you restock the ET tubes and the bag valve masks too," Regina said, as if they'd been talking about the airway cart the entire time.

For a second, Ellie looked as if she was about to playfully salute. "Will do, Doctor."

Regina gave her another curt nod, then turned toward Beth. "Enjoy your mustard sandwich." She strolled away without waiting for a reply, her entire focus on not walking as if she'd slammed into a wall—or had amazing sex with Ellie Fisher all night long.

Chapter 9

ELLIE YAWNED AND SHUFFLED INTO the kitchen for a much-needed cup of coffee. After three exhausting twelve-hour shifts in a row, she had slept until eleven on her first day off.

Just as she flipped the switch on the coffee machine, her phone chirped.

After some searching, she finally found it under the pizza flyer she'd left on the counter the previous night. With a few quick swipes, she unlocked the screen and tapped the messages app.

Ooh! She had a text from Regina!

Baking is a go, it said. *Tomorrow 4 p.m.*

"Hi to you too, Regina," Ellie muttered. "Why yes, I'm doing well and enjoying my day off, thank you so much for asking."

She waited, watching the screen to see if Regina would add more, but no new messages appeared.

Do you want us to carpool? she wrote back. *Taking two cars for a 1.5-hour drive seems like a total waste of resources.* If she'd learned one thing by working together for seven months, it was that Regina was a big believer in efficiency, so if she phrased it like that, Regina might say yes.

Okay, came the expected reply. *Will pick you up at 2.30.*

No question mark. She'd used a period. Regina had just decided that was how they would do things, without consulting Ellie at all.

Yeah, no. Ellie shook her head and tapped decisively with both thumbs. *Why don't I pick you up instead?*

It took only seconds for Regina's answer to arrive. *Because you don't know where I live.*

We could remedy that, Ellie typed back. *After all, we're dating, so shouldn't I know where you live?* She added a smiley face with a shit-eating grin.

We are not dating, Regina replied. *We are going on a couple of dates for a good cause.*

And I'm the one who's spending my hard-earned money on that good cause, so shouldn't I get a say in who's picking up who? No way would she let Regina walk all over her and call all the shots.

This time, it took Regina a full minute to type four letters: *Fine.*

Fine? I get to drive?

Don't rub it in, or I'll change my mind.

Ellie chuckled. Texting with Regina was equally infuriating and fun. *Okay, okay. Text me your address.*

Nothing happened. No address or Google Maps link appeared on her screen.

Ellie turned toward the coffee machine to give Regina a minute.

Before she could place a mug under the nozzle, her phone chirped again.

This isn't because of last week, is it?

Ellie stared at the message. *Not sure what you mean.*

You insisting on driving, Regina replied. *It's not because I had a moment in the car last week, is it?*

That hadn't even occurred to her, but apparently, Regina was still thinking about it. Clearly, having Ellie see her like that was still gnawing at her.

No, Ellie typed hastily. *Not at all. I still feel safe with you.*

No reply came.

Ellie reread what she'd written. *Still feel safe with you...* That sounded as if she was talking about something much deeper than just being a passenger in her car, didn't it? She quickly added, *With you as the driver, I mean.*

Good, Regina replied. *Because I call dibs on driving on our next date.*

Ellie grinned. Of course Regina had to have the last word. *All right. Where do I pick you up tomorrow?*

Within seconds, a link popped up on her screen.

Ellie tapped on it. Her Google Maps app opened, displaying the location of Regina's home.

Ooh. Regina lived two blocks west of the Plaza, in one of the historic apartment buildings lining 48th Street.

Ellie couldn't wait to see her apartment! She nearly sent back a text saying so but then stopped herself.

It might sound too much as if she looked forward to seeing not just her home but also Regina herself, and that, of course, wasn't true at all. Regina was still Dr. McIcy, she reminded herself. The woman had stopped by her table in the cafeteria, not to say hi but to request she restock the airway cart, for Christ's sake!

See you at 2.30, she finally texted back.

A thumbs-up emoji was Regina's only reply.

Regina placed a mini marker where her disc had been and put her right foot behind it.

The basket of the last hole was next to the tennis courts, and the path toward it was clear, with no trees or bushes to navigate around.

Dylan, her disc golf partner, waited quietly somewhere behind her, out of her line of sight, so he wouldn't disturb her focus.

She took up her putting stance and lightly gripped the disc as she visualized its elegant arc toward the basket. When she could see it clearly and could almost hear the clank of the chains, she brought the disc down and back toward thigh level. Then she pushed off with her back leg, shifted her weight forward, and extended her arm.

Just as she was about to release the disc, her phone chirped, breaking her concentration.

The disc sailed through the air, hit the rim of the basket, and bounced off. It landed in the grass about a yard from the basket.

Damn. Regina pulled the phone from her pocket. She rarely put it on silent because it wasn't necessary. The only one who ever called or texted was work if they were looking for someone to cover a shift.

"This better be an emergency," she muttered and slashed her finger across the screen to unlock it.

It was a text from Ellie. *Hey there.*

Regina glared at the message. She'd failed to make the putt for *hey there*? She stabbed at the tiny keyboard. *What is it?*

Three little dots appeared, then disappeared, as if Ellie had deleted what she'd written. *Did I catch you at a bad time?*

Regina huffed out a breath. *The worst. Right at the release point.*

This time, neither a reply nor the little dots appeared, as if Ellie didn't know what to say to that.

What was so hard to understand about the importance of timing? But then again, Ellie probably wasn't familiar with disc golf and had never heard terms like release—

Regina froze with her thumbs over the screen. "Oh, shit."

"Work?" Dylan asked behind her. "Do you have to go?"

"No, I just need a minute." Regina typed furiously. *DISC GOLF*, she wrote in all caps. *I'm on the disc golf course, trying to time the release of the putter disc just right.*

The three little dots danced below her sent message for quite some time.

Either Ellie was writing an essay, or she couldn't decide what to write. Finally, merely four words appeared: *Disc golf. Of course.*

Regina could easily imagine the blush coloring her cheeks. A grin tugged up her lips as she wrote back. Her perfect throw had been ruined, but at least she could have some fun. *Yep. Did you think I was doing something else?*

This time, the answer came in about half a second. *No. Disc golf. That's what I was thinking of.*

It was tempting, so tempting to shoot back a teasing reply, but Regina reined herself in. That kind of teasing came dangerously close to flirting, and that was out of the question with Ellie. *Right. What can I do for you?*

Ellie took a while to answer, as if she'd had to redirect her thoughts. *There's a slight change of plans tomorrow.*

Want me to drive after all? Regina replied. *Sure, I can do that. No problem.*

No, that's not it. Would you mind if I brought Ally along?

Regina stared at Ellie's last message. What the…? Her grip on the phone tightened. *You want to bring another woman to our date?*

Ellie sent a message containing a smiley face with a toothy grin and a single word: *Jealous?*

Please! Regina kicked at a branch in the grass with her sneaker. *Not in the slightest. I'm just not sure how open the auction sponsors are to pics of a happy thrupple.*

Don't worry. I have a feeling they'll love it. Number three in our thrupple is too cute to resist. I think it's those soulful brown eyes. Or the cute eyebrows.

What on earth? Why was Ellie swooning over some woman's eyebrows? Regina was not jealous. But that didn't mean she appreciated Ellie interrupting her disc golf round to fawn over another woman. This Ally person and her eyebrows could be cute someplace else.

Wouldn't you agree? Ellie texted. A photo appeared below the message.

Wally was looking directly at the camera, an eager doggy grin on his face. Since his head was cocked to the side, one tuft of hair above his eyes was higher than the other, giving him the appearance of raising one eyebrow.

You're talking about your dog?

Of course. Did you think I was talking about someone else? Ellie asked, repeating the sentence Regina had typed earlier almost exactly.

You said Ally. Not Wally.

That was autocorrect, Ellie answered. *And your reaction was just too cute to clear it up right away.*

Regina pinched her eyebrows together. The only thing more annoying than Ellie calling another woman cute was Ellie calling *her* cute.

Dylan cleared his throat and fake-coughed.

Regina shot him a look. "Hold your horses. I'll be right there." He was about to lose anyway, so why was he in such a hurry? She returned her attention to the phone and typed, *You want to bring your dog to baking class?*

Just to Fair Oaks, Ellie replied. *Normally, he goes to Grandma and Grandpa's house on Tuesdays, but my parents are out of town. I reached out to Sasha, and she said to bring him.*

Sasha? Regina asked.

Ms. Peterson, Ellie replied. *She told me to call her Sasha. She was super nice and said Wally can hang out with her girlfriend's and her aunt's dogs while we bake.*

Their baking instructor was gay too? *All right. You can bring him.*

Thank you for your generous permission, Your Majesty.

Ellie really didn't let her get away with anything. Regina wanted to find that infuriating but had to admit that she secretly liked it. *I have to go. See you at 2.30 on the dot.* She put her phone away without waiting for a reply.

Ignoring Dylan's curious stare, she placed her mini marker where the putter had landed, picked up her disc, and stepped back to get out of his way. "Your turn."

Dylan strolled toward his own marker. "Boyfriend?" he asked casually.

"As if," Regina muttered under her breath.

"Girlfriend?"

"No."

Dylan stopped at his marker and turned back around to face her. "But you are gay, aren't you?"

"What I am is eager to win this round, so…" She waved at him to throw his disc.

"Come on. You show up here last year, proceed to kick the ass of everyone in the league, and expect us not to be even a little curious about you?"

Regina tapped her disc against her thigh. "Has nobody ever told you that curiosity killed the cat?"

"Well, yeah, but cats have nine lives, so…" He gave her a disarming smile.

"I'm here to play disc golf, not to chat about my love life."

"Ah. You said *love life.*" Dylan grinned. "So it *was* your girlfriend."

Regina didn't dignify that with a response. "Take your shot."

Still grinning, Dylan turned around and faced the basket. "You should bring her sometime," he said over his shoulder.

"Take—your—shot." Regina put a harsh note into her voice—the one that made first-year residents shake in their bootie-covered sneakers.

She would not bring Ellie to disc golf. They would check off the four dating activities Ellie had been promised by the auction, and that would be it. The last thing she wanted was to let Ellie into what little bit of a personal life she had.

Chapter 10

THE LAST PATCHES OF SNOW had melted away, and the vivid green grass of the park to Ellie's left made it feel as if spring was just around the corner, even though the official first day of spring was still three weeks away.

Wally followed her down Roanoke Parkway with his tail wagging, always eager to go on an adventure.

Ahead of her, on the other side of the street, she could already make out the historic building at the corner, where she thought Regina lived.

When she reached the pedestrian crossing, the orange hand flashed, so she paused and used the delay to study Regina's apartment building.

The number above the white front door confirmed she was in the right place. Ellie had remembered correctly: Regina lived in one of the Literary Apartments—a cluster of historic buildings named after famous writers and poets. The name of this one, Washington Irving, was carved in stone above the entrance, which was flanked by two spiral columns.

The building's red brick exterior gave it a stately look, while the white cornerstones, terracotta ornamentations, and arched windows beneath the roof line added a certain elegance. A tower with a clay-tile roof rose up above the seven stories.

Somehow, the building seemed to fit Regina—it was economical, yet attractive.

Attractive?

Well, yeah, okay, no doubt Regina was hot. Objectively speaking, of course.

The light turned green, and she stepped off the curb—or rather, she tried to.

Instead of following her, Wally strained in the opposite direction, down 48th Street.

Oh no. It finally occurred to her why he'd been extra eager as they'd headed down the street from where she'd parked. This was the route they took when they went to Three Dog Bakery to get his favorite treats! He must have thought that was where they were going.

"Wally, no! We're not going to the bakery. I have a date at another bakery, and if you make us late, Regina will be pissed. We don't want that; believe me. She can be one scary lady when she's pissed."

Wally seemed unimpressed. His Yorkshire terrier half asserted itself as he stubbornly dug in his heels and tugged on the leash.

People veered around them, then glanced back over their shoulders to see who would win the fight.

Sweat broke out on Ellie's forehead. How embarrassing! She prayed Regina wasn't watching from one of the balconies or windows facing the intersection.

"Wally, come on!" She clucked her tongue and patted her thigh to get his attention. "There's a cute French bulldog and an adorable golden retriever waiting for you."

Finally, just as the orange hand started to flash, he gave in and followed her.

Ellie had to jog the last few yards to make it across the intersection in time. Once they were safely on the sidewalk, she wagged her index finger at him. "Don't do that in front of Regina, okay? I don't want her to think you're a badly behaved brat."

He tilted his head to the side, and his floppy ears twitched as he listened to her.

"You're lucky you're cute." She bent to ruffle the wiry fur on his head, then led him up two short sets of stairs toward the front entrance, which was located where the two wings of the building's L-shape met. She looked up at the Juliet balconies on the top floor but couldn't make out anyone.

Phew. Regina hadn't been watching from up there.

When she lowered her gaze back to street level, she noticed the figure leaning against one of the spiral columns flanking the door.

Great. The reason Regina hadn't been watching from up there was that she'd been down here. She straightened to her full height and peered down at Ellie with what seemed to be a mix of amusement and annoyance. "Did anyone ever tell you, you can pick up and carry a small dog like him?"

For a few seconds, no answer came to mind. Maybe because her brain was busy taking in Regina's outfit instead of trying to process language.

She was wearing a pair of light-blue jeans that clung to her legs, making them appear even longer. As usual, she hadn't bothered with a scarf or hat, and the long, black leather coat she wore didn't seem warm enough for the last day of February, but Ellie had to admit it looked good on her.

Incredibly good.

Ellie's libido sat up and took notice without her approval.

There should have been a rule that forbade wearing a leather coat—or a leather *anything*—on a date that wasn't actually a date. It was common knowledge that the sight of it triggered some kind of Pavlovian reaction in most lesbians.

Right. It's the coat, not the woman wearing it. Ellie would keep telling herself that. She forced her gaze away from Regina's legs and that distracting leather coat. "Why would I carry him around? He's a dog, not a purse."

Regina's lips twitched as if she was struggling to hold back a smile. "I noticed. A dog who was intent on heading the other way."

Ellie ducked her head. "He's usually much better-behaved, but the bakery that makes his favorite T-R-E-A-T-S is just down the street. Sorry to tell you, but in his book, their lick'n crunch cookies beat a visit with you."

Now that Wally had caught sight of Regina, he seemed to have forgotten about the Three Dog Bakery altogether. He rushed toward her as if he remembered her, forcing Ellie to follow.

Regina crouched down to pet Wally, who was sniffing her hands, yowling, and trying to lick her fingers as if she were an old friend. She cocked her head and glanced up at Ellie. "Lick'n crunch?"

Her crouching position brought her head level with Ellie's navel, which was as distracting as the coat. The way "lick" rolled off Regina's tongue, all smooth and sensual, sent heat swirling through her body.

No, no, no! Regina was still Dr. McIcy. The only heat she was allowed to produce in her was that of anger. Ellie tugged on her scarf, pulling it away from her neck, and tried to sound completely casual as she said, "I didn't name the cookies. I just buy them."

Regina gave Wally one last pat, then rose. "Shall we?"

It took Ellie's brain a second or two to grasp what she meant. *Oh.* Regina wanted to leave right away, which meant she wouldn't get to see her apartment. Was that why Regina had come down instead of waiting for her to ring the doorbell? "Um, sure."

Regina walked past her and headed down the stairs. "Where are you parked?"

"By the Park Plaza Building. Parking around here is a nightmare." Ellie jogged down the steps to catch up with her.

Wally trotted between them as they walked toward the intersection, tail wagging.

Oh, please, please, don't think we're going to Three Dog Bakery, buddy. Ellie really shouldn't care what Regina thought, but she didn't want her to assume her dog was a spoiled, misbehaving rascal.

Luckily, Wally seemed completely taken with this interesting new person. When Regina turned left toward the Park Plaza Building and purposefully strode down the street, Wally followed without even glancing in the direction of the bakery.

Figures. Apparently, leather coats didn't just have a magnetic effect on queer women; they worked on dogs too.

The magnetic effect seemed to work a bit too well on Wally. When Regina climbed into the passenger seat of Ellie's car, Wally tried to jump in after her.

"Wally, down! You know you're not allowed in the front seat."

With a sad huff, he dropped down.

"Hop up." Ellie patted the backseat and, once he jumped up, secured his dog harness to the seat belt.

"He's quite the character," Regina said when Ellie got in on the driver's side.

Ellie wasn't sure if it was a criticism or a neutral comment. Regina was still hard to figure out, but she chose to assume it was the latter. "Yeah, he is. He's a borkie—a beagle/Yorkie mix—and I happen to think he's got the best traits of both breeds. Do you like dogs?"

Regina gave a one-shoulder shrug. "I don't not like them."

Ellie started the car and cast a quick, disbelieving look at her.

"What?" Regina said. "I didn't say I eat dogs for breakfast, did I? I simply haven't had a chance to develop an informed opinion."

An informed opinion on dogs? Laughter threatened to bubble up, but Ellie held it back. She had to admit the way Regina had phrased it was kind of endearing. "Never had a dog?"

"No."

Ellie waited for her to add something, but Regina fell silent. She didn't say a word as Ellie steered the car around the park, then north on Madison Avenue. Regina stretched out her legs and seemed content to look out the window and watch the world go by, even though there wasn't a single thing of interest as far as Ellie could see.

Ten minutes later, when Ellie merged onto northbound Interstate 35, Regina still hadn't said anything.

Only Wally's quiet snores from the backseat interrupted the monotonous hum of the engine.

Oh boy. It would be a long, long trip to the bakery.

After a while, Ellie couldn't stand it anymore. She cleared her throat. "Have you ever been to Fair Oaks?"

"Why would I?" Regina asked. "There's nothing interesting there, is there?"

Ellie chuckled. "Tell that to millions of Jenna Blake fans worldwide. She lives there, you know?"

Regina made a thoroughly unimpressed sound.

"Let me guess. You haven't developed an informed opinion on Jenna Blake yet?"

"No, I have."

"Which is?" Having a conversation with Regina was like playing tug-of-war with an elephant.

"A few of her newer songs are okay. The rest of her music is kinda meh."

Ellie took her gaze off the road to stare at her. "Meh? You can't be serious! How can you not love her music? The woman won five Grammys. She's a legend!"

Regina shrugged again. "All those sentimental love songs are just not my cup of tea."

So Regina didn't only have a problem with Valentine's Day and heart-shaped decorations; she also detested love songs. "Bad breakup?" Crap. The question had slipped out before she could think about it.

But, truth be told, she had wondered why Regina had left California for a while now. Could a bad breakup be the reason? According to hospital gossip, she had worked at Cedars-Sinai in LA, which ranked in the country's top ten of best hospitals. Why had she left and come to KC of all places?

There was a story there. Ellie sensed it, and the more time she spent with Regina, the more curious she became.

Regina sighed. The sound came from deep within her chest. "Do we have to do this?" She waved her hand back and forth between them.

"Do what?" Ellie asked.

"Play the twenty-personal-questions game."

"If it's too personal, we can talk about something else," Ellie said softly. After what had happened the last time they'd been in a car together, she didn't want to put her finger into another open wound.

"Is not talking at all an option?"

"For the next 1.5 hours?" Ellie gave her voice a faux-horrified note. "You did promise I wouldn't get bored on our dates, remember?"

Another sigh escaped Regina. "No breakup. I just needed a change of scenery."

"And why KC of all places?"

"Would you believe it was for the lovely Midwestern weather?"

"Compared to the balmy Californian temperatures? Nope."

"Okay, it was for the disc golf."

"Disc golf?" Ellie echoed.

"Sure," Regina said, her face so impassive that Ellie couldn't tell whether she was joking. "Kansas City is among the top fifteen disc golf destinations in the US."

Ellie burst out laughing, then stopped when Regina didn't join in. "Seriously? You moved here to play golf?"

"Disc golf. Well, not just for that, obviously. I want to be Chief of Emergency Medicine sooner rather than later, and it's going to be easier to achieve that at a smaller hospital."

Ambitious career plans fit Regina, and it all sounded logical, but Ellie could tell there was more to it. She sensed that Regina had reached her limit, though, so she didn't ask.

For a while, they drove without speaking.

As they passed beneath an overpass, the sounds of the tires on the asphalt seemed to grow louder, emphasizing the silence between them.

Okay, time for her emergency plan.

"Could you open the glove compartment?" Ellie asked.

Regina glanced up at the overcast sky. "You don't need your sunglasses, do you?"

"No. You'll see."

Regina popped open the glove compartment.

A small bag of Cheetos spilled out.

Regina caught it before it could end up on the floorboard. She stared down at it as if she were holding a bunch of chocolate-covered grasshoppers. "What is that?"

"Road trip snacks." Ellie did a little shimmy behind the wheel.

Regina eyed her skeptically. "You think Cheetos make a good road trip snack?"

"You prefer snap peas and cauliflower florets?" Ellie shot back.

"I prefer something that doesn't stain the car seats orange."

Ellie tilted her head in acknowledgment. "Okay, I'll give you that. But there's other stuff in there too."

Regina pulled the packages from the glove compartment one by one. "M&Ms, goldfish crackers, licorice, Twinkies." She sounded as if she were ranking a list of deadly diseases. "You know that we're not doing a cross-country trip, right? We're just going to a bakery that's an hour and a half away—a bakery where we'll probably get to eat whatever we'll be baking."

"Have you heard the advice to never go grocery shopping when you're hungry?"

"Of course I have. But you apparently didn't follow that advice when you went shopping for these." Regina jostled the bags on her lap.

Ellie chose to ignore that remark even though it was true. "That's also valid advice for baking. The last time I baked on an empty stomach, I ended up eating half of the raw dough and nearly threw up afterward. So it's medically advised to have a snack before baking."

"Is that your professional advice as a registered nurse?"

Ellie nodded sagely. "It is. Does the doctor concur?"

"Well…" Regina tossed the Cheetos back into the glove compartment. "My mentors have told me repeatedly not to dismiss the advice of an experienced nurse, so…" She ripped open the pack of Twinkies and handed Ellie one.

That was a surprise on so many levels. "Huh. I figured you for a goldfish woman."

Regina shook her head and bit into the Twinkie. "If I'm doing this, I might as well do it right," she said as soon as she'd swallowed. She ran her tongue around the creamy white center of the Twinkie, then slowly dipped it in.

Oh. My. God. Ellie nearly choked on a bite of her own Twinkie as a hunger of a different kind roared to life. She squirmed in the driver's seat and quickly looked away, pretending the nearly empty road ahead required her full attention.

Maybe Regina had been right. Road trip snacks were a bad idea. An outright *dangerous* idea.

She focused on her own snack and the road ahead for a full minute before risking a quick glance to the right to see if Regina was done seducing the Twinkie.

But Regina was either the slowest eater in the universe, or she was enjoying Ellie's discomfort.

Yeah. Discomfort. Keep telling yourself that.

The way Regina curled her tongue to tease out the cream filling made desire curl low in her belly.

Finally, she couldn't stand it any longer. "You're doing that on purpose to get back at me for asking too many questions!"

"Me?" Regina drawled. "Doing what on purpose?"

"Having tongue sex with that"—Ellie stopped herself before the word *lucky* could slip out—"damn Twinkie."

Husky laughter drifted across the middle console. "Tongue sex? It's called oral, Ellie."

Oh God. The way Regina had said her name, teasing and sensual, right after the word *oral...* A flush swept through her entire body. "I know what it's called." She tried to sound unaffected, but even she could hear the hitch in her voice.

"Good to know," Regina said, then added, "I mean, providing sexual health education is part of your job every now and then, right?"

"Right," Ellie rasped out.

Regina popped the remainder of the Twinkie into her mouth, then licked a bit of cream off her finger.

Ellie suppressed a groan. Maybe she should have brought cauliflower florets. No one could do sexy things with those.

But then again, Regina would probably have managed. Ellie could only hope that Sasha would have them bake an entirely unerotic pastry. Visions of what Regina would do to a lava cake and its moist core danced in front of her mind's eye.

Ellie's mouth felt parched. She flicked on the turn signal and took the next exit in search of a gas station. "Water," she croaked out in explanation. "I forgot to bring water."

Regina just smirked.

Fields, pastures, and a few stands of trees were all Regina could see as Ellie drove north on a narrow two-lane highway that barely deserved the name. The asphalt was cracked and patched up, and Ellie's attempts to avoid the potholes and bumpy spots reminded Regina of trying to find a good vein on an eighty-year-old dialysis patient.

Every now and then, they passed a farm building, but other than that, there was nothing to see.

"Are you sure we aren't lost?" Regina finally asked.

"I'm sure."

Ellie didn't add anything else. She hadn't said much since the Twinkie incident.

Regina knew she shouldn't have done that. But she hadn't been able to resist. It had felt too good knowing she was having an effect on Ellie.

That flush on her cheeks and the way she had chugged down the water they had stopped to get, as if she was about to overheat…

Regina wasn't even sure why the sight of it had made her want to devour a second Twinkie so she could see Ellie like that again.

Probably just the thrill of the game, right? It was great to know she hadn't lost her touch after everything she'd been through in the past year. She'd played games like that before, seduced women just because she could, when she'd felt low after Amber had broken up with her. Maybe it shouldn't have surprised her that she was falling back into old habits after Riley's death had turned her life upside down.

But Ellie wasn't someone she could play with. She was someone she worked with and therefore off-limits.

Plus Regina sensed that, beneath all her spunk, Ellie was a sensitive soul. A romantic who hung paper heart strings and listened to Jenna Blake songs on repeat.

So as much fun as it had been to tease her, she needed to cut it out and go back to being a professional.

It surprised her that the thought triggered an unexpected amount of resistance. She really didn't want to be strictly professional with Ellie, and that had never happened before.

Finally, a large, white sign appeared to the right, announcing *Welcome to Fair Oaks, hometown of Jenna Blake.*

Ellie sat up straighter behind the wheel and slowed to a crawl, moving through the tiny town at a much slower pace than the posted thirty miles per hour.

Was she looking for the bakery? Regina sent her a quizzical glance. "Sasha said to turn left once we passed Casey's." She pointed to the gas station ahead.

"I know. I just thought maybe I'd see…" Another rosy blush swept into Ellie's cheeks. "Oh, forget it."

"Ah, now I get it! You were hoping to catch a glimpse of Jenna Blake!"

Ellie's face went from rosy to pomegranate red, confirming Regina's suspicion.

Normally, Regina had no patience for immature, starstruck behavior, but she still felt a bit guilty for the Twinkie incident, so she said nothing. Besides, the way Ellie was blushing was kind of adorable, even though Regina would never tell her that.

Ellie sped up a little and turned left.

The red brick spire of the courthouse rose up before them. All the local businesses seemed to be clustered around it: a hardware store, a diner, a mom-and-pop grocery store, a pharmacy, a flower shop, and a beauty salon.

"Oh, there it is." Ellie pointed to the right, at an old brick building.

On a sign above the door, cursive letters read *Slice of Heaven*.

They parked in front of the building and got out.

Regina peered through the large window. She could make out a counter, a display case, and a seating area with several small tables and chairs, but the bakery seemed to be empty. When she tried the door, it was open. She stuck her head in but didn't enter to avoid Wally rushing in after her. "Hello?"

The double doors at the back of the room swung open, and a tall, solidly built woman in a white baker's apron walked toward them. A thick braid dangled over one shoulder, and instead of a traditional baker's cap, a red bandanna covered the rest of her hair. She held the door open with a broad grin. "Hi! You must be Ellie and Reggie. I'm Sasha."

Ellie burst out laughing.

Regina glowered at her, then at their host. "Regina."

"Oh. Sorry. I must have misunderstood on the phone. I could have sworn she said you prefer Reggie." Sasha's gaze went to Ellie.

Wow, that little... You just wait, Ellie Fisher. Maybe she would eat that second Twinkie on the way back after all.

"Um, yeah, must be a misunderstanding." Ellie shook the taller woman's hand, her smaller one nearly disappearing in Sasha's. "Sorry we're a bit late. I, um..."

"My friend here was a little parched, so we stopped for water," Regina threw in.

Ellie stared at her with wide eyes.

"What?" Regina asked. "It's true. You were about to overheat."

"Yeah, but... You just called me *friend*."

Shit, had she? Regina normally didn't toss around words like that lightly. She had made few friends as an adult and never someone she worked with. This entire auction thing had her so off-balance, it wasn't even funny. She shrugged. "Figure of speech."

Sasha's braid swung to the side as she tilted her head and looked back and forth between them. "Ah."

Regina narrowed her eyes at her. What the hell was that supposed to mean? Their baking class wasn't off to a good start.

Before she could say something, the double doors opened again, and a second woman stepped out.

"Hi." She flashed them a warm smile. "You must be Ellie and—"

"Regina," Regina said with a warning glare at Ellie.

"Right. I'm Ashley."

"My assistant for today's baking lessons," Sasha added with a grin.

"Oh no. Don't listen to her. I'm her girlfriend, not her assistant." Ashley walked over to Sasha and gave her a light swat. Her fingers lingered and curled around Sasha's biceps in a familiar gesture. She was blonde where Sasha was brunette, several inches shorter and more slender, but as she leaned against Sasha's side, they seemed like a perfect fit.

Regina rolled her eyes at herself. Perfect fit? There was no such thing. Apparently, she'd been spending too much time with Ellie lately. If she wasn't careful, Ellie's romantic streak would start to rub off on her. She shuddered at the thought.

"I'm just here to take the photos for social media," Ashley added. "I won't do any baking. Any time I help with the baking, we end up in a food fight."

"Nothing wrong with a good food fight." Sasha's already deep voice dropped another register.

As she and Ashley looked into each other's eyes, they seemed to forget that they had visitors.

Regina folded her arms across her chest. *Great.* She'd ended up in Romance Central. No doubt they'd bake heart-shaped cupcakes. She pointed at the doorstep, where they were still rooted to the spot. "Are you going to ask us in?"

Ellie elbowed her. "Be nice," she whispered. More loudly, she said, "I brought Wally, so I don't think we can come in."

Ashley let go of Sasha's arm. "Let me take him. I'll drop him, Casper, and Snickerdoodle off at my friends' house, then come back to take the photos."

Ellie laughed. "Snickerdoodle? How did he—or she—end up with that name?"

Sasha grimaced. "Don't ask. Let's just say it's way better than what my aunt wanted to name him."

Ellie handed over Wally's leash and watched Ashley get acquainted with him. As the blonde led him away, the look on Ellie's face resembled that of a mother who had dropped off her kid for their first day of preschool.

The impulse to pat her arm and tell her the dog would be fine gripped Regina, but she ignored it. Yeah, she was definitely spending too much time around Ellie. Sentimental reassurances like that weren't normally her style.

"Let's head to the kitchen." Sasha led them through the café part of the bakery and held open one side of the double doors for them.

Regina entered first.

The bakery kitchen was noticeably warmer, and the scent of cinnamon and yeast hung in the air.

A huge wooden worktable formed the center of the room, while a stainless-steel sink, an industrial-sized dishwasher, and several ovens lined the walls, along with shelves filled with every piece of baking equipment known to mankind.

Ellie glanced around, her cheeks already flushed, either from the heat emanating from the ovens or from excitement. "So, what are we going to bake?"

"I was thinking of Sweet Kisses," Sasha said.

"Yeah, I could tell from the way you looked at your girlfriend," Regina murmured under her breath.

But apparently, Ellie had an amazing sense of hearing. "Behave, or I'm gonna tell her to call you Gina."

"They're my most popular baked good around Valentine's Day," Sasha added. "They're heart-shaped chocolate cupcakes with salted caramel frosting."

Oh hell. They really would be making heart-shaped cupcakes! Regina struggled not to grimace.

"But I'm flexible if you want to try something more challenging," Sasha said.

Regina was always up for a challenge, especially if it spared her from having to participate in Valentine's Day-related baking. "Like what?"

"A lava cake, for example."

Ellie started coughing as if she'd swallowed wrong. "No!" she gasped out when she could speak again. Her eyes were wide, as if Sasha had suggested they make deep-fried chicken-foot cake pops. "Um, I mean, no lava cake please."

"Not a fan of chocolate?" Sasha asked.

"No, I am. It's just…" Ellie shifted her weight from one foot to the other. "A lava cake might be too much for me right now. Uh, I mean, too rich."

Regina took a closer look at her face. That wasn't only the heat from the ovens staining Ellie's cheeks scarlet, was it? She would have paid her back the nine hundred dollars Ellie had spent at the auction to find out what was going through her mind right now.

"Okay, no lava cake." Sasha thought for a few seconds. "How about a rainbow layer cake? With its bright colors, it will look great on social media, plus it's an opportunity to show the world that happy, cake-eating queer people exist." She paused and slid her bandanna up while glancing back and forth between them again. "You two are queer, right? You didn't just bid on her for a good cause, did you, Ellie?"

"We're both lesbians," Regina said. "But she was just trying to kill a fly."

Ellie let out a groan. "You'll never let me forget that, will you?"

"No," Regina said cheerfully. In Sasha's direction, she added, "A big one."

Sasha laughed. "Ooh, you'll have to tell me that story while we're baking."

"There is no story," Ellie said. "I didn't mean to bid. It was an accident."

Ellie had told her that several times. It should have been old news by now, something that didn't bother her at all. But knowing Ellie hadn't meant to bid on her still grated. Not that she had wanted Ellie to bid on her, of course.

Regina clapped her hands to chase away the distracting thoughts. "All right. Let's get started."

Two minutes into their baking class, Ellie mentally added bandannas to the growing list of garments that shouldn't be allowed to be worn on a date that wasn't a date.

Sasha had handed each of them a bandanna to keep their hair away from their faces—and from the kitchen equipment.

Ellie had a feeling she looked like a kid in a cheap Halloween costume wearing hers, while Regina managed to look effortlessly sexy. The gray bandanna emphasized her amazing cheekbones and the color of her eyes.

It also made the tiny wrinkle between her brows stand out even more. With every instruction Sasha gave them as they gathered the ingredients, Regina's frown deepened. Clearly, she didn't like not being the one calling the shots.

Ellie bit back a grin. Baking class promised to be highly entertaining.

"You know what?" Regina said as Sasha placed a huge bowl on the counter between them. "Why don't we make this a little more interesting?"

"Um, more interesting...how?" Ellie asked. That challenging glint in Regina's eyes didn't bode well.

"How about a bake-off? We both make our own rainbow layer cake, and whoever manages to make the better one wins."

Ellie couldn't help laughing. Leave it to Regina to turn what the auction had intended as a romantic baking lesson for two into a competition. "Do we even have enough ingredients for two cakes?"

"We do. This is a bakery after all," Sasha said. "And there's no such thing as too much cake. That is, if you're sure that's how you want to do this. You're the winning bidder, after all, so it should be your choice."

Ellie hesitated. The auction probably had something different in mind—them working together to create a shared vision.

"Scared to lose again?" Regina asked in a challenging tone.

"Again? Ha! No. I'm just thinking of your poor wallet since you already owe me one drink. But if you insist... You're on."

They took up position on opposite ends of the counter and nodded at each other while holding eye contact, like two gunfighters about to draw their weapons.

"Do I need to hire additional cleaning staff?" Sasha asked with a chuckle. "I have a feeling my kitchen might end up looking worse than after that first food fight Ash and I had."

"Nah," Regina said, her gaze still on Ellie. "Just give me another bowl and tell me how to get six perfectly even layers."

Ellie stepped in front of her so she was in Sasha's line of sight. "Tell *both* of us. No helping just the competition allowed."

"Competition, huh?" Amusement colored Regina's tone.

Ellie nodded. "You wanted a bake-off; you got a bake-off. I'm not going to phone it in and let you win."

When Ashley returned from dropping off the dogs a few minutes later, they were working furiously, each whisking together flour, sugar, eggs, and the rest of the ingredients.

"Oh wow." Ashley paused one step into the bakery kitchen. "What's going on here?"

"I have no idea." Sasha laughed. "Somehow, my romantic baking class turned into *The Great American Baking Show*."

Ellie didn't look up from her sponge cake batter as Ashley started to take pictures. She reached for the vanilla beans, but instead, her fingers met warm skin.

Regina had reached for the same ingredient at the same time.

A tingling sensation danced along Ellie's nerve endings, running up her fingers and through her entire arm.

"Sorry," Ellie croaked out.

"No worries."

In the middle of their intense competition, they both paused, their hands lingering on the jar with the vanilla beans.

The camera sound of Ashley's phone finally wrenched Ellie out of her trance.

Vanilla beans. Batter. Baking competition. Right.

She pulled the jar out from under Regina's hand, stealing it for herself.

"Hey," Regina protested three seconds too late.

While Ellie fished a vanilla bean from the jar, Regina lingered behind her, waiting for her to be done with the ingredient she needed. Ellie could have sworn the temperature in the kitchen went up a degree or two as Regina's body heat seemed to engulf her.

At work, Ellie was usually the nurse everyone called when they needed to start an IV or draw blood from hard-to-find veins, but now she had difficulty keeping her hands steady.

Having Regina so close was really distracting. She hoped Regina wouldn't have the same effect on her once they were back at work.

Finally, she handed Regina the jar, very careful not to let their hands brush this time.

As they continued to work, they kept bumping into each other—their shoulders or arms brushed in passing, or their hands touched as they reached for the same item.

She had no idea how it kept happening. The bakery kitchen wasn't small at all, and the worktable was long, giving them plenty of space.

Yet it seemed any time she needed the scales, a pinch of salt, or the baking powder, they were on Regina's side of the counter.

Ellie was starting to believe Regina didn't emanate only heat but some weird magnetism too.

Or maybe she was just more aware of Regina's physical closeness after the tongue acrobatics she had performed on the Twinkie in the car.

She tried to concentrate on her cake, but she couldn't help glancing over at Regina's side of the worktable every now and then.

Well, of course she had to glance over. They were competing against each other after all, so she had to check on Regina's progress. It had nothing to do with the expression of fierce focus on Regina's face as she weighed her six bowls, making sure each contained an equal amount of batter.

"Don't add too much, Ellie," Sasha said. "A little of the gel food coloring goes a long way."

Oops. Ellie wrenched her attention away from Regina's side of the worktable, put the squeeze bottle down, and stirred with a spoon. The batter turned a shockingly bright shade of orange. *Okay. Looks like I'll go for really intense colors.*

Regina slid the cake pans with her colorful batter into the oven seconds before Ellie did and flashed her a triumphant grin.

"We aren't competing for who'll finish first," Ellie called over to her. "The person with the best cake—not the fastest one—will win."

"I'm aiming for both," Regina called back.

Of course she was. With a shake of her head, Ellie closed the oven door and turned toward Sasha for more instructions.

Ellie smoothed the long spatula over the final layer of buttercream one last time, trying to keep the spatula as flat as Sasha had shown her. When the top layer and the sides of the cake were evenly covered, she let a handful of rainbow sprinkles rain down on it.

Then she stepped back to admire her creation, spread her now-empty hands wide, and declared, "Done!"

"We aren't competing for who'll finish first," Regina mumbled from where she was still working on her own cake. "The person with the best cake—not the fastest one—will win."

"I'm aiming for both." Ellie turned toward her with a grin.

She had managed to keep her gaze off Regina's side of the worktable for the last fifteen minutes, focusing on her own frosting. Now she caught a glimpse of Regina's nearly finished creation for the first time.

Her mouth dropped open.

Regina had refused to put sprinkles on her cake. Instead, she had armed herself with a pastry bag, and now she was piping a line of red buttercream around the side of the cake.

Hers was square, not round like Ellie's. Lines of velvety buttercream decorated the sides, starting with purple, then blue, green, yellow, orange, and red. Each one looked like delicate scrollwork.

Regina expertly held the piping bag in one graceful hand, applying steady pressure, while using the other to guide the star-shaped tip along the surface of the cake.

Wow. Ellie closed her mouth and swallowed.

As Regina guided the tip toward the last side, her shirtsleeve slid forward, threatening to brush along the buttercream art. She couldn't pull it back without interrupting the piping.

"Wait. Let me help." Ellie took a step forward, into Regina's space, and slid the sleeve up Regina's forearm.

Slender muscles bunched beneath her fingers as Regina froze.

Ellie cleared her throat. "There."

"Thanks."

They stood rooted to the spot for several heartbeats longer, then Ellie moved back. "You're welcome."

Regina turned toward her cake and frowned at the now slightly uneven line. She finished the last string of buttercream, then placed two strawberry halves in the middle of her cake before turning toward Sasha. "So? What do you think, Judge?"

Sasha walked closer to the cake stands and made a show of studying both creations from all sides. "I think," she finally said, "neither of you needed baking lessons. Clearly, you've done this before."

"I wish." Ellie chuckled. "I'm usually the queen of box cake mixes."

"Well, then I guess what they say is true: competition is really good for business," Sasha said. "You outdid yourself. Both of you did. Right, Ash?"

Ashley snapped several close-ups of both cakes. "Yeah. They turned out amazing!"

"Let's see which one tastes better." Regina reached for a knife and sliced into her cake with the precision of a surgeon, revealing its colorful layers.

Ellie cut a piece of her own cake and presented it to Sasha, then cut three more.

Soon, each of them had a plate with two samples of cake.

Ellie slid the first forkful into her mouth. *Oh yum.* Not only did her creation look great, it actually tasted wonderful too!

She tried a bit of Regina's cake and could barely tell the difference, other than maybe Regina having used slightly more vanilla. *Who would have thought. Regina is a fan of vanilla.* She grinned around another forkful of cake.

Sasha smacked her lips like a sommelier at a wine tasting. "I think it's a tie. They're both award-worthy."

Regina put down her fork and gave a grudging nod. "They're both… edible."

Ellie gave her an incredulous look. "Edible?"

Regina shrugged. "Better than the Twinkie."

A forkful of cake nearly went down the wrong pipe. "Uh, right," Ellie managed to get out, but her libido insisted that nothing would ever beat that Twinkie.

Shut up, she told it firmly and took another bite of cake.

They were sitting in the café section of the bakery, enjoying their cake, when the bell above the door jingled.

Regina looked up.

Two strangers entered the bakery.

The shorter one—a curvy redhead—greeted them with a warm grin and pointed over her shoulder at a red jeep parked outside, where Wally and two other dogs were pressing their noses to the window in the back. "Anyone interested in trading a pack of dogs for two apricot-orange cream scones?"

Ellie laughed. "I'll trade you a slice of rainbow layer cake for my borkie."

"Deal. I'll never say no to cake." The redhead shook Ellie's hand and tugged her companion forward with her other hand. "I'm Holly, dog sitter extraordinaire, and this is my wife, Leo."

Huh. Regina leaned back in her chair and regarded them with interest. Who would have thought they would meet not one but two same-sex couples in a tiny town like this?

"Hi. I'm—" Ellie turned her attention toward the taller woman for the first time. Hand extended toward her, she froze and let out an ear drum-piercing shriek. "Oh my God! You're Jenna Blake!"

Regina glared at her and clutched one ear, hoping it would stop ringing in a second. She studied the taller woman. So that was the famous singer? She didn't get why people made such a big fuss over her—or celebrities in general. In a pair of worn jeans and with what seemed to be graphite dust from a pencil on her cheek, Jenna Blake didn't look like a superstar at all.

"Leo, please," the singer said. "I've never been Jenna here in Fair Oaks." She reached across the table to shake Ellie's still-extended hand.

Ellie delicately gripped Leo's fingers, as if she didn't know whether to shake her hand or kiss it. Her cheeks were as red as they'd been during the Twinkie incident. "Leo. Of course. It's so great to meet you. I'm a big fan."

"She really couldn't tell," Regina muttered.

Ellie reached over and slapped her arm without ever taking her gaze off Leo.

Regina smirked. She would never admit it, nor did she fully understand it, but seeing Ellie fangirl like a teenager was kind of cute. Still silly, but cute.

"Thank you," Leo said. "That means a lot. I wouldn't say no to a piece of cake either."

Regina shoved her chair back and stood before Ellie could jump up and fall over her own feet. "I'll get you one of mine. Ellie would probably go into cardiac arrest and need CPR if you ate a piece of hers."

"You made two cakes? Wow, you city folks are real overachievers." Leo rounded the counter and got two plates, apparently very familiar with where things were kept in the bakery.

"*You* city folks?" her wife repeated. Her vivid blue eyes twinkled. "So you're a small-town gal now?"

Leo paused with the empty plates in her hands. "Damn. I just said that, didn't I?"

"Yep," Sasha said.

"You sure did," Holly added with a soft smile.

"Come on. Admit it," Ashley said. "You love this little town."

"I love Holly and being wherever she is," Leo said. "But yeah, I admit there might be a thing or two that I like about Fair Oaks. Its bakery, for one thing."

"Of course. I mean, what's not to love about this bakery?" Sasha spread her arms, showing off her establishment as well as her impressive wingspan.

"Or its owner," Ashley added quietly.

Oh Christ on a bike. Something had to be in the water in this tiny town. Something awfully sweet that made people lovesick. Regina took the first plate from Leo's hand and deposited a large piece of cake on it, then plopped a slice of Ellie's cake onto the other. At least if they were eating, the Fair Oaks folks couldn't be spewing sentimental love declarations.

"Thanks." Leo took the plates from her and carried them to the small table where her wife had taken a seat. "So what's your story?" She looked from Regina to Ellie. "I hear this is all part of a singles auction package?"

"It all started with a fly," Sasha answered before either of them could. "A big one."

Regina fixed the singer with a threatening stare. "If any of this makes it into a love song, I'll be back."

Ellie doubled over laughing. "You'll have to excuse my friend here. She's a romance grinch."

Friend. Now it was Regina's turn to get stuck on the word. Had Ellie used it as a figure of speech too, or was that how she saw her now? Regina didn't like it, she decided. Not one bit.

It had nothing to do with wanting to be "more" than a friend. She just preferred keeping a professional distance from the people she worked with; that was all.

She dropped onto her chair. "I'm not."

Ellie set her fork down on her plate, tilted her head in a way that reminded Regina of her dog, and gave her a questioning look as if to say, *Not your friend?*

Regina could imagine the hurt in her big, dark eyes if she nodded in confirmation. "I'm not a romance grinch." She snapped her mouth shut. *Damn.* Why had she said that? Since when did she care about doe-eyed looks and trying not to hurt someone's feelings?

"Hmm." Leo swirled her fork through rainbow-colored frosting. "The romance grinch. That would actually make a good song title."

Regina groaned while everyone else burst out laughing.

Chapter 11

"Oh my God, oh my God, oh my God" was all Ellie could say for the first ten minutes of their trip back to Kansas City.

Usually, when women said that in Regina's presence, she'd been the cause of it, not meeting some celebrity. But she bit her tongue and abstained from saying so. *Professional. Be professional around her.*

Ellie bounced in the driver's seat, making Wally lift his head from where he had been asleep in the back of the car. "We met Jenna Blake!"

"Leo," Regina said. "We met Leo."

"Yes! Isn't it great that she allowed us to call her that? And she ate our cake! Can you believe it?"

"Yes," Regina said. "I can. By the way, it was *my* cake she ate, yet I'm not about to have a commemorative plaque made."

Ellie glanced over for a moment. "You don't get it at all, do you? Have you truly never had a little crush on an actress or a singer?"

"No, never. Why would I?"

"Not once? Not even as a teenager?"

Regina shook her head. "I had no time for silly infatuations. By the time I was Riley's age, I knew I wanted to go to Harvard Medical School."

Ellie flicked her gaze over to her again and gave her a startled look.

At first, Regina thought it was because she'd gone to Harvard. Most people were suitably impressed when she mentioned it. But it wasn't admiration on Ellie's face, and the expression of surprise had flashed across her features a second before Regina had name-dropped her med school.

Riley. The realization slammed into Regina with the force of a battering ram. She had said the name out loud without even noticing. She had meant Caitlin's kid, not her brother, but still… It was the first time she'd casually mentioned his name since he'd died.

What a weird moment, made even weirder by the fact that the sharp stab of pain she'd expected never happened—more like a dull ache.

That made her feel worse instead of better. She couldn't be over him. Shouldn't be over him. She was the one who had failed him.

Ellie loosened her grip on the steering wheel with the hand closer to Regina, as if she was about to reach over and touch her.

"I was focused on my own goals," Regina added quickly. Her voice was too loud, but at least the volume helped her push back thoughts of Riley. "Not on some Hollywood starlet or some Grammy winner. Mooning over people I knew I'd never meet made no sense to me, even then."

Ellie was silent for several seconds, then returned her hand to its initial position on the steering wheel as if deciding to let it go. "Well, we just met Jenna…Leo, so…"

The tension in Regina's shoulders receded. "All right, I'll give you that. Still, I never understood all the hype around a person just because they can carry a tune."

"Carry a tune?" Ellie echoed. "She's one of the world's best singers!"

"So? I'm great at my job too, yet you don't see anyone throwing their bra at me."

Ellie laughed. "So you have bra envy?"

"That's not a thing."

"Apparently, it is. You've got bra envy!" Ellie drew out each word in a delighted singsong.

"Nonsense. You've seen what I can do with a Twinkie. If I wanted women to throw their bras at me, they would."

Ellie's laughter ended abruptly. An audible gulp echoed through the car.

For the next mile or two, Regina rode along with a triumphant grin on her lips. She loved winning arguments—and she was growing to enjoy that blush on Ellie's face just as much.

"The Plaza looks weird without the holiday lights, doesn't it?" Ellie pointed to their left, down 47th Street.

Regina made a vague sound of agreement.

"Especially this year, when they stayed on for six weeks longer than usual," Ellie added.

Another "mm-hmm" came from Regina.

Conversation had flown better on the way back from the bakery, but the closer they got to KC, the quieter Regina had become. The teasing banter from earlier had stopped.

Was Regina just tired and peopled out? Or was more going on?

Maybe being back in the city reminded Regina that this date was drawing to a close, with only two more activities to go before they'd be back to being just co-workers who could barely stand each other.

Ellie hadn't figured out how she, herself, felt about that fact, so maybe Regina was thinking about it too.

A car pulled out of a parking space along the curb next to Regina's apartment building.

"Ooh!" With a triumphant cry, Ellie pulled in as soon as the other car had vacated the spot. She set the parking brake, turned off the engine, and gave Regina an expectant look. Would Regina ask her in—maybe invite her up for that drink she owed her?

"Thanks for dropping me off." Regina released the seat belt and reached back between the seats to give Wally a pat on the head. She balanced the bakery box containing several pieces of cake in one hand while opening the passenger-side door with the other.

Apparently, no invitation was forthcoming.

"Wait," Ellie said quickly.

One foot already out the door, Regina turned her head toward her. "What? You want to walk me to the door? I'm not going to kiss you, if that's what you thought."

"No!" Ellie spluttered. "That didn't even cross my mind." And it hadn't. But now that Regina had mentioned it, Ellie's overactive imagination showed her flashes of what it might be like to rise up on her tiptoes and press her lips to Regina's. *No, no, no, no. This is a charity date. No kissing involved.*

"Then what is it?" Regina asked.

"Um, would you mind if I came up with you and used your bathroom? I drank too much water."

It was true. Well, half true. She could have held it until she got home, but if she was being honest with herself, she had to admit that she was curious to see Regina's apartment and didn't want to miss the only chance she might ever get.

"My bathroom?" Regina repeated as if it were a foreign concept.

The little line between Regina's brows made Ellie bite back a grin. Clearly, she didn't have visitors asking to use her bathroom often. "Yes. You do have one, don't you?"

"Of course I have one. All right. Come on up."

Ellie didn't have to be asked twice. She unclipped Wally's safety harness, and they followed Regina to the front door.

Even though the building had to be nearly one hundred years old, the security system was state-of-the-art. Regina unlocked the door with a key fob and led her over to an elevator that looked brand-new. She pressed the button for the top floor.

No surprise there. Ellie smiled to herself. Regina wasn't the only bossy doctor she knew who lived on the top floor of their apartment building.

Within seconds, the elevator doors slid apart on the seventh floor.

Regina marched toward an apartment in the back of the building, facing west, not toward the park. She cradled the bakery box against her chest and unlocked the door. Unlike the one downstairs, this one didn't have modern technology that gave her access at the tap of a key fob. The beautiful wood, arched shape, and the *art nouveau* peephole had an old-fashioned charm.

Instead of pushing the door open, Regina paused as if considering whether she really wanted to invite Ellie into her home.

"Don't worry if you didn't have time to clean," Ellie said softly. "When I work three or four twelve-hour shifts in a row, cleaning is the last thing on my mind, so I completely understand."

"It's not that," Regina said.

"Ah. You don't have a lot of visitors, do you?"

"You're the first."

The first? Ellie froze. Maybe asking to come up had been a bad idea. She should have known Regina wasn't a big fan of having people in her space. "If it makes you uncomfortable, I can just hold it until I get home."

"No," Regina said. "Waiting too long to empty your bladder could lead to UTIs and kidney infections, and as a doctor, I don't want to encourage such unhealthy habits."

Ellie bit the inside of her cheek to keep from laughing. Who would have thought Regina could be so adorable? "Is that geeky doctor speak for 'Please come in'?"

"Guess so." Regina shrugged, pushed the door open, and went inside.

A second later, the ceiling light flared on.

The apartment door opened into a large living room.

Regina set her keys and the bakery box onto a small table to the right of the door and moved farther into the room.

Wally ran after her, tugging Ellie forward.

Lack of cleaning really hadn't been the issue. Regina's apartment was spotless. The light reflected off the gleaming hardwood floors that looked as if they had been freshly waxed and polished. Not a single cobweb hung from the very white walls, the high ceiling, or the beautiful crown moldings.

Straight ahead, a four-panel French door led to a Juliet balcony. Wally sniffed at a blue couch to the left of the entrance. Beyond it, the two doors of a built-in closet stood open. Regina had turned it into a workstation with a desk, a computer, and a shelf full of medical tomes. She probably spent a lot of time in that cozy little doctor cave.

A thought occurred to Ellie, eliciting a giggle.

"What?" Hands on her hips, Regina glowered at her. "Is my humble abode not to your liking?"

"No, no, it's great. I like it. I just didn't think you'd be a closet lesbian."

"Closet lesbian?" Regina repeated. "What's that supposed to mean? Just because I prefer not to talk about my private life at work and don't hang up rainbow flags in my apartment doesn't mean I'm in the closet."

God, she was so serious all the time. Always in defensive mode. "Relax. Why do you always think I'm attacking you in some way? I'm kidding, okay? I was talking about this." Ellie pointed at the desk inside of the closet.

Regina managed to give the impression of arching her eyebrows without actually doing so. "You have the great honor of being my first visitor, and yet you chose to insult my choice of furniture placement?"

Ellie opened her mouth to protest. Then she realized Regina's glare lacked real conviction. She was teasing her right back!

Maybe Regina wasn't the only one who got overly defensive when they were around each other. With the way they interacted at work, she hadn't expected Regina to banter back and forth with her. None of her fellow nurses would ever believe how playful Regina could be. And maybe that was a good thing. If anyone knew about the Twinkie incident…

Ellie staved off the wave of renewed heat rushing through her. "Oh, come on. You secretly love being teased."

This time, Regina did arch her eyebrows in an "oh please" expression. But one corner of her mouth curled up the tiniest fraction of an inch.

Ellie probably wouldn't have noticed it if she hadn't been focused on Regina's lips. Not because of how amazingly soft they looked. Of course not. The only reason she was glancing at Regina's mouth was the green stain on her bottom lip.

"What is it? Any other piece of furniture you want to comment on?" Regina's gaze trailed over the coffee table, then went to Ellie's mouth as if unconsciously mirroring her.

"Um, no. You've got a little something…right there." Ellie touched her index finger to her own bottom lip. "Probably green food coloring from the cake frosting."

Regina rubbed the pad of her thumb across her lip.

The gesture's unexpected sensuality hit Ellie low in her belly. Her own lip began to tingle as if Regina had touched it instead of her own mouth. She quickly looked away.

"You let me meet Jenna Blake like this?" Regina grumbled, still wiping at her lip.

"Ha! So you're not completely immune to celebrities after all! You did want to impress her."

"I didn't say that. But neither do I want to inspire her to write a song about a green-lipped baking contest winner."

Ellie laughed. "First of all, we both won. Second, I don't think she saw you like this. It must have happened after Leo and Holly left, when we boxed up the cake and you got some frosting on your fingers and licked it off."

"You saw that?"

Ellie's cheeks burned. "Um, what can I say? I'm very observant. Comes with being a nurse."

"Right," Regina said with a smirk on her still-stained lips.

Ellie squirmed beneath Regina's knowing gaze and finally remembered why she had come up here in the first place. "Um, bathroom?" She really needed to splash some cold water onto her overheated face.

Regina pointed at an arched doorway to the right. "Through there and to the left."

"Thanks. Be right back." Ellie handed over Wally's leash and rushed off before Regina could protest.

She stepped into a broad hall or maybe more of a second, smaller living room. An open door on the right revealed a glimpse of a narrow kitchen with granite countertops and white cabinets, which looked as pristine as the rest of the apartment.

Ellie reached for the doorknob to her left.

"That's the closet," Regina called after her. "Try the second door— unless *you* are the closet lesbian between us."

"Hahaha. Don't give up medicine to become a comedian." Ellie hurried to the second door.

Regina's bathroom was tiny—the bathtub took up the entire length of one wall, and as she sat on the toilet, she could touch the tub if she stretched out her leg. Her upper arm brushed against the sink.

A second door led to the bedroom. It had been left ajar, and Ellie craned her neck to glimpse inside. The bedroom seemed to be small too. A queen-sized bed, made with military precision, filled most of the space, with only a nightstand fitting next to it.

Ellie squinted into the semi-darkness. Was that a stuffed animal next to the novel on the nightstand? It looked like a cow with long, shaggy fur.

She pressed a hand to her mouth to keep quiet. The prickliest doctor at CMC slept with a stuffed animal! That discovery alone had been worth the subterfuge.

Still chuckling, she washed her hands. She didn't dare snoop around, but she did study the items lined up on the small ledge above the sink.

Apparently, Regina was a no-fuss kind of woman when it came to her beauty regimen. Hand sanitizer, a stick of deodorant, toothpaste, some lotion, and a bottle of perfume were the only things Ellie found. *Whitewater Rapids,* the label said. A weird name for a perfume, but it fit the bold, crisp scent. She had a feeling a person could easily get trapped in the maelstrom and plunged underwater if they got too close.

"There are clean towels on the shelf," Regina called through the door.

Ellie jumped. "Thanks." She reached for the towel on top of the stack and dried off her hands.

When she left the bathroom, the sounds of Wally lapping up water drifted out of the kitchen. Regina must have filled a bowl for him.

A smile tugged on Ellie's lips. For a woman who insisted that she didn't have an informed opinion about dogs, Regina seemed to have a soft spot for canines.

Ellie crossed the hall toward the living room. To the left of the arched doorway was a beautiful built-in open cabinet. It held the only personal knickknacks—other than the stuffed cow—Ellie had seen in the apartment.

They were trophies, she realized as she got closer: debate club awards, science fair ribbons, academic achievements, and disc golf medals, most of them in gold.

Ellie couldn't help being impressed. It seemed Regina was used to being successful in whatever she tried her hand at...maybe other than her personal life.

One item on the middle shelf stood out. It was a framed photo of a much younger Regina in a high school graduation gown. Her dark hair that spilled out from under her mortarboard was longer than she wore it now, but her gray eyes were just as intense, as if she was ready to take on the world.

She was flanked by a proudly smiling couple that could only be her parents. The woman was much shorter than Regina but shared her stunning cheekbones, and the man had her height, black hair, and light features.

A boy of maybe seven or eight was posing in front of Regina, grinning into the camera, showing off a gap where he'd lost a baby tooth. He was slightly leaning back into Regina, who had her hand on his shoulder.

Something—maybe a low sound or the scent of *Whitewater Rapids*—made Ellie look away from the photo.

Regina stood behind her. The green stain on her mouth was gone now and her bottom lip redder than usual, as if she'd rubbed at it to remove the food coloring. She wasn't glancing at Ellie; her focus was on the picture. The expression in her eyes made her look more vulnerable than Ellie had ever seen her.

A lump lodged in Ellie's throat, and she had to swallow twice before she could speak. "Is that…?"

"Yes." After a beat, Regina added, "That's Riley."

They stood in silence and studied the photo of the boy for a while.

Then Ellie turned toward Regina again. "I'm sorry you lost him." Ugh, that sounded as if he were a set of keys or an umbrella she had lost somewhere. Why was it so hard to find the right words? "I can tell you were close."

Warmth against her fingers made her look down. She hadn't meant to touch Regina, but apparently, she had reached out and taken a hold of Regina's hand.

They both stared down at her fingers, wrapped around Regina's.

Um. Ellie swallowed again. What now? Should she let go? Or hold on?

"Not really." The words burst out of Regina before Ellie could make a decision.

Ellie's gaze darted up from their fingers to Regina's face.

It was startlingly pale. She pulled her hand from Ellie's gentle grip and pressed her knuckles against her mouth as if trying to push the words back in.

Clearly, she hadn't meant to say that. Maybe Ellie's touch had thrown her off-balance too.

"You weren't close?" Ellie glanced at the picture—at the way the boy leaned in to Regina's hand on his shoulder. Some people did the happy family thing just for photos, but this didn't seem staged. "This looks like you were."

Regina hesitated as if debating how much to tell her...or whether she wanted to answer at all. "Well," she finally said, her voice raspy. "We were, back when that photo was taken. But I left for college soon after, and..." She opened and closed her fingers in a helpless gesture.

Ellie waited for her to continue, but Regina didn't, so Ellie filled the silence for her. "There was a big age gap between you."

Regina tilted her head. "Ten years."

"That's a lot," Ellie said. "At least at that age. I bet it's hard to stay close when you're at such different stages in life."

"It certainly didn't help," Regina mumbled. "Neither did the drugs."

Oh no. Ellie drilled her nails into her palms. "Did he...?" Her chest felt tight, and she realized she was barely breathing, so she sucked in a lungful of air before she whispered, "Overdose?"

Regina didn't answer for so long that Ellie thought she either hadn't heard the question or chose to ignore it. "No," Regina finally said. "It doesn't matter. Nothing we can do about it anymore." She straightened her shoulders and strode past the framed photo, back into the living room.

Wally's nails click-clacked across the hardwood floor as he trotted after Regina.

Ellie's soft footsteps followed more slowly, as if she wanted to give Regina a moment to compose herself.

Which Regina immediately did. She couldn't believe she had let her guard down like that. The night Riley had died, she had vowed to never show her vulnerabilities again, yet now it had happened around Ellie *twice.*

By the time she faced Ellie in front of the apartment door, her most impassive expression was firmly in place—the one she had perfected all those times she had to tell an anxiously pacing family their loved one had died.

Ellie's dark eyes were full of compassion. She opened her mouth, maybe to tell her again how sorry she was or to ask more questions about Riley.

Regina didn't want to hear either. "Are you working tomorrow?" she asked before Ellie could speak.

Ellie blinked. "Um, yes. Our nurse manager scheduled me for the same shifts you cover this week to make it easier to find a time for our third date."

"How...considerate," Regina said, when what she really meant was *awkward*. She would have preferred to have a couple of days with no contact to get her equilibrium back. "Guess I'll see you tomorrow, then."

"See you tomorrow." Ellie reached her arm back and felt around for the doorknob without looking away from Regina, as if there was something else she wanted to say. "Thanks for a great day. I had fun."

Regina wasn't sure what to say to that. It wasn't something Ellie said only to be polite. Regina could tell. And, dammit, as hesitant as she was to admit it, she had actually had fun too. She just hadn't meant to end the day like this.

"Don't worry about it," Ellie said quietly, as if she could read her thoughts.

Was she that transparent now? "About what?"

"I don't know... Whatever you're worried about. Me not respecting you as a doctor maybe, just because you're a human with feelings." Ellie nodded in the direction of the shelf with Riley's photo.

Regina wanted to say she hadn't been worried about that. She hadn't been, right? After all, her status as an excellent physician wasn't in question. Instead, what came out was "Some days, I prefer being a doctor to being a human with feelings." Most days, actually.

Ellie's gaze was kind and understanding. "I get that. But not today, I hope. Because I bid on the human, not the doctor."

"You didn't bid on me," Regina said, glad to change the topic before she said more things that she hadn't meant to reveal. "You swatted at a fly."

"A big one," they said together.

Ellie smiled at her, and Regina found herself grinning back.

Jesus, these auction-prescribed date activities were bad for her. She wasn't the smiling-at-people type, and she'd never had little inside jokes with anyone before.

But as Ellie said good night and the door closed behind her and Wally, a new voice piped up in the back of Regina's mind. Maybe spending some time with Ellie wasn't all bad.

Because she'd also never before been able to smile after the complicated mix of grief, guilt, and anger had raised its ugly head.

Chapter 12

A FEW MINUTES BEFORE THE start of their next twelve-hour shift, Ellie and Jasmine sat in the break room, enjoying a moment of quiet.

"So?" Jasmine asked around a mouthful of the rainbow layer cake Ellie had brought in to share with her colleagues. "How was baking class?"

"It was great. I learned a lot of little tricks from Sasha, our instructor, and we got to meet Jenna Blake!"

Bright orange cake crumbs rained down on the break room table as Jasmine started coughing. "*The* Jenna Blake?"

Ellie nodded. "The one and only. She was amazing and so down-to-earth. Did you know her wife is a nurse too?"

Jasmine finally stopped coughing and wiped away the mess she'd made. "Oh, cool. I had no idea, but I'm not surprised. Obviously, she's a woman of great taste. I mean, what's not to love about nurses?"

Grinning, they clinked coffee mugs.

"Did anything else interesting happen?" Jasmine asked while slicing off the next forkful of cake.

"Getting to meet my favorite singer isn't enough?"

"You weren't on a date with Jenna Blake. I want to know what happened with Dr. Novak."

Ellie had known she'd have to answer questions like this. The staff in the ED was a tight-knit team, and everyone in the hospital knew about their dates, so at least a few of her colleagues were bound to ask. She tried to imitate Regina and put on her most impassive expression. "About what you'd expect," she said as vaguely as possible. "She turned our baking class into a competition."

"Aaand?" Jasmine drawled.

"And Sasha declared it a tie," Ellie said.

Jasmine glanced toward the ceiling as if sending up a prayer for the romantically hopeless. "I'm not talking about the baking. Did you heat up the kitchen with something other than the ovens, or was she her usual frosty self?"

"Um, no." There had been nothing frosty about the way Regina seduced the innocent little Twinkie or about the rasp in her voice when she'd declared, *It's called oral, Ellie.*

"No to what? I asked you a two-part question, so you can't just say— Wait, you're blushing!" Jasmine waved her fork. "What happened? Did the two of you—?"

"Nothing happened," Ellie said firmly.

Jasmine eyed her the way she would a lab report that cited normal troponin levels despite the patient showing all symptoms of a heart attack.

"Do I have to put an official statement in the staff newsletter before you believe me?"

Jasmine laughed. "I'd love to see Dr. Novak's face if you did."

Ellie shook her head. "I doubt it would be as amusing as you think." Clearly, Regina hated having her personal life being discussed at her workplace—which was exactly why Ellie wanted to get out of this conversation. "I think I'd better get some work done now. I want to take down the Valentine's Day decorations while we aren't busy."

"Oh, come on. You've been on two dates with Dr. Novak now, and you expect me to not be curious about what she's really like? Can't you at least tell me one thing about her?"

Truth be told, Ellie could understand her friend's curiosity. For the most part, she had agreed to go through with their dates because the money was for a good cause and the sponsors expected to get some social media pictures out of it. But part of the reason was also that she had wondered what Regina might be like away from the hospital. She went over the previous day's events in search of something she could tell Jasmine.

Telling her about Riley, Regina's brother, was out of the question. Any time Ellie thought about the pain in Regina's eyes, an iron band tightened around her ribs.

Maybe she could tell Jasmine about the stuffed cow on Regina's nightstand or about her masterful seduction of the Twinkie. These were harmless little details.

Okay, the plush animal was harmless. The Twinkie thing had been anything but—at least to her libido.

Ellie went over the list of things she had learned about Regina over the course of their two dates but ended up discarding them all. Jasmine was her friend and closest co-worker, yet telling her anything felt wrong, like a violation of Regina's trust.

Which was silly. Regina probably didn't trust her at all.

Still, Ellie felt protective of her. That might be even sillier. Regina was intimidating. A force to be reckoned with. She didn't need her protection.

Memories flashed through her mind—the way Regina had trembled in the car when she had first mentioned her brother's name, the hollowness in her voice when she'd talked about not being close…

Maybe even intimidating Dr. Regina Novak needed a bit of protection every now and then, even though she might not think so herself.

Ellie put her empty mug into the dishwasher and turned to head back to the nurses' station. "She has no informed opinion about dogs," she said back over her shoulder.

"No informed opinion about dogs?" Jasmine called after her. "That's all I'm getting?"

"You're also getting cake." Ellie waved cheerfully and left the break room.

Ellie glanced up at the American Heart Month poster she'd hung behind the curved desk at the nurses' station more than two weeks ago. On the banner, a woman's hands protectively cradled a red plastic heart.

For a moment, it made her think of the wave of protectiveness that had swept through her when Jasmine had quizzed her about Regina.

"Okay, no more cake for you," she told herself. Apparently, all that sugar was messing with her brain.

She climbed up on one of the plastic chairs, slid her finger beneath the poster, and pried it loose. Then she replaced it with a banner for Multiple Sclerosis Awareness Month, which had just started.

The string of paper hearts was next to come down.

Thankfully, the emergency department was still amazingly quiet as she stood on her tiptoes on top of the chair and stretched to the right to reach the end of the string.

A pair of sneakers squeaked to a stop behind her. "What did I tell you about workplace safety?"

Ellie dropped to her heels and peeked over her shoulder. A sense of déjà vu overcame her.

Regina stood behind her, arms folded across her blue scrub top, and scowled at her.

Just two weeks ago, Ellie hadn't thought anything of that scolding gaze. It had been part of her everyday interaction with the aloof doctor.

Today, Regina had treated her the same way as always. Coolly. Strictly business.

Ellie didn't know what she had expected. Maybe just a hint of warmth? An acknowledgment that they had formed a little bit of a connection the day before?

But apparently, it was all one-sided.

Okay, good. Two could play that game. She would be all business too. Ellie turned back around to hide her expression. "I'll be right down," she said, as she had two weeks ago. "Just need to get those paper hearts down first."

This time, instead of storming off with an indignant huff, Regina stepped closer. Her hands, warm and strong, settled on Ellie's hips.

A jolt went through Ellie. Not one of surprise. It was as if her body had expected the touch, which was even sillier than being hurt that Regina was all business.

"Um, what are you doing?" Ellie asked. Crap, her voice sounded squeaky. So much for being cool, calm, and collected around Regina.

"Following safe workplace practices," Regina said.

If that was what Regina was doing, it was having the opposite effect. Regina's hands on her hips weren't safe at all. The heat of her fingers filtered through the thin fabric of Ellie's scrub pants, making her legs feel as wobbly as if she had spent an hour on a trampoline. "Oh, so you're the hospital's workplace safety inspector now?" She couldn't help the annoyance—both at her own traitorous body and at Regina's coolness—from leaking through.

"I'm the person who'd have to treat you if you fell off and broke something."

"Who says you'd get to treat me? There are other doctors around who—" Ellie stopped herself before she could say, *Have a better bedside manner.* No way did she want to even think about Regina's bedside manner while Regina was still touching her.

"Who what?" Regina asked, a challenge in her tone.

Her touch continued to burn through Ellie's scrub pants. "Who, um, could treat a fracture. Not that I'll get one." She stretched up on her tiptoes, ignoring her body's demand to lean back, into Regina's strong arms.

Regina followed her movement and leaned even closer—so close that Ellie thought she could feel her breath on her lower back. Her grip on Ellie's hips tightened.

The tack that held the piece of string in place escaped Ellie's unsteady fingers. Finally, on her second attempt, she managed to grasp it and pulled it out.

The string of paper hearts dropped down on one side and dangled from the other tack.

Oh no. They would have to repeat this procedure on the other side.

"Are you coming down?" Regina asked.

How long had she stood on the chair without moving? Ellie mentally kicked herself into motion. "Of course." She turned to jump down.

Instead of letting go and backing away, Regina kept her hands in place, as if she intended to lift Ellie down.

Ellie wanted to tell her she didn't need any help.

But as she turned, Regina's fingers slid along her belly, making speech impossible. The muscles in her abdomen quivered. She half jumped, half stumbled off the chair.

"Whoa!" Regina couldn't step back in time to make space for her.

Their bodies collided.

If Ellie had thought that moment at the ice rink, when Regina had been pressed against her from behind, had been the extent of unwanted attraction she would have to suffer through, she'd been wrong.

Way, way wrong.

That situation was lukewarm in comparison to the heat that engulfed her now.

Regina stumbled back to absorb Ellie's momentum until the edge of the curved desk stopped her.

Somehow, Ellie ended up cradled between her thighs, with their fronts tightly pressed together and Regina tilted backward, as if Ellie were laying her back on the desk to have her way with her.

Holy shit!

This wasn't how Ellie had imagined this. Um, not that she had imagined this or anything like it at all.

Regina was still holding on to her, but instead of cupping her hips, her hands were now on Ellie's back. Her fingers clutched the fabric of Ellie's scrub top as if she wanted to rip it off.

Ellie was overly aware of every inch of Regina's body touching hers.

"You okay?" Regina's voice was raspy. Her warm breath fanned across Ellie's face.

A jittery "mm-hmm" was all Ellie got out. It sounded suspiciously like a moan.

Get yourself together and get off her. You're at work!

But before she could get her legs to work, footsteps approached. Then a pair of sneakers screeched to a stop.

"I was just about to ask how your date went, but I can see it went really well." Dr. Kayla Vaughn stood next to the nurses' station and regarded them with a wide grin.

Ellie disentangled herself from Regina and jumped back. "We… It's not… I fell."

"Wow. Congratulations. It's a bit fast, but who am I to judge? It only took me a few dates to fall for my husband too."

"What? No! From the chair!" Ellie gestured wildly toward the ugly orange thing. "I was taking down the paper hearts."

Regina straightened and brushed her hands down her scrub top as if to smooth out any wrinkles—or maybe wipe away the imprint Ellie's body had left on her own.

Or maybe Ellie was projecting, because Regina seemed entirely unaffected, her expression as impassive as ever.

How infuriating, especially when every nerve ending in Ellie's body was still dancing a jig…or perhaps more of a slow, sexy tango.

Regina gave Dr. Vaughn a cool look. "What can I do for you? Aren't you covering fast-track today?" She gestured at the area where they treated patients with lacerations and minor fractures. "Need a refresher on suture techniques?"

"No, thanks. One of the residents said there's cake, but I just checked, and it's all gone."

Regina shrugged. "Well, what did you expect? You know the first rule of working in the ED. If there's food around, eat it right away, or it'll be gone."

"Yeah, but I thought you made two cakes. Don't tell me both are gone already!"

"How do you know we made two cakes?" Regina asked.

"Insta."

Their baking adventure had made it to Instagram? Sasha must have posted some of the photos Ashley had taken.

"Well, I didn't bring the cake I made." Regina reached for the electronic chart tablet she must have put down on the desk earlier and walked away with barely a nod in Ellie's direction.

Dr. Vaughn followed. "Why not? The rest of us bring in snacks all the time. You'd be way more popular with the nurses if you did the same—although it seemed you're pretty popular with one nurse in particular already."

"This is work, not a popularity contest," Regina's sharp voice drifted back to Ellie. "And I shouldn't have to bribe the nurses into doing their jobs."

Ellie's overheated body cooled instantly. *Ouch.* There she was—Dr. McIcy. Bringing in cake or donating a few dollars for the nurses' candy drawer, as many of the doctors did every now and then, couldn't be considered bribery. It was a little appreciation for a job well done.

As the distance between them grew, Ellie didn't catch what else Regina said.

Maybe it was better that way. Ellie didn't want to know what else Regina had to say about nurses.

What an ass. She couldn't believe she'd felt drawn to her for even a second.

She shoved every thought about what Regina's body had felt like against hers to the back of her mind, but the memory of the vulnerable look in Regina's eyes as she'd talked about her brother was harder to forget. Resolutely, Ellie marched over to where the string of paper hearts dangled from the wall.

No way would she climb onto the chair a second time, risking Regina rushing back to provide workplace safety.

One anger-fueled tug and the tack popped out of the wall. It catapulted across the ED, barely missing the charge nurse.

Crap. Dr. Regina Novak was definitely not good for workplace safety.

It was a miracle humankind hadn't gone extinct yet. Regina's latest patient—a case of food poisoning from a spoiled oyster—was just one in a long list of avoidable disasters.

Eating raw shellfish… Regina barely abstained from shaking her head at him. Who the hell had decided that was a bright idea, especially in a place so far from the ocean?

Not that her own decision-making had been all that sound lately.

After the night before, she had been determined to put some distance between herself and Ellie.

That plan had been a complete and utter failure. Instead, they had ended up pressed together, half on top of a desk. *Distance, my ass!*

Why hadn't she just let Ellie do whatever she was doing up on that chair? As Ellie had pointed out, she wasn't the hospital's workplace safety consultant, so she should have walked by and minded her own business. But no, she had to go over to keep her safe.

Putting her hands on Ellie topped eating bad oysters. At least getting the spoiled shellfish out of her system would have been faster.

Most of their shift had gone by, yet even nine hours later, she could still feel Ellie pressed against her.

Regina didn't get it. At work, she had always been fully focused on her patients and on gathering the information she needed to make the decisions that might save their lives.

Not once had any of the nurses, doctors, or EMTs she worked with registered as more than a colleague. She barely would have been able to describe them.

With Ellie, every detail was burned into her memory as if she had prepared to give a description for a missing person report. She vividly remembered how wide Ellie's eyes had gone and how appealing the curve of her lips had looked when they had formed a startled "O" as she had landed half on top of Regina against the desk.

How infuriating that she couldn't ban those details from her mind. This wasn't like her at all!

It didn't help that this patient was one of Ellie's, so Regina had to work with her instead of avoiding her for the rest of the shift.

"You should start to feel better once we've replaced the fluids and electrolytes you lost." She pointed at the IV in his arm, then nodded in Ellie's direction without looking at her. "Ellie will collect a stool sample from you to help us find out what bacteria or toxin it was that made you sick. Do you have any questions?"

Her patient weakly shook his head. "No. Thanks."

Regina turned and slid back the privacy curtain around his cubicle.

"Oh, nurse?"

Regina took another step.

"Nurse?" the patient called again.

She stopped and glanced over her shoulder to see why Ellie wasn't reacting.

He wasn't looking at Ellie. His gaze was on Regina. "Could you bring me a blanket? It's a little cool in here."

Not again. Regina didn't have the energy or the patience to deal with this misogynist bullshit.

She rarely wore a white coat that would help identify her as a doctor. It was too restricting, plus they were terrible fomites and could spread bacteria and viruses.

Still, the letters MD on her name badge should have given him a clue—as should her introducing herself as Dr. Novak earlier. She hated patients who instantly assumed any woman in scrubs had to be a nurse. Her male colleagues never had to deal with that assumption, despite the fact that female physicians outnumbered them in the emergency department.

She had to unclench her jaw to answer. "It's Doctor." She tapped her name badge with one stiff finger. "I'm not a nurse. I'm sure Ellie would be happy to bring you a blanket."

"Of course. I'll be right back." Ellie gave the patient a friendly smile, which disappeared the moment she turned away from him and marched past Regina, giving her a heated glare.

What the hell is her problem? Regina stared after her.

What an arrogant jerk! Ellie barely resisted the urge to close the curtain in Regina's face after storming past her. *I'm sure Ellie would be happy to bring you a blanket,* she mentally parroted what Regina had said. *Because Ellie is just a lowly nurse, while I'm too good to perform mundane tasks like that.*

It wasn't the first time Ellie had seen a female doctor react with indignation when they'd been mistaken for a nurse. Most of the time, she managed not to take it personally, but now it got under her skin.

She got under your skin, an annoying voice piped up in the back of her mind. She ignored it and marched toward the supply closet that held the blankets.

"Ellie," Regina called after her. "Wait up."

As soon as they were out of earshot of their patient, Ellie snapped around to face Regina.

"What was that?" Regina's eyes, gray and hard like granite, held her gaze in a silent challenge. "Do we have a problem?"

Ellie glanced left and right to make sure no patient could overhear them.

Thankfully, it was a slow afternoon in the emergency department. The only person around was Jasmine, who was charting at the nurses' station, seemingly engrossed in her paperwork.

"I don't." Ellie refused to look away. "But apparently, you do."

Regina's eyes sparked, and her cheeks flushed as they faced each other in the middle of the ED. "And what problem, pray tell, may that be?"

Even pissed off as Ellie was, a part of her couldn't help thinking how hot Regina looked like that—and that annoyed her even more. What on earth was going on with her? She had never found asshole doctors who thought they were better than the nurses even vaguely attractive before.

She drew in a slow breath. "You acted as if being called *nurse* is the worst insult ever."

"Nonsense. I merely corrected his assumption that every woman in scrubs is a nurse."

Ellie clutched the stethoscope in her pocket. "*Just* a nurse—isn't that what you mean?"

"Stop putting words into my mouth. I—"

The crackle of the EMS radio interrupted Regina mid-sentence. "We're coming in with a seventy-two-year-old male in acute respiratory distress. O_2 sats were 78% on room air. After nebulized albuterol and eight liters of oxygen, it's only 89%. ETA is six minutes."

Immediately, they gave up their standoff.

"Noah, could you bring Mr. Bauer in exam three a blanket?" Ellie called to one of their nursing assistants.

"Sure," he said.

Ellie gave him a thumbs-up as she and Regina rushed past him toward an open trauma bay to glove and gown.

They waited side by side.

No one said anything. Regina's expression was professional and intent, and Ellie focused entirely on the patient they were about to receive too.

Their argument seemed silly now, even though Ellie knew she might not think so later, once the adrenaline pumping through her veins had receded.

The wail of a siren pierced the air, and it wasn't long before two EMTs rushed a gurney into the trauma bay. One of them rattled off the patient's history and stats.

Ellie took in the pale, weathered face beneath the oxygen mask. Her step faltered. It was Paul! "I know him. He's got a history of asthma. Ends up here every couple of months because he can't always afford his medication."

It wasn't fair that he was lying there, gasping for breath, when his asthma flares could have been kept in check if only he had the money. Her fist curled around the edge of the gurney.

"On the count of three."

Regina's calm voice brought her back to the moment.

Ellie pushed back her anger and helped transfer him from the gurney to the trauma bed. *Help him now. You can get angry later.*

She focused on Regina's controlled voice, her precise orders as she guided the team.

Despite the tension between them, they worked together like the cogs in a finely tuned machine.

She squeezed in between Regina and a resident to get Paul hooked up to the cardiac monitor while Jasmine got an IV started. Ellie's hands were steady as she placed their own leads and pulse oximeter.

Everyone glanced at the monitor.

Crap. O² sats, BP, heart rate… All his vitals were terrible. His face looked ashen; his lips had taken on a bluish tint, and his respiratory rate was much too high. His chest heaved as if he'd just finished running a world-record-breaking sprint. His eyes were closed, and he had reacted neither to the transfer to the bed nor to anything the team had done so far.

This wasn't like any of his previous asthma attacks.

Ellie pushed back her sense of dread and focused on her part in their efforts to save him.

"GCS 3. We need to intubate him," Regina said.

Ellie had no idea if he could still understand her, but she leaned over the head of the bed. "We're going to sedate you and put you on a ventilator to help you breathe, okay?"

"Give him 125 milligrams of methylprednisolone IV and start the nebulizer with albuterol and ipratropium," Regina ordered as soon as the breathing tube was in.

Everything was textbook, but nothing worked.

Paul's lungs kept spasming, and his oxygen saturation levels plummeted even further.

His heartbeat slowed—then stopped.

"Stop compressions." Regina flicked her gaze toward the clock, then back to the cardiac monitor, which still showed a flatline. "We're calling it. Time of death: 17:02."

She gave each member of her team a nod as they cleared out of the trauma bay until only Ellie remained.

A damp lock of brown hair was plastered to her forehead. Her shoulders slumped, either with defeat or with exhaustion. Probably both. Even though the team members had alternated, Ellie had taken more than her share of turns doing compressions for the past thirty minutes.

Regina wanted to say something, but what? Good job? It seemed inappropriate since their patient had died. Giving in to her impulse to put a hand on Ellie's shoulder was out too.

Finally, she resorted to what her mentor had told her when she'd been a resident. "You can't save everyone."

Ellie looked up from their patient. "What?"

Shit. That hadn't come out the way she had meant it. "Sometimes, you lose a patient, no matter how good you are or how hard you try. It's not possible to save everyone."

Ellie sighed. "I know. But dying like this"—she nodded down at him—"because our health-care system is broken… It sucks."

"Yes, it does."

They stood in silence for a few moments.

With a final sigh, Ellie straightened. "Do you want me to tell his wife since I know her a little?"

It was tempting. So tempting. Telling a stranger a loved one had died had always been the hardest part of her job, but since she'd had to call her parents and tell them Riley had died, it always felt personal. It was like reliving that night over and over again.

Ellie's gaze on her was soft—bare of the anger from earlier—as if she could sense her hesitation and knew the reason for it.

Regina hated feeling so transparent. She squared her shoulders. No, she couldn't—wouldn't—say yes. She put on her attending face. "No, that's my responsibility."

Ellie's face fell.

Oh, hell. Not another round of *it's your responsibility because you're a doctor and I'm just a nurse.* She hadn't meant it like that.

"Right," Ellie said. "I'll prepare him for the family."

She sounded neutral. But was she really okay?

Usually, Regina didn't care whether she had hurt anyone's feelings or not. She didn't have the time or energy to cater to anyone's delicate sensibilities.

But Ellie…

But nothing, she firmly told herself. Ellie was a nurse. A nurse she had gone on two unusual dates with, but that shouldn't matter.

However, Ellie knew the patient's wife. Having a familiar face in the room when she received the horrible news might help. "You know what?" Regina said before Ellie could walk off. "Why don't we talk to his wife together? She might take it better if you're there."

Ellie nodded instantly. "Thank you."

She might be the only person who had ever said thank you at being saddled with such a hard task. But then again, maybe that wasn't what Ellie had thanked her for.

Regina pushed away the thought. "Let's go and get this over with."

Chapter 13

ELLIE'S SHOULDERS ACHED FROM DOING compressions as she pushed a small bag of chips along the cafeteria's steel rail on an otherwise empty tray.

It was barely more than an hour until the end of their shift, but the charge nurse had told her and Jasmine to take a break after they had lost Paul.

"I need coffee." Jasmine steered her over to the coffee station. "I'm going to my goddaughter's dance recital after work, and I won't make it through the evening without caffeine."

Ellie gave her a commiserating look. "Ugh. The only place I'm going is my couch…or maybe even straight to bed."

"And the shower, I hope."

Ellie dragged up a smile. "Are you saying I reek?"

"You reek," Jasmine said. "And so do I."

The cafeteria worker behind the coffee station laughed. "You nurses always have the best conversations," he said. "What can I get you?"

"A quadruple shot of espresso or whatever is the strongest caffeinated beverage you have," Jasmine answered.

Within a few minutes, he set down a huge paper cup of steaming black coffee in front of Jasmine, then slid a smaller cup toward Ellie.

She held up her hand. "Oh, no, thanks. No coffee for me."

"You want this. Trust me." He gave the cup another nudge toward her.

Reluctantly, she picked it up. It was hot chocolate. She blew across its surface, then took a careful sip. *Oh yum.* It was the extra creamy one, made with milk. "I thought the hot chocolate made with water was the only one you had?"

"We ran out."

"You ran out of water?"

He shrugged, then waved them away when they tried to pay. "Already taken care of."

"By whom?" Ellie asked.

He shrugged again.

"You know what they say about gift horses. Come on." Jasmine led the way toward one of the small tables.

Ellie dropped onto a plastic chair. Just being off her aching feet made her feel better, and the hot chocolate helped too. She cradled it with both hands and inhaled its sweet scent. "Just what the doctor ordered," she murmured into the steaming beverage—then paused. *Wait a minute!* Had Regina somehow arranged for her to get this?

Grinning, Ellie took another sip. "Apology accepted."

"Why would I apologize?" Jasmine asked around a mouthful of potato chips.

"Not you. I was talking about…" Ellie hesitated. Regina already had a reputation for being cold and arrogant among the nurses, and she didn't want to add to that by telling Jasmine about their argument. Again, the wave of protectiveness surprised her, but she was too tired to question it. "Talking to the universe."

"You're talking to the universe over a cup of hot chocolate?" Jasmine chuckled. "Damn, that must be some amazing hot chocolate!"

Ellie hid her smile behind the paper cup. "Mm-hmm. It is."

Regina missed the Californian weather, but there was one good thing about no longer living in an area that was in a drought for most of the year: she could take a guilt-free long shower after a day like this.

Just as she was drying off, her phone rang in the living room.

Who the hell was that?

Hopefully, the hospital wouldn't dare call her for anything after a shift like that, and all of her disc golf team mates knew she preferred to text.

Clad in only a towel, she marched into the living room and snatched her phone from next to the door.

Ellie Fisher flashed across the screen.

Her thumb hit the *accept* button before she could consciously think about it. She lifted the phone to her ear. "Just FYI: I hate talking on the phone."

The silence lasted all of a second, then Ellie laughed, obviously unimpressed. "I would have texted you, but I wanted to thank you in person. Well, kinda in person."

"What for?" Regina asked, even though she had a pretty good idea what Ellie was talking about.

"The hot chocolate."

Ah. Good. So her co-conspirator from the hospital cafeteria had carried out her instructions. "I have no idea what you're talking about. If someone sent you a hot chocolate, maybe it was one of your friends among the hospital staff. Someone who understands how tough it is to lose a patient, especially if it's someone you knew."

"I'm sure it was," Ellie said.

They were silent for a few moments.

"So since you didn't have anything to do with the hot chocolate, it's fair to say it doesn't count as the drink you owe me," Ellie finally added.

"Yes. Which is just as well since it's *you* who owes *me* a drink."

Ellie muttered something that contained the word *delusional,* then was uncharacteristically silent for a while. "I didn't just call to thank you for the hot chocolate you know nothing about. I called because I think I owe you an apology too."

"Too?" Regina echoed. "I didn't apologize."

"You bought me a hot chocolate even though you consider it beneath you to 'bribe the nurses.' If that's not an apology, I don't know what is."

Shit. So Ellie had heard that, and of course she would call her on it. She hadn't even meant it like that, for crying out loud! Well, she did think she shouldn't have to bring in snacks to get into the nurses' good graces. Doing her job well should have sufficed. But she had said it mostly to get Kayla off her back, so she wouldn't have to admit why she hadn't brought her cake to work.

After Ellie had left the night before, the last thing on her mind had been the silly cake. She had simply forgotten that it was still sitting on the table next to the door. Even this morning, she'd been so preoccupied that she must have walked by it without seeing it. But she didn't want to admit that because then Ellie would think she'd been a grieving mess.

"I thought we established that I didn't have anything to do with the hot chocolate," she finally said.

"Right. Do you want to hear my apology anyway?"

"All right." Regina headed toward her bedroom. "Let me put on some clothes before you start groveling."

"You're...*naked?*" Ellie squeaked out. "Like, completely unclothed? Right now?"

Regina couldn't help grinning. She enjoyed Ellie's reaction a little too much. "Well, strictly speaking, I'm wearing a towel."

An audible gulp echoed through the phone.

Regina knew she really shouldn't play with Ellie like that, but it was so much fun, so she added, "A short one."

"I can call back," Ellie blurted. "Or, better yet, just text you since you don't enjoy talking on the phone."

"But I enjoy listening to apologies, so give me two seconds." Regina tossed the phone onto her bed. While she put on a pair of yoga pants and a faded Harvard Medical School T-shirt, she gave herself a stern talking-to.

Ellie is someone you work with, not someone to flirt with, dammit!

Finally, she picked up the phone again. "I'm back."

"Are you decent?" Ellie asked.

Regina reined in her tired brain, which immediately came up with half a dozen flirty replies to that question. "I'm wearing clothes. Why?"

"We could FaceTime," Ellie said. "It's always nicer to see the person you're talking to, don't you think?"

"No, I don't think that at all." Getting through this conversation would be much easier if she didn't have to look into Ellie's big, brown eyes. "So? Didn't you mention an apology?"

"Um, right." Ellie audibly inhaled, then exhaled. "I still think you should have tried not to sound so insulted at being called *nurse*, but I admit I overreacted. I was in a shitty mood for most of the day, and when I heard you tell the patient that you're a doctor, not a nurse... I took it personally. I'm sorry." Her tone wasn't meek or grudging. It was straightforward and genuine.

Wow. Regina couldn't remember ever receiving an honest apology like that. In her world, an apology was a weakness she couldn't afford. From the time she had entered med school, she had been taught that doctors should never apologize or admit to having made a mistake, because it could be used against them in a malpractice lawsuit. Female physicians in particular had to keep up the facade of always being right, or they would lose the respect of colleagues and patients. "I don't know what to say. All right, I guess?"

"How about: I apologize too?"

Regina scratched her neck. Did she really want to say that? *Could* she do it?

"Let me guess." Ellie sounded amused, not annoyed. "You never mastered the art of apologizing?"

"Well, naturally, since I'm right most of the time."

Ellie burst out laughing.

A vivid image flashed through Regina's mind: Ellie tossing her head back, exposing the graceful line of her neck, her eyes sparkling with mirth. The corners of her own mouth curled up in reaction. "I guess I was in a pretty shitty mood too," she finally said.

There. That would have to do.

"As opposed to your sunshiny usual self?" Ellie muffled a noise that sounded suspiciously like a giggle.

"Yes," Regina said. "Opposed to that."

"So what put you in that extra shitty mood?" Ellie asked.

Damn. Now she would have to reward Ellie's honesty with a lie. She couldn't very well tell her that trying to put some distance between them—and failing horribly—was what had put her in such a bad mood. "Oh, you know how it is. Paperwork. Starting a string of twelve-hour shifts. A patient coming in because of a stuffy nose. How about you?"

"Um, same."

Regina had a feeling Ellie wasn't telling the full truth either, but it was safer to let it go.

"So that was all it was—you being in a grumpy mood?" Ellie finally asked. "It wasn't that you consider being called *nurse* a challenge to your ego?"

Regina huffed. "My ego is very much intact, thank you very much."

A laugh escaped Ellie. "True."

Regina ignored the remark. "I'm not embarrassed to be called *nurse*. It's just not what I am. I worked as hard…scratch that; I worked harder than any of my male colleagues to earn those initials after my name. I gave up a lot to become a doctor, and to be called *nurse*… It invalidates all those sacrifices."

Ellie didn't say anything for a while. "Time with Riley," she finally whispered.

A weight settled on Regina's chest. When had the conversation taken this turn? The night before, she had decided to never make herself vulnerable in front of Ellie again. Yet here they were, talking about Riley once more. "Yeah." She cleared her throat to get rid of the scratchiness. "Among other things," she added because those other things didn't hurt as much. "Anyway, I'm not putting up with misogynist bullshit. Plus it could get the hospital into legal trouble if patients later insist they were never seen by a doctor, 'just' nurses."

"I get that, but there has to be a way to stand up to that BS and avoid misunderstandings without being dismissive toward nurses," Ellie said. "Let's roleplay."

Regina flopped onto the bed. "Roleplay?" she repeated. The only kind of roleplay that came to mind was one she had no business thinking about while talking to Ellie.

"I meant, let's brainstorm what you could say next time someone mistakes you for a nurse."

"What else am I supposed to say other than 'I'm a doctor, not a nurse'?"

"How about: 'Oh, you needed a nurse? Let me grab one for you.'"

Regina's lips curved into a sensual grin. "Grab a nurse, huh?"

"Get a nurse. Get!"

Regina's grin widened. She had a feeling Ellie was blushing. This roleplaying thing was actually fun. "Other suggestions?"

"How about: 'I'm sorry. I'm *just* a doctor.'"

"I'm gonna hang up now," Regina said.

Ellie laughed. "Okay, okay. I'm kidding. It's not so much about what you say but how you say it. Don't make it sound as if being a nurse is a big step down from being a doctor. I got enough of that reaction when I dropped out of med school."

"I know it's not a step down; it's a completely different path." Then Regina's brain caught up with what Ellie had just said. She sat up in bed as if that would enable her to hear Ellie better. "Wait, you went to med school?" She'd had no idea. Maybe she should start listening in on the hospital gossip every now and then.

"Not for long," Ellie answered. "I dropped out after the first semester."

"What happened?" Regina wasn't usually one to ask personal questions, mostly because she didn't care to find out the answers. But now she had a hard time reining in her curiosity.

"Thanks for not assuming I dropped out because I couldn't keep up."

That thought hadn't even crossed Regina's mind. Ellie was smart, dedicated, and determined. But Regina wasn't one to hand out compliments, so she asked instead, "So why did you drop out?"

"My grandmother got sick, so I took a semester off to help care for her."

"Why you?" Regina asked. "Why didn't your parents do it?"

"Why not me? My grandmother and I were always close. Of course my parents and Vickie helped, but my mom was still trying to get her cleaning service off the ground, and Dad was helping her while still working at his old job." Ellie paused. "And to tell you the truth, I needed a time-out to think about where I was going with my life. After my grandmother died, I decided not to go back and get a nursing degree instead."

"Just like that?" Regina didn't get it. Becoming a doctor had been her number one goal—her only goal—for as long as she could remember. For Ellie to give up on that dream…

"It wasn't an easy decision, believe me. But I think it was the right one," Ellie said. "My grandmother was in the hospital a lot, and when I watched her nurses, I realized that was the kind of interaction I wanted with patients—more hands-on time, not just dropping in for a quick diagnosis or to prescribe a treatment."

Just "dropping in" was exactly what Regina loved about being an emergency medicine physician. She didn't have to spend a lot of time with the same patients. There were always new challenges around the corner, and people she treated were either released or sent upstairs as quickly as possible, so she didn't get attached to anyone. "And you never thought about going back and finishing med school?"

"No."

The certainty in Ellie's voice stunned Regina.

"I love being a nurse," Ellie added. "Well, most of the time. It really grates on me that everyone sees me dropping out of med school to become a nurse as a failure. It was the right choice for me, even though not everyone agreed."

"Your family wasn't supportive?"

"I wouldn't say that, but I know, deep down, my parents were disappointed. They both worked hard to give me and my sister all the opportunities they never had. They wanted me to have a successful career and a comfortable lifestyle. But in the end, they respected my decision. Which is more than you can say for my girlfriend. She broke up with me the week after."

Regina flopped onto her back. "Ouch." She didn't know what to say to that. So that was why it was such a sore point for Ellie when someone implied that being a nurse was somehow less than being a doctor.

"Yeah, ouch. She was the first girl I fell in love with. I was convinced we'd be together forever." Self-deprecating humor colored Ellie's tone, but Regina could hear that it concealed old hurt. "You know how it is."

Actually, Regina didn't. Not once in her life had she thought about growing old with one of her girlfriends. The concept of *forever* had only ever applied to her job, not to her relationships. "But your ex wasn't the forever type of girl?"

"She was. Chelsea had mapped out our entire future before we even graduated high school, including where we would live—New York City, how many kids we would have—two, and where we would vacation— Saint-Tropez in summer and St. Moritz in winter."

Regina let out a low whistle. "Posh." She couldn't see down-to-earth Ellie in either place.

"Yeah." Ellie laughed. "Apparently, Chelsea didn't know me as well as I'd thought. She envisioned herself as the wife of a wealthy surgeon, not someone who has to get by on a nurse's paycheck."

"Huh. Maybe we should date each other's exes," Regina muttered. "Mine was the opposite."

"She would have preferred you becoming a nurse?"

Regina hadn't meant to talk about her own past relationship, but now that she had commented on it, she couldn't refuse to answer. To her surprise, she found that she didn't mind. "Pretty much. She constantly complained about how little time I had for her. When I was offered the position of chief resident before my last year of residency, Amber wasn't amused."

"I can see why," Ellie said. "With all the additional duties our chief resident has, I don't see how she has time to date."

"Yeah. Amber worked in hospital admin, so she knew that too. That's why she made me choose: her or being chief resident."

Ellie sucked in a sharp breath. "I'm sorry. Did she really think she would win if she made you choose?"

"Apparently, she didn't know me as well as she thought she did," Regina repeated almost exactly what Ellie had said earlier. Truth be told, she hadn't given Amber much of a chance to get to know her.

Ellie was silent for a moment. "You know what? I don't think I want her number. I prefer a partner who's supportive of my goals."

Regina usually didn't give a damn about what everyone else thought of her priorities, but having Ellie side with her felt unexpectedly good. "I don't think I want Chelsea's number either."

"Good," Ellie said.

"Good?" Regina asked with a grin. "You don't want me to date your ex? You're not jealous, are you?"

Ellie tsked. "Rein in your ego, Doc. I meant, it's good that you don't want to date her because she's happily married to Dr. Granger."

"Granger from ortho?"

"Yep."

Regina let out a disdainful huff. "Far be it from me to be judgmental, but she really downgraded."

Ellie burst out laughing. "Thanks… I think. So is that why you're single?"

How had she maneuvered herself into this conversation? Regina didn't do girl talk. She got up to grab a bottle of water from the fridge. "Being heartbroken over Amber?"

"Making work your number one priority."

Regina had told her parents that once or twice when they had worried about her being alone. But even though it probably didn't help, she knew that wasn't the only reason. "I don't date because I don't like it."

"You don't date?" Ellie echoed. "Like, at all?"

Regina clutched the phone between her ear and shoulder so she could open the bottle of water. "Not in the last couple of years. Why waste my time meeting someone I probably won't like?"

Ellie didn't seem to have an answer for that.

"Let me guess… You love dating and meeting new people."

"I love meeting new people," Ellie said. "Dating…not so much."

That was a surprise coming from someone who put up strings of paper hearts in an emergency department of all places. Regina paused in the middle of raising the bottle to her lips. "Oh?"

"Don't get me wrong. I love being in a relationship," Ellie added. "But dating feels kinda forced most of the time. More like a job interview. All of my relationships were with women that I met through a mutual friend when I wasn't even looking for love, just hanging out, and then it happened naturally."

Regina took a swig of water. "For a moment, I thought you might not be a starry-eyed romantic after all."

Ellie laughed unrepentantly. "Oh no, I am. If you want to find something we have in common, you'll have to keep looking."

"Why would I want to do that?" She didn't, right? If dating felt like a waste of time, surely she shouldn't want to find commonalities with someone she had no intention of dating.

"Right," Ellie said, all laughter now gone from her voice.

Oh hell. Regina shouldn't care whether she'd hurt Ellie's feelings. This was exactly why she didn't get involved with someone she worked with. Tiptoeing around people's sensibilities would make her much less effective at work. And yet she heard herself say, "I mean, since we already found one thing we have in common."

"We did?"

"Yes. We both hate dating."

Ellie chuckled. "True. Which is ironic considering we'll be going on another date this weekend."

"A not-a-real-date date," Regina said. "And we won't have to pretend to enjoy it."

"Nope. We can openly hate every second of it."

"Exactly."

"Just like you hated every second of talking on the phone," Ellie said. "For the last twenty-seven minutes."

Regina froze mid-nod. She pulled her phone from her ear to check the time. *Holy shit.* How had that happened? She had never talked on the phone for twenty-seven minutes to anyone. Hell, all phone calls she'd made in the past year put together hadn't even lasted for twenty-seven minutes! "Well, I didn't hate *every* second of those twenty-seven minutes."

"No?"

"No. Like I said, I do enjoy listening to apologies."

Ellie let out a noise that was half snort, half laugh.

Before Ellie could come up with a reply, Regina said good night and ended the call. She'd had the last word. But then why didn't she feel as if she had the upper hand at all?

Chapter 14

ELLIE REACHED FOR A STERILE dressing without taking her gaze off Regina's fingers, captivated by their confident movements as Regina stitched up a laceration that stretched across the patient's forehead.

Some of the ER doctors consulted a plastic surgeon for facial lacerations like this one, but Regina always handled them herself—and Ellie could understand why.

Regina's grip on the needle holder was steady and controlled. The needle pierced the patient's skin effortlessly, guided by Regina's practiced touch.

It felt like watching a master sculptor at work.

Oh, get a grip. She's a doctor, not Michelangelo.

Regina placed the last stitch, stepped back, and surveyed her work.

Ellie did the same. *Wow.* The precise row of stitches was a work of art. None of their plastic surgeons could have done a better job.

When Regina turned toward her, Ellie gently placed a sterile gauze pad over the sutured laceration and secured it in place with tape, making sure not to get any hairs trapped beneath it.

Regina gave her a curt nod, exchanged a few words with the patient, then turned to leave without the faintest hint of a grin or a secret wink for Ellie.

All business, as always.

It was as if their half-hour phone call the night before hadn't happened and they had never shared intimate details about their past relationships. Was she really just one of the nurses to Regina?

The thought shouldn't affect her, yet it did.

Ellie discarded the empty packages and used supplies, then ripped off her gloves with more force then necessary.

When she returned to the nurses' station, Regina was at one of the nearby workstations, making notes in the patient's electronic chart. She glanced up from the screen. Her eyes narrowed as she searched Ellie's face. "Something wrong with my sutures?"

Crap. Unlike Regina, Ellie didn't have a poker face at all. Or maybe Regina had become better at reading her facial expressions. "Oh, no, they're beautiful. Uh, I mean, you did a great job with them." She forced a smile. "Good thing I'm not the bra-throwing kind."

A line appeared between Regina's eyebrows.

Ellie's cheeks heated. "That's a reference to what you said about being good at—"

Regina held up a hand. "I know what it refers to."

Oh. So Regina had understood; she just didn't like any references to what had happened on their dates while they were at work. Would it be like this all the time once they had gotten their last date over and done with?

The charge nurse walked up to Ellie. "Would you bring Mrs. Rodriguez in exam three over to ortho? Unless Dr. Novak still needs you."

"No, I don't need her," Regina murmured and went back to her chart. "She's all yours."

"Sure." Ellie rushed to get a wheelchair. Getting out of here for a few minutes sounded like a good idea.

I don't need her. Regina's words echoed through her mind all the way to the orthopedic department. Okay, message received loud and clear.

After safely delivering Mrs. Rodriguez to the orthopedic department, she trudged back toward the ER, not in a hurry to face Regina again.

"Hey, Ellie!"

A shout from behind stopped her before she could reach the elevators. Ellie turned.

It took her a moment to make out who had called her name.

Caitlin waved at her with the arm that wasn't encased in a short arm cast, while a tall woman silently hovered next to her. "I thought that was you. I hope you don't mind me stopping you to say hi."

"No, of course not." Ellie walked over and gave her a warm smile. "How are you doing?"

"I'm great. Just got my cast." Caitlin knocked on the fiberglass.

"Ooh, I love the color you picked."

Caitlin smoothed her hand over the purple casting tape. "It's gorgeous, right? I didn't even know casts came in that color."

Her companion shook her head at them. "You do know it's not a fashion accessory, don't you?"

Caitlin grinned. "Yes, I noticed, thanks. Ellie, this is Mica—the friend I told you about. Mica, this is Ellie, one of my incredible rescuers."

Ellie turned her attention toward the woman next to Caitlin for the first time.

Mica looked like Caitlin's complete opposite in almost every possible way. With her soft features, upturned nose, and blonde locks, Caitlin exuded mom-next-door vibes, while her friend seemed to be the tough rebel type.

She wore her espresso-brown hair in an edgy side cut, shaved short on one side, but falling to her chin in a wild tousle on the other. Her face was as bold as her haircut, with sharp angles, an aquiline nose, and a strong jaw. Only a few freckles on her tanned cheeks added a touch of playfulness to her rugged appearance.

The cuffs of her black denim jeans were slightly frayed—not as a design choice but probably because she'd worn them a thousand times. A pair of scuffed hiking boots peeked out from beneath. Their thick soles added another inch to her already tall frame.

As she reached out to shake Ellie's hand, the sleeve of her worn dark-gray leather jacket slid up, revealing part of a tattoo.

But as tough as she seemed, she clasped Ellie's hand gently while her other hand kept resting on Caitlin's back in a protective gesture.

"Thank you for taking such good care of her and Riley." The look in her eyes was intense, as if Ellie had saved their lives, not just taken care of Caitlin's broken arm.

"I was glad to help," Ellie said. "How is Riley doing?"

Mica laughed, which made her seem a lot less intimidating. "Milking their lip for all it's worth."

Caitlin bumped her taller friend with her good arm. "Oh, like you weren't the one spoiling them after we got back from the hospital!"

Mica shrugged. "Hey, I didn't give them the tattoo they want; that has to count for something."

"You'd better not!" Caitlin let out a little growl that came across like a Chihuahua snarling at a Rottweiler. Then, looking at Ellie, she added, "Mica is a tattoo artist. Well, not just any tattoo artist. She's the best one I know."

"I'm the only one you know."

"Well, yeah, that too." Caitlin turned from her friend to Ellie. "Seriously, she's the best. If you ever want a tattoo, give her a call. I'm sure she'll give you a discount." She produced a business card from somewhere and slid it into Ellie's hand.

Her friend stared at her. "You took some of my business cards with you on a trip to the hospital?"

"Why not? Someone has to drum up business since you're so bad at tooting your own horn." Caitlin gave her a quick pat on the belly.

"Uh, yeah." Mica rubbed the spot as if she could still feel Caitlin's touch.

Ah. Ellie had a feeling Mica wouldn't be as enthusiastic about being set up with her as Caitlin had assumed. She gave Mica a commiserating smile. It took very little effort for her to recall how Regina's hands on her hips, then the brush of her fingers along her belly had felt, even twenty-four hours after it had happened. Not that their situation was in any way comparable otherwise. If the blush on Mica's tanned cheeks was any indication, she was quite smitten with her friend, while it was only Ellie's traitorous body that felt drawn to Regina. She didn't even like the woman most of the time.

"The offer is good for Dr. Novak too." Caitlin pointed at the business card in Ellie's hand, oblivious to what was going on with her friend. "Right, Mica?"

"Absolutely," Mica said. "If either of you ever want a tattoo, give me a call."

The mental image of Regina getting a tattoo made Ellie laugh. "Will do." She slid the card into the chest pocket of her scrub top. "I'd better get back to work. Take good care, okay?"

Mica nodded along with Caitlin, as if she was determined to keep her safe from any additional harm.

Being in love with a clueless straight friend had to be tough, Ellie mused as she headed back to the emergency department. Maybe Regina with her cynical attitude toward romance was right.

Sometimes, love sucked.

Regina usually preferred day shifts since they were busier and kept her on her toes, but unless it was summer, being on days meant that she sometimes didn't get to see the sun for half the week.

When she'd arrived at work this morning, it had still been dark, and night would have fallen by the time she would leave at seven.

Armed with a paper cup of coffee, she went outside to the staff's favorite break spot just past the ambulance entrance to catch some air.

The hospital's thoracic surgeon sat on a bench, smoking, but no one else was out here.

He really should know better than to chain-smoke. In his job, he would have seen all the damage it could do. Regina gave him a shake of her head but otherwise ignored him. She stepped out from beneath the ambulance canopy to enjoy the spring sun peeking out from behind gray clouds.

Regina looked across the staff parking lot to a small garden between two buildings while she sipped her coffee.

The surgeon got up and went back inside, acknowledging her presence with only a nod, which was the way Regina preferred it.

Her peaceful solitude was interrupted when the door behind her opened.

Annoyed, Regina glanced over her shoulder.

It was Ellie. She paused beneath the canopy, cradling a tall paper cup with both hands, and gave Regina an uncertain look. "Oh. Sorry. I didn't know you...anyone was out here. Do you mind if I join you?"

"I'm not renting the space, so..." Regina swept her arm in a join-me-if-you-have-to gesture.

Ellie moved out from beneath the canopy and took up a spot next to Regina. She tipped her head back and lifted her face into the sunshine. Her eyes fluttered shut, and a low sound of contentment escaped her.

Did she have to make noises like that and look so blissful? It did weird things to Regina's pulse. She dragged her gaze away and stared into the black depths of her coffee.

"Sometimes it's nice to come out here and be reminded that there's a real world out there, beyond the ED, isn't it?" Ellie murmured.

Most of the time, Regina didn't want to be reminded of that fact, so she gave a noncommittal grunt.

Ellie lowered her head and studied her as if she knew exactly what Regina's non-answer meant. The chocolate-brown shade of her eyes appeared even warmer in the sunlight.

Regina had braved confrontations with some of the most intimidating people in medicine. Why on earth would she struggle to hold the gaze of an overly romantic nurse?

Finally, it was Ellie who looked away. "Oh, by the way, Caitlin said to tell you hi."

"Caitlin?"

"Riley's mom," Ellie said. "I saw her in ortho earlier when she came in to get her cast."

"They didn't give her a plaster cast, did they?"

"No. It looked like fiberglass."

Regina gave a nod. "Good. Just in case it has to be X-rayed while it heals, they can do it through the cast."

"I know. I'm sure the docs in ortho took good care of her. Her friend is watching over her too. Oh, speaking of." Ellie switched the paper cup to one hand and reached into the chest pocket of her scrub top with the other. She held out a business card.

Regina took it, careful not to let their fingers brush, and squinted down at it. "Inkspiration? What am I supposed to do with a business card from a tattoo studio?"

"Get a tattoo," Ellie said with a grin. "Caitlin's friend, Mica, owns the studio, and she offered us a discount on our first tattoo."

"What makes you think I don't already have one?" Regina couldn't resist saying.

Ellie nearly inhaled a sip of coffee and started coughing. "You do?" she wheezed.

Regina kept her face impassive. "Possibly."

Ellie's cheeks had taken on a burgundy tint. Was it from coughing, or was she imagining where on Regina's body the tattoo might be?

It was so hard to resist the impulse to say something that would deepen that blush. Regina cleared her throat. "Will you take her up on that offer and get a tattoo?"

Ellie instantly shook her head. "No. I'm not too fond of needles."

"You're a nurse."

"Okay, then let's say I'm not too fond of being on the receiving end."

Regina bit the inside of her cheek so she wouldn't make a joke about Ellie being into giving, not receiving. When had flirting with Ellie turned into her catnip? She said nothing and handed back the business card.

Ellie slid it into her chest pocket and smoothed her hand over it.

What a weird gesture. Almost as if Ellie wanted to make sure the card was securely inside. Why would it be important not to lose the card if she didn't plan to take Caitlin's friend up on her offer to get a tattoo at a discount? Unless Ellie intended to call her for another reason. "Are you going to call her?"

Damn. She hadn't meant to ask. What did she care whether Ellie went out with the tattoo artist, as long as she waited a bit?

"For a tattoo appointment? No. Like I said, I'd rather avoid the business end of a needle."

"For a date," Regina said impatiently. "She's the friend Caitlin offered to set you up with, isn't she?"

"I assume so."

"So?" Regina drew out when Ellie didn't add anything.

"Hmm. I don't know." Ellie trailed her thumb along the edge of her scrub top pocket. "She seems like a fascinating person, so maybe I should. My family and friends are always on my case about me not dating enough. Even if we don't vibe as anything more, I might make a new friend."

Regina frowned. Why would Ellie need another friend? Surely she made friends wherever she went. "Just don't rush into it."

A smile spread across Ellie's face. "Aww, how sweet. Are you worried about me?"

Ellie's amused tone made Regina scowl. "I'm worried about my reputation."

"Your reputation?" Ellie set her paper cup down on a concrete post as if to give Regina her full attention. "What does me calling Mica have to do with your reputation?"

Wasn't it obvious? "Everyone knows you bid on me at the auction. It's appropriate for you to wait at least a few weeks before you show interest in anyone else."

"Appropriate?" Ellie echoed. "Says who? *The Handbook of Singles Auction Etiquette?*"

Against Regina's will, laughter burst from her chest. It sounded strange in her own ears—like a violin that had sat unused and untuned in a closet for a year. She pressed her hand to her sternum at the unexpected sensation. "Yes. It's right there in chapter two: The winning bidder shall be seen pining for the bachelorette they bid on for a period of at least twenty business days before accepting date requests from other parties."

"Pining?" Ellie was clearly trying to sound appalled, but she had to choke out the word between chuckles. "You want me to make googly eyes at you from the nurses' station?"

The lightness bubbling inside of Regina died down. "No. That's not what I meant at all. We agreed to keep things strictly professional at work, so googly eyes are out. Just don't appear too eager to get involved with someone else."

"Ah." The grin was back on Ellie's face. "You want everyone to think you were the one who ditched me instead of the other way around. You"—she reached over and poked Regina's shoulder—"really have an ego problem, dear doctor."

"Nonsense." Regina smoothed her hand over her scrub top to remove any wrinkles Ellie might have left. "It's only logical to let everyone think I was the ditcher, not the ditchee."

"How, pray tell, is that logical?"

"Easy," Regina said. "You forked over nine hundred bucks for a few dates with me, so clearly, you're smitten with me."

Ellie let out a long-suffering sigh. "Clearly. Right. I told you it was—"

"A fly."

"An accident," Ellie said.

"Yes, but no one else knows that. They assume you bid on me because I'm hot, smart, and—"

"Super modest," Ellie threw in.

Regina gave her a nod and struggled to keep her face expressionless and not return that teasing grin. "Now you're catching on. So if you go out with someone else before the ink on the check you wrote for our dates is even dry, everyone will think my dating skills aren't up to par."

"Of course we can't have that."

"No, we can't."

Ellie seemed to think about it for a moment. "Well," she finally said, "as I told you before, you'd better make sure I have the best time ever on our last two date activities."

Was it just Regina's imagination, or was there something other than merely a playful challenge in her tone? Whatever it was sent a thrill through her body.

Oh, come on. She was teasing. Maybe she really needed to check her ego. "Oh, don't worry, I will."

"So where are you taking me on our surprise date?"

"Surprise date?"

"Yeah. Didn't you listen to the emcee or read the information package the auction sent along? It says the date package includes one surprise activity the bachelorette plans for the generous bidder."

Regina had barely even skimmed the information package, not wanting to spend more time than strictly necessary on anything to do with the auction, so this was the first time she had heard about a surprise activity. But, of course, she would never admit to that. "Oh, that. Don't worry. The generous bidder will be very surprised." Very, very surprised. It was so much of a surprise that even Regina had no idea where she would take her.

Ellie picked up her coffee and took a sip. "Good."

"So you agree not to call the tattoo artist lady before, let's say, April?"

"Actually," Ellie said, "I'm not sure I will call her at all. I have a feeling she wouldn't be interested in me anyway."

"Why wouldn't she be interested?" *Ugh.* That had come out all wrong, as if no queer woman would be able to resist Ellie. Which wasn't the case at all. Regina resisted her just fine. "I mean, you're gainfully employed and your features are reasonably symmetrical."

Ellie's hand went to her cheek as if to assess the proportions of her face. "Reasonably symmetrical? If that's your idea of a compliment, it's no wonder you're single."

"It wasn't a compliment. I was merely pointing out facts. So, I repeat, why wouldn't Caitlin's friend be interested?"

"I could be wrong, but I had a feeling she has a thing for Caitlin."

Regina pondered it for a second. "Huh. Isn't Caitlin straight?"

"I think so. But it's not like Mica can control who she has feelings for. No one can."

Regina shrugged and emptied her coffee. The dregs tasted bitter. "I've always managed to follow my five ground rules."

"What five rules?"

"No straight women. No clingy girlfriends. No cheaters. No relationship drama." Regina ticked them off on her fingers, then paused before adding the most important one, "No co-workers."

Ellie lowered her gaze into her cup and swirled around the remainder of her coffee.

Before she could say anything, the door behind them swished open and Jasmine burst outside. "EMS just called in. They're en route with a suspected drug overdose. Six minutes out."

Regina crushed her empty paper cup in her fist and, already striding toward the doors, tossed it into a trash can. Her mind immediately went over the checklist of things to do to save this patient. "Call—"

"RT." Ellie jogged to catch up with her. "I'm on it."

Chapter 15

REGINA CLICKED OFF HER HEADLAMP so it wouldn't interfere with her night vision as she walked up to the tee pad and peered through the darkness.

In the distance, the basket was lit up like a Christmas tree. Well, if Christmas trees were illuminated by glow sticks.

Ellie would like this.

The thought came unbidden, and she brushed it off with an annoyed shake of her head and instead focused on mentally mapping out the glow disc's flight path.

She started her run-up and did a quick x-step. As she reached the end of the tee pad, she rotated her hips, swung her arm forward, and unleashed a powerful throw.

The glow disc streaked across the dark sky like a comet.

Like a comet? She snorted at her own thoughts. *Please! You've been spending too much time with Ellie.*

She followed the disc's path toward the basket with her eyes. For a few seconds, it looked as if it might be a hole-in-one, but then the glow-in-the-dark disc veered a little to the right and dropped into the grass a few yards from the basket.

Behind her, Dylan let out a sharp whistle. "Great drive!"

She moved back behind the tee pad, making room for him to tee off. "So," she said as he ran his UV flashlight over his disc to charge it up, "any plans for the weekend?"

He paused as if surprised she would ask, but then groaned and answered anyway. "Getting my taxes done."

Since they had met up for a glow round after work, she had subtly dug for anything that might give her an idea where to take Ellie on their surprise date, but so far, Dylan had been pretty much useless. "What about last weekend? Did you do anything fun?"

He looked up from his disc and peered through the darkness as if trying to make out her face. "Since when are you interested in what I do in my spare time?"

"I'm not," she replied. "Just trying to find out what the locals do for fun around here."

Dylan slipped the flashlight into his backpack and dropped it behind the tee. "This local went axe-throwing with a few buddies."

"Axe-throwing? At a medieval festival?"

He laughed. "No. Believe it or not, there are places with axe-throwing lanes. It's kinda like darts, only with bigger weapons. We had a blast."

Hmm. Taking Ellie axe-throwing would fit the surprise activity bill. Regina made a mental note to look up those axe-throwing places as soon as she got home.

After a short run-up, Dylan sent his glow disc down the fairway. In the dark, it graced the branches of a tree and dropped into the grass half-way to the basket. "Shit. I'm not gonna beat you this time either, am I?"

"I'm not planning on it."

They clicked on their headlamps and walked toward their discs, carefully watching their footing.

He directed the beam of his lamp her way. "Your sudden interest in my weekend activities doesn't have anything to do with you looking for date ideas, does it?"

"I don't date," Regina answered.

"Good. Because as much fun as *Bury the Hatchet* is, I don't think it can be considered romantic."

Not romantic. Perfect. They were definitely going axe-throwing, then, because romance with Ellie Fisher was the last thing she wanted.

"Ha!" With a triumphant cry, Ellie thumped the puzzle piece she'd been searching for into place—only to realize it didn't quite fit after all.

A loud ping from her phone drowned out her audiobook. She hit the pause button, stopping her favorite narrator mid-sentence, to check the new message.

It was from Regina.

I'll pick you up tomorrow at 4.30. Prepare to be surprised.

"Yes, 4.30 works for me, thanks for asking," Ellie muttered.

Vickie glanced up from where she was lounging on the couch. "Pardon me?"

"Oh, nothing. Just Regina being Regina." Ellie waved her phone, then lowered it to answer. *Good surprise, I hope.*

It comes highly recommended by my local sources, Regina answered.

Ellie gave the screen a doubtful look. *Do you even know any locals?*

Of course I do. Regina had added a haughty-looking emoji, which had one eyebrow raised.

Ellie countered with the monocle emoji to convey her skepticism. *Oh yeah? Provide a list.*

Number one: Ellie Fisher, Regina replied. *Number two: Rick the security guy.*

Nick, Ellie typed before Regina could send her number three. *His name is Nick. And please tell me you did not ask our security guard for date ideas. He's on his third divorce!*

That means he managed to convince three women to marry him, so his date ideas can't be that bad, Regina shot back.

Hmm, can't fault that logic. Except we both know you didn't ask anyone at work. Regina seemed hell-bent on keeping work and her private life in neatly separate boxes, and Ellie couldn't see that changing anytime soon.

Regina didn't answer for a while.

Crap. Ellie had enjoyed bantering back and forth, and now her careless comment had put a stop to it.

True, Regina finally replied. *So you're safe from Nick's dating activity suggestions.*

Ellie blew out a breath. *Do I get any hints on where you're taking me?*

Wouldn't be much of a surprise if I told you. But I'll give you one clue.

Ellie leaned closer to the small screen and sent an ear emoji to indicate she was all ears.

Wear sensible shoes, Regina's next message said. *No heels. No sandals.*

Where on earth are you taking me?

You'll have to wait and see. After a slight pause, a second text popped up. *Oh and Ellie? You might want to wear something flannel.*

"Flannel?" The word burst out of Ellie.

Vickie looked over again. "Are you exchanging what-are-you-wearing messages already?"

Ellie threw one of the puzzle pieces at her sister. "Haha. Regina wants me to wear sensible shoes and something flannel for our date tomorrow."

"So? It's the lesbian uniform, isn't it?"

Ellie hurled a second puzzle piece in her direction, then reached for her phone again. *You do know that lesbians loving flannel is just a stereotype, don't you?*

So are you saying your closet is completely flannel-free?

I might have a pair of flannel pajamas, Ellie replied.

Aaaand?

Ellie wasn't about to admit to owning a plaid flannel shirt. *And I look damn cute in them.*

I bet.

Ellie's cheeks warmed. She hadn't expected that reply. *You don't really expect me to wear flannel, do you?*

A smirking emoji was Regina's only response.

Regina???

Another smirking emoji arrived.

Ellie leaned her forehead onto the table. "Oh God. This woman will be the death of me."

Chapter 16

AT EXACTLY FOUR THIRTY THE next afternoon, Regina got out of the car, walked toward Ellie's charming little two-story home, and jogged up the five steps leading to the tiled porch.

At the front door, she paused and ran her gaze down her outfit—blue jeans and a burgundy button-down blouse with a twist hem. Flannel had never been her style, but she'd put on a pair of chocolate-brown leather desert boots to complete her lumberjane outfit.

She adjusted her belt so it was centered and tucked her hair back behind one ear, then realized what she was doing and snatched her hand away.

This felt annoyingly similar to a real date. Maybe it had been too long since she'd gone out with a woman, so she'd forgotten what it actually felt like.

Let's get this over with. She rang the doorbell.

Barking sounded from inside, then the door swung open.

Instead of Ellie, her sister stood in front of Regina. With a smirk, she took in Regina's outfit. "No flannel? Ellie will be so disappointed."

Regina sighed. This was why she didn't date women she worked with. Especially not women whose sister she also worked with. Not that she and Ellie were dating, of course. "I'm sure she'll live."

"Come on in. Ellie is still getting ready." Vickie opened the door farther and invited her in.

Regina made her way inside. With Wally jumping around her, tail wagging, it was like navigating an obstacle course.

The front door opened into the living room. With its hardwood floor, cream-colored walls, and a fireplace flanked by built-in bookshelves, it looked cozy and inviting—exactly the way she had imagined Ellie's house would look.

The living room flowed into the dining room, where most of a long table was taken up by a half-done puzzle. The image of an avenue lined by cherry trees started to take shape, the pink blossoms forming a soft carpet.

"So," Vickie said, "last date, huh?"

"Mm-hmm," Regina answered but kept her attention on the puzzle so she wouldn't invite a conversation. A hole in the sea of pink blossoms caught her attention, where a puzzle piece was missing. She walked over, glanced at the pieces laid out on the table, then picked one up and plugged it in.

It fit.

Vickie seemed unbothered by her refusal to make small talk. "Unless, of course, you plan to ask Ellie out again," she added.

Oh for Christ's sake! Apparently, Vickie hadn't gotten the memo that they were merely fulfilling their obligations toward the auction. This was heading into what-are-your-intentions-toward-my-sister territory, and Regina absolutely wouldn't go there. She turned away from the puzzle and fixed Vickie with a hard stare. "Why would I do that?"

Vickie's mouth dropped open.

A creaking sound made Regina look away from her.

Ellie stood at the bottom of the stairs, which led to the second floor.

Shit. Regina's throat felt as if she'd tried to swallow a hard-boiled egg without peeling it. Then the egg slid down her esophagus, spreading pressure to her chest. Had Ellie heard? Should she add something? Explain? Apologize?

What? Why the hell would she apologize? She hadn't apologized in at least a decade. She hadn't even told Riley how sorry she was for not being more present in his life. No way would she apologize now.

And what was there to explain? She had no intention of asking Ellie out. Surely Ellie had known that already, and if she hadn't, setting clear expectations was a good thing.

Ellie paused on the last step and gazed at her across the living room. For the first time since Regina had met her, her usually warm and open expression shuttered.

Oh yeah. She heard. Great. Now Regina felt like an evil witch torturing a puppy. The egg plunked into her stomach. By now, it was so big that it must have been laid by an ostrich.

Or possibly a dragon.

"Maybe," Ellie said quietly, "because of my reasonably symmetrical features." One corner of her mouth curled into a crooked smile.

See? Ellie was smiling. No big deal. If Regina's comment had hurt her feelings, she'd get over it.

Ellie stepped down into the living room. "Ready to go?"

"Yes." Regina strode past Vickie, ignoring her heated glare.

It was only when she led Ellie to the car that she noticed what Ellie was wearing.

Flannel—but not the way Regina had envisioned. Instead of an oversized flannel shirt, Ellie was wearing a black-and-yellow plaid suspender skirt.

Regina had always discounted outfits like that as silly—something worn only by schoolgirls or porn stars.

But *silly* was the last thought on her mind as she took Ellie in. The skirt hugged Ellie's curvy hips, then flared out at the bottom, ending an inch or two above her knees. It was the first time Regina had ever seen her legs—and she was seeing a lot of them.

She forced herself to look away, but taking in the top Ellie wore wasn't any better. Ellie had paired the skirt with a black, formfitting turtleneck. Detachable suspenders trailed along the outer curve of Ellie's breasts, framing them as if to invite her gaze.

Invite your gaze? The hell! You don't want to date her, so stop ogling her!

She opened the passenger-side door for Ellie and pointedly ignored her smooth legs as Ellie got in. Regina climbed behind the wheel and headed west toward Overland Park.

Silence settled between them.

Regina didn't mind. A lack of conversation had never bothered her, nor had she ever cared if she hurt someone's feelings. And she didn't care right now either. Her urge to clear the air was for entirely selfish reasons. As it stood, Ellie was more likely to ram the axe into her skull than throw it at the target, and Regina liked her head intact, thank you very much.

"Listen," she said. "What I said earlier about—"

"No need to repeat it." Ellie's voice was raspy. "I understood it the first time."

That dragon egg in her belly was back. It felt as if the fire-spitting brat was about to hatch. Regina tugged the seat belt away from herself. "I was only trying to correct your sister's misguided assumptions. I wasn't implying that there's no reason anyone would ever want to date you."

Ellie inhaled audibly but said nothing.

"There's nothing wrong with you. You're...um..." Regina flipped through her mental lexicon in search of a word that would describe Ellie. Kind, dedicated, smart, determined, witty, courageous, grounded, beautiful. All true, yet none of those words described Ellie to perfection, at least not by themselves. "Lovely," she finally said.

Then she winced. Lovely? Really? She had never used that word in her entire life—and she should have left it at that.

Ellie smacked her lips as if tasting the word. "Lovely? Is that like having symmetrical features?" A hint of warmth was back in her tone, as if she was teasing.

"*Reasonably* symmetrical features," Regina corrected.

Ellie didn't answer.

Shit. She had fallen back into their banter without thought, but clearly, it had been too soon for her to return the teasing. "What I'm trying to say—"

"Badly," Ellie interjected.

Regina flicked a glare at her. "What I'm trying to say is that it's me, not you. I don't date—"

"Which is a good thing," Ellie said. "Because that's the most unoriginal rejection line in the history of dating. It even tops 'I hope we can still be friends.' Or were you going to say that next?"

"No, of course not." Mostly because she wasn't sure she wanted to be Ellie's friend—*could be* both her friend and her co-worker. Her world had spun off its axis any time her work and private life had collided, and she had promised herself to never let it happen again. "What I'm trying to say is you don't like dating."

"Neither do you."

"Yes, but I hate it because I hate people. You hate it because you want a relationship—something deep instead of a superficial connection.

And I don't have that in me anymore, if I ever did. Especially not with a colleague."

Ellie was silent again.

God, she was fucking this up. Now she had said too much. There was a reason she usually shied away from an emotional striptease like that. Regina glanced over.

Ellie stared back with a stunned expression.

"Did I get that wrong?" Regina asked. "About you wanting more than a superficial connection?"

"No. That was… It's exactly right. Now that you said it, that's exactly what I dislike about dating. I just never put it into words, even to myself."

A weird feeling spread through Regina's belly, and this time, it wasn't related to the dragon egg. When had she gotten to know Ellie so well that she had started to sense things like that about her?

Ellie shook her head as if in response to something she'd been thinking about. Then she smiled. "Don't worry. I'm not searching for a soul-deep bond with you. All I want is my money's worth." The teasing undertone was back in her voice, then faded away. "And it would be nice to not be talked about as if you'd rather manually disimpact a dozen severely constipated patients than go on a real date with me."

Regina focused on the road ahead but could feel Ellie's gaze on her, as if Ellie was waiting for something. An apology, most likely. And she deserved one. But the words wouldn't come. "You're right," she said instead. "You deserve better."

"I do," Ellie said with a gentle fierceness Regina secretly admired. "Which is why you now owe me two drinks instead of one."

Regina snorted. "I'm sure what you meant to say is that we're now even when it comes to owing each other drinks. Besides, you don't want to drink too much where we are going."

"Where are we going?"

Regina gave her a mysterious grin. "A lady never…um, books and tells."

Regina's words—*why would I do that?*—still echoed through Ellie's mind as they got out of the car in Overland Park.

Or maybe it wasn't just the words but also the tone—as if dating her was the last thing Regina would ever do.

That had cut deeper than Ellie wanted to admit. Even after their conversation, she couldn't quite shake it, and she wasn't sure of the reason.

Why did she suddenly care what Regina thought? It wasn't as if she wanted to date her…was it?

But if she really wasn't interested at all, why did it bother her? Before the auction, she would have thought *What a bitch* and moved on.

Was it possible she didn't dislike Regina quite as much as she'd thought and was actually starting to like her?

"Ellie?" Regina had stopped in front of an oval building and held the glass door open for her, as if this were a real date.

Don't read anything into it. Very likely, Regina was just trying to provide the perfect date because Ellie had challenged her. "Oh. Thanks." She shoved back her distracting thoughts. There would be time to figure it out later.

Regina's Whitewater Rapids scent engulfed her as she stepped past her into a large, warehouse-like room. The smell of sawdust and the thump of steel sinking into wood greeted her.

She paused and looked around.

A plastic skeleton dressed in a *Bury the Hatchet* T-shirt and a Viking helmet sat on a throne next to the front desk.

Wood-paneled walls gave the room a warm, rustic feel. Several high-top tables and barstools took up the center, while about a dozen lanes resembling batting cages spread out on either side. At the end of each hung a circular wooden target, and wood chips were scattered across the floor underneath.

A guy took up position in the cage closest to Ellie, lifted an axe behind his head with both hands, and threw it at the target. Ellie couldn't see where the axe landed, but he let out a whoop and shouted, "Killshot!"

"Axe-throwing?" Ellie cast a disbelieving look over her shoulder at Regina. "For our surprise date activity, you took me to a place where people are hurling sharp tools? I'm pretty sure that's not covered in *The Handbook of Singles Auction Etiquette.*"

Regina shrugged. "I've never been the grand prize at an auction before, so excuse me if I'm unfamiliar with the protocol."

"Grand prize?" Ellie laughed. "Someone has a high opinion of herself. Let's see if that's still the case once I've beat you at axe-throwing."

"You're welcome to try." With a confident grin, Regina strode past her toward the front desk.

Ellie followed. "Um, shouldn't we wait for Mitch?"

"Mitch?"

"The auction photographer. You did call him, right?"

"Oh, him." Regina's nose crinkled as if she'd opened a Tupperware container that had gotten lost at the back of the fridge for months. "He'll meet us at the restaurant later. I've been told our instructor would be happy to take a few pictures for us."

Had Regina taken a dislike to the photographer, or did she hate him documenting their date for the world to see?

"Welcome to Bury the Hatchet." A staff member greeted them with a friendly smile, then had them fill out a waiver of liability.

"First time I've had to do that on a date," Ellie whispered to Regina as she signed it.

"Me too," Regina answered. "Although some of the dates I've been on should have come with that warning about risk of serious injury."

A bearded guy in a T-shirt that said *axe master* approached them. Obviously, he had overheard what Regina had said because he laughed. "No worries. I'm JT, your instructor, and I'm here to make sure the only body part you might lose on this date is your heart."

Ellie firmly shook her head. She would not lose any body parts on this date, period. Especially not her heart.

JT led them over to their designated lane and walked them through the safety rules, then showed them how to throw an axe. "Some people prefer to take a wide stance; some prefer to put their dominant foot forward; some take a step forward as they throw." He demonstrated each option. "Try it all out to see what feels best for you. Grip the axe at the bottom with your dominant hand. The other hand goes on top. Line it up with your arms straight ahead of you, then bring the axe back, behind your head. Now bring it forward and release it right when it's at eye level."

His axe flew through the air, rotated once, then thumped into the wooden target, where it stuck close to the bull's-eye.

He walked over, removed the axe, and slid it into a wooden box at the other end of the lane. "Who wants to try first?"

Ellie and Regina looked at each other.

Regina waved her arm in a you-go-first gesture.

Swallowing, Ellie entered the cage. She wiped her damp hands on her skirt before she picked up an axe.

It was heavier than she'd expected. She hefted it a few times to get used to its weight before she took up position at the twelve-foot mark, as JT had shown them.

JT moved back behind the table. "You don't need to throw it that hard. Axe-throwing is not about strength. It's all about having the correct technique."

With a two-handed grip, Ellie moved the axe in front of her, as if taking aim with a revolver. Then she lifted it behind her head, squinted at the target, and hurled the axe toward it.

The weapon rotated too much. The axe head hit the target, bounced off, and landed in the wood chips scattered at the end of the lane.

"Don't worry. Most people don't stick the axe on their first try," JT said. "But you've got a good eye. On your next try, step forward a bit. That way, the axe won't overrotate. As long as one of your feet is behind the twelve-foot line, you're fine."

Ellie retrieved the axe, then joined JT behind the table so Regina could step into the lane.

"Can I do this one-handed?" Regina asked as she pulled an axe from the wooden box.

"Sure. That was next on my list of techniques to show you." JT walked back around the table. "Keep your elbow straight, pull the axe back until the head almost touches your shoulder, then bring it forward." He demonstrated, then retrieved the axe and joined Ellie again.

Ellie had no clue about axe-throwing, but as Regina took up position, it looked like the perfect form to her.

Regina held the axe as loosely as if it were no heavier than a dart. She had rolled up her shirtsleeves, so Ellie could see the slender muscles in her arm flex as she lifted the axe.

Ellie licked her dry lips. Did they serve drinks at the axe-throwing range? She kept her gaze on Regina instead of turning her head to ask JT.

In a fluid motion, Regina swung her arm forward and released the axe. It rotated once, then embedded itself into the wood half in the bull's-eye, half in the inner ring.

"Yes!" JT pumped his fist. "Either I'm the world's best teacher, or you've done this before."

Regina calmly walked toward the target to retrieve the axe. "Nah. I'm just very motivated to win."

"Why's that?" JT asked. "Are you playing for a special prize?"

Regina looked back over her shoulder and met Ellie's eyes.

For a moment, Ellie thought she'd say something like *a kiss*.

But, of course, that was silly. Regina had made it clear she didn't want to date her, so she probably had no desire to kiss her either.

"A drink," Regina said and tugged the axe free with more force than JT had shown them.

Regina had thought she would win that drink easily, but Ellie had given her a run for her money.

JT had introduced them to several different games, and Ellie had improved with each round. Once she had gotten the feel for it, she managed to stick the axe with almost every throw, each one inching closer to the bull's-eye.

Her face was a study in concentration as she passed Regina on the way to the throwing lane.

Ellie seemed so easygoing, as if she didn't care whether she won or lost. Of course, Regina should have known better than to assume that meant she would just roll over and give her an easy win.

Any time they'd butted heads, Ellie had never backed down, even at work, and Regina admitted to herself she liked that about her.

"I think I've figured it out now," Ellie murmured as she lined up the axe in front of her. "My release point is still a bit too low, isn't it?"

Regina discussed her release point with her disc golf buddies on a regular basis, and it had never sounded the slightest bit sexual to her. Yet when Ellie said it, she had to take a big gulp of her beer to douse the heat simmering in her belly. "Um, yes, I think so too. Release it when it's slightly above the bull's-eye."

Ellie had switched to one-handed throws a while ago too, and now she looked like a pro at it as she swung the axe backward toward her shoulder.

For a moment, Regina wondered how she might fare at disc golf.

Hell, no. Ellie was a co-worker, she firmly reminded herself. She did not belong in that part of her life.

Ellie brought her arm forward in an elegant arc and released the axe with perfect timing.

It rotated once, then thumped into the wood exactly in the middle of the bull's-eye.

Ellie jumped up and down as if she had won the axe-throwing world championship. Her skirt twirled with every leap, making her look girlish and sexy at the same time. Her "Oh my God! Yes, yes, yes!" made Regina go for her beer again.

Since when did she find the girl-next-door type sexy? But there was no denying that Ellie's breathless voice sent a jolt of desire through her—or that her antics made her smile.

"Can you take a picture to preserve this important moment for posterity?" Ellie asked.

"Sure." Regina reined in her libido. At least taking a photo gave her an excuse to look at Ellie without her noticing.

Ellie took up position half in front of the wooden target and pointed at the axe sticking out of the bull's-eye with both index fingers. The biggest grin curved her lips, and her eyes shone. She was radiating joy.

It was silly. Totally over the top. It was just one bull's-eye, after all. Regina had hit several of them already, so there was no need to get this excited over it.

Even sillier was that she couldn't bring herself to say any of that. Not even one sarcastic comment would cross her lips, all because she didn't want that smile to dim.

Pathetic.

Regina stabbed at the screen of her phone to take several photos in a row.

Finally, Ellie turned toward the target, gripped the handle, and wiggled it up and down to remove the axe the way JT had shown them.

But apparently, the blade was deeply embedded in the wood and didn't budge.

"Need some help?" Regina called over.

"No, it's fine. I—" With a final tug, the axe came free. "Ouch." Ellie let out a startled gasp and clutched her hand.

Adrenaline shot through Regina's body, and her muscles responded before she could think about it. She rushed toward Ellie, prepared for a gushing cut or possibly even a severed finger.

Ellie cradled the hand that still gripped the axe, so Regina couldn't see a thing.

Was there blood? Regina pressed closer. "Let me see."

JT ran over. "What happened? Did anyone get hurt?"

"No, no," Ellie said quickly. "It's just a splinter."

A splinter? A breath whooshed from Regina's lungs. "Let me see," she said again.

"Nothing to see. I told you it's just a splinter." Ellie pushed against Regina's shoulder with the hand that wasn't holding the axe. "Stop the emergency medicine doctor mode, Regina. You're scaring JT."

Scaring JT? Regina snorted. Her heart rate was only now returning to normal. "I bet he'd be a lot less scared if a qualified doctor took a look at your finger."

JT took the axe from Ellie. "Actually, yes." He glanced from her to Regina. "Do you want me to see if we have a pair of tweezers?"

"Don't encourage her, or she'll insist on you getting an entire tray of surgical instruments," Ellie said.

Regina ignored them both. She cradled Ellie's hand in hers and lifted it to eye level to examine it. "Every time we go out on a date, someone gets hurt. Maybe the universe is trying to tell us something."

"It's a splinter, Regina, not a chopped-off limb. Besides, no one got hurt during baking class."

"You mean other than your near heatstroke on the way to Fair Oaks," Regina said with a smirk, but her attention was on Ellie's hand. Even though the axe-throwing range was well-lit, she couldn't find the splinter. She ran the pad of her thumb along Ellie's index finger to feel for it. The only thing she noticed was how incredibly soft Ellie's skin was. *Cut it out.*

The softness of Ellie's skin was hardly relevant diagnostic information. "Is this the right finger?"

Ellie cleared her throat. "Um, yes. But I actually can't feel the splinter anymore."

"What do you know?" JT chuckled. "A miracle healing!"

Regina pierced him with her most intimidating glare, making him flinch. He might have been kidding, but she didn't see the humor in Ellie getting hurt. "Do you want us to stop and head to the restaurant?"

"Stop?" Ellie shook her head and gently tugged her hand free of Regina's grip. "I'm not stopping before I beat you at least once. At axe-throwing," she added as if she knew Regina had been about to tease her about finally admitting that she had lost the ice-skating race.

Did Ellie really know her that well already? She wasn't sure how she felt about that. "Well," she drawled, "you can certainly try. But be careful with that axe, okay?"

"Aww, how sweet of you to worry."

Regina arched her brows. "Nothing sweet about it. I just don't want to be the one to explain to the director of nursing how our best nurse lost a finger."

Ellie grinned. "Best nurse, huh?"

"Well, best among all nurses who went on an axe-throwing adventure this weekend," Regina added.

"Oh, no. You can't take back a compliment."

"I don't do compliments, remember?"

"Right." With a smile, Ellie stepped back behind their table.

Chapter 17

IF SOMEONE HAD ASKED ELLIE this morning, she never would have listed axe-throwing as a good date activity, but it had actually been fun, and hurling the three-pound axe at the target had gotten her heart rate up.

Right. The axe was what made your heart beat faster. Not the way Regina trailed her thumb along your finger.

She could still feel her touch as they parked the car in the River Market neighborhood and strolled toward The Meadow.

Mitch, the auction photographer, was waiting for them in front of the historic four-story brick building. "Hi, lovebirds."

Regina gave him a cool look. "Mike."

"It's Mitch."

Without any indication that she'd heard his correction, Regina held the door open for Ellie, then followed her in without doing the same for him.

Wow, the woman sure knew how to hold a grudge. Apparently, she still hadn't forgiven Mitch for snapping photos of them taking care of Riley and Caitlin at the ice rink.

Regina gave her name to the hostess and added, "The Heart-to-Heart Auction made our reservation."

"Ah, yes. Your table is ready, Dr. Novak," the hostess said. She gave Regina a nod that seemed oddly conspiratorial. "Right this way."

As they followed the hostess, Ellie leaned close to Regina and whispered. "What was that?"

"What was what?"

"The hostess." Ellie gestured at the woman's back. "She gave you a weird look. You don't know her, do you?"

"No. She was probably just flirting with me."

Ellie laughed. "God, you've really got an ego."

The hostess led them to a quiet table in a small room separate from the main dining area.

The reddish-brown hardwood floor, timber posts, low lighting, and exposed brick walls on two sides gave the restaurant a rustic but cozy atmosphere. A beautiful mural of a wildflower-dotted meadow covered one wall. Candles flickered on wooden tables for two. Soft music drifted over from the main room, where a small band was playing live.

The ambience was a lot more romantic than Ellie had expected. Maybe it was a good thing they had Mitch as a chaperone.

Ellie reached for her chair, but Regina beat her to it.

Their hands brushed on the back of the chair, renewing that tingly feeling that had just started to fade.

Ellie quickly snatched her hand away.

Regina pulled the chair out for her and waited until she was seated before she sat across from her.

The waitress instantly came over, took their drink orders, and left them with the menus while Mitch snapped a few discreet pictures of the restaurant.

In the main dining room, the band started playing a different song.

It took only two bars for Ellie to recognize "Holly's Song" by Jenna Blake. She tilted her head to listen. "They're playing my favorite song by my favorite singer! What an amazing coincidence."

"Yes," Regina said. "Amazing."

Something in her tone made Ellie study her more closely. Regina wore her usual impassive expression, but Ellie had spent enough time with her now to sense it was a mask. "Their choice of music isn't so coincidental after all, is it?"

Regina nonchalantly took a sip of water. "Maybe. Maybe not."

"How did you do that?"

"It's this newfangled invention called a phone."

"You called and arranged for them to play my favorite music?" So that was why the hostess had given Regina that conspiratorial look. Ellie couldn't figure her out. Regina could be standoffish and say things that cut deeply, but then she went and did something sweet like that.

Regina clinked the ice cubes against the edge of her glass. "Actually, I called Jenna…Leo and tried to get her to sing here tonight, but she said it's impossible to arrange the security on such short notice. So this"—she nodded toward the band in the main dining area—"was the next best thing."

Ellie struggled not to gape at her. "You called a five-time Grammy award winner to come sing for us?"

Regina shrugged. "You challenged me to provide the best date ever, so I had to deliver."

Ellie studied her in the candlelight. Regina made it sound as if it was all about her competitiveness, but was it really? She was starting to suspect that Regina cared about her enjoying their date for more than strictly selfish reasons.

The click of Mitch's camera made her look away from Regina. He had returned and snapped a photo.

"Can we order first before you take photos?" she asked him.

"Hungry?" he asked with a smirk.

"Very. We've worked up quite an appetite."

He lowered his camera. "Oh. Sure."

The corners of Regina's mouth twitched up into an amused smile. She leaned across the table, closer to Ellie. "You do know that he now thinks we've had hot, bed-breaking sex, don't you?"

"What? Why would he—? Oh!" Ellie's cheeks burned. "Axe-throwing," she said loudly enough for Mitch to hear. "We've worked up an appetite playing with axes."

Regina's grin only broadened. "That's not helping. Double-headed axes have been a symbol of lesbianism for ages. Now he thinks 'playing with axes' is a euphemism for—"

Thankfully, the waitress's return saved Ellie. She set Ellie's drink—a red ale from a local microbrewery—down in front of her and refilled Regina's water glass. "Are you ready to order, or would you like more time?"

Ellie hadn't even opened the menu, much less perused it. "We need a little more time, please." To Regina, she whispered, "You are very distracting."

She scanned the menu, but the more she read, the less she knew what to get. Everything sounded great, and every dish she could see being prepared in the open kitchen looked mouth-watering.

Finally, she decided on the thyme-roasted chicken breast with mashed potatoes and glazed carrots, while Regina ordered the KC strip steak with mac and cheese and Parmesan broccoli.

Ellie stared at her.

"What?" Regina asked as she handed the waitress her menu.

"I don't know… I thought you'd order the salmon fillet or something."

"I like salmon just fine, but I'm more of a steak kind of woman, and I can never resist mac and cheese."

Never in a million years would Ellie have guessed that. "I nearly ordered that too. Maybe I can try some of yours."

"Sorry." Regina took a sip of her water. "I never share my food."

Ellie gaped at her. "You're not serious, are you?"

"Like a brain aneurysm," Regina said.

"Fine," Ellie muttered. "In that case, you're definitely not getting any of my breast."

Regina's impassive expression gave way to a sensual grin. "Who said I was interested in your breasts?"

"Chicken breast, singular. I was talking about the tender, juicy piece of chicken breast I ordered, okay?" Ellie pressed the back of her hand to her overheated cheek. "You really enjoy making me blush, don't you?"

"It's been the highlight of every date," Regina said cheerfully.

Apparently, Mitch enjoyed it too, because he lifted his camera and zoomed in on Ellie's face.

Regina held up a hand to stop him. "Why don't you take a cigarette break or something?"

"I don't smoke," Mitch said.

"I don't care. Come back when there's food to photograph on the table."

Mitch scowled, but Regina held his gaze, unimpressed, until he slung his camera over his shoulder and marched toward the bar.

Mitch had taken what felt like a hundred pictures of their food and them sampling it.

Finally, Regina's patience snapped. She pointed her fork at him. "Unless you're planning a documentary on the importance of chewing your food thoroughly, I think that's enough."

Camera still raised, he glowered at her.

"Thanks, Mitch," Ellie added more softly. "It was nice to see you again."

Her tone was friendly, but it was a clear dismissal too.

Mitch put his camera away, said goodbye, and left.

Huh. Guess there's more than one way to skin a cat. Satisfied, Regina watched him go. She couldn't even say what bothered her about him. Maybe just his mere presence. It reminded her this was an auction-arranged evening and the last of their dates. Once it ended, she and Ellie would no longer have a valid reason to spend time together outside of work. A few weeks ago, that thought would have left her relieved, but now she felt strangely disappointed.

She realized she'd zoned out for a moment and turned back toward Ellie.

So far, all of their dates had consisted of activities—ice-skating, baking, and axe-throwing. Now that they were sitting across from each other and Mitch was gone, there were no more distractions. She was supposed to talk to Ellie.

"So," she finally said, "how's your breast?"

Ellie paused with a square of meat lifted halfway to her lips. "Chicken breast. Which you definitely won't get to sample since you're not sharing your food." She glanced at Regina's KC strip steak with big doe eyes. A playful pout formed on her full lips. "Your really delicious-looking food."

"Fine. Here. Have some before you trip over that stuck-out lip of yours." Regina cut off a bite-sized piece of her steak and deposited it on Ellie's eagerly held-out plate, along with a forkful of mac and cheese.

With a happy grin, Ellie nudged a square of chicken breast and a forkful of mashed potatoes onto Regina's plate in exchange. As she dug into her food, she let out little hums of enjoyment.

Regina took a big gulp of her ice-cold water and tried to focus on her own plate instead of the sounds coming from across the table.

Finally, Ellie paused in her enthusiastic appreciation of their food. "Since we've now officially buried the hatchet…" She made a motion with her left hand that mimicked throwing an axe.

Regina's knife screeched across her plate. "Wait. You thought I took you to Bury the Hatchet as a symbolic act to end all the conflicts we've had at work?"

"You didn't?"

"No! I didn't pay attention to the name of the axe-throwing place when I booked the lane."

"Oh." Ellie looked down and drew a pattern into her mashed potatoes with her fork. Then she glanced back up. "Can I ask you a question anyway?"

Every muscle in Regina's body tensed. It was such a stark contrast to how she'd felt before that she realized how much she'd started to relax in Ellie's presence. She heaved a sigh. "If you must."

Ellie laid her fork down. She moved it to the right, then back to the left. "Why were you so hostile to me from the moment you first started working at CMC?"

Regina had been sure Ellie would ask about her brother. It took her several seconds to process the unexpected question. "Hostile?" The word burst out of her. "Oh, come on. Just because I'm not the warm and fuzzy type doesn't mean I was hostile."

"You didn't even introduce yourself." Ellie's voice was soft, not confrontational, but she wasn't backing down either.

"Oh for the love of…" Regina clenched her fingers around her fork. "I was a little too busy saving lives to care about social niceties."

Ellie held her gaze. "It wasn't even a particularly busy shift."

"Maybe not for you," Regina ground out through gritted teeth.

A flush swept up Ellie's neck. "Are you implying you think we nurses sit at the nurses' station all shift, sipping coffee, while you doctors do all the work?"

Regina threw her fork onto her plate with a loud clank. "No! That's not what I'm saying!"

"What are you saying, then?" Ellie's voice was infuriatingly quiet.

Shit. Ellie had her cornered. She could either let her assume she didn't think much of the nurses' work ethic, or she had to bite the bullet and tell her the truth.

Are you out of your mind?

She had never allowed herself to show any weakness at work, and she wouldn't start now.

Yeah, but you're not at work. And as much as she wanted to keep seeing Ellie as just someone she worked with, deep down she knew Ellie was so much more.

Less than a month ago, she wouldn't have even considered telling Ellie the truth. She would have let her think whatever she wanted.

But now...

She met Ellie's eyes in the candlelight.

Dammit.

"It was my first shift as an attending, okay? And all the first-year residents and med students were new too. I had my hands full keeping the greener-than-green residents from killing anyone, so I, um, might have lost track of whom I'd already introduced myself to and who I hadn't met yet."

Ellie stared at her. Then a slow smile spread over her face. "Oh my God! Regina Novak had new attending jitters!"

"Nonsense! I did not!"

"Hey, it's nothing to be ashamed of. Going from being a resident to being the one in charge is a huge jump."

"I didn't have jitters," Regina repeated. "I was focused on my patients, not the staff." Truth be told, before discharging the first patient on her own, she had read his chart three times to make sure she hadn't missed anything—even though he'd merely had a rash. It had taken her a month to stop overtesting and trust her training.

"Mm-hmm," Ellie said, still grinning.

"Stop it."

"Stop what?" Ellie asked with an innocent expression.

Regina pointed at her full lips. "That grin."

The corners of Ellie's mouth curled up even more.

That smile was annoying! The urge to lean across the table and kiss it off her lips gripped Regina.

Oh hell, no! Remember your number one rule? No co-workers. And especially not this co-worker. Ellie was a starry-eyed romantic—someone who hung strings of paper hearts for Valentine's Day and wanted deep, forever kind of love. A kiss wouldn't be only a kiss to her. And, unlike Regina, she was a people person. She was friends or at least friendly with every nurse, every EMT, and every resident in the entire damn hospital. Getting involved with her would create one big mess at work.

No, thanks.

Finally, Ellie sobered. "What about afterward?"

"Afterward?" Was Ellie asking what would happen after this date? They would go back to being just co-workers. That's what they had said from the start and what they both wanted…right?

"Yeah," Ellie said. "After you were no longer struggling to make it through your shift."

Oh. That's what she meant. "I never said I was struggling."

"Right." Ellie's lips twitched. "But even after you settled in, you made no bones of the fact that you didn't like me."

"I like you just fine," Regina muttered.

Ellie paused. She wasn't grinning now. Her gaze searched Regina's face.

"I mean, I don't *not* like you, even though you can be infuriating."

Ellie tapped her chest with both hands. "Me?"

"Yes, you. You questioned my competency and undermined my authority from the start."

"What? I never—"

"Yes, you did. You went right over my head and complained to the chief of the emergency department when you didn't like the order in which I treated the patients."

Ellie's palms slid off her chest. She pressed them to the table. "Okay, I did that, and maybe it wasn't the best solution, but I've worked with the chief since he was an attending and I knew he would take me seriously—while you didn't. You blew me off when I told you the patient with the abscess should be next. You skipped right over him because he was unhoused and a drug user."

"What?" Regina barked out the word. "You think I delayed his treatment because he was a drug user?"

Ellie faced her across the table. "What else was I supposed to think? None of the patients you treated ahead of him was sick enough to warrant seeing them first. You failed to help him in a timely manner and…"

Blood roared through Regina's ears so loudly that she didn't hear the rest of Ellie's sentence. Unfortunately, even the roaring couldn't drown out the echo of Ellie's words: *You failed to help him.* Bile rose up her throat, and a whirling sensation gripped her as if she were being sucked into a tornado. "Excuse me for a minute." She had no idea whether she was shouting or barely rasping out the words.

Her chair screeched across the hardwood floor, shattering the sudden tense silence between them, as she shoved it back and jumped up.

Ellie's eyes were wide and dark against her pale face. "Regina…"

Regina forcefully held up her hand. She couldn't face whatever was in Ellie's eyes—accusation, shock, pity, too many questions. "I said give me a minute." She whirled around and marched toward the restrooms.

Ellie stared after Regina's quickly retreating back. Her heart thudded wildly against her rib cage. What had just happened?

She had expected Regina to matter-of-factly explain her reasoning for treating other patients first. At the most, she had thought Regina might pierce her with a death glare and tell her she didn't have to justify her decisions to her. Never in a million years had she expected Regina to storm off, looking as if Ellie had stabbed her in the chest with a fork.

Should she go after her or give Regina a minute, as she had requested, and wait for her to return to the table? Was she even coming back?

"Is everything okay?"

A voice from next to the table made Ellie jerk her gaze away from the restroom door, which had fallen shut behind Regina.

A striking woman in a crisp, white chef's uniform stood in front of her, raven-black hair pulled back with a white bandanna. "I'm Nadia Jamison, one of the co-owners here at The Meadow," she said with a faint French accent. "If the food isn't to your liking, I can get you something else." She gestured at their still half-full plates going cold on the table.

"Oh, no, no. The food is great. Excellent, really." But Ellie couldn't imagine eating another bite. Her stomach felt as if it had been scrubbed with steel wool. "Please don't think this is a reflection on your restaurant. Everything has been wonderful, and your staff is incredibly attentive. It's just… My friend isn't feeling well. I think it's best if I take her home." That was, if Regina didn't refuse to follow her anywhere.

"I'm sorry to hear that. I hope she feels better soon. Let me box this up for you"—Nadia gestured at their half-full plates—"and get you some dessert to go." She hastened back to the kitchen before Ellie could decline.

Ellie directed her attention back toward the restroom door. It had been way longer than a minute since Regina had disappeared behind it.

With her heart in her throat, Ellie left a generous tip on the table, grabbed her purse, and slowly made her way to the restroom. She pulled open the door—and collided with Regina, who'd been about to step out.

Ellie clutched Regina's hip to keep her balance.

Up close, the scent of Whitewater Rapids made her head spin, so she held on even more tightly. Her body tilted toward Regina, and her fingers curled into one of Regina's belt loops.

"What are you doing?" Regina asked, her voice husky.

Ellie shook herself out of her trancelike state and pulled back. "Um, checking on you."

"No need for that. I assure you I've been going to the restroom on my own since I was three." Regina's impassive poker face was back in place. Her gray eyes—like clouds on a stormy day just minutes ago—were now an impenetrable stone wall keeping her out. She brushed past Ellie and strode back toward their table, where a waitress had deposited a huge bag with the restaurant's logo. Their plates and glasses had disappeared.

Regina stopped abruptly. "What the hell is going on? Are they kicking us out for getting into an argument? We weren't even that loud!"

"No." Ellie latched on to her arm before Regina could confront the poor waitress. "I told them you aren't feeling well, so I'm taking you home."

Regina shook off her hand. "What? I'm fine, and you're not taking me anywhere."

Ellie hoped Regina was just saying that because they had taken Regina's car, not because she refused to spend another minute with her. "Okay, then *you* can take *me* home."

Regina glared for a few more seconds, then snatched her purse from the back of her chair and marched toward the exit.

Ellie grabbed the bag with the food and hurried after her.

Outside, the sun had set, but there was still some light in the sky.

Regina didn't say a word as they made their way to the car, nor as she unlocked it and jerked her head toward the passenger-side door for Ellie to get in.

Ellie reached out, then stopped.

If she got in, that would be it. Regina would maneuver the car to Brookside with a stony expression and drop her off with a terse "good night."

She didn't want the evening—their last date—to end like this. "Can we walk?"

Regina stared at her in the twilight. "To Brookside?"

"No. Just to the riverfront."

"It's nearly dark, and it'll be cold by the river."

Ellie gave her a pleading look. "We don't have to stay long. It's not far, and it's a good place to talk."

"We've done enough talking for today," Regina muttered.

"Please," Ellie said quietly.

A string of curses pierced the air, then a beep as the car doors locked.

The weight on Ellie's chest lifted a little. But then again, just because Regina wouldn't abandon her in the near darkness didn't mean she was willing to talk.

Ellie led the way down Main Street.

It wasn't long before the Town of Kansas Bridge appeared before them in the dusky light.

Their steps—oddly in sync despite the tension between them—echoed loudly on the weathered gray wood planks of the elevated walkway. Somehow, it only emphasized the silence between them.

In the middle of the bridge, Ellie couldn't stand it anymore. "What happened?"

"I don't have to justify my decisions to you, but if you really want to know…"

That wasn't what Ellie had meant. Mostly, she wanted to know why Regina had fled to the restroom, not what had happened in the hospital last summer. But this might be a start, so she nodded. "I do."

"It was a busy shift. The waiting room was bursting at the seams. We were one walk-in away from examining patients on gurneys in the hallway. I was trying to clear some beds by seeing the patients with FOOSH injuries, strep throat, and other quick discharges first."

Ellie had to admit it was a solid strategy, even though she didn't like making patients wait longer because they didn't have a straightforward diagnosis. "Okay, but don't you think you could have communicated your reasoning a little more clearly to the rest of the team—or at all?"

"Like I just said, I don't have to justify my decisions to you," Regina replied.

Her icy tone cut deep. "No," Ellie answered, "you don't have to. But if you did, I never would have jumped to the conclusion that you delayed treating a patient because you look down on unhoused drug users or that you put off draining his abscess because you don't like the foul smell."

A wooden observation deck opened up in front of them, but Regina didn't spare a glance at the dark, broad band of the Missouri River below or the lights reflected off the water. She whirled around and glared at Ellie. "You think I care about the smell? I would have gladly drained a thousand abscesses if—"

She cut herself off mid-sentence.

The light of the lamps to their left and right gave Ellie a good look at her expression. Ellie's thoughts raced as she tried to make sense of what she was seeing.

Regina's face was stony, her jaw muscles tight. She was no longer glancing at Ellie; her gaze veered into the darkness beneath the bridge, where a freight train slowly passed.

A few weeks ago, Ellie would have assumed Regina was furious—and clearly, she was, but there was also something else underneath all the anger. Regina looked as if she were clenching her core muscles because Ellie had hit her in the gut and she expected another punch. However, she didn't raise her hands to ward off the imaginary attack.

Ellie's stomach churned. "Regina?"

Regina turned away as if to study the last traces of orange that lit the clouds and the arches of the Buck O'Neil Bridge from below, yet Ellie had a feeling she wasn't seeing any of it.

Slowly, Ellie took a step forward until she was right next to Regina at the shoulder-high railing, then inched closer.

It reminded Ellie of that evening after their baking class, when they had stood side by side in front of Regina's award shelf and looked at her graduation photo. At her brother's picture.

"This is about Riley." She didn't phrase it as a question, because certainty swept over her, leaving no room for doubt. Usually, nothing could penetrate Regina's armor. The only times Ellie had seen her shaken were when it involved her brother.

Regina flinched as if Ellie had defibrillated her. "We're talking about the patient back in August."

"Are we?" Ellie asked quietly.

"Let it go." Regina's voice was low and rough, her tone somewhere between a warning and a plea.

Ellie knew she could press on—ask her to confirm some of the many assumptions running through her mind. Once, Regina had said her brother hadn't died of an overdose. Had it been an untreated abscess? She wanted to know, but not at the price of hurting Regina further. "Okay."

Regina glanced at her out of the corner of her eye as if she couldn't believe Ellie was backing off just because she'd told her to. "Okay?"

"Yeah. Of course it's okay. I wasn't asking to satisfy my curiosity. I want to understand what's going on with you. But if you're not yet ready to tell me…"

Not yet. The words hung between them. They sounded as if Regina might tell her at some later time, but that wasn't likely to happen. After tonight, they would only see each other in the ED, where Regina would wear her professional armor and would never talk about her personal pain.

Regina said nothing. She braced her upper arms on the railing as if the tension had drained from her muscles and she needed the support.

Ellie leaned against the metal next to her.

They looked toward the illuminated arches of the bridge to their left and watched as the last glimmer of orange disappeared from the horizon and the first stars twinkled.

"So," Regina said after a while, "what's in the bag?"

Ellie stared down at the bag that dangled forgotten from her left hand. "Oh. They boxed up our food. And added dessert."

"Are there spoons?"

Regina wanted to have dessert now? Here? Ellie searched her face.

Their gazes met.

Ah. Regina didn't want to talk about her brother, but she didn't want to go their separate ways and end the evening on this half-sad, half-angry note either.

"I don't know." Ellie dug through the bag so hastily that she nearly dropped it. With a triumphant grin, she held up two plastic forks.

Regina waved for her to hand over the bag. "Let's see what we've got." Her tone was back to confident and commanding, without a trace of vulnerability.

But now Ellie had an idea of what lurked beneath. Without looking away from Regina, she reached into the bag and pulled out the container on top.

Their fingers grazed as Regina took it from her hand. Both paused with their fingers lingering.

Heat spread up Ellie's arm, warding off the chill of the night.

Then Regina pulled the container toward her and interrupted the contact. She popped open the lid.

Ellie glanced down—and started coughing.

Of all the desserts in the world, Nadia had to pack them a huge piece of lava cake. The tip of the slice had broken off, and liquid chocolate oozed out.

"Isn't this the one you said you don't like?" Regina asked.

"I never said I don't like it." After the Twinkie incident, she merely hadn't been ready to see what Regina might do to the moist core of a lava cake. "I like it just fine."

Regina peeked into the bag. "What else is in there?"

Ellie pulled out another container and opened it.

Regina immediately sliced off a bit with her plastic fork as if claiming the cake. She slid it into her mouth and let out a low moan as she pulled out the fork.

And Ellie had been worried about lava cake. Whatever cake that was seemed to be just as dangerous. She fought the urge to fan herself and instead sliced off a bite for herself. The aroma of cinnamon, vanilla, and lemon mingled on her tongue. Her eyes fluttered closed. "Mmmmm. It's like a cheesecake and an apple pie had a love child."

Regina cleared her throat. "Let's make it an orgy." She dragged a forkful of the cheesecake/apple pie through a puddle of chocolate in the other container.

"Ooh." Ellie dug in and tried the same combination. "Oh my God. We invented culinary perfection. We're geniuses."

With each of them holding on to one container, they traded bites of cake until only traces of the chocolate sauce remained.

"Will you marry me?"

Ellie nearly choked on her last mouthful of cake as she sucked in a sharp breath. "W-what?" she wheezed.

Regina let out a laugh. Then she stopped and touched her own throat as if surprised that she could laugh after memories of her brother had nearly ruined their evening. She pointed at one of the hundreds of love locks attached to the railing's crisscrossing metal bars.

Ellie squinted to read the inscription in the light of the lamp above them. *Will you marry me?*

"You didn't think I was proposing, did you?" Regina asked with obvious amusement.

"Well," Ellie said, "I did share my cake, so…"

"*Your* cake?"

Ellie nodded. "I forked over nine hundred dollars for our date package, which means I paid for dinner and dessert."

"Hmm." Regina cocked her head, then dipped her index finger into the chocolate sauce and slid it into her mouth to lick it off.

Jesus. Nine hundred dollars. Worth every cent.

"Why do people hang these things?" Regina pointed her newly licked finger at the love locks. "*Locked in love*," she read from one of them. She snorted. "Half of them have probably broken up by now."

Ellie ignored the sarcastic comment. "Because it's romantic."

"About as romantic as an epidemic," Regina muttered. "They had to remove all the locks people added to the Pont des Arts in Paris because the extra weight threatened the structural integrity of the bridge."

"Seriously?"

"Mm-hmm." Regina dragged her finger through the chocolate sauce again.

Ellie took the container from her and stuffed it into the bag before Regina could continue the erotic spectacle. "I still think it's romantic."

"Of course you do." Regina tossed the other container and her fork into the bag too. "We should go."

Ellie nodded. It was getting cold on the observation deck. Or, more likely, it had been cold all along, and she hadn't noticed earlier because she'd been so focused on what was going on with Regina. Despite her long-sleeved top, goose bumps prickled all along her arms, but she still found herself reluctant to return to the car.

Side by side, they strolled across the bridge. Neither said anything until they reached the end of the walkway, but this time, the silence wasn't heavy.

"You're pretty clever," Regina said.

Ellie looked over, but Regina had waited until they had passed the last lamp on the bridge, so she couldn't make out her face in the near darkness. "Pardon me?"

"You probably have a good idea of what happened to Riley."

Ellie swallowed. "Yes," she whispered. "I think so."

"It was an abscess from injecting heroin."

That was one of the scenarios Ellie had thought might have happened, but she hadn't expected Regina to say it.

"A stupid abscess," Regina repeated. "A simple incision, a clean bandage, and some antibiotics and he would have been fine. But he didn't go to the hospital. Not until it was too late. His arm had turned purple. The infection spread through his body, and he went into septic shock. His blood pressure crashed. His kidneys shut down. His heart failed."

She listed it off as if reading symptoms from a medical textbook, but Ellie knew she was hiding her grief behind her professional mask.

Oh God. And she had dug her fingers into that open wound by practically accusing Regina of delaying treatment for a patient with an abscess—a patient just like her brother. Tears burned in Ellie's eyes. "I'm so, so sorry."

Sorry he had died and sorry she had made it worse. But she didn't know how to say that, not without making Regina's pain about her.

Instead, she reached over and found Regina's hand in the darkness.

Regina flinched.

Crap. That had been the wrong thing to do. She'd made it worse—again.

But just as Ellie was about to let go, Regina closed her fingers around her own and squeezed softly. Her hand was warm despite the chilly air. Its heat traveled up Ellie's arm and chased away the goose bumps—only to be replaced with a rush of new ones when Regina trailed her thumb along Ellie's index finger.

"Thank you," Regina said so quietly that Ellie could barely hear her over the sound of a train in the distance. Then she let go, shoved her hands into her pants pockets, and strode toward her car. "Come on. Let's get you home."

Fingers still tingling, Ellie rushed after her.

Chapter 18

Usually, Regina found dating as boring as watching the weather forecast and couldn't wait for the date to end.

But as she walked Ellie to her front door, that feeling was strangely absent, maybe because too many other emotions were tumbling through her.

She couldn't believe she had told Ellie about Riley. Her skin prickled as if she'd rubbed it raw—had said too much and made herself too vulnerable. Or maybe it was remnants of the tingly sensation that had spread through her when Ellie had taken her hand. It had been an innocent gesture, yet somehow, it felt more intimate than a kiss. She still couldn't believe she had returned the gesture and held hands with Ellie, a co-worker, for a moment.

Ellie shuffled her feet on her front porch. "Do you want to come in?"

Regina wrenched her gaze to Ellie's eyes, which made her realize she'd been looking at her mouth.

"For a drink," Ellie added.

Regina allowed a grin that felt mostly authentic to spread across her face. "So you admit you lost the ice-skating race and owe me a drink?"

"Ha! No. But you did win all but one of the axe-throwing games, so…" Ellie swept her arm toward the front door.

Regina hesitated. The annoying photographer was gone, and all of her auction obligations were fulfilled. There was no reason to prolong this—other than she really wanted to.

Her stomach lurched at the realization.

No. Tell her good night and thanks for bidding on a good cause. If she left now, she'd be fine by tomorrow. In the fluorescent lights of the ED, she would be able to put this entire whirlwind of an evening into the right perspective. Ellie would be just one of the nurses again.

Yeah, right.

"Um, thanks, but I'd better go." Regina vaguely gestured toward her car. "I'm working tomorrow." It was a feeble excuse, considering it was only eight thirty and Ellie would be working the same shift.

Even in the dim light of the porch, Regina could see Ellie's face fall.

"Me too, so you're right. We'd better call it a night." Ellie set the bag from the restaurant down and reached into her purse, probably looking for her keys. "Ouch."

Damn. Now she'd hurt Ellie. What a mess. "I didn't say no to hurt you. I just... Me coming in... Not a good idea."

"Oh, no, no. Not you." Ellie pulled her hand with the keys out of her purse and tapped her index finger. "I thought the splinter from earlier was gone, but I just felt it."

"Let me see."

"In this light?" Ellie shook her head. "You wouldn't be able to find an entire branch sticking out of my hand, much less a tiny little splinter. I'll pull it out once I'm inside."

Regina arched her brows. "With your left hand?"

"I'm sure I'll manage."

"*Managing* isn't good enough," Regina told her. "Not when you have CMC's most talented emergency physician at your service."

"At my service, huh?" The grin was obvious in Ellie's tone. "Does that mean you're coming in after all?"

Instead of a verbal reply, Regina took the key from her and unlocked the door.

"You do know I live with an EMT, don't you?" Ellie asked, even as she led her into the house. "I'm not sure my sister is home, but even if she isn't, she can take care of it later."

There was no light on in the living room, so Regina hoped Ellie's sister had gone out. She would remove the splinter and be out of here within five minutes, tops. "EM doctor trumps EMT. Where's your first aid kit?"

"In the upstairs bathroom." Ellie turned the lights on, set the bag from the restaurant on a small table next to the door, and climbed the stairs.

Regina followed.

The stairs creaked, interrupting the silence between them.

Ellie opened the first door they came to and turned on the light.

The bathroom was small but as cozy as the rest of the house, with bath mats and towels in bright colors and a shelf filled with bath salts and candles. Apparently, either Ellie or her sister liked to soak in the tub after a long shift. A white vanity and a sink were set flush against the tub.

Ellie pulled open the mirrored door of a white medicine cabinet above the sink, revealing neat rows of over-the-counter medications, Band-Aids, cough syrup, antibiotic ointment, and a bottle of rubbing alcohol.

Regina gave an approving nod. She thoroughly washed her hands with a bar of soap that smelled of roses, then watched as Ellie did the same. "Tweezers?" She held out her hand.

Ellie disinfected the small instrument with rubbing alcohol, waited a while, then placed it on Regina's palm.

Their familiar roles—a doctor and the nurse assisting with a procedure—soothed Regina's frazzled nerves.

But as she reached for Ellie's hand, the feeling of Ellie's skin against her own wasn't medical at all. She was much too aware it was Ellie's hand she was cradling, not the appendage of a random patient.

Focus!

She couldn't make out the splinter because Ellie wasn't fully under the light coming from the ceiling. Gently, she placed one hand on Ellie's shoulder and turned her until her back was against the sink and her hand directly beneath the lamp.

She lifted Ellie's hand and brought it closer to her eyes and the light—so close that her breath probably tickled Ellie's palm.

Reflexively, Ellie's fingers curled and brushed Regina's thumb, reminding her of the moment on the bridge earlier.

Regina swallowed, suddenly aware of how small the bathroom was, how tight the space between the wall and the vanity—and how close Ellie was.

Get it over with before you do something you will regret.

Finally, she detected a tiny splinter embedded in the tip of Ellie's index finger. It was beneath the skin, with no part of it sticking out, so she couldn't grab it with the pair of tweezers.

"Do you have a needle or a—?"

Ellie pulled a little basket off the shelf and presented a hypodermic needle.

Regina wasn't surprised. Most health-care professionals had all kinds of medical supplies at home. Hypodermic needles came in handy for things like splinter removal, especially since they were sterile and sharper than a sewing needle. She ripped open the packaging and gently pierced the top layer of skin with the needle until the end of the splinter was exposed.

In the ED, Regina's hands were always rock-steady, even when she was woken up in the middle of the night for an emergency. But now her entire body felt jittery, as if she had existed on nothing but coffee all week. It took her three tries until she managed to grab the splinter with the pair of tweezers.

Carefully, she pulled it out at the same angle it had gone in. Once it was out, she trailed her finger along Ellie's to feel for any other splinters that might be buried beneath the skin.

Ellie let out a breathy little sound.

Regina looked up to make sure she hadn't hurt her.

Their faces were inches apart. While Ellie's cheeks were flushed and her pupils wide, Regina didn't think it was from pain. Ellie wasn't even glancing down at her hand; she was staring into Regina's eyes with startling intensity.

As they lingered close to each other, time seemed to slow to a near standstill, then sped up when Ellie's gaze darted to Regina's mouth.

A groan escaped Regina.

The tweezers clattered onto the tiles as she gripped Ellie's hips with both hands.

Their bodies crashed against each other; their lips collided.

There was nothing tentative about the kiss. It wasn't a gentle first exploration; it was hungry and raw—as if a dam had burst, flooding them with a pent-up passion that swept away all reason.

Regina urged Ellie's mouth open. She tasted of chocolate, vanilla, and cinnamon. Perfection. The softness of her lips, the heat of her tongue, the scent of her skin… Ellie filled all of her senses.

Ellie instantly responded and deepened the kiss. When she moaned into Regina's mouth, it was the sexiest sound Regina had ever heard. Ellie ran her hands over Regina's back, into her hair, then back down. She clutched at her blouse, tugging desperately until she could finally slide her fingers over Regina's bare skin.

Her nails set off sparks along Regina's back, a counterpoint to the pressure building low in her belly.

God, she wanted to feel Ellie's skin too. Urgency gripped her. She pulled one suspender down, nearly tearing the button in her haste.

Neither of them cared.

But the damn suspender skirt didn't budge.

With a groan of frustration, Regina trailed one hand down Ellie's skirt-covered thigh, searching for the hem.

Ellie gasped and arched against her. Their bodies were molded together from their knees to their breasts. The heat of Ellie's body filtered through the thin layers of their clothing.

Regina bunched the skirt up in her hands, pushed it up around Ellie's hips, and—

"Ellie?"

The voice from downstairs brought Regina crashing back to reality.

Shit. Ellie's sister.

They froze; both of them breathing heavily; Ellie pinned against the sink with her skirt around her hips and her hands beneath Regina's blouse; Regina with one hand halfway up Ellie's thigh. Her very bare thigh.

Jesus. What were they doing? She'd been five seconds away from lifting Ellie onto the vanity and—

Regina roughly shook her head to drive the vivid image from her mind.

"Ellie?" Vickie called again. This time she sounded closer, as if she was climbing the stairs. "Are you home?"

They jumped apart.

Regina bumped her elbow against the wall and bit back a curse. Hastily, she shoved the ends of her blouse into her jeans and tried not to watch as Ellie fumbled to pull the dangling suspender up and push her skirt back down.

"Um, yeah." Ellie's voice was raspy and shook. "I'll be down in a minute." She searched Regina's face.

That sunburned feeling, as if Ellie could see beneath her skin, returned. "I…I'd better go. See you at work."

She stormed out and took the stairs two at a time, past Ellie's gaping sister, who had been on her way up. "Make sure she puts some antibiotic ointment on her finger," she told Vickie in her best doctor voice but didn't pause.

"What's wrong with her finger?" Vickie called after her.

"Nothing," Regina answered, more to herself. She could still feel the touch of Ellie's fingers on her back. "Absolutely nothing." Too bad the same couldn't be said about Regina's head.

Ellie's head spun. She grabbed the edge of the sink with one hand and gave the still-open medicine cabinet door a tap with the other.

The mirrored door swung closed, revealing her reflection.

She stared at her flushed cheeks and reddened lips. *Wow.* She looked as dazed and out of control as she felt. Regina's taste lingered, and she could still feel her mouth on her own in an intoxicating amalgam of silky softness and hard, demanding pressure.

"Ellie?" Vickie asked from the doorway. "What happened?"

Ellie wished she knew. Right now, she wasn't sure of anything, not even if she'd ever been kissed like that before.

Okay, who was she kidding? She knew she hadn't. She'd certainly never kissed anyone like that.

"Ellie?" Vickie's increasingly alarmed voice came from right behind her now. "Are you hurt?"

Yes. No. For a second, she didn't know the answer. Regina rushing out as if a pack of growling wolves were after her had hurt. "I'm fine," she finally forced out.

"What happened?" Vickie asked again.

"Nothing." Ellie sounded about as convincing as the actors in a soap opera. She kept her back to Vickie and lowered her head so her sister couldn't see her reflection in the mirror since she knew her poker face was nonexistent. "We went axe-throwing, and I got a splinter. Regina was just removing it."

"Oh, is that what they're calling it now? She looked like the only thing she wanted to remove was your clothes."

Ellie's cheeks flamed hot. She could still feel Regina shoving up her skirt, her fingers sliding up her leg. If Vickie hadn't interrupted them…

"Ellie?" Vickie sounded as if she'd called her name more than once already. She gripped Ellie's elbow and urged her around. "Are you sure you're okay? That bitch didn't hurt you, did she?"

"No! She didn't. And she's not a bitch."

"Could have fooled me," Vickie muttered. "The way she talked earlier, when she picked you up… I did not appreciate that, and I don't appreciate her playing with you."

Ellie pulled her elbow free of Vickie's grip. "Oh, please, cut the protective big sister routine. I'm an adult and can take care of myself."

"Did you tell her you're not into one-night stands or bathroom hookups?" Vickie asked.

Heat returned to Ellie's cheeks. "We weren't… She didn't…" She slumped against the sink.

Yeah. That was exactly what it would have been if they had gone any further. Merely a quick, meaningless hookup. Because, as Vickie had just reminded her, Regina had made it clear she didn't want to date her. And as much as her body had insisted otherwise, Ellie really wasn't into one-night stands. This frenzied make-out session in a bathroom, with someone she wasn't dating, was completely out of character for her.

Vickie gave her a quick hug, then reached past her and opened the medicine cabinet. "Come on. Let's put some antibiotic ointment on your finger before Dr. McIcy starts spreading rumors at work about how incompetent the local EMTs are."

Work. Oh God. She would have to work with Regina tomorrow, and she had no idea how to face her.

Chapter 19

FOR THE FIRST TIME SINCE she'd started working as a nurse, Ellie volunteered to restock the resuscitation rooms—and instantly regretted it.

Her arms and shoulders ached from her axe-throwing adventure the day before, so reaching up to the top shelf to stow away supplies was not fun.

But at least it gave her a few minutes alone, with no chance of running into Regina.

Each time she saw her—which had been twice since their shift had started—her cheeks heated with a mix of arousal and embarrassment.

Regina, however, appeared completely professional, as if she didn't even remember what had happened the night before.

Ellie heaved a box of IV fluids from a cart and dropped it onto the shelf with more force than necessary. Her muscles protested, and she let out a groan.

Jasmine looked over from where she was wiping down one of the trauma beds. "What's up with you?"

"I'm fine, just very sore," Ellie said. "I must have worked some muscles I didn't even know I had last night."

"Oh?"

Jasmine was the only person Ellie knew who could make a single syllable sound like sexual innuendo.

Ellie reined in the urge to throw a box of gloves at her. "Nothing like you're thinking." Okay, it had been a little like Jasmine was thinking. But she didn't have to tell her that. "Regina took me axe-throwing as the surprise activity part of our last date."

"Ah. Is that why she's extra prickly today? Because she's hurting all over?"

"Is she? Extra prickly, I mean." To her, Regina had seemed like always, as if she shared passionate kisses with women every day, then went back to business as usual.

Jasmine laughed. "Are you kidding? Cardiology was giving one of the residents a hard time, refusing to come down for a consult, and she took the phone from him and ripped them a new one. Someone from cardio showed up to see our patient three minutes later."

For a moment, Ellie wished she'd witnessed it—Regina passionately advocating for a patient, eyes flashing. Then she shook off the thought. She would not make googly eyes at Regina while at work. Scratch that. She wouldn't make googly eyes at Regina at all.

When Chelsea had dumped her, she had promised herself to never again get involved with someone who wasn't proud to be seen at her side.

She would forget she had ever bid on a date package with Dr. Regina Novak. And maybe use the downstairs bathroom at home for a while to avoid any flashbacks.

Resolutely, she shoved several laceration trays into the cupboard, then pushed the door shut with her shoulder.

Regina had never been the EMTs' favorite doctor. Hell, she'd never been *anyone's* favorite doctor. Frankly, she didn't care.

But the glare Ellie's sister had just given her before pushing her empty gurney back to the ambulance…

What had Ellie told her about what had happened between them?

"What was that?" Kayla pointed at the ambulance as it pulled out of the bay.

Regina schooled her features into an impassive facade. "What was what?"

"Vickie gave you a look as if you kicked her dog…or her sister." Kayla widened her eyes. "Oh shit. Your last date with Ellie didn't go well, did it?"

Great. Now her colleagues would be wagging their tongues behind her back, making wild speculations about how their date had ended.

She had known that would happen. Getting involved with someone she worked with would only lead to complication upon complication. The night before, she had lost track of that for a minute. All she'd been able to think about had been touching Ellie.

But she wouldn't lose sight of the consequences again. "It went just fine." It had gone a little too well, actually.

"So what now?" Kayla prompted.

"Now we'll do sign-out rounds; you'll take over, and I'll go home," Regina answered.

"That's not what I meant."

Regina walked toward one of the treatment rooms, leaving Kayla to scramble after her. "Ms. Lukowski in room two has acute appendicitis. Surgery insisted on confirming it with a CT because—and I quote—'women tend to exaggerate their pain.'"

"You're really not going to tell me anything?"

"Oh, I'll tell you everything you need to know. That Ms. Lukowski's very real pain is under control, for example. She has received antibiotics and is waiting to go to the OR."

Kayla sighed but finally gave up as Regina continued to discuss each of her patients.

Regina was extra thorough, informing Kayla of every little detail regarding their patients she could think of. Then she even hung around for another half hour and caught up on paperwork.

She had timed it all perfectly, just so she and Ellie wouldn't leave the hospital at the same time.

But her clever plan hadn't taken into consideration that Ellie might stay longer too, either because she needed to catch up on charting or because she was trying to avoid having to talk to her on the way out as well.

As Regina headed toward the staff exit, she nearly collided with Ellie.

"Whoa!" Ellie grabbed hold of Regina's forearm to keep her balance.

The touch set off sparks along Regina's skin even through the fabric of the long-sleeved top she wore beneath her scrubs.

Ellie snatched her hands away.

"You okay?" Regina asked. Only once she'd said it did she realize her question could be interpreted to mean more than Ellie nearly losing her balance.

Shit. She really didn't want to discuss this at work. Or at all.

Ellie nodded but said nothing. She looked pale and tired, as if she hadn't slept.

Was she okay? Regina bit her lip so she wouldn't ask a second time. *Don't flatter yourself. She's fine. It's not like she's heartbroken just because you walked out on her.*

Or was she? Ellie was a romantic, not a woman looking for an almost quickie pressed against a bathroom sink.

They left the building and walked to the staff parking lot without saying a word.

The path leading away from the staff exit was lined with light fixtures, which bathed Ellie's face in a warm glow.

It reminded Regina so much of the previous night's walk across the bridge that she nearly expected Ellie to reach over and take her hand again.

Ridiculous. She clenched her fingers around her car keys. This nonsense had to stop. Right now.

As they approached their cars, which were parked just a few spots away from each other, Ellie fiddled with her own keys as if readying them so she could jump in and speed off as soon as they reached her car.

"Listen," Regina said. "About, um, yesterday…"

Something that looked like defiance sparked in Ellie's eyes. "The kiss."

Did she have to say it out loud? Here of all places? "Yes," Regina said through gritted teeth. She glanced left and right to make sure no colleague could overhear them. "The kiss. It was—"

"A mistake," Ellie said before Regina could decide how she wanted to finish her sentence. "Totally." Her head bobbed in several rapid nods. "Just a heat-of-the-moment thing we got swept up in."

Regina opened her mouth, still not sure what she was about to say.

But it didn't matter because Ellie was on a roll, doing all the talking. "Seriously. I get it." Her tongue darted out and traced her full lower lip, distracting Regina from finally getting a word in. "It was an emotional evening that brought up a lot of stuff for you. Stuff you're not ready to deal with. So you needed to get out of your head."

Regina stared at her. Was that what had happened? Why it had happened? As much as she didn't want to admit it, Ellie was right. Kind of. She had desperately needed to stop thinking, and kissing Ellie had provided one hell of a distraction. She hadn't thought of Riley even once for the rest of the night. Scary that Ellie had grasped what mind space she'd been in. All the more reason to put some distance between them.

But a part of her balked at agreeing with Ellie that it had been merely a distraction, as if Ellie were replaceable, just a hot body to blow off some steam with. *Jesus, Regina! She's giving you an out. Take it!*

Regina cleared her throat. "Right. Plus you did challenge me to provide a spectacular date experience." She forced her lips into a teasing smile. "I'd like to think I delivered."

A blush shot all the way up to Ellie's earlobes, which Regina found entirely too enchanting. "Well..." Ellie smacked her lips as if her mouth had gone dry. "It was a nice kiss."

"Nice?" Regina knew she shouldn't linger on how amazing the kiss had been, but she couldn't help it. "Merely...nice?" She narrowed her eyes at Ellie. No one had ever described her kisses that way. Earth-shattering. Heart-stopping. Scorching hot. But a boring, mediocre *nice*? Never.

"Okay, fine. It was *very* nice. The auction organizers won't get any complaints from me on that section of the feedback form."

Regina arched her brows. "There's a feedback form? Like an exit interview for dates?"

"What's the matter? You don't have performance anxiety, do you?"

"No. More like paperwork anxiety." It was much too easy to slide back into their banter. Finally, Regina sobered. "So, on the 'on a scale from zero to ten, how likely are you to repeat the experience' question, we're both checking zero, right?"

Why was she asking? She should be *telling* Ellie they couldn't repeat any of this.

"Because as hot as the kiss was, it can't happen again," she added before Ellie could answer. "It crossed a line I'm not comfortable crossing. Mixing business and pleasure never ends well."

A muscle twitched in Ellie's face at the word *pleasure.*

What? They had just agreed that the kiss had been intensely pleasurable, hadn't they?

"So?" Regina prompted when Ellie was slow to answer. "Are we on the same page?"

"Of course." Ellie gave a firm nod. "We're adults."

Adults who had nearly done very adult things with each other, Regina's mind helpfully supplied.

"We can keep things professional," Ellie added. "Consider the kiss on the do-not-repeat list." She stuck out her hand, and they shook on their declared kiss boycott.

Sticking to it should be easy. Regina was a professional. A professional whose pulse sped up as Ellie's fingers wrapped around her own, but that was beside the point.

They'd agreed to go back to being just co-workers. That was great. A relief. Exactly what she wanted.

Which was why she did *not* feel a weird sense of loss and light-headedness as Ellie let go of her hand, climbed into her beat-up car, and drove off without looking back.

No. Definitely not. And if she did, it was probably low blood sugar.

Ellie gripped the steering wheel so hard her knuckles ached.

Even though she had turned up the volume of her car stereo, she didn't hear the music. Regina's words were still echoing through her mind.

It can't happen again. Mixing business with pleasure never ends well.

She had expected her to say that, of course. If Regina hadn't said it first, she would have.

They were better off as co-workers. Just co-workers. She could do that. Totally. After all, she had done it for the first seven months she had worked with Regina. She would go back to that. A few dates she hadn't even meant to bid on and a make-out session in a bathroom were hardly life-changing experiences.

All she had to do was scrub that kiss and the way Regina's hands had felt on her skin from her memory.

Easy, right?

Chapter 20

A WEEK LATER, RIGHT AFTER Ellie had prided herself on not having thought about their kiss for several hours, she was part of the team that helped Regina transfer a heavy patient from an ambulance gurney to a treatment bed.

"On three," the resident whom Regina had allowed to take command said.

Several team members crowded around the gurney, and each grabbed a corner of the sheet beneath the patient.

Regina squeezed in next to Ellie instead of claiming her usual position, leaving the space at the head of the gurney to her resident.

"One, two," the resident counted. "Three."

Everyone lifted, and the patient abruptly slid over onto the bed.

The momentum jerked Ellie off-balance, and her shoulder bumped against Regina's. Her heart sped up, and she knew it wasn't just adrenaline. She was glad to get a minute to collect herself as a tech set up the portable X-ray machine, and everyone backed away from the bed.

Ellie flattened herself against the wall at a safe distance from the source of radiation—but not from Regina, who squeezed in between her and the resident.

Ellie's breath hitched, and she struggled not to lean in to the heat emanating from Regina.

So much for it being easy to forget about the kiss and go back to being just co-workers. Even a week after their no-kissing deal, she was flashing back to those moments in the bathroom at the most inopportune times. She knew she shouldn't be so hung up on a simple kiss. Except there had been nothing simple about it.

As soon as the tech had shot the X-rays, Regina pushed away from the wall. She was the first at the X-ray machine and studied the monitor. "Hemothorax." She glanced at the resident. "What do we need to do?"

While he seemed to ponder the right answer, Ellie grabbed everything necessary to put a chest tube into the patient's thorax to drain the blood that had accumulated in his pleural cavity.

"Call surgery?" The resident's answer sounded more like a question than a statement.

Regina shook her head. "Chest tube." She gave an appreciative nod at the instruments Ellie had laid out before turning back to the resident. "Watch and learn." She ripped open a surgical gown package, then scrubbed her hands at a stainless-steel sink. "Can someone tie me up?"

Why did she have to phrase it like that? It didn't help with Ellie's focus. She sent Jasmine a look, hoping she'd assist Regina with putting on the surgical gown.

But Jasmine was busy cleaning the area where the chest tube would be inserted with Hibiclens and placing sterile drapes, so Ellie would have to assist Regina with the gowning.

No problem. She had done this a thousand times for various doctors over the years. She could do this in her sleep.

Regina pushed her arms through the gown's sleeves but kept her thoroughly scrubbed hands inside instead of poking them through the cuffs.

Careful not to touch the sterile outside, Ellie took up position behind her and pulled the gown up over Regina's shoulders. Since she could only touch the inside, her hands were beneath the gown. Her fingers brushed Regina as she closed the Velcro strap at her neck, then tied the band at her lower back. She grasped a piece of fabric at the bottom of the gown and gave a light tug to settle it more comfortably around Regina's shoulders.

Regina stood very still. Her expression was focused as she donned her gloves and tugged one of the two waist ties free of the paper tag attached to their ends. When she handed Ellie the paper tag with the other tie, their gazes met, then veered apart as Regina spun in a counterclockwise circle, wrapping the waist tie around herself.

Once she faced Ellie again, she took back the tie Ellie had held on to and tied the two ends at her waist.

The entire process was like an elegant dance routine, with both of them knowing the steps by heart.

Regina gave her the shortest of nods before turning toward their patient.

Ellie released a shaky breath, then hurried around the bed to help. Her last stray thought before she focused fully on her job was: Thank God Regina could remove the gown without her assistance later. That would have been way too much like undressing her.

Ellie Fisher was everywhere. Every time Regina set foot into a treatment room, headed to the nurses' station, or went to the cafeteria, Ellie was there. Or maybe it just felt like it because Regina was now overly aware of her presence.

The Sunday after their no-kiss agreement, in the middle of a very busy shift, Regina hastened to the women's locker room to get a granola bar from her bag, knowing she wouldn't have time to grab something from the cafeteria.

When she entered the code into the keypad and pushed the door open, she somehow wasn't surprised to find Ellie in the locker room.

What did surprise her was Ellie's state of dress—or rather undress.

She stood next to one of the benches in only her scrub pants and a sports bra. Her glossy brown hair was out of its usual ponytail and fell onto her smooth, winter-pale shoulders. The light-blue scrub pants rode low on her full hips. She looked up and froze with her hands on the pants' drawstring. Her breasts strained against the bra as she sucked in a breath.

The door slid from Regina's grasp and banged shut.

While most staff members rarely used the shower, preferring to get out of the ED as quickly as possible after their shift, Regina had walked in on colleagues changing several times.

It wasn't a big deal. No one who worked in the ED had time to worry about something as inconsequential as modesty. Everyone kept their eyes to themselves and continued the conversation.

Except that Regina's brain failed to stick to that unwritten rule. Her gaze traveled down Ellie's body. *What are you doing?* She turned her head away.

"Uh, hi. I, um, needed a shower." Ellie waved at her body, drawing Regina's attention back.

"Me too." Regina bit back a groan. She had not just said that, had she? She definitely needed a shower—a cold one. "I mean, a granola bar. I need a granola bar." She marched past Ellie toward her locker. *Dammit.* It was a work-appropriate sports bra, not sexy lingerie. Nothing that should make her pulse race.

"By the way, I can diagnostically confirm that the kid in exam three has a stomach bug," Ellie said.

"Let me guess," Regina replied, proud at how calm her voice sounded. "He threw up all over you?"

"Yep. Thankfully, vomit isn't my one thing."

Regina took her time opening the padlock and searching her bag for a granola bar, hoping Ellie would be fully dressed by the time she turned around. It surprised her how unaffected Ellie seemed by this situation. "One thing?"

"The one bodily fluid that grosses me out. Most nurses have one. You?"

The only bodily fluids Regina could think of while standing next to a half-naked Ellie didn't gross her out at all. "I don't think I have one." She risked a peek over her shoulder.

Ellie had put on a long-sleeved T-shirt and a new scrub top—in a way that made Regina do a double take.

A grin tugged up the corners of Regina's mouth. So much for Ellie being unaffected. She took a bite of her granola bar and walked past Ellie. At the door, she paused, glanced back, and pointed at Ellie's top. "You might want to take that back off."

Ellie blinked. "You…you want me to take my shirt off?" Her cheeks reddened, making Regina's grin grow.

"Yes. Because you put it on backward." She waited a beat. "And inside out."

Ellie's blush deepened as she stared down at the tag of her T-shirt, which rested right below the hollow of her throat.

Chuckling, Regina popped the rest of her granola bar into her mouth and strode out.

Chapter 21

"COME ON, ELLIE," JASMINE SAID as they sat at the nurses' station, charting, two days later. "It's one date."

Ellie didn't look up from her patient's chart. "Sorry. Can't make it this weekend. I've got plans."

"Really?"

Ellie tossed a pen at her. "Don't sound so surprised."

"Who are you going out with?"

"I said I have plans, not that I'm going out with anyone." Ellie's gaze veered to the calendar on the desk. The twenty business days of pining over her bachelorette before accepting date requests from other parties weren't up yet. But, of course, that wasn't the reason she didn't want Jasmine to set her up on a blind date. She just wasn't in the mood to go out with anyone. "I've been meaning to declutter my bookshelf for ages."

Jasmine took both hands off her keyboard and stared at her. "You can't go out with my new friend from yoga because you're decluttering your bookshelf?"

Okay, that didn't sound like a good enough reason. "I might also go see the St. Patrick's Day parade with my family on Friday. Besides, two women aren't necessarily going to hit it off just because they're the only lesbians you know."

"Who says I don't know any other lesbians?" Jasmine said. "For starters, I think we've established that Dr. Novak is a lesbian too."

"How, pray tell, have *we* established that?" The only thing she had told Jasmine about her dates with Regina was that she had no informed opinion about dogs.

Beth walked past Ellie's workstation on the way to the printer. "Oh, the newsletter definitely established that. And it also explained why Ellie won't go out with your friend, Jazzy."

"What newsletter?" Ellie twisted her chair around.

Beth pulled several sheets of paper out of the printer and dropped them on Ellie's keyboard. "The staff newsletter."

Ellie had seen that in her inbox when she had checked her email this morning, but she hadn't yet had the time to read it. She leafed past department meetings, tips from their clinical documentation specialist, and a page celebrating career milestones of various staff members. In the back, probably as this month's feel-good piece, were two pages about the Heart-to-Heart Auction with a recounting of her and Regina coming to the rescue of two people who got hurt ice-skating.

She could imagine Regina's reaction to being portrayed as a hero for patching up someone's busted lip. She would roll her eyes so hard she might need the help of an ophthalmologist to get them unstuck.

Then Ellie took in the photos that accompanied the article.

One was of their artfully arranged food at The Meadow, while another presented the two rainbow cakes side by side. A third showed Ellie beaming as she pointed at the axe sticking out of the bull's-eye.

All completely harmless, fun pictures—even though she knew the photo of Regina in the bakery, with a green lip from the cake frosting, would not go over well with Regina. Well, Ellie thought it looked adorable.

She turned the page and couldn't help staring.

Mitch had captured the moment at the ice rink when Regina had bumped into her from behind, catapulting her against the low wall. However, in the picture, it didn't give that impression at all. It seemed as if Regina was embracing her from behind, cradling her gently in her arms.

She glanced up at Beth, then at Jasmine. "It's not what it looks like," she blurted out, then winced. *Ugh.* Why had that horribly clichéd sentence been the first thing that had popped into her head?

"Mm-hmm." Jasmine and Beth exchanged knowing glances.

"No, really," Ellie said. "We collided, and Regina caught herself with her hands to my left and right so we wouldn't somersault over the wall."

"Oh, so then this one is not what it looks like either?" Beth pointed at another photo.

It had been taken during their baking competition, when they had both reached for the vanilla beans at the same time. But the glass jar was barely visible, so it seemed as if they were holding hands. "Yes. No. I mean, we were just reaching for the same ingredient."

"Then I'm sure you'll have a good explanation for this too." Beth tapped the picture at the very bottom of the page.

This one had been taken in the restaurant. Candlelight softened their features as they gazed into each other's eyes as if they had forgotten anything else existed. Regina was grinning while Ellie pressed one hand to her clearly flushed cheek.

Ellie caught herself before she could touch her fingertips to the smile on Regina's face.

Jasmine nearly fell out of her chair as she craned her neck to get a glimpse of the picture. "Oh wow! I almost didn't recognize her with that smile on her face!"

"Regi—Dr. Novak smiled. So what?" Ellie said as dismissively as she could manage.

"She smiled *at you*," Jasmine said. "She certainly never smiled at me like that." She lowered her voice. "I didn't even know Dr. McIcy could smile."

Ellie mentally went over their date activities. Regina had smiled like that a lot. And Ellie had blushed a lot.

She studied the photo again.

It wasn't a pre-arranged picture, staged to show everyone how much fun they'd had and to drum up interest for the next auction. Truth be told, Ellie had completely forgotten about Mitch and the auction.

Crap. It finally dawned on Ellie that her constant flashbacks to their kiss weren't the only reason she found it hard to go back to being just colleagues. She also struggled to accept that she would possibly never get to see a grin like that on Regina's face again. Regina might allow a superior smirk or a sarcastic curl of one corner of her mouth, but this kind of softer smile wasn't part of her professional repertoire. It would be forever lost to Ellie.

"What the hell is this?" Regina ripped the printed-out pages from the staff bulletin board in the break room.

"What's what?" Kayla asked.

"This!" Regina shook the pages in her clenched fist.

Kayla carried her coffee mug over, gently tugged the wrinkled paper free of Regina's grip, and smoothed it out on the table. "The staff newsletter."

"I know that," Regina snapped. "But why am I…are we in it?"

Kayla frowned. "They told you they would take photos for promotion purposes, didn't they? It's even in the paperwork you signed."

"For promoting our sponsors, sure. I couldn't care less about that. But putting photos of us and this sappy piece of writing into our staff newsletter, where every doctor, nurse, PA, RT, and unit clerk I work with can see it… I should rip them a new one for this bullshit!"

"Whoa, calm down! It's for a good cause."

"The nine hundred dollars Ellie paid were for a good cause. This"—Regina stabbed at the newsletter—"is just gossip."

Kayla shrugged. "It's a harmless feel-good piece."

"It's not harmless," Regina ground out, emphasizing every single syllable. "It's an invasion of my privacy, and it doesn't make me feel good at all." After her former colleagues had watched her break down when Riley had died, she couldn't stand to have everyone talking about her. Never again. That was why she had moved across the country. And now it was happening here too.

"Come on. You're overreacting." Kayla tapped a picture of Regina with a green lip. "It's cute."

Regina growled. Cute was a word people used for kittens, baby penguins, and rabbits with twitching noses. Okay, maybe for Ellie too. But not for her. She needed people to take her seriously, for Christ's sake!

"Honestly, what did you expect?" Kayla asked. "For them to post photos where you two are looking bored out of your minds?"

"No, but…" If she were honest, she had to admit that there hadn't been any moments when she'd been bored during any of their dates.

"Then what's the problem? These"—Kayla touched the last picture and the photo in which they were both cradling the vanilla beans, then pressed her palm to her chest—"are wonderful promo for the auction. They'll make every single person on staff think they should bid on someone next year. You two look so…um, cozy."

"It wasn't cozy! It was a baking contest! They tricked us by making it look like—"

"Like two people who like each other? Or who might even have—"

Regina huffed loudly, drowning Kayla out because she didn't want to hear whatever else she had to say about her and Ellie. "When have you ever known me to like someone?" She wrinkled her nose. "I barely even tolerate people."

"Right. So you weren't smiling at Ellie in that last picture; you were showing your teeth to intimidate her."

Regina didn't dignify the comment with a response. She snatched the newsletter up from the table and stomped to the trash can.

Her gaze fell onto the last page Kayla had looked at.

Damn. She *had* been smiling at Ellie. Not a reluctant flash of her teeth for PR purposes, but a full-out, genuine grin that crinkled the edges of her eyes. She couldn't even remember the last time she had smiled like that in any photo.

Knowing everyone had seen it made her stomach churn. That kind of vulnerability had no place in her professional world. She crumpled up the pages between both hands, bunched them up into a tight ball, and slam-dunked it into the trash can.

"There," she said with grim satisfaction. "And if I catch anyone else pinning a copy of the damn tabloid newsletter to the bulletin board, I'll do the same with their head! Feel free to spread the word." Without waiting for a reply, she stormed out.

Chapter 22

THE SOUND OF BAGPIPES AND drums echoed down Broadway, nearly drowning out the click-clack of the Irish dancers' hard shoes and the excited buzz of the crowd.

Dylan leaned close to Regina so he could be heard over the ruckus. "Bet you didn't have this in California!" He swept his arm in a wide arc that indicated the elaborate floats, the marching bands, and the green classic cars passing by.

"We also didn't have freezing temperatures in the middle of March!" Nearly two weeks ago, when she had taken Ellie axe-throwing, temperatures had been well into the fifties, but now they hovered around freezing. The chilly wind made it feel even colder, and the bright sunshine barely helped.

The crowd lining the street huddled in thick jackets and green wool hats. Others had dragged lawn chairs to the curb to watch the St. Patrick's Day parade and covered themselves with blankets.

"You have to think of ways to stay warm. Moving to the music, for one thing." Dylan tapped his feet to the rhythm of the drums. "Putting on a beard helps too. Want to have mine?" He tugged on his fake, clover-green beard.

Regina grimaced. "No, thanks. I'm not into facial hair."

When Dylan burst out laughing, she glared at him.

"Lighten up and have some fun! Your mood is darker than Darth Vader's helmet." He shook his head at her. "Not that you're usually Little Miss Sunshine or anything."

It reminded her of something Ellie had once said about her *sunshiny usual self*. Regina glared harder.

"You okay?" Dylan asked, the teasing now gone from his voice.

Regina gave a dismissive wave. "Why wouldn't I be?"

"You've complained about the weather being too cold, the crowd being too peoply, and the bagpipe music being too depressing."

"So?" Regina shot back. "They are." It wasn't just the sorrowful sound of the instruments that annoyed her but also the kilts the pipers wore. They reminded her of the skirt Ellie had worn on their last date—the one she'd shoved up around Ellie's hips when they had made out in the bathroom. "Besides, I warned you that I wouldn't be pleasant company, but you didn't listen and insisted I come."

She wasn't sure why she had let herself be talked into it. Maybe so she would stop thinking about how it had felt to kiss Ellie, but so far, that attempt had been a complete failure.

Dylan sighed. "That'll teach me. I thought this would cheer you up." He pointed at the group marching past now.

It was an animal shelter. Each human led a dog on a leash—a border collie with a string of green beads, two mixed breeds with green bandannas, and a basset hound with a tiny green felt hat.

Regina gave a casual shrug. "Well, I guess they are less depressing than the music." Her gaze followed a French bulldog wearing a headband with two antennae that ended in sparkly shamrocks.

The animal veered slightly off-route to sniff one of the spectators.

Regina did a double take.

It took her several seconds to be sure she wasn't just imagining things; it was really Ellie petting the dog, then swaying to the music as the animal shelter group continued on and a marching band followed.

She wore an oversized leprechaun hat that kept slipping down over her eyes, forcing her to reach up and push it back each time.

"I knew it!" Dylan gave her shoulder a friendly tap with his fist.

Regina forced her gaze away from Ellie to narrow her eyes at him. "What?"

"I knew the dogs would make you smile."

"I'm not smiling."

"Right," Dylan said. "Your lips are forming a U shape because you hate dogs."

"If my lips form weird shapes, it's because they're about to freeze off from the balmy sixty degrees you predicted for St. Paddy's Day." Regina glanced across the street again.

Apparently, Ellie wasn't attending the parade alone. Regina recognized her sister, who had painted shamrocks onto her cheeks.

Ellie said a few words to a couple around sixty, making them laugh. Something about their warm, unrestrained laughter made Regina think they might be her parents.

Mid-chuckle, Ellie looked up and right at her.

Shit. "Is it too late to accept your beard?" Regina mumbled.

"What?"

"Forget it."

Ellie stared at her for several seconds, then she slowly lifted her hand in greeting.

Regina bit her lip. *Great.* If she returned the gesture, Dylan would ask all kinds of awkward questions, so she pulled out her phone instead and sent her a text. *What are you doing here?*

The green hat fell over Ellie's eyes again as she typed out a response. She settled it back into place with a toss of her head, not taking her hands off the phone.

A second later, her answer arrived: *Watching the parade.*

No shit, Sherlock, Regina typed back.

Ellie answered with an emoji that stuck out its tongue and a one-word question: *You?*

I'm only here for the beer I've been promised afterward.

Fair warning: It'll probably be green, Ellie replied.

Amazing how normal their interaction felt—as if the kiss and that damn staff newsletter had happened in another world…and maybe they had. Or maybe being separated by an entire brass ensemble, with neither of them able to cross the street, made communication easier because if they were actually face-to-face, Regina wasn't sure she would know what to say.

She had barely finished the thought when one last float and a black stretch limousine passed by. Then the stream of people and vehicles cut off, leaving the space between Regina and Ellie empty.

Both stopped typing to stare at each other.

Ellie wouldn't be coming over, would she?

Nah. Ellie had probably seen the staff newsletter and would prefer to keep her distance too. She would lift her hand and wave; Regina would return the gesture, and then she would drag Dylan away to go get a green beer…or several.

Ellie said something to her family, straightened her leprechaun hat again, and stepped off the sidewalk.

Shit. She was coming over.

~~~♡~~~

Ellie couldn't believe Regina was here, at the parade. She also couldn't believe she was crossing the street to talk to her after avoiding her for the majority of their last shift.

But she knew she couldn't keep that up. They worked together and had to get along. Saying "hi" was the polite thing to do. Maybe it would help ease them into a better relationship.

Working relationship, of course, because that was all Regina wanted. Ellie had accepted that. Or tried to. No way would she be the needy masochist who chased after an emotionally unavailable woman.

The closer she came to the other side of the street, the more her steps slowed. Her gaze zeroed in on Regina.

Even in this crowd, Regina stood out—not only because of her height or because she was the only one not wearing green in a sea of emerald. Her presence was magnetic.

Finally, Ellie reached her. "Hi."

Regina gave a nod. "Hi."

For the first time in her life, Ellie's usually excellent social skills deserted her. If only Regina didn't look so attractive with her cheeks flushed from the chilly weather.

Luckily, the guy next to Regina stepped in. His brown eyes twinkled above his fake green beard as he eyed her with interest. "Who's your friend?"

Regina glanced at him as if only now remembering his presence. "This is Ellie. We're co-workers."

Ouch. Being just co-workers was what they had agreed on, but Regina's emphasis of the word implied they weren't even friends. That hurt. Only now did Ellie realize it wasn't a new wound. Their conversation in the staff parking lot had felt like a rejection—as if she was once again not good enough. Just a co-worker. Just a nurse. Not someone Regina would ever consider an equal, not at work and certainly not as a partner in her private life.

Ellie's hat slipped forward, covering half her face. This time, she was glad about it because it gave her a moment to school her features into what she hoped was a neutral expression.

"Ellie, this is Dylan." Regina's voice was controlled. "We play disc golf together."

Ellie pushed the hat out of her eyes and shook the hand he held out to her as if she were on autopilot.

"Play together is a euphemism for her slaughtering me every time," he said with a laugh. "If you ever want to see a guy be totally humiliated, you should come watch us play. Oh, hey, we've got a tournament next weekend. Only an amateur one, without any big names, but it's fun. You should come. It's on Saturday at 9 a.m. in Bonner Springs."

Ellie glanced at Regina out of the corner of her eye.

She stood stiffly, a wrinkle between her brows, and didn't say anything.

The message was clear. Ellie was just a co-worker. Regina had drawn a big, fat "stay out" line, possibly even barbed wire, around her private life.

All right. Fine. If that's what she wanted, Ellie would happily play her silly game. *See if I care.* She had plenty of friends and a date offer from Jasmine's yoga acquaintance. She did not need Regina Novak. It had been only a few dates for a good cause. It wasn't as if she had invested her heart in Regina.

"Thank you. I'll think about it," she said to Dylan. Then, with only a quick look at Regina, she added, "I guess I'll see you at work" before turning away.

"See you," Regina said from behind her.

Ellie's foot hovered over the empty space at the curb. So Regina would let her walk away, dismiss her without a kind word?

Despite what Ellie had just told herself, she couldn't let it go. Not like this.

She whirled back around. "Can I talk to you for a minute?"

Regina's face remained impassive, but her eyelashes fluttered almost imperceptibly. "Sure."

The crowd around them was dispersing, so they walked a few steps until they were out of earshot.

As soon as Regina faced her, whatever Ellie had wanted to say fled her mind.

"You're not Irish, are you?" Finally, it was Regina who broke the silence. She pointed at the *Kiss me, I'm Irish* button pinned to Ellie's coat.

"Oh. No." Ellie covered the button with her hand. "My sister put it on me. She says everyone's Irish today."

Regina said nothing, but her gaze trailed from the button to Ellie's face. She bit her lower lip as if struggling to keep herself from doing what the button requested.

Nonsense. Regina barely acknowledged her existence; she did not want to kiss her. "So we're just co-workers?" The words burst out of Ellie without her having time to think about them.

Regina hesitated. She lifted both hands, then dropped them to dangle at her sides. "That's what we agreed on, right?"

"Right." Raw hurt saturated her voice. Ellie hated being so transparent, making herself even more vulnerable. She should walk away before she made it worse.

But she couldn't. When Chelsea had broken up with her, she had promised herself to never allow anyone else to dismiss her so carelessly again. Not even Regina Novak.

Especially not Regina Novak.

"No!" she said, then lowered her voice when she realized how loudly she had spoken. "It's not right at all. I won't let you treat me like that!"

"Like what?" The flush from the windchill was gone from Regina's cheeks now, and she looked pale.

Ellie forced herself not to say something nice to smooth over the situation. "Like you're too good for me and I'm not worth acknowledging as anything but a co-worker. You don't want anything to ever happen between us again? Fine. I'm more than good with that. But that doesn't mean you get to pretend you hardly even know me!"

Regina moved her jaw left and right as if she had taken a blow to the chin. "I... Look... It's not personal."

Ouch. Of all the things Regina could have said, she'd chosen the most painful. Ellie wished the hat would drop down to cover her face, but for once, it stayed put.

"I mean, I don't really have any friends," Regina added. "Never had time—or any desire—for them. I always just had colleagues, study partners, and team mates. And the occasional girlfriend, although they barely deserved that title. But they never overlapped. Work was work, and my private life was private. Any time these two areas collided…" She shook her head firmly. "Not situations I'd like to repeat. So I'm at a loss at how to handle this." She waved her hand between them.

Ellie gaped at her. Maybe coming from anyone else, this wouldn't be much, but for Regina, it was a huge concession. "Is that an apology?"

"It's an explanation."

Right. Regina Novak didn't do apologies. Ellie shouldn't have expected one. She looked away.

"For why I said something that wasn't very nice," Regina added.

Ellie glanced back up. "Nice? Since when do you do nice?"

"I don't. Not usually. But maybe I should have made an exception this once."

The words were not exactly what Ellie wanted to hear, but there was something in her tone—a hint of…maybe regret or possibly an acknowledgment that Ellie wasn't just a colleague after all and deserved better than this.

But she wasn't about to let Regina get away with it this easily. "Maybe?" she repeated.

Regina sighed. "All right. Definitely. I definitely should have been nicer about it. You're right—you do deserve to be acknowledged. But Dylan knowing anything about another compartment of my life…" She shook herself. "It creeps me out. And not because he's a creep or anything."

"He seems nice," Ellie said because she didn't know what else to say to Regina's not-quite-an-apology.

Regina gave a nod.

"But don't worry. I don't have to come to your tournament just because he invited me."

Regina hesitated. "Hmm. No."

Ellie had known Regina didn't want her there, but hearing a no still made her struggle to hide a flinch.

A noticeable jerk went through Regina. She looked like a person who had forced herself to step forward, straight into a room full of the things that scared her most. "No," she repeated slowly. "You should come."

Ellie's head jerked up. "Did you just say…?"

Regina shrugged as if it were no big deal, but a muscle in her face twitched, giving her away. "Yes. You should come."

This was big for Regina. Huge. The hospital gossip said she had set the staff newsletter on fire, nearly making the smoke detectors go off, just because there had been photos of the two of them together in it. She had made it clear she wanted no interaction outside of the emergency department. Why had she suddenly changed her mind? Was it because she felt guilty for being an ass? "I appreciate it, Regina. Really. But I don't want a pity invite."

"Pity invite?" Regina echoed.

"Yeah. You don't have to—"

"I want you to come." Regina's eyes widened as if she had accidentally swallowed a bug. "Um, I mean, I'm always happy to introduce people to disc golf. It's an interesting sport. One that you don't get to see every day. It's not like you'd be coming just to watch me."

"No, of course not. If I decide to come, it will be to see Dylan win," Ellie said with the tiniest grin.

Regina huffed out a laugh. "Ha! You'd better prepare to be disappointed, then, because I fully intend to take that trophy home."

There she was again—the confident, sometimes even arrogant Regina Ellie knew from work. And she really was both, but she was also so much more.

Yeah, but you are not going to the tournament to discover more of her layers.

Just because she had forced Regina to finally acknowledge what had happened between them didn't mean they would repeat it.

She pointed across the street to where her family waited, pretending they weren't watching her and Regina but not being very convincing. Her father looked as if he was seconds away from coming over to introduce himself to Regina. "I'd better get back before they file a missing person report."

Regina nodded. After an almost unnoticeable hesitation, she asked, "So, are you coming to the tournament?"

Ellie wanted to say yes so much it scared her. If she attended…then what? Wouldn't they be exactly where they were now? With Regina being fun, bantery Jekyll one moment, then reverting back to cool, dismissive Hyde at work. No way would Ellie put up with that hot-and-cold treatment. She looked at Regina to tell her that.

Regina's gray eyes weren't dismissive or cool right now. Her face was as impassive as usual, but she couldn't hide the hopeful expression in her eyes.

"Text me the exact location, and tell Dylan I'll see what I can do," Ellie said against her better judgment. Regina inviting her, telling her she wanted her there, had been a big concession. Maybe she should meet her halfway. If they hung out for a while, they might be able to get to a point where they weren't so awkward around each other. "I'm off on Saturday. If I can find a dog sitter for Wally, I'll be in the stands, rooting for him."

"There aren't any stands in disc golf. The fans usually follow a group of players around the course."

Ellie nodded. "Fine. Then tell him I'll be there to follow him."

Regina let a lopsided grin curve her mouth. "I'll tell him you like hopeless cases."

Maybe that wasn't far from the truth, Ellie thought as she waved at her and crossed the street. Because Regina was pretty hopeless at any kind of interpersonal relationship. In fact, she had the potential to hurt her badly, and yet here Ellie was, going back for more—even though she wasn't sure what she was going back for.

Chapter 23

THE AIR HORN SOUNDED TWICE, warning the players that the tournament would start in two minutes.

Usually, at this point, Regina was laser-focused on the first hole and the line she would have to hit. Instead, her gaze went from a small group of spectators watching her group to the parking lot.

Still no sign of Ellie anywhere.

Had she decided not to come?

It would really be for the best. Regina had never invited anyone to a tournament. Not even to a casual practice round. Ellie coming to watch wouldn't only distract her, it would also complicate their relationship.

She was breaking her most important rule or at least bending it totally out of shape, and she wasn't even sure what had prompted her to do it. Just because she knew she had hurt her and couldn't bear to do it again by telling her not to come?

"You okay?" Dylan asked from next to her.

He was one of her card mates for the tournament, and she wasn't sure if she should be relieved or disappointed about that either.

"Yes, of course. Just thinking about the best strategy." She pointed toward the basket, which was uphill and around the bend. As casually as she could manage, she added, "Hey, can you text Paige and tell her to keep an eye out for Ellie, in case she's running late?"

"I already texted her twice when you told me to." He gave her a curious look, but before he could comment, a longer blast sounded, announcing the start of the tournament, and everyone fell silent so the first player to tee off wouldn't be distracted.

Regina focused on him, not allowing herself to glance toward the spectators or the parking lot again.

It seemed to take him forever to line up his shot, and as everyone took their turn teeing off, it wasn't only him.

Regina had forgotten how much she disliked the slower pace of tournaments compared to casual rounds. As they continued to the second hole, they even had to wait until the group ahead of them had finished. It left her with too much time to dwell on any small mistake...and to wonder if Ellie really wasn't coming.

It messed with her focus, and her disc ended up under a cedar tree twenty feet from the basket. She had to get down on her knees and putt from an awkward position.

Luckily, it went in, but it did not improve her mood.

She rammed the disc into her backpack with more force than necessary.

"Lighten up, will you?" Dylan told her as they walked toward the next hole. "This is a C-tier event, not the PDGA World Championship. We're here to have fun. Even you can't shoot an ace at every hole."

Regina didn't answer. She couldn't tell him that she wasn't annoyed with herself for her unfocused play or at least not *just* for that. If she was being honest with herself, she was mostly pissed that she wasn't relieved that Ellie hadn't shown.

Just as she was trying to decide whether she should try a flex forehand for the third hole, Dylan nudged her with his disc. "Looks like Paige found her."

Regina peered over her shoulder to where he was pointing.

Next to Dylan's fiancée, standing behind the tee pad so she wouldn't distract the players, was Ellie.

The thrill that had been missing at the sound of the air horn earlier went through Regina.

Ellie was dressed perfectly for the event—jeans, a pair of hiking boots that would be great for following them around the wooded course, and a light-gray fleece jacket that she hadn't zipped up. Her cheeks were flushed, either with the excitement of watching her first disc golf tournament or from rushing along the mulch path to catch up with Regina's group.

Ellie waved and mouthed something, maybe "hi" or "sorry" for being late.

Regina lifted her hand and returned the greeting.

"Who's that?" Justin asked.

Regina glanced back. *Damn.*

The three other players on her card had noticed her distraction. Now they were all staring at Ellie.

"New girlfriend?" Justin asked.

Unease prickled across the nape of Regina's neck. She hated revealing any kind of personal information to guys she was competing with. Well, to anyone really. "No. She is not my girlfriend."

Justin looked from Ellie to Regina, then nodded toward Scott. "Um, I was talking to him."

"Right." Regina lifted her hand to run it through her hair, then let it drop when she remembered she was wearing a baseball cap. *Shit.* She was losing her cool. "Well, she's not Scott's girlfriend either. She's—" She stopped herself before she could again say *a co-worker.*

Ellie was right. She deserved better.

But what was an accurate description of who Ellie was to her? *The woman who accidentally bought a series of dates with me, who got me to talk about Riley, who makes me smile and tear my hair out, and who made me forget every bit of reason in a damn bathroom of all places?*

Finally, her gaze still on Ellie, she said: "That's my friend Ellie. Now can we play some disc golf, gentlemen, or are you scared to lose to a woman?"

Justin snorted and strode toward the tee pad.

Regina held back a smirk. *Men. So easy to distract.*

She picked a disc from her bag and eyed the uphill slope of the fairway. *Let's see if I can get an ace.*

The tournament had an ace pot, after all, and she wouldn't say no to winning three hundred dollars. It had nothing to do with wanting to impress Ellie at all.

Dylan's fiancée hadn't stopped talking from the moment she had rescued Ellie from the parking lot. Apparently, Paige had attended many disc golf tournaments, and now she was trying to catch Ellie up on the rules.

Ellie's head spun at all the terms, most of which sounded remarkably similar to regular golf. She barely grasped half of what Paige was saying, mostly because she was too busy watching Regina, who took up position at the end of a concrete rectangle and looked out across the pond below.

Since Ellie couldn't even see the basket, she kept watching Regina.

She looked different, like a professional athlete, not a competent doctor, dressed in a white baseball cap, a light-blue athletic shirt, and a pair of stretchy gray golf pants that made her legs appear even longer.

Her hands were as steady as they were in the ED, every movement precise and controlled. She swung her arm around in perfect timing with her hips and the rest of her body.

Half a dozen spectators who had gathered to watch Regina's group cheered as the disc shot across the pond and made it to the other side.

"She's got great form, doesn't she?" Paige said. "She makes good use of her hips."

An image of Regina's hips against hers, pressing her against the sink, flashed through Ellie's mind. "God, yeah. Um, I mean, as far as I can tell. I really don't know the first thing about disc golf." She pulled her water bottle from her backpack and took a big sip, both because her mouth had gone dry and to hide her flushed cheeks.

She watched the other players send their discs across the pond too. They didn't look as elegant and in control as Regina, but they launched their discs with a more explosive strength, so some of them flew farther. "Do men and women always compete against each other in disc golf?"

Paige shook her head. "Women can play in any division, either mixed or female-only. But it's hard for them to keep up with the driving distance of the men, so pretty much all of the women I know play in female-only tournaments, especially at the pro level."

"But not Regina," Ellie said. Somehow, she wasn't surprised. It fit Regina's personality to not just want to be the best woman; she wanted to be the best, period.

"Not Regina," Paige repeated as they followed the players to where their discs had landed. "At first, I wasn't sure what to make of it. I thought maybe she might be entering the mixed tournaments so she could play with Dylan. I mean, why else would she put herself in a position where she was always losing?"

"Regina keeps losing?" Ellie echoed. She couldn't imagine that.

"That's what took me a while to realize. She actually wins her fair share of rounds and tournaments. Some of the men might be able to outdrive her, but her putting is better and her throws are more accurate, so on a heavily wooded, less open course like this one, she has a good chance of beating the guys."

As if to prove her right, the chains clanked as Regina propelled her disc directly into the basket from thirty feet away on her next throw.

Ellie let out a little whoop.

Paige grinned at her. "Well, it's good to see that I've really got nothing to worry about."

"Worry?" Ellie looked away from where Regina was heading toward the basket to get her disc so she could study Paige, not sure what she meant.

"Um, yeah. Dylan has been spending a lot of time with her, you know? They meet up for a glow round after work several times a week and even went to the parade together when I was out of town. It's not that I don't trust Dylan, and I know it's silly, but..." Now it was Paige who blushed. "Sometimes, I feel a little insecure, and Regina is an attractive woman..."

Yeah, there was no denying that. Ellie's gaze went to Regina again, and she almost missed Paige's next sentence.

"So I have to admit it's good to see that her interests lie elsewhere."

For a moment, Ellie nodded along, convinced that Paige was talking about Regina's lack of interest in men.

"And you two make such a cute couple," Paige added.

Ellie froze mid-nod. "Um, no, no, we're not."

"Oh, come on. Regina packed a cooler and brought three different sandwiches for you because you might not know to pack a lunch and she wasn't sure what you liked. That's totally cute."

Aww, it actually was. But Ellie was determined not to read anything into it. Just because Regina didn't want her to starve didn't mean they were dating. "We're not a couple. I'm a co-worker."

Ugh, now she had basically used the same words she had nearly decapitated Regina for using. But then again, how was she supposed to explain when she wasn't sure why Regina had invited her and what her intentions were beyond this one disc golf tournament? Did Regina want to be friends? Go back to being just colleagues? Or—?

"Oh, I'm so sorry. I didn't mean to make any assumptions just because…" Paige looked from Regina to Ellie. "I really misread things."

"It's okay." She couldn't blame Paige. After all, her libido and, admittedly, her heart didn't know how to read the situation either. "Come on. They are getting too far ahead of us." She nodded toward their group of players and followed them to the next hole, hoping Paige would get the hint and go back to chatting about disc golf.

Regina was just about to step onto the tee pad at the last hole when Dylan walked over.

"Do you want to know your standing?" He pointed at his phone. As the designated scorekeeper of their group, he had the UDisc app open.

Usually, Regina didn't want to know her score while she was playing. It messed with her focus. But something in Dylan's tone made her think she needed to know. "Tell me."

"You and Brodie Malone are tied for the lead, and he's got one hole to go too."

Damn. No pressure or anything. That meant if he managed to finish his last hole under par and she didn't, he would be in the lead.

After two steadying breaths, she took up position at the end of the tee pad and tried to tune everything out—her card mates, Ellie and the other spectators watching her, and even the birdsong in the trees around her—as she visualized her throw.

At a hundred and forty feet, it was a short hole, but a tricky one. The fairway sloped uphill, and the basket was positioned right behind a narrow gap between two large trees.

If her drive arched just a foot too much to either side, her disc would ricochet off one of them and might end up in the brush or roll downhill.

Was it better to play it safe and aim for a spot to the left or right of the trees to make it past them instead of trying to hit the gap?

But then again, she had invited Ellie to attend the tournament. Nothing about this event was playing it safe.

She peered through the gap and imagined the perfect trajectory that would lead her disc directly into the basket. Then, omitting an x-step run-up in favor of more precision, she launched her disc.

It soared past a slender tree and directly toward the gap.

"Ooh," Justin said from behind her, "it's looking really—"

Regina twisted around and hurled a glare at him that made him snap his mouth shut mid-sentence.

Disc golfers were as superstitious as folks working in the emergency department. If someone complimented a shot before the disc landed, that was akin to mentioning how quiet it was in the ED. All hell was sure to break loose within seconds.

The basket's metal chains clanked.

Had the disc glanced off them, or—?

Regina whirled around.

The orange disc had landed squarely in the basket.

Yes! Regina pumped both fists.

"No way!" Justin shouted.

The spectators' cheers echoed through the forest behind them. One voice rang out louder than the others, and Regina didn't need to turn around to know it had been Ellie.

Regina adjusted her baseball cap so the brim shielded her face and jogged toward the basket to retrieve her disc.

As she pulled it out and held it up in the air, the spectators clapped, cheered, and whistled.

Again, Regina could easily make out Ellie's voice.

She wasn't sure how she felt about Ellie's enthusiastic cheering. It was kind of embarrassing, especially since she knew it might make the other players jump to conclusions again.

Yet at the same time, Ellie's unbridled joy at her success made her feel all warm inside.

Since when was she the type to get sentimental because someone was rooting for her?

But then again, she couldn't remember the last time someone… anyone had been rooting for her.

When she rejoined the other players, Dylan high-fived her.

"Your not-girlfriend is incredibly loud!" Justin laughed and playfully clutched his ears.

"You're just jealous because you can't make a woman scream," Scott said.

Regina sent them a lethal glare. "If you two don't shut up, I'll show you how I make a man scream."

They quickly decided selecting discs from their bags required their full attention.

Once the last player in Regina's group had landed his disc in the basket, they joined the small gathering of spectators, mostly consisting of family and friends.

Ellie watched Regina approach, and their gazes held the entire time, despite the chaos of greetings, hugs, and high-fives around them.

Paige threw her arms around Dylan and kissed him as if he were a victorious warrior returning from battle, which made the situation even more awkward for Ellie because she had no clue how to greet Regina.

Finally, Regina paused in front of her and hooked her thumbs behind the straps of her disc golf backpack, demonstrating that she had no intention of hugging or casually touching Ellie. The brim of her baseball cap shielded her eyes, so it was hard to make out her expression. "Hi." Her voice was soft, though, not the coolly professional tone from work.

"Hi. That was amazing!" Ellie gestured toward the last basket but stopped herself before she could continue gushing. "I'm sorry I was late and missed the first two holes."

"Did you have trouble finding it?" Regina asked.

"No, that wasn't it at all. My sister was supposed to have the day off, but she was called in to cover a shift for a sick colleague at the last minute, so I had to make a detour to my parents' house to drop off Wally." That plus Vickie had tried to talk her out of going to the tournament up until the second she had left for work, calling Ellie a glutton for punishment and warning her that she would get hurt.

Ellie hadn't even been able to tell her she was wrong.

"I'm starving," Dylan said. "Let's go get our lunch."

They headed to the parking lot, and Regina got a big cooler from her car.

"I didn't know it would be an all-day event, so I didn't bring anything," Ellie said.

"No worries. I've got you covered."

So Paige was right. Regina had brought sandwiches for her. Ellie bit back a smile.

Their group claimed one of the picnic tables next to a soccer field for themselves, and everyone unpacked their coolers.

Regina set a bottle of water and three foil-wrapped sandwiches in front of Ellie. "Ham and Swiss cheese. Chicken-avocado. Mozzarella-tomato. Pick whatever you like."

"Wow. You went all out."

Regina waved her hand as if it were no big deal. "Well, I owe you dinner, so…"

"Dinner? Was I upgraded from you owing me a drink?"

Regina huffed. "You're the one who owes *me* a drink or two. But I do owe you dinner since we left The Meadow before you could enjoy your meal."

The reference to their last date was a surprise—a good one. At least it meant Regina no longer pretended they had never spent a moment together outside of work.

The others at the table sent them curious glances. The guy who had introduced himself as Justin even lifted an eyebrow.

Oh no. They probably thought she and Regina had abandoned dinner and rushed home to ravish each other.

Which was far from the truth, but not so far from how the evening had nearly ended.

Ellie cursed her tendency to blush. Regina, however, looked as cool, calm, and collected as ever, so Ellie aimed to appear just as nonchalant. "I hate to tell you, but a sandwich doesn't make up for missing out on dinner at one of the best restaurants in the city." She kept her tone teasing. "You still owe me."

"Well, in that case, I'll take these back." Regina pulled the foil-wrapped packages to her side of the table.

"Hey!" Ellie lunged for the chicken sandwich.

Their fingers grazed.

The fleeting contact seared down to her toes, touching every spot in between.

The wrapped sandwich landed on the table as they both let go at the same time.

Regina grabbed her water bottle and took a long draw, then wiped a droplet off her bottom lip.

Jesus. A simple drop of water had no business looking so sexy. Ellie snatched up the sandwich and tore off the wrapper as if she were starving.

Regina had assumed it would feel awkward to have Ellie at a disc golf event, but it wasn't. At least not for Ellie.

Within minutes of their group sitting down at the picnic table, Ellie debated the merits of mustard versus mayo with Justin, showed Scott pictures of her dog on her phone, and teased Dylan about barely recognizing him without his fake green beard. She had even exchanged phone numbers with Paige.

Ellie seemed to fit right in, and Regina wasn't sure how she felt about that.

It was unsettling, especially since Ellie's involvement kept drawing her into the conversation too.

Normally, she used the lunch break between rounds to go over her mistakes and think of ways to improve her game, more or less ignoring the other players.

But it was more than not being able to focus on the second round. Watching two of her neatly separate worlds collide left her uneasy.

Truth be told, it wasn't really a collision—more like a smooth slotting into each other.

Maybe that was the most unsettling aspect because it wasn't what she had expected at all.

Don't trust it. That peaceful alignment wouldn't last.

But for the moment, she would allow herself to pretend otherwise and enjoy it.

She washed the last bite of her sandwich down with a sip of water. The spring sun warmed her stiff shoulders as she watched the weird but admittedly cute way Ellie ate her sandwich.

Ellie pinched off a piece and popped it into her mouth. Sunlight fell through the leaves of the tree next to the picnic table, painting a pattern of light and shadows onto her face and making it look incredibly soft.

Regina itched to reach out and touch her cheek. "Maybe you should have been a surgeon after all," she said to distract herself. "You're dissecting the poor sandwich."

Ellie paused mid-chew. She swallowed slowly and pursed her lips into a smile, but it wasn't the teasing, almost affectionate grin that usually accompanied their banter.

A few weeks ago, Regina might not have noticed, but now it was as glaringly obvious as a flashing neon sign. *What did I—? Oh.*

She had put her finger right into Ellie's wound by telling her she should have become a doctor, not a nurse. It had been a joke, of course. With anyone else, Regina would have brushed it off as them being too sensitive.

But with Ellie, she couldn't do that. She wasn't ready to admit it, but dammit, she liked Ellie's sensitivity.

Should she…apologize?

But Paige and the players on her card were already eyeing them with curiosity, clearly trying to figure out the nature of their relationship.

Yeah, good luck with that. She hesitated but couldn't bring herself to show that kind of weakness in front of her card mates. Finally, she said instead, "Not that nurses can't dissect a sandwich, of course."

The corners of Ellie's mouth curved up again, and this time, the smile reached her eyes, as if she understood exactly why Regina had said that. "Well, this nurse can and will." She pulled a slice of pickle from her sandwich and popped it into her mouth.

"Oh, you're a nurse?" Scott asked. "Do you work with Regina?"

Great. Just when she had decided to forget about the fact that they worked together for the day. Regina wiped her hands on a paper napkin and got up. "I'll go find out where our starting hole for the second round is. Be right back."

Before one of the guys could offer to go instead, Regina walked away from the table.

The sound of footsteps followed her almost immediately. "Wait," Ellie called. "I'll go with you."

Regina suppressed a sigh. She slowed down, allowing Ellie to catch up.

For several seconds, they walked toward the small tent that held registration without saying a word.

"Are you okay?" Ellie asked after a while.

"I'm fine," Regina said. "Although I admit I'll be exhausted by tonight."

"I bet. But I wasn't talking about how you are physically." Ellie glanced at her, then away. "If this isn't working for you…"

Regina's step faltered. Had Ellie misunderstood her invitation? She knew this wasn't a date, didn't she? "This?" She struggled to keep her voice even.

"Um, I mean, me being here."

Ah. "No, it's fine." Regina squeezed her eyes shut for a second. *Way to make her feel welcome.* "I'm, um, glad you came."

They reached the registration tent. A short line had formed where the starting holes for round two were posted.

Ellie turned toward her and searched her face with an intensity that caused the sunburned feeling that was starting to become familiar when she was around Ellie. Then her gaze softened. "Me too."

They looked into each other's eyes, and Regina found herself leaning closer, drawn in by the warmth in Ellie's brown irises.

"Hey, Regina, heard you threw an ace at the last hole," someone in line behind them called.

Regina wasn't sure whether she should kick him or hug him for interrupting. She turned toward him. "Heard you almost got one too, Brodie—if only that damn tree didn't come out of nowhere."

He laughed. "Well, now I know where all the trees are, so I'll beat you easily in the second round."

"In your dreams." They reached the head of the line, and Regina checked where her group would start the next round.

"Speaking of the second round," Ellie said when they made their way back. "I won't be able to stay until the end. I didn't know the tournament would last all day, and my parents can only watch Wally until four."

It was better that way, Regina told herself. No awkward goodbyes in the parking lot. Definitely no kisses at Ellie's front door. She probably would be so busy playing disc golf she wouldn't even notice Ellie was gone.

But then again, having most of the spectators—or at least the loudest one—behind her had given her a little extra energy at each tee-off. She would miss that.

"That's okay," Regina said as calmly as possible. "I'll send you a picture of the trophy."

Ellie laughed. Her eyes twinkled. "Careful with that ego."

Yeah, careful. That was good advice. But it wasn't her ego or the tournament Regina was worried about. Throwing an ace through a tiny gap between two trees was easy in comparison to navigating this situation and deciding where to go from here.

Ellie was stretched out on the couch with Wally, debating with herself whether she should watch another episode of *The Last of Us* or do the reasonable thing and go to bed, when her phone chirped.

She picked it up from the coffee table and tapped the screen.

It was a message from Regina—just a photo, no text.

The snapshot showed Regina's trophy case. On the middle shelf, surrounded by science fair ribbons and other medals, was a new award, a golden figurine about to throw a disc.

Ellie grinned and quickly tapped a reply. *You won! Congratulations!* She added an emoji with a party hat.

Of course I did, Regina answered.

Two months ago, Ellie would have thought the answer was unbearably arrogant, but now it made her grin broaden. *Of course. Did Brodie encounter another tree?*

No. Believe it or not, I won without any interference from cedars or oaks.

Ellie scrolled up to study the photo Regina had sent. Right next to the new trophy was the framed picture of Regina flanked by her parents, one hand on Riley's shoulder.

Regina could have snapped a photo of the award before placing it on the shelf, and it warmed Ellie that she hadn't. Letting her have even that tiny glimpse of Riley was a huge sign of her trust.

Thank you, Ellie typed. *For sharing that with me.*

It took a while before Regina's next message arrived. *Are you working tomorrow?*

Yes, Ellie replied, allowing the change of topic. *You?*

No. I always try to get the day off after a tournament so I can sleep in.

Ellie sent her a crying emoji. *Mentioning that is cruel when I have to get up at 5:30.*

I'd better not keep you up, then, Regina replied. *I just wanted to send you the picture, as promised.*

Thanks, Ellie typed back. *And thank you for inviting me to the tournament.*

Again, Regina took her time answering, as if she didn't know what to say to that. *You're welcome.*

Three dots appeared, indicating that Regina was writing something else, but no second message followed.

Ellie wrestled down her disappointment. What had she expected? For Regina to ask her out? That would never happen, and she wasn't sure she would want it to.

Clearly, Regina had a lot of rules and issues around dating, and despite what Vickie might think, Ellie wasn't a glutton for punishment.

Good night, she finally typed. *Enjoy your day off.*

Good night. Have a good shift.

Just when Ellie wanted to toss the phone onto the coffee table and go to bed, another message arrived.

It wasn't from Regina.

Paige had sent her a video of Regina playing the last few holes Ellie had missed and the award ceremony.

Ellie held out for all of three seconds before she pressed play.

Maybe she was a glutton for punishment after all.

Chapter 24

REGINA'S DAY OFF WASN'T GOING well. For the past few hours, she had buzzed around her apartment like a mosquito on speed.

After the tournament the day before, she wasn't in the mood for disc golf. Cleaning the apartment had kept her busy only for an hour. She tried reading but tossed aside her crime novel after less than a page, and the latest issue of the *Journal of Emergency Medicine* couldn't capture her interest either.

For a second, she thought about calling her parents, but that would hardly improve her mood. Since Riley's death, she had called them only a handful of times and kept each call short. She couldn't stand the silent accusations in their voices. They hadn't come right out and blamed her, but it was clear to Regina anyway.

No, she couldn't deal with that.

When her phone dinged, she immediately reached for it. Maybe it was Ellie. She should be home from work by now. Perhaps she wanted to continue the text conversation from the previous night.

But the message wasn't from Ellie. It was from Kayla.

Congrats on winning the tournament, her colleague had written.

Regina clutched her phone more tightly. Had Ellie told Kayla she had attended the event? Had she even shown her the photo of the trophy, right next to Riley's picture?

No. Ellie wouldn't do that. While Regina hadn't told her everything, Ellie knew enough to understand she didn't want to share that photo with anyone else.

How do you know I won? Regina typed back.

It took a few minutes until an answer appeared. *My cousin plays disc golf. He was the guy who won third place.*

Small world. Which was exactly why any attempt to be friends—or more—with Ellie was doomed to fail. Every hospital employee would know within a shift.

Yeah, very small. Sometimes, you'd think KC is a tiny little village. We just had to send one of the nurses home because she's friends with the burn victims we treated today.

Regina's stomach churned. For a few seconds, the memory of Riley being rushed in through the ambulance entrance played through her mind in full HD. She would never forget that horrible moment when she had realized it was her brother on the gurney.

She chased away the images with a rough shake of her head and focused on Kayla's text. One of the nurses? What were the chances of it being Ellie? She ached to find out, but then Kayla would think she was taking a special interest in Ellie.

Which, of course, she totally wasn't. She rolled her eyes at herself.

Burn victims? she asked instead.

An entire family—mom, dad, two kids—in serious condition after a house fire. The mom might not make it.

How awful! Regina swallowed. She had to know. *Who was the nurse who's friends with them?*

Mel Schneider, Kayla replied. *Ellie called Mel's husband to come get her and stayed longer until we got the family stabilized and transferred to the burn center.*

Regina's grip on the phone eased. It hadn't been Ellie's friends. Still, she'd had a horrible shift. Burn victims were always tough, especially when kids were involved.

She said goodbye to Kayla, then sat with her phone still in her hand for quite some time.

The urge to reach out to Ellie and find out if she was okay gripped her and wouldn't let go, no matter how often she told herself Ellie was fine. She was a professional. She was not Regina's responsibility on her day off.

But then again, her day off was already as relaxing as an M&M conference, and she did owe Ellie dinner.

She jumped up and strode to the door without giving her rational mind an opportunity to poke holes into that flimsy excuse.

Ellie held on to the door of the fridge as if for dear life and stared inside without seeing the contents.

Her stomach rumbled, but she didn't have the energy to cook. Even slapping a sandwich together seemed like too big of a task. Food didn't sound appealing anyway. The cloying smell of burnt skin and flesh still seemed to cling to everything, even after a half-hour shower.

What she really needed wasn't food; it was a hug. But Vickie had left a note, saying she'd be home late. She had taken Wally with her to visit a friend.

When the doorbell rang, Ellie jumped and hit her head on the fridge door.

Quickly, she slammed it shut, plodded to the door, and opened it.

Wow. She really needed to eat. Low blood glucose was making her see things. It couldn't possibly be Regina standing on her porch, holding up a plastic bag like a shield between them.

Ellie blinked, rubbed her eyes, then looked again.

The view in front of her hadn't changed. Regina stood there, looking better than anyone had a right to in a hoodie and a pair of jeans with a ripped knee.

"What are you doing here?" was all Ellie got out. "Is everything okay?"

"I'm fine, but you look a little worse for wear." Regina took in every inch of her. "Have you eaten?"

"Does a handful of potato chips at lunch count?"

"I'll take that as a no." Regina squeezed past Ellie, who still stood frozen, kicked the door shut with her heel, and continued to the kitchen as if she did it every day. "Plates? Silverware?"

Ellie hurried after her, still not sure what was going on. "Um, in the cabinet right in front of you and in that drawer." She leaned in the doorway and watched as Regina pulled containers from the bag and heaped food onto a plate. "You brought me dinner?"

Regina shrugged as if it were no big deal. "Mac and cheese and Parmesan broccoli from The Meadow."

Comfort food. Thank God Regina had opted for the vegetarian version. Ellie didn't think she could stomach a sizzling steak after dealing with burn victims. For the first time all day, a smile found its way onto Ellie's face. "Wait a minute. They don't do takeout."

"They do if you left a lasting impression on the owner."

Ellie would have thought Regina would never set foot in The Meadow again after the way she'd stormed out on their last date. And yet Regina had braved it—for Ellie.

Regina carried the heaping plate and a bottle of water over to the dining room table and pulled out a chair for her.

Ellie sank onto it. Her head still spun as she reached for the knife and fork Regina laid next to the plate and tried the mac and cheese. It was still hot and creamy and the best thing she had experienced all day—with the exception of finding Regina on her doorstep. She lowered her fork and regarded Regina, who had taken a seat across from her. "Why?"

The simple question hung between them for a few seconds.

"Well," Regina said, "you insisted sandwiches don't count, so I owed you dinner."

Regina's tone was light, even teasing, but Ellie wasn't in the mood to turn this into a joke.

"You know, one day, we will run out of excuses," Ellie said quietly.

Regina studied the nearly finished puzzle at the other end of the dining room table.

She took so long to answer that Ellie was convinced she would pretend not to understand what she was talking about.

Finally, Regina looked into Ellie's eyes and tilted her head in acknowledgment. "I know. But not today. So eat."

Ellie stared at her. She really hadn't expected Regina to admit that owing her dinner was only an excuse; she had come because she wanted to spend time with Ellie. But what did it mean going forward? Clearly, Regina wasn't ready to figure it out. Ellie picked up her fork and continued to eat. Within a few bites, her appetite returned, and she basically inhaled dinner.

"Wow," Regina said when Ellie had all but licked the plate clean. "Looks like I saved a life even on my day off."

"You did. This was exactly what I needed." Even more than the food, Regina's company was what she had needed, but, of course, she didn't say that. "I had the shift from hell."

"Yes, I heard."

Ellie glanced up from where she had put her empty plate into the dishwasher.

"Kayla told me about the burn victims," Regina added. "Want to talk about it?"

So that was why Regina had shown up on her doorstep with comfort food. She had found out Ellie had had a tough day and wanted to be there for her. She'd even been thoughtful enough to skip the steak. For a moment, Ellie blinked back tears. She didn't trust her voice, so she nodded, led Regina over to the couch, and flopped down onto it.

Regina took a seat next to her—not all the way at the other end but also not close enough to touch. She regarded Ellie without hurrying her along, giving her as much time as she needed.

"It was horrible. All of it. The mother was worst. She had third-degree burns over eighty percent of her body."

They looked at each other. Both knew what that was likely to mean.

"What hit me most was that she was fully alert. It was almost surreal. She knew what was happening, and the way she looked at me—" A shiver ran through Ellie. She wrapped her arms around herself.

Regina slid closer. "I don't think she felt any pain since the nerves in all her skin layers have been destroyed."

Ellie knew that, and Regina was probably aware of that but had no idea what else to say.

Regina cleared her throat. "Do you feel like a hug would help?"

Again, Ellie couldn't help staring. She wasn't so much surprised that Regina had a caring side—she had seen glimpses of it several times during their dates—but that Regina was willing to reveal it to her after insisting they could only be co-workers.

The way Regina had phrased the offer, as if she were discussing a treatment option, made a small smile form on Ellie's lips, driving back some of the horror and the sadness. She knew she should resist, but after the day she'd had, she didn't have the will to fight it. "Worth a try, I guess."

Regina's gaze darted over Ellie's arms and shoulders, as if it had been years since she'd hugged anyone and she had no idea where to put her hands.

Ellie curled her legs under herself so she could face Regina fully.

Both hesitated, lingering inches apart.

Ellie knew she should tell her it wasn't a good idea, but her vocal cords refused to work.

When Regina wrapped one arm around Ellie and drew her close, the words fled Ellie's mind. Every bit of hesitancy evaporated, and she sank against her. She buried her face against the crook of Regina's neck and breathed in her scent. God, she smelled so good.

Regina put her other arm around Ellie too and held her close, sheltering her. At first, her stance felt rigid, the hands on Ellie's back unmoving and the arms holding her taut with tension. Gradually, Regina relaxed, her body becoming a soft yet solid resting place.

Ellie's eyes fluttered shut as she burrowed more deeply into her. She fought the urge to tug the neck of Regina's hoodie down so she could press her lips to her skin and connect with even more of her.

Regina shuddered as if she had read her thoughts.

They really should stop this. She should pull away. But instead, she wrapped her arms around Regina and clutched the small of her back. Her heart beat against Regina's…or maybe hammered was more accurate.

Finally, Regina eased away a few inches, touched her fingertips to Ellie's jaw, and gently tipped her head back just enough to see Ellie's face. "Better?" she murmured, one arm still around Ellie.

"Mm-hmm." Ellie couldn't glance away from Regina's eyes. The gray of her irises looked like sun-warmed rocks, drawing her in.

"Good," Regina said, her voice husky. She brushed her thumb along the line of Ellie's jaw in a featherlight caress.

Neither of them let go.

Ellie tightened her fingers in the fabric of the hoodie and pulled Regina toward her. Or maybe she had leaned forward. She wasn't sure. All she knew was that Regina's lips were on hers and she was kissing her and Regina was kissing her back.

It was nothing like the hot, desperate make-out session in the bath-room. This time, Regina's lips caressed hers slowly, with an almost aching softness. Her fingers still rested on Ellie's face, cradling it tenderly.

Ellie brought her hands up as well and cupped Regina's cheeks to keep her mouth against her own.

A low sound escaped Regina, and she brushed her tongue along Ellie's bottom lip.

Desire spiraled through Ellie. Her lips parted on a gasp, and as their tongues met, soft turned into urgent.

Ellie threaded her fingers through Regina's hair and deepened the kiss. Regina's taste was as intoxicating as her scent. More. She needed more.

The thought pierced the haze of arousal. She wouldn't get more from Regina. Maybe a hot night of passion that helped her forget everything for a while, but by tomorrow morning, nothing would have changed. They would be back to Regina insisting she wanted to keep things professional.

With a groan that had nothing to do with desire, she pulled away and broke the kiss.

When Ellie retreated abruptly, Regina caught herself against the back of the couch so she wouldn't fall forward. Ellie's move away, the kiss, the entire situation between them had completely unbalanced her, not just physically, but emotionally too.

"I'm sorry," Ellie said, her voice hoarse and barely above a whisper. "I shouldn't have kissed you."

"It's okay." It was the only thing Regina could think of to say. "You had a tough day."

Ellie sighed and looked away, but not before Regina had seen a flash of hurt in her eyes.

Damn. We're really running out of excuses, aren't we? She had meant to give Ellie an out, not to upset her, but maybe Ellie didn't want an out—and Regina was no longer sure she wanted one either, as scary as that thought was.

"I can't keep doing this." Ellie pointed a trembling finger at Regina, then herself. "You kiss me back like it means something, then tomorrow you'll push me away and act like I'm just a co-worker. I can't… I won't let you play with my feelings like that."

At the word *feelings*, Regina's heart jumped against her rib cage as if trying to break free. She clutched a fistful of the couch to keep herself steady as a barrage of conflicting emotions slammed into her. Part of her wanted to leap forward, pull Ellie into her arms, and kiss her again, but another part shouted at her to jump up and put some distance between them.

Calm down. She's not talking about love or anything. But if she was being honest with herself, she knew they could have something special, and she was the one who was too chickenshit to let it happen. "I'm not playing," she got out. "And hurting you is the last thing I want."

"I know you're not doing it on purpose, but that doesn't mean I won't get hurt by that hot-and-cold treatment."

"No, you're right." Regina knew she had a reputation for being arrogant, but she was self-aware enough to realize she sucked at interpersonal relationships. "I have an award or a medal to show for pretty much anything I ever tried my hand at—school, medicine, sports. But there's one thing I've never excelled at."

"Relationships," Ellie said quietly.

Regina had meant to say *dating*, but maybe the word Ellie had used was more accurate because she had no problem sweeping a woman off her feet as long as nothing got too serious. "Yes. I was never great at them. Never made an effort to be even passable. After…" She forced herself to say it without looking away. Ellie deserved that much from her, even if she couldn't give her anything else. "After Riley's death, it only got worse. I've barely pieced my life back together, and getting involved with anyone…with you…could unravel it all."

Ellie pulled a throw pillow onto her lap and then pressed it against her chest. "I get it."

She really does, Regina thought, and that made it even harder.

They paused, both at a loss.

Understanding and acceptance shone in Ellie's eyes, but Regina could also see the sadness.

She was hurting Ellie even now. There was only one thing left for her to do. For Ellie's sake, she had to pull back completely. No more teasing banter. No more invitations to disc golf. No more delivering comfort food. No more arranging for Ellie to get a hot chocolate with real milk.

The thought sliced through her like a scalpel. The sharp feeling of loss surprised her. She had known Ellie for only nine months and spent time with her outside of work for just two of them. How could Ellie have become so important to her in such a short time?

She had merely meant to fulfill her auction obligations—just a few dates for a good cause. Nothing that would be hard to give up. And yet she could hardly get out the words she knew she had to say. "I should keep my distance," she murmured, not sure if she was talking to Ellie or herself. Her chest squeezed tighter with every word, making it hard to breathe. "But the thing is… I really don't want to." She had struggled with that for a while without fully admitting it even to herself, but now, as Ellie had said, she had run out of excuses.

Ellie stared at her, eyes wide and unblinking as if she didn't want to miss the tiniest shift of her facial expression. "W-what do you want?"

Regina swallowed against a mouth as dry as a bowl of flour. Just like at the tournament, she had a choice to make: play it safe or risk it all. But this time, there was so much more at stake than a shiny trophy. "I…" Her fingers went numb from clutching the edge of the couch with all her strength. "I want to try. To date you. For real."

The pillow slid from Ellie's hands. "Regina…" She said her name like a mix between a warning and a groan of longing.

Regina squeezed her eyes shut. She shouldn't have said that. Shouldn't have made herself so vulnerable. "Bad idea. I know. Forget I said that." She waved her hand as if to wipe away her words.

"No!" Ellie shouted, then ducked her head, a flush rising up her neck. "I mean, I really want that too, but what about your number one rule? I doubt you would quit your job, and I'm certainly not going to quit mine."

"I know. I would never ask you to. But maybe we could take it slow. See where things are going. And keep it out of the ED." Regina couldn't believe the words were coming out of her own mouth, yet she knew it was what she wanted. She had wanted it for a while and finally that want had become bigger than her fear. With every sentence, the faint glimmer of hope in her chest grew. Maybe they could make it work after all.

Ellie pulled the side of her bottom lip between her teeth. "Keep it out of the ED," she repeated. "What does that mean? That you'll go back to pretending you barely even know me as soon as we are at work?"

"No," Regina said, even though she wasn't sure what exactly it meant. "Just that I'm not ready to send out a notice in the staff newsletter."

The corner of Ellie's mouth twitched up into a tiny smile. "Yeah, I heard you set it on fire, nearly setting off the smoke detectors."

Regina huffed, the hint of teasing in Ellie's tone easing her gut-clenching tension. "You really shouldn't trust the hospital rumor mill. I merely crumpled it into a ball and slammed it into the nearest trash can."

"So what you're saying is no steamy sex in the on-call room, no quickie in the supply closet, and no sexy lingerie pinned to the staff bulletin board." Ellie's tone was humorous, but her gaze searched Regina's face for answers.

Answers Regina didn't have yet, so she huffed again. "Please. This isn't *Grey's Anatomy*. As if we ever have time for that in the emergency department anyway." She lowered her voice to a husky drawl. "Because trust me, if we were to do any of that, it wouldn't be quick."

A noticeable shiver went through Ellie. "God, Regina, you really are the queen of mixed messages. How do you expect us to take it slow if you talk to me in that sexy tone?"

Regina sobered. "So we are doing this?"

Ellie looked at her, all her emotions—mostly hope, affection, fear, and desire—plain to see in her eyes. "I'm willing to risk it. Are you?"

Regina forced herself to keep eye contact, even though her skin itched with that sunburned feeling, warning her she was making herself too vulnerable. "I am," she got out through the lump in her throat.

They stared at each other.

Regina couldn't believe it. How had they gotten from her dropping off dinner to agreeing to date for real? But she would not take it back.

"What now?" Ellie asked.

Somehow, it felt good to know Ellie was just as uncertain as she was. "Well, I brought dessert, and we could finish your puzzle afterward." That wasn't really what Ellie had been asking, but Regina needed to ease off the emotional intensity. She went to the kitchen, pulled a container from the plastic bag, and carried it back to the dining room, along with a fork.

Ellie opened the lid and peeked in. Laughter burst from her, as if she had needed an escape valve too. "Lava cake? Woman, you'll be the death of me."

"I hope not." The thought of hurting Ellie in any way made her stomach lurch. She hopped off the couch and went to get a second fork for herself.

Ellie would have normally finished her puzzle in less than an hour, but now she fumbled with the pieces and afterward could barely tell whether the motif had been Antelope Canyon or the Eiffel Tower.

She was still trying to process that Regina wanted to date her for real!

Yeah, but she also wants to keep it out of the ED. It should have been a big red flag—one that made Ellie back out. At the very least, she knew she should be careful and not jump in with both feet, but she couldn't help herself. Something about Regina made her want to abandon all caution.

Distractedly, she reached into the box containing the last pieces.

Her fingers brushed Regina's, who had been going for a puzzle piece too.

Goose bumps rippled up Ellie's arm. Her entire body buzzed, and it wasn't a sugar high from the lava cake they had shared earlier.

It was the sixth time it had happened, even though the box wasn't that small.

"Are you doing that on purpose?" Ellie asked.

"Doing what on purpose?" Regina's poker face was firmly in place.

Ellie knew her well enough by now to read it as a confirmation. "Reaching into the box at the same time I do."

"Well, you are the puzzle pro, so correct me if I'm wrong, but isn't it the goal to get the pieces from the box into their rightful places?"

"Mm-hmm."

"And wouldn't that require reaching into the box?"

"Mm-hmm." Ellie gave her a faux strict look but wasn't sure how convincing she was because she secretly loved their teasing banter, especially after all the tension earlier. "You know, if you want to touch my hand, you could just ask."

Regina arched her brows. "Is that so?"

"Try it."

Regina held out her hand, palm up. Their gazes connected, and the look in Regina's eyes was confident and enticing, as if she played flirty games like this every day, but there was also a well-hidden vulnerability that revealed she hadn't done anything like this in a long time.

Ellie wanted to continue their banter and tell Regina she hadn't asked yet, but her hand moved as if on its own accord. She slid her fingers onto Regina's palm.

Regina lifted Ellie's hand up, closer to her face, and studied it intently. She trailed her thumb along the top of each finger, caressing each knuckle, each joint, and each spot in between. Once she reached her pinkie, she turned Ellie's hand over and touched the tip of her index finger to Ellie's.

Each touch made Ellie shiver. She pulled her lip between her teeth to hold back a moan as Regina traced a line down the inside of her finger, across the palm, and down her wrist.

Jesus. Regina was touching her wrist. Just her wrist. Why was her breath catching as if Regina were trailing her fingers up her inner thigh?

"You were right," Regina murmured, still busy finding the most sensitive spot on the inside of Ellie's wrist. "I might have approached the puzzle all wrong. This is much more effective."

Maybe not for completing the puzzle, but it was definitely doing things to Ellie. "Much more. Here's another tip from the puzzle pro: You can complete the puzzle faster if more hands are involved." She turned hers and captured Regina's. Tantalizingly slowly, she caressed up one side of each long finger and down the other. "Has anyone ever told you, you've got beautiful hands?"

"A few people might have mentioned it." Regina held very still, as if entirely unaffected, but her voice was raspy. "They also mentioned the fact that I have beautiful lips."

"Oh, did they?" Ellie looked from Regina's smoldering eyes to her full lips. "Hmm, let me see."

Fingers intertwined, they leaned toward each other.

A second before their mouths met, a key rattled in the door.

Nooo! Not now, Vickie! Her sister had the worst timing. With a low groan, Ellie sank against the back of her chair.

Glowering, Regina grabbed the last puzzle piece and hammered it into place with her palm. "I'm really not sure I like your sister," she muttered.

Apparently, that feeling was mutual. While Wally gave an excited yip and bolted toward Ellie, Vickie paused one step into the house and glared at them as if she had caught two burglars. "What's this? Ellie?"

Ellie busied herself petting Wally, who was wagging his tail, whining, and trying to lick her hands as if he hadn't seen her in months.

Regina rose calmly. "I believe it's Antelope Canyon in Arizona." Her gaze brushed Ellie, and the ice in her gray eyes melted the tiniest bit. "Beautiful place."

Ellie tightened her fingers in Wally's fur so she wouldn't reach out and touch her. "Hmm. Yeah."

"I'd better go," Regina said. "I'm working tomorrow."

"Me too." Ellie jumped up and walked her to the door, ignoring the warning look Vickie gave her. She stepped onto the porch and pulled the door closed behind them for some privacy. "I'm sorry. I'll try to get her to stop the overprotective sister routine."

"It's okay." Regina glanced toward her SUV as if she couldn't wait to climb behind the wheel and get out of there, but she didn't. Instead, she turned to face Ellie. "I hope you can sleep."

It took Ellie a second to realize she was talking about the tough shift she'd had. So much had happened since then that it barely felt like the same day! "I'm sure I will. Sweet dreams to you too."

"Thanks." Regina hesitated. Her gaze darted toward the closed door, then back to Ellie's face. Her lips.

Ellie didn't move, neither toward her nor to step back. She sensed that this had to be Regina's choice since Vickie was part of her professional life and she wasn't sure Regina would be comfortable with any PDAs while Vickie was nearby.

Regina dipped her head. Her warm breath tickled Ellie's cheek, making her eyes flutter shut in anticipation of being kissed.

Oh God, yes. Please.

Regina's soft lips brushed the corner of Ellie's mouth, then slowly retreated.

Ellie blinked her eyes open and forced a smile. It wasn't the kind of kiss she'd wanted, but any gesture of affection with Vickie on the other side of the door—or maybe even watching them through the window—was probably a big deal for Regina.

"See you at work." Regina lifted her hand, hovered in front of Ellie for a few seconds longer, then turned and walked toward her car with her long-legged stride.

"See you," Ellie murmured. She watched Regina get in and, after one last look back and a wave, drive away. Sighing, she turned toward the house.

Crap. She had forgotten to grab her keys and had locked herself out. No way to avoid Vickie now. She knocked twice.

The door swung open immediately. Vickie stood in the doorway with her arms folded. "What are you doing, Ellie?"

Ellie had known she would have to face that question eventually, but she had hoped to have time to discuss it with Regina before it happened. Regina had made it clear she wanted to keep their relationship—if that was where this was headed—out of the emergency department, but surely that didn't mean she was supposed to lie to her sister just because she was an EMT, did it?

"What everyone is always telling me to do," Ellie said with a hint of defiance. "Dating."

"We didn't mean you should date *her*!" Vickie stabbed her finger in the direction where Regina's car had disappeared down the street. "Don't you remember what she said when I asked her if she planned to ask you out for real? She looked as if I'd told her to reach into a bucket of horse poop, and now suddenly, you're dating her? Jesus, Ellie, you'll end up getting hurt. It'll be Chelsea all over again."

Ellie pushed past her sister into the house. "She's nothing like Chelsea."

"Right. She's worse." Vickie rushed after her, grabbed Ellie's shoulder, and pulled her around. "Remember Malik, the newbie on my rig? He used to work with her in LA, and when he tried to talk to her, she acted as if she had never seen him before! She can be a real bitch."

Ellie's hackles rose. "Stop calling her that! You have no idea. You don't know her the way I do."

"Yeah, because she doesn't let people get to know her. That's my point! She'll shut you out and crush your heart."

"That's a risk I'll have to take. But it's my risk to take. Mine!" Ellie thumped her chest and glared at her sister. "And I decided she's worth it, so let me make my own decisions and stop butting into my relationship!" *Crap.* She hadn't meant to call it a relationship quite yet, especially not in front of Vickie, but she wasn't about to take it back.

Vickie's hand dropped from her shoulder. "You feel so strongly about it? About her?"

Ellie pressed her lips together and nodded.

"Now I'm even more worried."

"I know you are. But please, Vickie, don't make it any harder than it already is by confronting her at work."

"Okay, okay, I won't," Vickie said. "But if she hurts you, I'll ambush her in the staff parking lot or something."

Ellie gave her a little shove, partly playful but also with some real irritation. "No, you won't."

Vickie shoved back. "Yes, I will."

With Wally barking and trying to get in on the weird game, they shoved each other through the house until they ended up in the kitchen, where Vickie paused and pointed at the discarded container that had held the lava cake. "Ooh! You got dessert from The Meadow? I thought they didn't do takeout."

"They don't. At least not for us mere mortals. But Regina has her ways."

"She got you dinner?"

"I told you she's nicer than you think."

Vickie drew in a long breath, then blew it out noisily. "For your sake, I hope you're right."

Chapter 25

THE NEXT DAY AT WORK, Regina felt as if she had a neon sign on her forehead, flashing the words *Dating Ellie Fisher* in big letters.

But, of course, that was nonsense.

No one knew. No one *could* know because she was a professional, behaving professionally.

When Ellie clocked in and stepped out of the locker room, Regina was already at work, studying the lab report of an elderly patient, one of their frequent fliers who was in a nursing home after having a stroke.

"Good morning," Ellie said as she walked over.

Regina glanced up, pretending she had seen her only now, even though she'd been aware of Ellie's presence as soon as she had entered the emergency department. "Morning."

The smile Ellie gave her looked exactly like the smile she gave all of her colleagues. Okay, maybe not *exactly* like it, but close enough that it wouldn't be obvious to anyone else.

But Regina doubted that any of her co-workers felt the same buzz of excitement that was coursing through her when Ellie approached.

"Hey," Ellie said, hovering just out of touching distance. "Beth told me Mrs. Dodson is back."

"Yes. This time, it's a UTI. She's dehydrated and running a fever." Very aware of a resident charting at a nearby workstation, Regina tried to sound as if Ellie were any other nurse. "I've admitted her, and now we're waiting for a bed upstairs. Beth already started an IV with fluids and antibiotics before she clocked out, but Mrs. Dodson still seems to be pretty uncomfortable and confused. She keeps trying to climb out of bed."

"I'll go check on her."

"Thanks."

When Ellie walked away, it took all of Regina's considerable self-control to turn back toward her screen instead of watching her.

How disturbing. Regina hadn't expected that she would be the one struggling to focus on her job.

Well, taking care of Mrs. Dodson was part of her job, so it was entirely professional for her to head over to exam room two in ten minutes' time, right? She was checking on a patient after all, not on her girlfriend.

The word made her pause for a second. But yes, that was what she wanted Ellie to be. She wouldn't have broken her number one rule and gotten involved with a co-worker if it wasn't serious for her.

Quietly, she slid back the privacy curtain so she wouldn't scare Mrs. Dodson.

Ellie was at her bedside. She had repositioned the elderly woman, probably to find a more comfortable position for her stiff joints, and was dipping a swab in ice water and moistening the patient's mouth.

Oh, great idea. While the IV would take care of the dehydration, it didn't get rid of the nagging thirst.

Mrs. Dodson had stopped trying to climb out of bed. For the first time since the EMTs had brought her in, a drowsy smile spread across her face, and she looked as if she was peacefully resting instead of being agitated and uncomfortable.

Regina paused half in, half out of the room and took in what Ellie had done for their patient. It was nothing lifesaving, but the little things added up and made a huge difference for Mrs. Dodson's well-being.

If she was being honest, Regina had to admit that she, like any other doctor, might not even have thought of these little things because she was focused on treating the causes of her patient's health problems.

God, she's a fantastic nurse. Regina had always respected Ellie's profession, but never before had she seen so clearly that Ellie had made the right choice when she'd quit med school. As a nurse, Ellie could make a difference for their patients in a way that Regina, as a doctor, couldn't.

Maybe she should tell Ellie about that realization. She had a feeling Ellie needed to hear it. While Ellie was proud of being a nurse, her ex, her parents, and all the other people who had nudged her to go back to med school had left wounds, and Regina wanted to help heal them.

But was it really professional to say something? She had promised herself not to treat Ellie any differently at work just because they were dating. Back in LA, she had worked with an attending who'd been involved with one of the nurses, and he had always given her preferential treatment. Regina had despised it, and she vowed to never be like that.

On the other hand, if she stayed silent because they were dating, she would be treating Ellie differently. It wasn't as if she'd let their personal relationship cloud her professional judgment. Anyone with eyes could see that Ellie was a damn good nurse.

And she would tell any other nurse if they'd done a good job too, wouldn't she?

Okay, she had never done that before. Maybe she should.

God, what was happening to her? Being with Ellie was changing her. Now she was seriously considering complimenting the nurses! What was next? Bringing them donuts and snacks? No way. She would draw the line there.

Mrs. Dodson's eyes drifted closed.

Regina tiptoed backward and quietly drew the curtain shut.

Ellie's favorite break spot was empty when she went outside.

At the end of March, the temperatures hovered in the fifties, but the sun was out, making it feel warmer. The first crocuses and daffodils pushed through the ground in the small garden between two buildings. Even the air seemed to smell differently.

She leaned against a concrete pillar, cradled her paper cup of coffee with both hands, and enjoyed the moment of peace.

When the door behind her opened, she was surprised to see Regina step out from beneath the ambulance canopy. Truth be told, she had secretly hoped Regina might see her slip out and join her so they could have a few minutes alone, but she hadn't thought Regina would actually do it.

"Hey there." Ellie finally allowed herself the kind of smile that she had wanted to give Regina all morning instead of dimming her grin to a collegial level.

"Hi." Regina paused next to her, a cup of coffee in her hand.

At work, Regina didn't wear perfume, but Ellie thought she could still detect faint traces of it. Or maybe she was just imagining it, and what she really sensed were the tumultuous ripples of her own emotions surging through her—her very own whitewater rapids, caused by Regina's closeness.

She studied Regina, who looked as professional as always in unwrinkled, stain-free scrubs. A pen, a marker, and a penlight stuck out of the breast pocket of her scrub top, like soldiers ready to report for duty. She seemed distracted, though, shifting her paper cup from one hand to the other.

"Are you doing okay?" Ellie asked. She reined in the urge to reach out and run her hand along Regina's arm.

"Hmm? Yes. Busy morning."

That wasn't what Ellie had meant. She had wanted to find out how Regina was doing *with them*. Or was Regina so much in work mode right now that the fact that they were dating had faded into the background for her?

Ellie, however, couldn't forget about it for even a second.

Before she could think of a way to ask, Regina cleared her throat. "I've been meaning to tell you something."

Oh no. That sounded serious. Ellie's heartbeat sped up.

"I was watching you with Mrs. Dodson earlier."

Part of the tension drained from Ellie's muscles. Apparently, this wasn't about them; it was about work. "Yeah? Did I miss something in her care?"

"No. Quite the opposite. You made a big difference, not only for her, but for all the patients under your care." Regina glanced into the depths of her coffee, then into Ellie's eyes. A hint of a smile played around her lips as she added, "I guess what I'm trying to say is if I were the bra-throwing kind, I'd throw mine at you because you're great at your job. If you had become a doctor, your patients would have missed out because you are doing things for them that I can't."

A lump lodged in Ellie's throat, and her eyes burned as she struggled to fight down tears. Jesus, what was wrong with her? She couldn't cry at work, just because Regina had been nice and paid her a compliment.

But it wasn't just any compliment. Others had mentioned she was great at her job before, but no one had ever told her that her quitting med school hadn't been a loss—that it had been a gain for her patients. Hearing it from Regina felt like applying ointment to a festering wound. It soothed an ache she hadn't even been aware of.

"You do know you're making it incredibly hard not to throw my arms around you and kiss you, don't you?" she choked out past the lump in her throat.

Regina's gray eyes seemed to warm from the inside out. She hesitated, then reached out and wrapped her hand around Ellie's wrist.

The touch was tender and supportive, and it also reminded Ellie of the night before, when Regina had trailed her fingertips over her wrist in a tantalizing caress.

"Sorry," Regina said with a lopsided smile.

"No, don't be sorry. What you just said…" Ellie's voice ended on a strangled whisper. She pressed her free hand against her own chest. "It means the world to me, especially coming from you."

Before Regina could reply, the door behind them swished open.

Regina quickly let go of Ellie's wrist. She gripped her paper cup with both hands and took a step back. "So if you could get me a urine sample from Mr. Eklund, that would be great, thanks," she said to Ellie as if they'd been in the middle of discussing a patient.

"Oh, um, sure," Ellie got out. Her throat constricted again, but now for a different reason.

The circle of skin where Regina's fingers had rested around her wrist felt cold as she watched Regina give a nod and stride back inside.

Jasmine paused just outside the door and glanced over her shoulder, following Regina's rapid retreat. "She's bothering you about getting a urine sample while you're on a break? And I thought she would go easier on you after you've gone on a few dates. Guess you were right. She was only doing it for a good cause, not because she's interested."

Ellie's shoulders slumped. "Yeah, I guess so." That wasn't it, of course, but what else was she supposed to say? She could barely form words because her head was spinning from the emotional whiplash—flying high after Regina's incredible compliment, then shattering into a million pieces as she crashed back to earth.

Quietly, she finished her coffee, which tasted bitter now, before going back inside. She got a specimen cup and headed to room three to tell Mr. Eklund they needed a urine sample. Hopefully, Regina hadn't just said that to make Jasmine believe they'd been talking about a patient, not having a very private conversation.

When she returned, Regina stood near the nurses' station but didn't look up from her lab report as Ellie passed her.

The night before, she had promised Ellie she wouldn't treat her like a near stranger, and yet that was exactly what she was doing now.

Ellie fought to maintain a neutral expression and not show how much it hurt to be shut out, especially after that tender moment between them. She went to her computer, pulled up an electronic chart, and stared at it without seeing any of the information.

Footsteps approached, hesitant and slow, and Ellie didn't need to turn around to know it was Regina.

"Ellie…" she said very quietly.

Tension knotted Ellie's shoulders. When she looked up, they were more or less alone since Jasmine was on break now. Only a unit clerk was cursing at the printer a few steps away.

Regina took a deep breath as if having to brace for what she was about to say. "I…I think we need to talk." She lowered her voice to a whisper and glanced at the unit clerk, who was still focused on the misbehaving printer. "But not here. Can I come over after our shift?"

We need to talk. Those four dreaded words had never heralded a lottery win, a marriage proposal, or any other good news, and this conversation would probably not be an exception.

Ellie had a feeling she already knew what Regina wanted to tell her: that she had decided she couldn't do this after all and wanted to break up. Deep down, Ellie had been afraid of it coming all day, yet hearing her fears confirmed made nausea swirl through her stomach. "Um, yes, but my sister will be there."

"Maybe you should come to my place instead." Regina lowered her voice even more. "I think it would be better if we had privacy for this conversation."

Ellie's eyes burned. She kept facing the screen to hide her expression from Regina. "I'll be there."

Regina shuffled her feet. "I—"

The dispatch radio squawked with a call from an incoming ambulance. "We'll talk later," Regina said.

Ellie tried not to think about what would happen later. For now, she would take a page from Regina's book and try to forget her worries by focusing on work.

Ellie's stomach lurched as the elevator carried her up to Regina's apartment, and it wasn't because it was moving too fast.

We need to talk. Regina's words had echoed through her mind for the rest of their shift and on the short drive over.

On shaky legs, she stumbled out of the elevator.

Regina was waiting by the open front door, her impassive doctor mask firmly in place. While Ellie had showered and changed into street clothes at work, Regina was still in her scrubs, and maybe that was part of her armor too.

No, this was not going to be good.

"Thanks for coming," Regina said as she led her into the apartment. "Can I offer you something to drink?"

They had shared so many personal things, and now Regina was hiding behind polite small talk. It hurt. Ellie shook her head. She couldn't draw this out for another minute.

Regina swept her hand toward the couch. "Please, take a seat."

Ellie sank down onto one end, while Regina remained standing.

She started pacing—two long steps to the left, an abrupt turn, two long steps to the right. She gestured with both hands as if she was having a discussion in her mind, putting together the perfect words to let Ellie down gently.

But that wasn't possible. They had officially dated for only a day, and yet Ellie knew she would take this hard. Every second Regina remained silent made her even more nervous. "Just say it and get it over with."

Regina stopped pacing. "What?"

"I've always been the ripping-the-Band-Aid-off-fast kind of woman. If you can't do this"—Ellie waved back and forth between them—"and want to break up, just tell me."

Regina's already fair features blanched even more. "What? No! Shit, I really messed up if I made you think that!"

Ellie flopped against the back of the couch as every muscle in her body seemed to turn into an overcooked noodle. "Y-you don't want to break up?"

"No! I want to…you know…talk. And…" Regina dragged in an audible breath. "To apologize." She blew the lungful of air back out. "I know I hurt you, and…I'm sorry."

Still sunk back against the couch, Ellie stared up at her. An apology from Regina Novak. She had not been prepared for that. And Regina hadn't just said it, she looked as if she meant it too. "Wow. I… I know that was hard for you to say, and I really appreciate that you said it anyway. But you know what? I think this time, I'd prefer an explanation."

Regina started pacing again. "I'm…struggling, okay? We agreed to keep this…us out of the ED, and then we touched, and someone saw, and I didn't know how to handle it." The words shot out of her in one long sentence.

"I know this is hard for you, and I'm trying to be patient, but we also agreed you wouldn't treat me like a stranger. It's not like we were making out in the middle of the break room or something. I've touched Jasmine, Beth, and most of my other colleagues like that a thousand times at work."

"Yes, but that's you! I'm not like that. Everyone knows I keep my distance. If anyone saw us touch, no matter how innocently, they would instantly know something's going on between us."

"So?" Ellie shot back. "Would that really be so horrible? As much as you sometimes like to pretend otherwise, you're not my boss, and we would hardly be the first doctor/nurse couple in the hospital. There's nothing in the employee handbook that keeps us from dating. I checked."

"It's not about the damn handbook!" Regina growled.

"Then what is it about? It's not about Amber, is it?" Regina's ex had worked in the same hospital, and the relationship hadn't ended well, but so far, what little Ellie had learned about Amber hadn't made her think that Regina had been heartbroken.

Regina shook her head. "She confirmed my belief that it's better to keep work and my private life separate, but no, it's not about her."

Ellie peered up at her, trying to make sense of it.

Shadows of emotions darkened Regina's eyes, like a churning sea during a storm.

"This is about Riley," Ellie whispered with a sudden clarity. Nothing else in Regina's life had the power to shake her like this.

Regina's jaw muscles clenched and unclenched. She nodded.

Ellie stood, stepped into Regina's path, and took her hands. Wordlessly, she drew her to the couch and pulled her down with her. She didn't let go of Regina's fingers, even though they were clammy. "Tell me."

"It's a long story," Regina said.

"I love long stories if they help me understand you better." Ellie squeezed Regina's hands. "Please."

Regina pulled one hand back to tuck a strand of hair behind her ear but left the other in Ellie's gentle grasp. "When I was little, I was close to my parents—mostly because I didn't want to play with kids my age. I could never relate to them."

Ellie could easily imagine that. "I bet you were trying to boss everyone around even as a toddler." She gave Regina a nudge with her shoulder to show her she was teasing to lighten the mood.

Regina didn't move away, letting her shoulder rest against Ellie's. "Probably. Everyone assumed I would be the boss one day and take over my parents' architecture firm. As a child, I spent a lot of time there, hanging out in one of their offices while they worked."

No wonder Regina didn't know how to relate to her peers. It sounded as if she'd spent most of her time among adults, in a work context—which might be why that was where she felt most comfortable. "I really can't see you as an architect."

"Me neither. Creating drawings of buildings bored the hell out of me, but I only realized that later." The hint of a smile that had played around Regina's lips faded away. "When Riley was born, everything changed. He was born prematurely and was in and out of the hospital a lot—that was when I first became interested in medicine. My mom stopped working, and my dad stopped taking me to work with him. They both focused on him a lot. He got all the attention because he struggled in school, while I was a straight-A student."

Ellie laced their fingers together. "I'm sorry. That's not fair. Is that why you and Riley weren't as close as you could have been?"

"It made things difficult. I wanted to be a big sister to him, you know? And there were moments when we were close, but overall… How can you protect and be there for someone who's already protected and given everything he could ever need by both of his parents?" Regina shook her head. "It left no room for me."

What a lonely childhood that must have been, especially after being close to her parents those first years! Ellie leaned her shoulder more tightly against Regina's.

"It wasn't as great as you might think for Riley either," Regina continued after a while. "He started smoking weed when he was only thirteen and then doing harder stuff a few years later. His entire life quickly became consumed with getting high. My last year of med school, I went home for a visit over Christmas, and he stole my laptop, then lied to my parents about it. And they covered for him. Not once, but again and again. They made excuses for him and gave him money, and when I told them they were making things worse, I was suddenly the bad guy."

There was so much bitterness and pain in Regina's voice that it was hard to listen to. Ellie closed her other hand around Regina's too, cradling it protectively.

"So finally I had enough of all the drama and stopped going home." Regina shrugged as if it were no big deal, but the hoarseness of her voice gave her away. "Easy to do since I was busy with my residency anyway."

Ellie swallowed. For the first time, she understood that Regina hadn't just lost her brother; she had lost her entire family to Riley's addiction.

"I worked long hours, but I didn't mind," Regina continued. "Work was…"

"Your safe place, where your family's problems couldn't touch you," Ellie finished when Regina trailed off. She remembered what Regina had once told her: *Some days, I prefer being a doctor to being a human with feelings.*

Regina nodded. "My area of competency. At least it was—until Riley died. After that, no one looked at me as if I was a competent doctor anymore."

Ellie didn't get it. "Why wouldn't they? Most people on staff have lost someone. Why does that—?"

"Not on their watch," Regina said sharply. "He died in my ED. During my shift. While I was chief resident." She stabbed at her chest with her free hand. "And I couldn't save him." Her voice broke on the last four words.

"Wait, what?" Ellie kicked off her shoes and curled her legs under her so she could face Regina more fully. "You were the one who treated him?"

Regina nodded shakily. "It was a busy night. My attending took over as soon as he became available, but by then, it was too late."

Ellie didn't know what to say. "How did he end up in your ED of all places?" she finally asked one of the many questions racing through her mind.

"I have no idea. I didn't even know he was living in LA. But I should have known. I should have reached out. If I had, I would have caught the infection in time, before he became septic."

Ellie squeezed Regina's hand hard to draw her out of the maelstrom of self-accusations. "No, Regina. That's not on you. He was an addict, and you had every right to protect yourself against that vicious circle."

"He was my brother, and I couldn't save him." Regina hung her head. Her chin-length hair fell forward, covering her expression. "I couldn't even save my reputation as a physician."

Ellie reached over and stroked several strands back behind Regina's ear. Her hand lingered against Regina's cheek. "What do you mean?"

"That night, after my attending had called the code, I broke down." Regina leaned into Ellie's touch, but her cheek was dry, as if she had spent all her tears that night. "In front of all my co-workers. Nothing was the same afterward. Everyone suddenly looked at me with pity."

"Pity?" Ellie echoed. "They were your colleagues, Regina! I'm sure they were looking at you with compassion."

Regina shrugged. "Tomayto, tomahto. They looked at me as if I were fragile and might shatter any moment, not as if I was someone they trusted to save lives. I was vulnerable in front of them that night, and it cost me their respect. Their trust. My safe space. I couldn't work with them anymore." She pulled back from Ellie's caress and searched her eyes. "Do you understand now why this…you…us is so hard on me? Being with you…it makes me soft. It requires making myself vulnerable, and I can't do that at my workplace again."

Ellie struggled to process it all. She clung to Regina's hand because she was afraid to lose that connection. Regina's last sentence made it sound as if she was ready to give up on them, despite saying she didn't want to break up.

No! She wouldn't allow that. Regina had lost her entire family to her brother's addiction; she wouldn't let her lose what they had too.

"That's not true." The words burst out of Ellie without having been planned.

Regina blinked as if the unexpected outburst had shaken her from the haze of grief and self-castigation.

Ellie took a steadying breath, struggling to continue in a calmer tone. "As a wise doctor once told me: Sometimes, you lose a patient, no matter how good you are and how hard you try. You can't save everyone."

"Yes, I said that, but—"

"That fact doesn't change just because the patient was your brother. Your colleagues knew that. They know you can't control everything, even though it's hard for you to accept. If they were looking at you, maybe it wasn't because they judged you or because they were waiting for the moment you'd break down again. Maybe they were simply trying to see if they could help. You just never found out because you walked away. But I'm not going to let you do that. Do you hear me?"

Regina stared at her. Then a noise that sounded like a mix between a sob and a laugh burst from her chest. "Um, yeah, I hear you. Kinda hard not to when you're shouting at me."

Ellie sucked in a breath. Her throat felt raw. *Oh my God.* She had really been shouting at poor Regina, after she had bared her pain to her. "I'm so, so sorry." She let go of Regina's hand and hid her overheated face behind her palms. "I shouldn't have—"

Regina pulled her hands down. The doctor mask from earlier was gone completely, and the emotions in her gray eyes—surprise, amusement, and a deep affection—were as clear to Ellie as if Regina had written them down for her. "No, you should have. You definitely should have. Because I really don't want to walk away from you. From us."

"You don't?" Ellie whispered.

Regina shook her head. Then she leaned toward Ellie and kissed her as if she had run out of words and needed a different way to express herself.

It was nothing like the frenzied encounter in the bathroom or even the kiss from the previous night, which had started gentle, then quickly turned urgent.

This kiss was deep and long and slow—a reassurance that there were good things in life even after all the pain Regina had been through. It was a promise she wouldn't run.

Without interrupting the kiss, Ellie threaded her fingers through Regina's hair, and Regina pulled her closer with both hands until Ellie's curled-under leg rested across her lap.

Even after they broke the kiss, gasping for breath from its emotional intensity, they hovered with their lips half an inch apart and held each other close.

Then Regina dipped her head and buried her face against the crook of Ellie's neck, exactly as Ellie had done to her the day before.

Oh wow. Regina was letting Ellie comfort her, showing her that she could make herself vulnerable with her, at least as long as there were no co-workers around. Ellie's chest expanded as her heart seemed to triple in size. She clutched Regina more tightly against her.

A loud gurgle from Ellie's midsection interrupted the moment.

Regina laughed and slid one hand down, between their bodies, to rub Ellie's stomach.

A hunger of a different kind flared up low in Ellie's belly, but she stopped her hips from rocking against Regina. This wasn't the right time.

Regina crawled out from beneath Ellie's thigh across her lap and pulled her up from the couch. "Come on. You can check if there's any-thing edible in my fridge while I take a quick shower."

Bellies full, they settled down on the couch, this time sitting close.

A bone-deep exhaustion swept over Regina. What a day!

"Regina?" Ellie said after a while.

"Hmm?"

"How do you feel about physical intimacy?"

A jolt went through Regina. Suddenly, she was wide-awake. She turned her head to stare at Ellie. "Now?"

"What?"

"Well, I admit I'm pretty beat, so I might not be up to my usual stellar performance, but I would be lying if I said I wasn't interested."

A flush tinged Ellie's cheeks. "Um, I… That wasn't what I meant. It was a tough day, so I was wondering if you'd like another hug…or a cuddle." Her blush deepened, but she looked into Regina's eyes as she added, "Although I'd also be lying if I said I wasn't interested in witnessing one of your stellar performances. But maybe that's better left for another day."

"Oh. Right." Regina rubbed her own cheek, which felt pretty warm. Not because she was blushing, of course—just because Ellie's words and her sensual tone had made her body temperature skyrocket. "To be honest, I wasn't much of a cuddler in my past relationships. I guess I was too driven, constantly on the go, to sit or lie still long enough."

"Oh. Okay." For a moment, disappointment flashed across Ellie's features.

It was surprisingly unbearable to be the source of that, so Regina added, "But I'm older and wiser now, so…" She stretched out on her back and pulled Ellie into her arms.

With a little sigh, Ellie slid one arm around Regina's hip and settled her head onto the spot between Regina's chest and shoulder. "Older and wiser, hmm?"

"Not that much older, but definitely wiser. At least I was wise enough not to run from this." Regina softly squeezed her. "That wouldn't have happened a year ago."

Ellie tightened her grip. "I'm glad the new you is a person of supreme wisdom, then."

Regina gave a hum of agreement and let her eyes drift shut. Her body buzzed from Ellie's closeness, but other than that, she felt very grounded—not as if she was getting impatient and wanted to escape at all.

Ellie rubbed her cheek against Regina's shoulder as if she could feel the cogs turning in her brain. She didn't try to talk, though.

Regina was grateful for that. She needed a few minutes to wrap her head around the unexpected turn of events. When she had decided she needed to apologize for the hurt she had caused Ellie, no matter how hard it would be for her, she had hoped Ellie would forgive her, but she hadn't thought the day would end like this. She especially couldn't have predicted her spilling her heart out to Ellie, telling her things she had never told anyone.

She had made herself as vulnerable as never before in her life, even before Riley's death, and she hadn't just survived it; she actually felt better. Ellie not only still respected her, she seemed to respect her even *more* for having bared her scars. She hadn't turned her back on Regina but was still here, snuggled against her.

And it felt wonderful.

Ugh. She was turning into a sappy romantic! Regina shuddered in halfhearted disgust.

The movement made Ellie lift her head. She peered at Regina, then at something on the back of the couch. "Who's your friend?"

"I don't have any friends."

"You keep saying that, but I think some of your disc golf buddies qualify as friends. Dylan in particular," Ellie said. "Dr. Vaughn…Kayla could be a friend too, if you'd let her."

Regina firmly shook her head. "It's already hard enough to break my number one rule for you. Making friends with anyone else at work is not in the cards."

"Hmm." Ellie reached up and pulled something from the back of the couch. "I still want to know who this is."

Regina lifted her head to make out the object Ellie was holding up.

It was Fergus. She stifled a groan. *How embarrassing.* Usually, she kept the stuffed animal in her bedroom, but she had moved him to the couch when she'd been cleaning the apartment on Sunday.

"That's a Scottish Highland cow." She aimed for a matter-of-fact tone, as if any reasonable adult kept a plush animal in their living room.

Ellie combed her fingers through his shaggy, reddish-brown coat, then turned him around. "No udder. I hate to tell you, Doctor, but your cow is a bull."

Had she said cow? Getting caught with a stuffed animal had thrown her off-balance. "I know. I've actually got great knowledge of anatomy, so I'm fully qualified to differentiate between an udder and other body parts." She trailed her hand down Ellie's side, gracing the outer curve of her breast.

A gasp escaped Ellie, and she pressed her body even more tightly against Regina's. "Don't think you can distract me with your anatomy knowledge," she said, her voice coming out lower than usual. "How did you get him?"

"Fergus was a gift." Regina cleared her throat. "From my brother. My parents bought him for Riley when he was four, but he insisted that I should have him. So I kept him."

Ellie smoothed an unruly lock of fur away from Fergus's big eyes. The touch held such tenderness, as if she were caressing Regina instead. Then she carefully placed the stuffed animal back where she had found him. "I'm glad you did."

"Mmh."

Ellie tucked her head beneath Regina's chin and made herself at home again.

Peaceful silence fell.

"Regina?"

She had nearly nodded off when Ellie's voice interrupted the stillness of the living room again.

"Hmm?"

"Can I ask you something, or are you all talked out?"

Regina felt as exhausted as if she had run a marathon. Maybe she was too tired to raise her shields, or she no longer had them around Ellie, because she found herself saying, "No, you can ask."

"What about your parents?" Ellie asked quietly. "Are you closer to them now that...?"

"I haven't talked to them since my mom's birthday in January."

Ellie raised her head off Regina's chest and looked at her with wide eyes. Clearly, she couldn't imagine going more than two months without talking to her parents. "Oh. Are you still angry with them? Do you blame them for what happened?"

"Me blame them? No. They enabled him in a way, but I try not to linger on it because I'm sure it would have happened anyway." Regina gently pulled Ellie's head back down so she couldn't see her expression. "They're the ones who blame me."

Ellie's head shot back up. "What? How can they do that? That's so—"

"They didn't come right out and say it. But I can hear it in their voices every time I talk to them. So I mostly don't. Call them, I mean. I'm already beating myself up, so I don't need them to do it too."

Ellie looked down at her and trailed her fingertips over Regina's forehead, making her realize she'd been frowning so hard that a line had formed between her brows. "Well, you were wrong about your colleagues. Maybe you are wrong about your parents too. Maybe they don't blame you at all."

Regina pulled Ellie's fingers away and kissed each of them. "*You think* I'm wrong about my colleagues. I'm not entirely convinced."

"Yet," Ellie added. "And that's okay. Because over time, I can be very…" She kissed the corner of Regina's mouth. "Very." Then the other corner. "Very convincing."

Regina lifted her head and kissed her, showing her with her lips and her tongue and a nip of her teeth how convincing *she* could be. If she weren't so exhausted, she would roll them over, cover Ellie's body with hers, and—

Ellie's phone chirped in the back pocket of her jeans. It was the third text she had received since they'd curled up on the couch.

Groaning, Ellie broke the kiss and leaned her forehead against Regina's. "I bet that's my sister. Again. I'd better get my tired ass home before she sends out the cavalry."

"Have I mentioned that I really…" Regina nipped Ellie's bottom lip. "Really…" Then kissed it. "Really don't like your sister?"

Ellie lightly smacked her shoulder. "Well, you'd better learn to like her."

"Oh, why's that?"

"Because you'll have to make it past her when you pick me up for our date," Ellie answered.

Regina found herself grinning, and it still astonished her that she could do that after nearly breaking down while spilling her guts about Riley. "Are you bidding on me again, Paddle Number Thirty-Three?"

"I never bid on you, Bachelorette Number Twelve," Ellie shot back. "It was—"

"A fly," they said together.

They smiled at each other.

Then Regina sobered. "I'd love to go on a date with you. A real one. But this time..." She leaned closer to whisper into Ellie's ear. "Don't wear flannel."

Chapter 26

A SENSE OF DÉJÀ VU overcame Regina as she got out of the car, headed toward Ellie's house, and walked up the steps to the porch.

At the same time, so much had changed since she had picked Ellie up for their axe-throwing date nearly a month ago. This date was the real deal, without an auction photographer around, and they weren't hiding their attraction any longer.

When Regina rang the doorbell, she squared her shoulders, tugged on her blazer, and braced herself for a confrontation with Vickie.

No barking sounded from inside the house. The door swung open, and instead of her sister, Ellie stood in the doorway.

They had talked on the phone for a few minutes every evening—with Regina slowly warming up to that style of communication—but they hadn't seen each other outside of work in the four days since she had told Ellie about the details of Riley's death.

Seeing Ellie sent a buzz through Regina's body.

Ellie had left her hair down, and it cascaded over her shoulders in soft waves. She wore a long, flowy lavender wrap dress with a sash that tied on the side and a V-neck that showed off a hint of cleavage. It clung to her curves, then swept playfully over her hips. She had paired it with a denim jacket—a combination that was both cute and sexy as hell. A pair of strappy heels—higher than Regina had seen her wear before—completed the outfit.

Regina returned Ellie's joyful smile. "Hi."

"Hi yourself. No flannel." Ellie tugged on her jacket, and her smile turned self-conscious.

"I noticed," Regina murmured. "You look beautiful."

"You're pretty easy on the eyes yourself."

Regina arched her eyebrows at her.

Ellie laughed. "Okay, okay, you look outrageously hot. I admit I have a secret weakness for seeing you in jeans, and don't even get me started on that semi-sheer lace blouse. Happy now?"

"Yes." Regina gave the most regal nod she was capable of while still taking Ellie in. Finally, she tore her gaze away and peeked past Ellie into the house. "Especially since your sister is nowhere to be found."

"She took Wally to the dog park," Ellie said.

"Hmm. I think I finally formed an opinion on dogs," Regina declared with a smirk. "I like them."

Laughing, Ellie gave her a light shove.

Regina nearly stumbled back because she hadn't been prepared for that. She grabbed hold of Ellie's arms to keep her balance, then didn't let go. "What does *The Handbook of Singles Auction Etiquette* say about kisses on the official first date when you've already been on several auction-mandated dates?"

Ellie leaned closer. Her lashes fluttered. "I'm not sure what the handbook says, but the winning bidder definitely votes yes on kisses."

"So does the bachelorette." Regina slid her arms around Ellie, drew her close, and kissed her. She immediately got lost in the softness of Ellie's lips. The murmurs of pleasure that escaped Ellie sent tingles down Regina's spine.

When they finally broke the kiss, Ellie clutched Regina's hips and blinked at her.

"What?" Regina's brain felt addled, so she had no idea what the look on Ellie's face meant.

"Oh, nothing. I just wasn't sure if you would be into public displays of affection." Ellie indicated the house across the street. Its occupants had a full view of the porch.

Regina shrugged. "I don't care what strangers think." It was the opinion of people she knew that she struggled with. She didn't say it, but Ellie's expression revealed that she understood anyway.

"Ready to go?" Regina asked.

Ellie stepped back into the house and grabbed her purse. "Ready. So, where are you taking me?" she asked as she followed Regina to the car. "The Meadow?"

Regina held the passenger-side door open for her. "That depends."

"On?"

Regina dropped her voice to a seductive rasp. "On whether you're going to let me sample your breast."

Ellie sank into the passenger seat as if her legs had given out.

Grinning, Regina closed the door, rounded the car, and got in on the other side just in time to catch Ellie's fading blush.

"What makes you think I'm interested in ordering the breast?" Ellie asked.

Regina ran a finger down the sheer top half of her own lace blouse, pausing at the point where the see-through part stopped an inch above the upper curve of her breasts. "Oh, you're interested." Her voice became lower and huskier with every word. "Very, very interested."

An audible gulp came from Ellie. "Maybe," she got out. "But you know, I doubt they have the breast I'm interested in on the menu."

Damn. Ellie might have just outdone her. Regina shook off the haze of arousal and started the car before she could decide the only place they were going was right to Ellie's bedroom.

The waiter glanced back and forth between Ellie and Regina. "Do you know what you want, or do you need more time?"

Regina looked up from the menu. The light reflecting off the glass candleholder sent a warm glow across her features. "I know exactly what I want."

A shiver went through Ellie. Regina was talking about the food options, she reminded herself, not about wanting her.

Or maybe she wasn't.

Regina was as confident and witty as she had been on all their auction-mandated dates, but one thing had changed: Their banter had a new note. More than just a note, actually. It was full of flirting and innuendo. While Regina had flirted with her every now and then on previous dates, she had released all brakes now. Her looks and comments had kept Ellie's body on a slow boil since Regina had picked her up earlier. How on earth could a woman who was admittedly bad at relationships be so good at flirting?

"How about you?" Regina asked.

"I've known all along. So I guess we don't need this." Ellie closed her menu and handed it to the waiter without breaking eye contact with Regina. "I'll have the chicken breast with mac and cheese and the Parmesan broccoli, please."

Regina snapped her menu shut. "Make that two, please."

"Excellent choice," the waiter said with a nod, then walked away and left them to enjoy their wine and each other's company.

"See? I told you you're interested." Regina's eyes twinkled in the candlelight.

Ellie shrugged, aiming for a casual gesture. "What can I say? If I find something I like, I don't mind eating it again and again."

Regina's gaze heated.

Ellie felt it on her skin like a searing touch.

"Is that so?" Regina drawled.

Ellie nodded and took a big sip of her chardonnay to wet her dry mouth. Then she looked into Regina's eyes and decided not to keep hiding behind flirty double entendres anymore. While she enjoyed the mutual seduction, it wasn't all she wanted. "I'm like that with women too."

A sensual smile curved Regina's lips. "Is that a reference to tongue sex?"

Heat suffused Ellie's cheeks, but she held Regina's gaze. "It's called oral, Regina."

Now Regina was the one who took a gulp of her wine.

"And I meant that I believe in forever," Ellie added.

Regina slowly lowered her wineglass back to the table but didn't respond with a flirty remark. She stared at Ellie without answering at all.

Oh crap. That had been too much, too soon. What had she been thinking? It was their first official date! Even counting the other dates they'd been on, it was much too soon to talk about forever, especially since Regina still had a lot of issues to work through. "In general, I mean," Ellie added quickly.

Someone walked up to their table.

Ellie turned her head, for once glad at the interruption. She expected to see the waiter or maybe even the owner who'd come out of the kitchen to greet them.

Instead, it was Sienna. "Hey, stranger," she said with a broad smile. "I nearly didn't recognize you out of scrubs, all dressed up."

Ellie rose to give her a hug. "Good to see you. Are you having dinner here too?"

"We just did. We were on our way out when I saw you." Sienna pointed at a man waiting behind her. "This is Jason, my boyfriend. Jase, this is Ellie, my friend and favorite ER nurse."

He stepped forward and shook her hand.

An awkward pause ensued, and Ellie knew it was her turn to make the introductions. She hesitated, not sure how to introduce Regina. As Dr. Novak? As a friend? As her date? Sienna worked in the ICU, so she was part of their professional world. How could something so simple be so complicated? Ellie glanced at Regina, hoping for some kind of hint.

The impassive doctor mask was back, and Ellie realized only now that she hadn't seen it all evening. Regina had let her guard down with her, but now her walls had snapped back into place.

Maybe that was her hint. Ellie decided to err on the side of caution. At least now she knew why Regina was struggling to reveal even the tiniest bit of personal information to someone she worked with, so it was easier to respect it without feeling rejected. "Sienna, this is—"

"Dr. Regina Novak." Sienna chuckled and addressed Regina. "You've got a bit of a reputation in the ICU. Um, for always sending up your patients well-cared-for and never exaggerating just to get your patients an ICU bed faster," she added. "Besides, I saw the staff newsletter."

Regina stiffened. It was almost imperceptible, but Ellie sensed it anyway.

"It looked like you two were having fun," Sienna continued. "Those rainbow layer cakes looked amazing. Speaking of cakes... If you're thinking of having dessert, try their lava cake. It's to die for."

A laugh burst out of Ellie, easing her tension. "I know. It's quickly becoming my favorite dessert."

The waiter interrupted by serving their meals.

"We should go. Enjoy your evening." Sienna bent down, kissed Ellie's cheek, and then walked away.

They watched them leave.

When Ellie turned back to face her, a line had carved itself between Regina's eyebrows.

"Who was that?" Regina asked.

"Sienna. CMC's best ICU nurse."

The line between Regina's brows deepened.

"Don't worry. She probably thought this"—Ellie waved her hand to indicate the two of them—"is still an auction date."

Regina picked up her fork and waved it dismissively. "I don't care what she thought."

A small smile formed on Ellie's face. She knew that wasn't quite the truth, but she appreciated the sentiment. Determined not to let meeting Sienna interfere with their date, she picked up her silverware too and took a forkful of the mac and cheese.

It was as creamy and delicious as she remembered.

Regina swirled her fork through the cheddar sauce but wasn't eating. "Did you and Sienna ever…?"

Wow. Regina continued to surprise her. Ellie hadn't thought Regina would pick up on that. For someone who insisted she wasn't great at interpersonal relationships, she had amazingly good antennae. "Um, yeah, kind of."

Regina gave her a skeptical look. "How can you *kind of* sleep with someone?"

"What? No! I didn't"—Ellie lowered her voice—"sleep with her. We went on two dates; that's all."

"Ah." The line between Regina's brows smoothed out. "What happened then?"

Wait! Ellie eyed her. Had that grouchy little line carved itself into Regina's skin not only because Sienna was someone from the hospital but also because she had thought Ellie had slept with her? She bit back a smile. "Then I had fulfilled the two-date obligation as that year's Bachelorette Number Three."

Regina's fork hovered over her plate. "She bid on you when you volunteered for the Heart-to-Heart Auction?"

Ellie nodded.

"So she's bi?"

Ellie nodded again.

"And yet she wasn't interested in asking you out on a real date?" Regina asked.

The note of bafflement in Regina's voice made Ellie grin. "Why's that so hard to believe? I remember a certain bachelorette who insisted she wasn't interested in me beyond our auction-mandated dates either."

Regina studied the broccoli on her plate as if it were the most fascinating vegetable ever. Finally, she glanced up and shrugged. "She lied. To herself mostly."

Ellie wanted to reach across the table and touch her so badly—so she did. She let her fingers hover over Regina's hand and tilted her head in a silent question.

In response, Regina reached up and drew Ellie's hand down, covering it with her own.

"When did you know you weren't as uninterested as you pretended to be?" Ellie asked.

Regina's gaze went out of focus as if she were fast-forwarding through a mental recording of their dates. "I didn't admit it to myself then, but probably during the car ride from the hospital, when you laid into me because you thought I was prejudiced against nonbinary people."

Ellie flushed, yet there was nothing but admiration in Regina's eyes. "That was after our first date!"

"What can I say? You left an impression. Boy, you were fierce." Regina squeezed her hand. "And then incredibly tender when I…"

When she had started to shake all over. Ellie didn't say it so she wouldn't embarrass her. She turned her hand over and stroked Regina's palm.

Regina took a big gulp of wine. Then she made eye contact again. "How about you? What was the moment you knew you wouldn't mind going out with me for real?"

"Well, at the risk of inflating your ego even further, I have to admit I was pretty wowed the first time I saw you. I accidentally dropped an emesis basin."

A pleased grin flashed across Regina's face. "Oh, did you?"

"Yeah. But then you were an arrogant ass, so my initial admiration instantly faded away."

"I wasn't an ass. I was—"

"Nervous."

"Busy surviving my first shift," Regina corrected.

Ellie nodded knowingly. "Right."

They smiled at each other, then withdrew their hands to focus on their meals.

Regina cut off a square of chicken breast and slid it into her mouth. "So," she said once she had chewed and swallowed, "how much did Sienna pay for those two dates with you?"

Ellie firmly shook her head and took a bite of her own meat. "I'm not telling you."

"Come on. Tell me."

"So you can brag about going for more money than I did? Nuh-uh."

"No," Regina said, the teasing tone in her voice now gone. "So I can tell you she didn't pay nearly enough."

Ellie almost melted on the spot. "God, you're so charming when you want to be."

"Yes, and I'm also right. So? How much?"

"If I tell you, will you go do a romantic touristy thing with me after dinner?"

Regina grimaced.

The exaggerated expression made Ellie grin. "What's that grimace for—the romantic part or the touristy part?"

"Take your pick," Regina said. "But all right, we'll go do your romantic touristy thing. How much?"

"Well, you have to remember that back then, we didn't have so many rich donors attend the auction. Most of the people bidding were underpaid and overworked CMC staff."

"How much?" Regina waved in an out-with-it gesture.

"One hundred dollars."

"One hundred dollars?" Regina forcefully put her fork down. "That's insulting! I hope you didn't kiss her good night!"

Ellie smiled. "I didn't."

Regina let out a satisfied huff. "Good."

"She kissed me."

The line between Regina's brows returned. "Even though the auction rules say the dates can stay completely platonic? That's bold!"

"Says the woman who kissed me at the end of our last date."

Regina pointed her fork at her. "Hey, you kissed me."

Ellie had never been able to figure out who had initiated that first kiss in her bathroom, but it probably didn't matter. "You kissed me back."

"Enthusiastically," Regina admitted with a smirk. "So did you kiss her back too?"

"Yeah. Much less enthusiastically, though." Sienna's kiss hadn't made her tingle the way even thinking about kissing Regina did. "We decided we were better off as friends."

"Good." Regina dug into her food.

With a fond smile, Ellie focused on her meal.

It was indeed a bit touristy and pretty romantic.

And actually not that bad, Regina admitted to herself.

They had gotten hot chocolate—the one with real milk—from a coffee shop that was still open and strolled across Crown Center Square hand in hand.

Now they stood not far from where they had ice-skated on their very first date and watched along with about twenty other people, most of them tourists, as the water show started.

Dozens of jets shot sprays of water high up in the air. Some arched up sixty feet, while others spouted lower and gracefully leaped in perfect rhythm with the recorded music of the Kansas City Symphony. The flutes and violins mingled with the gentle splash, and the water sparkled in the light shining up from the fountain's checkerboard-patterned surface.

The chatter of the people around them faded into the background as they watched the water show, still holding hands.

Ellie's lips formed an O, and she looked totally engrossed in the display, whereas Regina found herself more enthralled with her. The spectacle might have been breathtaking, but it paled in comparison to Ellie.

Ugh. Regina shook her head at the sentimental thought. She had never been like this in other relationships. With Amber and other girlfriends, she had rarely taken the time to do romantic things, and even then, she hadn't been fully in the moment, just letting herself enjoy it.

With Ellie, she didn't want to be anywhere else.

Yeah. Sentimental central. Next thing she knew, she would be the one hanging up paper hearts in the ED!

Ellie nudged her with an elbow and gave her a curious look. "Hey, it's over. Did you fall asleep?"

"No," Regina said. "The sugar rush from the hot chocolate kept me awake. Barely."

Ellie laughed. "Oh, come on. The water show wasn't boring at all. Admit it."

"All right. The show I was watching wasn't boring at all." Regina tucked Ellie's hand into the bend of her arm and set them off toward where she'd parked the car before Ellie could ask what exactly she meant.

When Regina placed her hand in the small of her back and walked her to the door, Ellie went weak-kneed. It wasn't only the physical touch but also the intimacy it conveyed. The gesture reflected the connection they had formed, despite the walls Regina surrounded herself with most of the time.

They paused on the porch and faced each other.

No lights were on in the house. Either Vickie had already gone to bed, or she was sleeping over at Brandon's. While her sister claimed they were just friends, Ellie had a feeling Vickie had a co-worker romance of her own going on.

"Thank you for a wonderful evening." Ellie found that she didn't want it to end.

"Thank *you*," Regina replied. "Just for the record, I would have paid a lot more than a hundred dollars for this date."

Ellie melted inside. It was always special whenever Regina revealed how sweet she could be. "I'm not after your money. But I'll accept a kiss."

With a smile, Regina stepped closer. She slid her hands beneath Ellie's unbuttoned denim jacket, settled them on her waist, and drew her closer. Each movement was slow and deliberate, as if she had thought about this moment and imagined it in detail on the entire drive over.

Heat seared through Ellie's dress where Regina's hands rested, and her breath hitched as Regina leaned toward her. Ellie wrapped her arms around Regina's shoulders and eagerly met her halfway.

Their lips touched, softly at first, then with more passion when Regina took control of the kiss. She trailed her tongue along Ellie's top lip, teased at the corner of her mouth, then nipped her bottom lip.

Little jolts of pleasure raced through Ellie. She sank her hands into Regina's hair and pulled her more firmly into the kiss.

Regina groaned and flicked her tongue against Ellie's. She tightened her grip on Ellie's waist and drew their hips flush together.

Being pressed against Regina's incredible body made Ellie's head spin. She felt drunk from Regina's kiss, which affected her more deeply than the wine she'd had with dinner. A shuddering moan passed from her mouth into Regina's.

Abruptly, Regina broke away. In the dim light on the porch, her eyes looked as black as the night sky above them. She kept one hand on Ellie's waist, stroking gently as if to calm her.

But her touch had the opposite effect. Ellie had to clear her throat twice before she could speak. "Do you want to come in for that drink I owe you?" She wasn't ready to say goodbye.

Regina's kiss-reddened lips curled up into a smile. "Oh, so you admit I won the ice-skating race?"

"Ha! No. But you won at axe-throwing, so…" Ellie swept her hand toward the front door.

Regina hesitated. "To be honest, I'm not in the mood for a drink."

Ellie tried not to let her disappointment show. "That's okay."

"But I could come in anyway," Regina added.

Her low, husky voice sent goose bumps down Ellie's body, so it took her a few seconds to grasp the meaning of her words. "Um, didn't you say…?" She had to push through the haze of want to remember Regina's words. "What about taking it slow?"

Regina slid her hand lower and traced circles on Ellie's hip with her thumb. The same desire that burned in Ellie's stomach crossed her features. "Overrated." She searched Ellie's eyes. "Unless you don't wan—"

Ellie pushed upward on her tiptoes and kissed her. "I want," she whispered against her lips. "I want you." Reluctantly, she tore herself away from Regina to unlock the door. Her hands shook with a mix of nerves and anticipation.

When the door swung open and Ellie flipped the light switch, everything remained quiet inside the house—no barking or noise coming from the TV in the living room.

"Mmm, looks like we've got the house to ourselves," Regina murmured only inches behind her. "We should take full advantage."

Visions of Regina taking her on the kitchen counter flared through Ellie's mind, making her gasp.

"You okay?" Regina asked.

Ellie nodded, not trusting her voice. She took Regina's hand and pulled her up the stairs. No kitchen counter. At least not this first time.

As soon as the bedroom door closed behind them, Regina toed off her shoes and dropped her blazer to the floor.

Ellie's jacket ended up on top of it.

Regina reached for her without giving the room even a fleeting glance. Her attention was entirely on Ellie.

"Wait!" Ellie hurried to her dresser, pulled out the top drawer, and grabbed a bra, which she then tied to the doorknob from the outside before she closed the door again.

Regina arched her brows. "Is that your signal for 'don't come knocking because the bed is rocking'?"

Ellie's cheeks warmed. "Something like that. I just realized I could have saved some time by taking off my bra and using it."

"No," Regina said, her voice fierce. "I want to be the one to take it off."

God. The things Regina could do to her with only a few words! "Be my guest," Ellie rasped out, equally proud and amazed that she could form a reply at all.

Regina stepped closer. Slowly, never breaking eye contact, she reached out and untied the sash at Ellie's hip with a single tug.

The front of the wrap dress parted.

Regina didn't push it off her immediately. She stood stock-still as her passionate gaze slid into the gap between the two halves, raking over Ellie's purple lace bra and the matching panties.

Ellie's pulse leaped even though Regina hadn't touched her yet.

"I think you were right," Regina murmured. "I might actually have bra envy." The corner of her mouth quirked up into a half-grin, but a fierce light burned in her eyes, drowning out the hint of playfulness.

"Bra envy?" Ellie's thoughts felt sluggish.

"Mm-hmm. I envy this bra because it gets to touch your skin. Cradle your breasts."

"Let's take it off, then," Ellie got out through a dry mouth. "I wouldn't want you to be jealous."

Regina stepped even closer—so close that Ellie could feel the heat emanating from her. She skimmed her hands inside the parted dress. Instead of going straight for the bra, as Ellie had expected, she trailed her fingertips up Ellie's sensitive sides.

Goose bumps spread over every inch of skin she touched.

Regina swiped her thumbs along Ellie's ribs right beneath the curve of her breasts. Then, with a groan as if she were the one being deliciously tortured instead of Ellie, she moved her hands up and cupped Ellie's breasts through the bra.

Ellie arched into the touch. She had never wanted anything more than to discard that bra, tear their clothes off, and sink onto the bed with Regina on top of her.

As if trying to grant part of her wish, the dress slipped off one shoulder.

Regina immediately pressed her lips to the newly bared skin.

Her hot mouth made Ellie's belly flutter. She reached for Regina, partly to steady herself, partly to drag Regina's blouse from her pants so she could feel her skin too. Eagerly, she slid her fingers up Regina's smooth back. *Mmm*, she felt so good.

The slim muscles along Regina's back twitched beneath Ellie's touch. Regina lifted her mouth off Ellie's shoulder and blinked as if struggling to keep her focus. Her gray irises were thin rings around her wide pupils. She held Ellie's gaze as she rasped her thumbs over her hardening nipples through the lacy fabric.

Stifling a cry, Ellie surged against her. "Regina!"

"Hmm?" Regina bent her head again and nibbled Ellie's shoulder, then the crook of her neck. With her thumbs, she drew circles over the lace, closer and closer to Ellie's nipples until she brushed them again.

Ellie's legs started to quiver. Or maybe it was her entire body. Her hips rocked against Regina's. She slid her fingers into Regina's hair, not sure if she intended to press her closer or pull her away so she could think. "If…uh…if you're not careful, you'll make me come."

Regina's hot breath fanned over her shoulder as she exhaled sharply. "That was the plan."

"Not like this. Not before I get to see you, to feel you too." More than anything, she wanted…needed to feel Regina's skin on hers.

All banter now gone, Regina backed away the tiniest bit. She pushed the dress off Ellie's other shoulder, then guided it down her arms.

The slow drag of the fabric along her oversensitized skin made Ellie shiver. When the dress fell at her feet, she stood in front of Regina in just her bra and panties.

She didn't get a chance to feel self-conscious because Regina drank her in with an appreciative look on her face.

"You're beautiful." Regina's voice held a wondrous note. "So incredibly beautiful."

Ellie's skin warmed beneath the compliment and the intensity of Regina's gaze on her. "And you're incredibly overdressed."

"Why don't you do something about it, then?" Regina asked with a playful challenge in her eyes.

Ellie didn't have to be asked twice. She ached to see Regina…to touch her. Her fingers shook as she tugged the front of Regina's blouse from her jeans and unbuttoned it. For the first time in her life, the urge to rip the top open and send the buttons flying gripped her, but she reined in her libido.

She wanted to take her time and experience every inch of Regina slowly—or as slowly as her growing need would allow.

Finally, the last button came free, and she eased the semi-sheer material off Regina's shoulders, not caring where it landed.

Then she stood and stared. Regina in just a pair of jeans, naked from the waist up, head held high in a confident pose, was the sexiest thing she had ever seen.

"No bra?" Ellie gasped out.

Regina shrugged, making her small, firm breasts rise and fall a bit. "The top of the blouse is see-through, so I can't really wear a normal bra with it, and I couldn't find my strapless one, so…"

Ellie wanted to tell her she didn't mind—in fact, she might hide all of Regina's bras if it meant she would go bra-less—but she couldn't make her vocal cords work. She took in Regina's perfect skin, her rosy nipples, her elegant collarbones, and her athletic shoulders. She wanted to imprint this view on her memory forever.

"As pretty as that bra is"—Regina traced her fingertips over the lace right next to Ellie's nipple—"let's take it off too." Before Ellie could reach around herself, Regina unhooked it with a quick flick of her fingers.

The straps slid down Ellie's arms, and the bra dropped onto the growing pile of clothes surrounding them.

Now Regina was the one staring. She trailed her gaze from Ellie's bare shoulders to her breasts, which were fuller than Regina's. Her tongue darted out to wet her lips.

Ellie's eyes tracked the movement.

When Regina reached out, Ellie caught her hand in her own. *Oh no.* If she let Regina touch her now, it would all be over much too soon. "Not yet. I want to feel all of you."

Their fingers brushed as they reached for Regina's belt at the same time. Finally, Ellie was the one who unbuckled it while Regina tore open the button on her jeans.

"Let me." Ellie reached for the zipper and drew it down. Her knuckle brushed a line down Regina's lower belly, making her suck in an audible breath. Hearing how she affected Regina sent her own desire spiraling even higher.

She dragged Regina's jeans down her incredible legs, stripping her panties off along with them.

Then Regina was completely naked.

"God," Ellie murmured, busy taking her in. "Do you have any idea how gorgeous you are?"

When Regina smirked and opened her mouth, Ellie held up a hand. "Actually, don't answer that." But Regina really was gorgeous. And Ellie was about to make love to her. She nearly couldn't believe her luck.

Then she paused. The words she had just thought reverberated through her brain. *Make love.*

Because that was what they were doing, at least for her. No matter how hot the sex would be, it would be more than sex to her.

The revelation wasn't a big shock. Deep down, she had known for a while that this was where she was heading emotionally.

But telling Regina was out of the question. She was too scared it would make her run. It was better to keep it to herself, at least for now, and enjoy what Regina offered.

And that was a lot.

"Your turn again." Regina traced her fingers down Ellie's side, to the lace at her hip. "These have to go." She slid her fingertips past Ellie's panties, though, down the outside of her thigh. "Mmm, I'm tempted to ask you to leave your heels on because you look hot as hell in them, but I expect things to get…heated, and if there was ever a time I didn't want to end up in the ED, it's tonight."

It was all Ellie could do to control her breathing and not hyperventilate as Regina hooked her fingers beneath the lace and eased her panties down.

When they pooled around her ankles, she kicked off her heels and stepped out of them.

Regina took her in for several moments and muttered something Ellie couldn't make out. It sounded like a string of curses—or maybe a prayer for self-control. Her eyes were hazy with desire. Then, with a sound that rose from deep in her chest, she crushed her lips to Ellie's.

Ellie moaned into her mouth. She stumbled backward without breaking the kiss, and when the back of her knees hit the mattress, she fell onto the bed.

Regina gave her just enough time to slide to the middle of the mattress before she followed her down.

Then they were thigh to thigh, hip to hip, breast to breast. Their hearts pounded in the same urgent rhythm.

Regina pressed her into the mattress with a deep kiss that sent all her senses into overdrive. She slid a long, athletic leg between Ellie's thighs.

A gasp escaped her, mingling with Regina's own as hot skin met Ellie's wetness.

Warmth flooded Ellie's body. She was so turned on already, she could barely keep herself from arching up and rubbing against her until she came. No one had ever made her feel so out of control so fast.

As if sensing Ellie's spiraling need, Regina eased her leg away.

Before Ellie could let out a sound of protest, Regina slid lower in bed and dipped her head. Her hair fell forward, tickling the sensitive skin of Ellie's throat. Then Regina's lips followed. Ever so slowly, she nipped, licked, and kissed a path down the side of Ellie's neck.

Ellie gasped at the feel of Regina's silky tongue against her overheated skin. She rasped her nails up Regina's back, eliciting a hiss, and threaded her fingers into her hair to press her closer. The gentle suction of Regina's talented mouth made her pulse throb.

With her fingers, lips, and tongue, Regina swirled patterns over her neck, then her collarbones as if she couldn't get enough of her feel and taste.

Then the excruciating caresses moved lower. Regina's warm breath feathered across her chest, and Ellie's breasts ached in anticipation of having Regina's mouth on them.

"Regina." She barely recognized her own voice.

But Regina apparently understood the plea in her tone. She slid to the side so she was half leaning over Ellie on one elbow and cupped one breast in her palm. Achingly slowly, she traced her thumb along the sensitive underside.

Ellie shivered with need.

Regina bent her head and swirled the tip of her tongue around Ellie's areola, closer and closer to where Ellie wanted her, until she took the nipple between her lips and flicked her tongue across it.

A jolt of sensation shot down Ellie's body. She tightened her fingers in Regina's hair and bowed her back, pressing herself against Regina's mouth.

Without stopping the slow strokes of her tongue, Regina slid one hand up to Ellie's neglected breast and caressed it. "How do you like it?" she whispered, her breath fanning over Ellie's wet nipple. "Gentle? Or a little harder?" She took one nipple between her fingers and gave it the tiniest twist while scraping her teeth lightly over the other.

A wave of arousal surged through Ellie. "Yes! Both! More!" More of either, as long as she didn't stop.

Regina captured one nipple between her lips and sucked.

Ellie moaned and dug her fingers into Regina's scalp. "Regina, please." As good as Regina's mouth on her breasts felt, she needed more. She was two seconds from sliding her own hand down and touching herself when Regina finally trailed her fingertips down her belly.

The sensual glide took Ellie's breath away.

With her fingertips lingering at the edge of Ellie's damp curls, Regina paused and looked up. As soon as they made eye contact, she smoothed her fingers lower, into Ellie's wetness. "God, you feel amazing," she whispered huskily.

"You," Ellie gasped out, nearly beyond words as Regina ran a finger along each side of her clit. "You…oh!…are the amazing one!"

Regina brushed across her clit with a barely there touch, and then it was all Ellie could do to hang on as Regina took command of her body and caressed her with long, sensual strokes that sent her into a frenzy.

Ellie's heart thudded faster. Her entire world narrowed to the feel of Regina's hands on her. "So good," she whispered, or at least she thought that's what she'd said. She couldn't think. All she could do was to writhe against Regina, looking for more friction.

Regina trailed one fingertip from Ellie's clit to her entrance. There she paused and stared down at her with a fiery gaze. "Yes?"

Ellie nearly came undone. Her entire body tightened with need. "Y-yes!"

When Regina eased inside, the feeling was so intense that Ellie cried out.

Regina stilled, an expression of awe and untamed desire on her face. "Okay?"

Ellie couldn't form words. She nodded weakly.

Regina withdrew and entered her with a second finger, deep and slow, her control perfect.

Oh God. Ellie surged up against her, seeking more contact.

Regina's control shattered. Hunger glittered in her gray eyes as she thrust deeper.

A pulsing heat spread through Ellie.

They moved in unison, faster and faster. Both breathed in the same rapid rhythm.

Pressure began to gather inside of Ellie. She clutched at Regina's head, her back, her butt in an attempt to hold on. She hovered on the edge of ecstasy.

But Regina knew just how to draw it out. She circled Ellie's clit with her thumb while her tongue did the same to Ellie's nipple.

Each sensation built on the last, driving her higher and higher with each of Regina's skillful touches. *Right...there.* Her thigh muscles started to quiver as she bucked up against Regina's fingers.

After one last swipe across Ellie's nipple, Regina surged up in bed and kissed her hot and hard and deep. She drove into her again while rubbing her clit with her thumb.

Pleasure rushed through Ellie. She cried out, into Regina's mouth, and arched up one last time before falling back against the bed.

Regina caressed her softly through her orgasm, prolonging it with whisperlike touches. When Ellie's body stopped shuddering, she gently withdrew her fingers, rolled to her side, and pulled Ellie into her arms.

Ellie slumped against her. Every muscle and every bone in her body seemed to have liquefied. With effort, she dragged her eyes open. She hadn't even realized she'd closed them.

Regina slid her fingers up Ellie's damp neck, into her hair, and kissed her gently, but with a barely contained heat that gave away her arousal.

Ellie sank into the kiss. Words wanted to tumble out—"that was incredible" or maybe "you're incredible," but she feared "I love you" wasn't far behind.

No. She couldn't say it, not when Regina probably wasn't ready to hear it. She would show her instead.

The need to touch Regina and make her feel just as good gripped her. She broke the kiss and roved her gaze over Regina's naked body.

Regina looked like a goddess, effortlessly sexy. Her stunning cheekbones were flushed with color, her hair disheveled from Ellie's fingers, and her skin glowed with a sheen of perspiration. A grin played on her lips—a bit smug, which she had every reason to be, but a hidden softness and a flicker of vulnerability lurked beneath it too. She stared back at Ellie with hooded eyes, and it was such a heady feeling to see the burning desire in Regina's gray irises and to know how much she wanted Ellie… needed her.

Ellie could no longer wait to touch her. She needed to know every part of her. Urgently, she pushed against Regina's shoulder until she rolled onto her back, with Ellie half on top of her.

Regina's body was taut beneath hers. Her skin was smooth and hot as Ellie caressed her jawline, traced the elegant arch of her eyebrows, then kissed the flush on her long neck. Regina's pulse pounded rapidly beneath her lips.

Ellie paused and deeply inhaled her scent, *Whitewater Rapids* mixed with Regina's unique essence. It made her head swim. She kissed her way lower, to the upper slope of one breast.

God, they were works of art. She stroked the smooth skin with the back of her fingers, then filled her hands with both of them.

The nipples hardened instantly beneath her palms.

"Mmm, that feels good." Regina put her hands on top of Ellie's, pressing them harder against herself.

A long groan escaped her as Ellie squeezed softly.

After a few moments, Ellie paused her gentle massage. She had to taste them. Now. She pulled her hands out from beneath Regina's, but Regina didn't remove hers. They remained on her own breasts, squeezing and rolling her nipples.

A new wave of arousal slammed through Ellie. She clenched her legs together and watched the erotic play of Regina's dexterous fingers for as long as she could stand it.

Finally, she pulled Regina's hands away and pressed them to the bed. "Mine," was all she got out before her mouth was on Regina's nipple.

Regina made a hoarse sound deep in her throat. She arched up, pushing her breast into Ellie's mouth. "Ellie!" One of her hands escaped Ellie's grip. She cupped the back of her head as Ellie swirled her tongue around the tight nipple. "Jesus, Ellie!"

A thrill went through Ellie. "I love how you say my name," she whispered. "Do it again." To encourage her, she licked more firmly across her nipple.

"Ellie," Regina groaned in a heady mix of warning, commanding, and begging.

That was even more exciting. "That's the hottest thing I've ever heard."

"I bet you can get me to make even hotter sounds," Regina rasped out, "if you touch me here." She took Ellie's hand that was still tangled with her own and guided it down her body.

The woman truly would be the death of her. "Patience," she said but didn't resist as Regina skimmed their hands down her flat belly.

"Not one of my many skills. Touch me. Now."

With her fingertips grazing dark curls that were damp with Regina's desire, Ellie paused, tilted her head, and sent her a challenging look.

Regina groaned. "Fine. Touch me…please."

Ellie gave her a tremulous smile. She was shaking all over, mostly with the excitement of getting to caress Regina intimately. She had been thinking—okay, more like fantasizing—about this for longer than she cared to admit.

She let her fingertips drift over the satiny skin along the inside of Regina's thigh, which began to tremble. Answering shivers zinged through Ellie as she eased her hand down.

Wetness coated her fingers, making both of them moan.

Regina had been right—that sound had been even hotter. But Ellie couldn't say it; couldn't find the words.

She watched expressions flicker across Regina's face as she started to move her fingers and tried to find out what she liked—soft or hard, slow or fast, circles or long strokes.

Regina's pupils flared wide. All barriers had come down. The raw desire on her face—desire for her—took Ellie's breath away.

She slid two fingers lower and dipped them just inside. "Do you—?"

Regina bucked her hips into Ellie's hand, driving her fingers deeper.

A sharp tingle danced up Ellie's spine. The stunning intimacy of being inside of Regina was overwhelming. "God. You have no idea how this makes me feel."

"I think—mmm—I have a pretty—oh!—good idea." Regina matched her every movement, rising and falling against Ellie in the same rhythm. Her breath came in ragged bursts already.

This might not last as long as Ellie wanted. She twisted her wrist, trying to find the angle that would make Regina moan her name again.

Encouraged by a low gasp, she curled her fingers.

"Fuck! Oh, fuck!" Regina thrust her hips faster.

Ellie's own body responded with a shudder of delight. The sounds of abandon coming from Regina, the way she fisted the sheet was so, so hot.

Regina dug her heels into the mattress and lifted up into each stroke, chasing her orgasm. Her head whipped from side to side, the muscles and tendons in her neck taut, and she squeezed her eyes shut.

"Please," Ellie whispered urgently. "Don't shut me out." She needed to see the look in Regina's eyes the moment she came undone.

Regina's lashes fluttered open.

Their gazes connected, increasing the intensity between them.

On her next thrust, Ellie pressed the heel of her palm against Regina's clit.

Regina drew in a breath between gritted teeth. "Ellie!" Her hips rose one last time, pressing her clit more firmly into Ellie's palm, then her inner muscles clenched hard around Ellie's fingers. A hoarse cry wrenched from her lips.

Ellie stilled and watched in awe as Regina's entire body shuddered.

Regina never looked away, letting Ellie see everything.

Finally, she loosened her death grip on the sheet and pulled Ellie against her. "Kiss me."

Ellie pressed herself against Regina's side, cupped her face with one hand, and kissed her. She reveled in the smooth stroke of Regina's tongue against her own for a while before she broke the kiss to stare down at her. "I have no words for how beautiful you just looked—still look," Ellie whispered against her lips.

Regina lifted one hand and smoothed Ellie's mussed hair back from her face. "Not half as beautiful as you."

Despite all the erotic and deeply intimate things they had just done to each other, a flush warmed Ellie's cheeks. The tenderness in Regina's eyes touched her deeply.

Regina grinned. "Have I mentioned how much I love making you blush?"

"Mm-hmm. You have."

Regina slid her lips along Ellie's jaw, then nipped her earlobe. "But not half as much as I love making you come," she whispered, her breath hot in Ellie's ear. She gripped Ellie's leg, which had come to rest across her thigh, and pulled it up around her hip, opening Ellie up to her as she started to rock her pelvis against her.

Ellie wanted to roll them over, tell her this probably wouldn't work for her, but then Regina smoothed her hands down over her hips and cupped her butt, pressing their bodies together.

A renewed wave of desire slammed into Ellie. Apparently, everything worked for her when she was with Regina.

Chapter 27

REGINA BLINKED HER EYES OPEN and squinted into the morning sunlight that streamed through the gap in the lacy white curtains.

Ellie was still asleep, curled up against her with one leg draped over Regina's, one arm tucked around her, and her hand resting on Regina's chest, right above her heart. She seemed to be trying to touch as much of her as she could while they slept.

The sunlight cast a soft glow over her face, and her features were open and relaxed. Despite the very adult things they had done all night, she slept like a child, deep and peaceful.

An almost physical tug pulled on Regina's insides as she watched Ellie sleep. She really didn't want to analyze what it was.

It had been quite some time since she had woken up in someone else's bed, cuddled against a warm body, but that wasn't the only thing that made this morning different.

No nightmares in which she tried to save Riley but failed. She had slept as peacefully as Ellie, without waking even once. Maybe it was just that she'd been exhausted after several rounds of the best sex she'd ever had. Or maybe the weight of Ellie's limbs across her body and Ellie's head on her shoulder had grounded her.

Now that she was awake, she still felt at peace, yet at the same time strangely unsettled. It shouldn't have been possible to experience these two things at the same time, but somehow it didn't surprise her.

Ellie had made her feel a complex mix of emotions from the very start, when she had sparked a fiery annoyance yet also a grudging admiration, whereas every other co-worker hadn't managed to raise even a blip on her emotional radar.

Now that annoyance had been replaced with something even more complex. Ellie made her feel vulnerable yet safe at the same time—safe enough to be vulnerable. That was the most stunning of all the new thoughts tumbling through her mind.

It was a lot. Too much for this early in the morning. She needed to clear her head. And get some water because her mouth was parched.

Gently, she extricated herself from Ellie's warmth and slipped out of bed.

She stood next to it and watched her for a few seconds—only to make sure Ellie would sleep on. Not because she was a sucker for this woman.

Right.

Ellie wrapped her arm around the pillow and mumbled something but didn't wake.

Regina tiptoed around the bed, gathered her clothes that were strewn all over the floor, and went to the bathroom, where she washed up and got dressed. The top button on her blouse felt a little loose, as if it was literally hanging by a thread, making her flash back to the way Ellie had eagerly undressed her. Her passion had matched Regina's own.

When she returned to the bedroom, Ellie was still asleep.

Regina couldn't find her shoes, so she padded to the door barefoot. Quietly, she opened it, slid out, and closed it behind herself. One of the stairs creaked beneath her, making her freeze.

A "woof" sounded from the living room, then Wally came bounding toward her.

Oh shit. She had forgotten all about him.

Luckily, he was wagging his tail and whining with excitement. The only danger he caused was potentially toppling her down the stairs as he jumped around her, trying to get some attention.

"Shh! Don't wake up Ellie—or Vickie." She really didn't want to deal with Ellie's sister, especially since she was fairly sure Vickie had heard them when she had come home late the night before.

The dog followed her back downstairs. His tail wagged even harder as he paused at the front door, where his leash hung from a hook.

Truth be told, Regina would have loved to snap the leash on his collar and take him outside, where the cool morning air might help clear her head. But her sleepover had been entirely unplanned. She and Ellie hadn't talked about any rights she had around the house—or whether she wanted to have any.

"Sorry, buddy." She scratched his head. "I can't take you for a walk."

Wally bounced and gave an excited bark.

"Shit. I said *can't*!"

A door opened upstairs, and steps approached.

Regina tensed. Maybe it was just her imagination, but she sensed it wasn't Ellie.

"Wally, why the hell are you making such a—?" Vickie paused on the last step, rubbing her eyes. She was wearing only underwear and a long T-shirt.

Of course, the top button of Regina's blouse chose that moment to fall off completely. It clattered to the floor.

Wally ran over to investigate, probably hoping she had dropped a morsel of food.

Quickly, Regina bent over and picked it up.

"I'll pretend I didn't just get an eyeful of your cleavage," Vickie mumbled.

"Then I'll pretend I didn't get an eyeful of your legs. Or notice that huge hickey on your neck."

Scowling, Vickie covered the side of her neck with her hand. "It's not a hickey; it's a bruise."

"Of course. Then I guess there's no way the burly EMT who was a bachelor at the auction will have a matching one on his neck, right?" It was a shot in the dark, but she wasn't as oblivious to the affairs and relationships of her colleagues as she let everyone believe. Just because she avoided getting involved in all the hospital drama didn't mean she hadn't seen the way he looked at Vickie.

"How did you…? I mean, um, I have no idea what you're talking about."

Aha! So she had been right. A triumphant smirk tugged on Regina's lips. "Right. Just like you have no idea where I spent the night. Do we have a deal?"

Vickie dropped her hand from her neck and stared at her. "Are you blackmailing me?"

"Blackmailing? Nah. I would call it a mutually beneficial non-disclosure agreement to ensure our privacy."

Vickie put her hands on her hips. "Do you seriously think I would gossip about my sister's sex life at work?"

Something about her words was like fingernails scraping across a blackboard. The way she'd called what had happened between them Ellie's "sex life" made Regina's hackles rise, even though she wasn't sure she was ready to call it "love life" instead.

Before she could respond, another door creaked open upstairs. "Regina?" Ellie whispered, her voice still rough with sleep.

"I'm here." Regina shot Vickie one last warning look, then walked past her, climbing the stairs.

Ellie stood in the doorway, her dress wrapped loosely around her like a robe and her hair a tangled mess.

The sight of her—equally cute and sexy—made Regina stumble and stub her bare toe. "Ouch."

Ellie rushed toward her. "Are you okay?"

"I'm fine." No way would she admit that her knees had gone wobbly just at a glimpse of her. She limped upstairs and closed the door behind them, shutting Vickie out.

"Let me take a look at your foot," Ellie said.

"It's nothing."

Ellie rolled her eyes. "You doctors really are the worst patients." She pointed at the bed. "Sit."

"You know," Regina said, lowering her voice to a seductive drawl, "if you wanted to get me back into bed, all you needed to do was—"

Ellie lightly shoved her backward, onto the mattress.

Regina blinked up at her. No one else had ever done something like that to her. "Is it wrong of me that I found that totally hot?"

"You did?" Ellie's voice came out breathless. She cleared her throat. "Don't distract me. Nurse at work here."

Regina relented with a smile, crawled up the bed, and held out her foot.

Ellie's fingers were gentle as she cradled her foot. "It's this one, isn't it?" She lightly touched the affected toe. "I think it'll bruise, but it's in normal alignment, not poking out at an odd angle, so I don't think it's broken."

"I told you it's nothing," Regina said.

But Ellie wasn't done with her examination. She slid up Regina's pant leg and palpated her ankle. Then she froze.

"What? I didn't bruise my ankle, did I?" Regina raised herself up on her elbows to take a look.

"No, it's fine. But I just noticed your tattoo for the first time."

"Didn't believe me when I said I have one?"

"That's not it. I just thought I had seen all of you last night." A charming flush rose up the gaping V of Ellie's dress. She traced the leaves of the dandelion curling around Regina's ankle, then followed the seeds blowing away in the wind, scattering across her skin.

A tingle went up Regina's leg. No one but her had ever touched the tattoo.

Ellie paused and leaned down, her face only inches from her ankle as she studied the ink. "Is that…?"

Regina nodded. If you looked very closely, one of the seeds formed the letter R to honor her brother.

Ellie touched her fingertip to it. "Didn't it hurt? The ankle seems like a painful place for a tattoo. So close to the bone, without any padding."

Close to the bone. Regina swallowed. "It did." With everyone else, she would have hated how scratchy her voice sounded. But with only Ellie here to witness it, she didn't mind as much.

Ellie looked into her eyes. "Ah. That was the point, wasn't it?"

Regina nodded again, no longer surprised that Ellie understood her so well. "After his funeral, I got drunk for the first and only time in my life. Or at least I started to. Then I realized I didn't want to feel numb. I had numbed myself to Riley's pain for too long already, ignoring it. So I put the booze away and got this instead." She waved at the tattoo.

Ellie caressed the delicate lines as if stroking away the pain. "Why a dandelion?"

"I don't know. I flipped through the tattoo artist's portfolio, and it just seemed to fit. Because it's fragile, I guess. There one second, then gone." Regina waved her hand at the wind-borne seeds.

Ellie firmly shook her head. "I hate to tell you, but you're wrong."

Regina arched her eyebrows. "I'm wrong?"

Chuckling, Ellie nudged her calf. "It happens every now and then. This is one of those rare times."

"So you're a dandelion expert?"

"Yeah," Ellie said. "I mean, my grandma was. Dandelions were her favorite flowers, so she told me everything about them. That's how I know they happen to be very hardy plants."

Another realization hit Regina: She also didn't mind being proven wrong by Ellie. Especially not because her serious dandelion-expert face was just too adorable. "Hmm. Right. They are weeds."

Again, Ellie shook her head as if she'd been personally insulted. "They are loaded with vitamins and have a lot of medicinal uses. Besides, they're wishing flowers. If you blow on one of the puffballs and make a wish, it will come true."

"Maybe if you wish for more dandelions to sprout," Regina muttered.

Ellie pinched Regina's big toe—which thankfully was not the one she had stubbed. "It's said that when you blow the seeds in the air, they carry your hopes and dreams to loved ones you lost. So I think you picked the perfect tattoo."

A lump lodged in Regina's throat. "That's not why I picked it," she got out.

"Doesn't matter. Some people even believe you're granted one wish for every seed that flies away."

"That's a lot of wishes," Regina said hoarsely.

"You deserve them," Ellie answered, all hints of playfulness now gone. "You deserve happiness, Regina. I didn't know Riley, but I have a feeling he would agree with me. He wouldn't want you to keep punishing yourself."

Regina wanted to tell her that wasn't what she was doing, but she was no longer sure. She had given up an attending position at one of the most prestigious hospitals in the country, and she had all but cut off contact with her parents and left behind mentors who would have supported her career and disc golf mates she gelled with. Maybe some of them had even been friends by Ellie's definition.

Her reasons for leaving had been complex, but maybe Ellie was right, and punishing herself had been one of them. Getting to have a life when she had failed to save Riley's had seemed wrong.

But her attempts to give it all up had brought her here—not only to KC, but to this moment with Ellie.

Maybe dandelions really were magical flowers.

Ellie cupped her hands around the dandelion. "Close your eyes."

"What are you doing?"

"Trust me and close your eyes."

Trust me. Ellie was asking for something Regina would have deemed impossible a few months ago. She dragged in a lungful of air and squeezed her eyes shut.

Ellie audibly inhaled and blew a warm breath across Regina's ankle, making a shiver run through her. "There." She pressed a kiss to it. "Now make a wish."

Regina opened her eyes. "Um, you blew on the dandelion, so isn't it you who should make a wish?"

Ellie held her gaze. A myriad of emotions flickered across the chocolate brown of her irises. "I already made one. But if it's true that you get one wish per seed, there are dozens left for you. Maybe hundreds."

Looking into Ellie's eyes, Regina could only think of one. She gave in. "Okay. Done."

"What did you wish for?"

"Oh no. I'm not telling you. If I do, it won't come true."

Laughing, Ellie tweaked her big toe. "Suddenly, you're a dandelion expert too?"

"What can I say? I'm a fast learner. But if it's true that I get one wish per seed, I've got another one that I'm willing to tell you."

Ellie's hands still cradled her ankle. "Yeah?"

Regina nodded. "I'd really like to kiss you good morning."

A little sigh escaped Ellie, as if she had been granted her one wish. "Well, dandelion wishes have to be taken seriously, so…" She caressed the tattoo one last time, then let go of Regina's ankle and crawled up her body.

Regina cupped her face and drew her mouth down to her own.

The previous night, their kisses had been passionate and demanding. This one felt different. Ellie's lips caressed hers tenderly, communicating something that wasn't urgent desire but just as intense.

Regina didn't think it had anything to do with dandelion magic; there was probably a scientific explanation for it, like where she was in her menstrual cycle, but this might be her favorite good-morning kiss of all time.

A buzzing sound finally made them pull apart, and it took Regina a few seconds to realize it wasn't a ringing in her ears.

It was her phone. The annoying noise came from the floor, where the device must have ended up in their rush to undress.

With a growl, Regina slid out from beneath Ellie and dove for the phone. "Someone better be dying!" she snarled into it without bothering to look at the caller ID.

Then she realized it might be the hospital. Maybe they needed her to cover a shift, and someone actually would be dying if she didn't show up.

"Uh, I might die of boredom while I wait for you." It was Dylan.

"Waiting for me? Why would you be—?" She moved the phone away from her ear so she could glance at the clock. *Damn.* She lifted the phone back into place. "Shit, I'm sorry. I was supposed to meet you for disc golf, wasn't I?"

"Yep," he said. "Twenty minutes ago."

That had never happened to her before. Apparently, it was a day for many firsts.

If she remembered correctly, they had agreed to meet at the Swope Park disc golf course. Ellie's place was actually closer than her own, so she could make it there in ten minutes.

Well, make that twenty. She definitely had to take a shower before she headed out. And kiss Ellie goodbye. Or kiss Ellie while they showered together.

Ellie.

She looked up, and Ellie gazed back at her with understanding in her eyes. "If you have to go, it's okay," she whispered.

She was making it easy for her.

Regina started to pace. A part of her wanted to take the out Ellie offered. She did need some time to herself so she could process what had happened between them. Spending the morning on the disc golf course, where the only emotions she experienced would be triumph when she hit her line and mild annoyance if she didn't, would be like a cooling compress on a fevered brow after the whirlwind of feelings tumbling through her.

But another part of her wanted to stay right where she was. She knew if she canceled, Dylan would ask questions the next time they saw each other. She might have to tell him about Ellie no longer being her not-girlfriend. But she would deal with that when the time came.

"Um, I hate being the person who stands up their disc golf buddy, but I won't be able to make it today. Something came up."

Dylan was silent for several seconds as if she had caught him off guard. "You not showing up for disc golf? Wow. Must be important."

Regina stopped pacing and looked at Ellie. "It is. *Very* important."

The smile spreading over Ellie's face mirrored her own happiness at the thought of staying and confirmed it had been the right decision.

"Guess I'll see you next week, then," Dylan said.

"Thanks. I owe you a beer."

"I'll take you up on that."

They ended the call, and Regina dropped the phone on the nightstand.

"You didn't have to do that," Ellie said.

"I know." Regina went to the bed, where Ellie had reclined while she had waited for her. "Looks like I'll miss my morning exercise today. Can you think of a physical activity that could replace it?"

Heat sparked in Ellie's eyes. "I sure can."

Regina pressed one knee to the bed next to Ellie's body. "Yeah?"

"Mm-hmm. We could walk Wally."

Regina froze above her and sent her a playful glare. "Walk Wally? You would prefer picking up dog poop to getting ravaged by me?"

Ellie looked as if she'd been about to burst out laughing, but at Regina's last few words, her pupils widened, and she licked her lips. "Ravaged?" She gulped.

"Mm-hmm. But if poor Wally can't wait—"

Ellie grabbed the front of Regina's blouse, popping another button, and pulled her down on top of her. "You should keep your foot elevated. I'm sure Vickie will walk him."

"Mmm. Win-win." Regina dipped her head down and nibbled on Ellie's neck, eliciting a long moan. "Because then she won't be able to hear us."

Chapter 28

THE DAY BEFORE, EVERYTHING HAD been easy. Ellie had somehow even made those moments when they had talked about Riley and her tattoo easy…or at least easier.

But now they were back at work, and everything was complicated.

Regina had no idea how to act around her in the ED. The only thing she was sure of was that she didn't want to hurt Ellie again by treating her like a person she barely knew.

But the alternative eluded her. After getting to touch Ellie so intimately, she wasn't sure she could interact casually. She was convinced that if she perched next to Ellie on the desk at the nurses' station and chatted with her, everyone would guess what they had spent the last twenty-four hours doing—and how she had felt doing it.

Her skin itched at the thought of revealing something so personal to her co-workers.

No, that was out. She could barely cope with the situation even while she and Ellie were the only ones who knew.

"Hey, you okay?" Kayla, who had entered the break room without her noticing, startled her out of her thoughts.

Quickly, Regina shoved her mug beneath the coffee machine and stabbed the button. "I'm fine. If I'm walking a bit funny, it's because of my toe. Not because…of other reasons."

"Um, what?"

"My toe. It's bruised. That's why I might be limping."

Kayla glanced down at Regina's feet. "Oh. I didn't notice. I wasn't talking about your toe. You seemed…I don't know…deep in thought."

Regina firmly shook her head. "I'm fully focused." Right. Just not on work. "But it's the first time I squeezed my foot into a shoe for longer than an hour since it happened, and it's not exactly pleasant." That much was true. Kayla didn't need to know why shoes had not been part of the dress code for most of the previous day.

"Do you want me to take a look at it?" Kayla asked.

"No!" Regina realized her voice had been too sharp and added, "Thanks, but a qualified health-care professional looked at it already."

At her toe and every other part of her body. Closely. Repeatedly.

And she really had no business thinking about it at work. She wrenched her mug out from beneath the coffee machine and took a big gulp, even though the beverage was much too hot.

Kayla turned toward Beth, one of the nurses, who sat at the break room table, and pointed at Regina. "She's how the rumors about us doctors being bad patients started."

Beth laughed. "What do you mean, rumors? That's a well-established fact."

So that was how Kayla interacted with the nurses? Regina had never paid attention before. Now she watched closely.

Kayla was grinning as if they were friends and having fun at work!

Regina really wouldn't mind making Ellie smile, even in the ED, but if she did it with her, she would have to do it with everyone else on staff too.

No, thank you. She couldn't see herself doing that. She would have to find another way to assure Ellie she was no longer just one of the nurses to her.

Coffee mug in hand, she crossed the ED toward her workstation.

Ellie was nowhere to be seen. She was probably still in exam three, talking to the stressed-out mom whose ten-month-old was running a high fever. While Regina had already treated the child, the mother needed as much attention, and Ellie was better at calming anxious parents than she was.

Poor Ellie hadn't even had time for a short break since the mom had rushed through the door with the crying baby, much less to go to the cafeteria for a bite to eat.

Hmm. Maybe that was something she could do for her.

Regina reached into the chest pocket of her scrub top and pulled out the blueberry granola bar she had meant to have with her coffee.

She went over to the workstation where Ellie's water bottle waited for her return. If she just left the granola bar, Ellie might not eat it because she would assume it belonged to someone else. She reached for a sticky note on the desk and grabbed a pen from a *Keep calm, I'm a nurse* pen holder.

Now what to write… She couldn't write what she wanted to—*thinking about you*. While it was true, it was also horribly sentimental, and more importantly, no one seemed to respect personal belongings around here. One of their nosy co-workers might read the note, so it had to be work-appropriate.

Just as she had scribbled down a message and was about to stick it on the granola bar, someone walked up behind her.

Hastily, she stuffed the snack and the note into her pocket and put on her best businesslike expression as she turned.

It was Jasmine, Ellie's best friend.

Shit. Did she suspect anything?

Jasmine gave her a curious look.

"Just needed a pen," Regina said calmly, held up the one she had taken from the pen holder, and strode away.

Focus, Ellie told herself for the fifth time since she had sat down to make notes in the electronic charts of the patients she had taken care of this morning.

But that was easier said than done when the scent of *Whitewater Rapids* seemed to linger in the air. It was probably all just in her mind since Regina never wore perfume while at work. Even if she were, she was nowhere near Ellie's workstation and hadn't been all day. So far, Ellie had seen her for all of five minutes since their shift had started.

Well, unless she counted the very vivid flashbacks she was having. Not even mostly to the time they had made love—okay, *several* times, each better than the one before—but to the moments they had spent out of bed.

Ellie had enjoyed those activities just as much as the more intimate ones, whether it had been walking Wally or having a very late lunch at Jalapeños. She had only meant to introduce Regina to her favorite restaurant and had instead discovered that Regina's seduction of the Twinkie paled in comparison to what she could do to cream-cheese-stuffed jalapeño poppers.

Get a grip. Ellie took one hand off the keyboard to fan herself.

Jasmine looked up from her own charting and studied her with a frown. "Are you coming down with something?"

"Uh, no. I'm fine." Ellie quickly lowered her hand back to the keyboard. "Just didn't sleep a lot the past two nights." That much was true. While Regina had gone home at six, Ellie had lain awake most of the night, going over each moment and wondering if the wish she had made on the dandelion would come true.

"Are you sure?" Jasmine asked. "You look a little flushed."

"I'm fine. Just a bit stressed because I'm *so* behind on my charting." That, too, was true, but Ellie still hated lying to her friend. She wanted to shout it from the rooftops and tell everyone the amazing Dr. Regina Novak was her girlfriend.

But Regina didn't want that.

Jasmine finally turned back to her work. She shuffled a thin stack of discharge instructions and leaned forward to grab a pen from her pen holder. "Damn, I keep forgetting that Dr. Novak stole my favorite pen. Same old, same old. It would take an act of God to stop the doctors from stealing our pens."

So Regina had been over here after all, probably while Ellie had been with Mrs. Stevens and her toddler. She wasn't avoiding Ellie, was she?

It hadn't seemed like it earlier, but Ellie couldn't be sure. The doctor mask had been back, and gone was the vulnerable woman who had wished upon a dandelion tattoo with her.

Regina was such a master at compartmentalizing her life. Maybe she, unlike Ellie, had an easy time focusing on work and wasn't thinking about her at all. The previous day and the night before that, Ellie had been sure that the blazing intensity in Regina's eyes had been more than physical desire. Even now, she still believed Regina cared about her—as much as she allowed herself to.

But maybe it was just Ellie who was head over heels, can't-think-about-anything-else in love.

God, I really am. She wanted to groan and bury her overheated cheeks in her hands, but Jasmine was still nearby, so she tried to focus on her chart instead.

It was the medical record of one of Regina's patients, though, so even now, she couldn't escape thinking about her.

She skimmed Regina's notes—then paused.

Oh, great. Now she was imaging erotica instead of diagnostic notes! She shook her head at herself and reread.

But the words were still the same. She hadn't imagined it.

Nipples equally round and reactive, Regina had written.

Ellie grinned. *Oh, really, Doctor?* Obviously, Regina had meant to write *pupils*, but then this Freudian slip of the keyboard had happened. Maybe she wasn't as unaffected and effortlessly focused on work as Ellie had thought.

"You're acting weird today," Jasmine said. "Why are you grinning like that?"

Ellie managed to rein in her smile. She closed the chart and stood. "Because I decided to go get your favorite pen back from Dr. Novak's clutches."

Jasmine pumped her fist. "My hero! I think she took it to her lair... um, office."

Like a woman on a mission, Ellie headed toward Regina's tiny office and knocked.

A muffled "come in" reached her ears.

Ellie's heart beat faster as she opened the door and entered.

It was the first time they had been alone at work since they'd slept together—the first time Ellie could take a moment to drink her in the way she had wanted to earlier.

Regina was flicking through a stack of papers at her desk, which filled up most of her closet-sized office. The pushed-up sleeves of the shirt she wore beneath her scrub top looked far sexier than they should. The slender muscles in her forearms flexed subtly as she twirled the stolen pen between her long fingers, drawing Ellie's attention.

Had scrubs ever looked so good on anyone else? Ellie didn't think so.

She stepped closer to the desk. Good thing the piece of furniture was between them, acting as a barricade, because she wasn't sure she could have kept herself from reaching out to touch Regina otherwise.

Just her hand. Just for a second. Only to reconnect.

But it was not what Regina had said she wanted, she reminded herself. She insisted on keeping their relationship out of the ED, so that's what they would do.

"Hi," she said, much too softly for a co-worker.

Regina glanced up from her paperwork, and her gray eyes warmed almost imperceptibly. "Hi." Her gaze fell on the chart tablet Ellie had grabbed on the way to her office.

For a second, Ellie thought she saw something almost like disappointment on Regina's face before she schooled her features.

Regina pointed at the chart. "Something I need to take a look at?"

Ellie nodded and tried hard not to smile. "Yeah." She pulled up the chart on the tablet and handed it over.

Regina scanned her notes. "I don't get what you're showing me. You don't agree with my diagnosis?"

"I'm sure your diagnosis is spot-on, but there's a tiny detail you might want to correct." Ellie leaned across the desk. Now she was so close that she could feel the heat emanating from Regina. She deserved an award— or at least a pay raise—for not brushing her fingers over Regina's as she reached out and pointed at the line in question. "Nipples. Apparently, your patient—or the person you were thinking of—had very round, very reactive nipples."

Regina's gaze darted to Ellie's face, then down to the chart. "Damn autocorrect! I wrote *pupils*." Almost under her breath, she added, "I think."

Now Ellie could no longer hold back her grin.

Still cursing autocorrect, Regina changed *nipples* to *pupils*, saved the chart, and handed the tablet back. "Thank you for bringing that to my attention."

The words were formal, but the soft look in her eyes was not—and neither was the hint of crimson coloring her stunning cheekbones.

Was Regina blushing? It was the cutest thing ever!

"Stop grinning," Regina grumbled. "It was autocorrect."

"Of course."

"Anything else I can help you with? Or was my embarrassment the sole purpose of this visit?"

That and I wanted to see you, Ellie would have liked to say but didn't. "No, that was all. Oh, I need that pen back because I promised Jasmine I'd go rescue it from your clutches." She gestured at it.

Regina tilted her head. "Clutches?" she repeated with a twinkle in her eyes. She looked as if she wanted to make an entirely unprofessional comment about her clutches but then didn't add anything.

Ellie nodded. "Clutches."

The unspoken words between them seemed to fill the tiny office and make it feel even smaller.

Ellie held out her hand, and Regina placed the stolen pen on her palm. As she withdrew, her fingertips grazed Ellie's skin.

It was an innocent, fleeting touch, yet Ellie felt it down to her toes.

They stared at each other.

If she had a dandelion now, Ellie would wish she could take Regina's hand. "God, this is hard." She dug her nails into her still-tingling palm. "Ugh. Sorry. I didn't mean to say that."

Regina nodded her understanding.

"I guess I will see you later?" Ellie didn't just mean that she would see her in a treatment room or at the nurses' station. She hoped to see her after work, where they could be themselves.

Regina nodded again. "You will."

Ellie slid the pen into her breast pocket and turned to leave.

"Ellie?" Regina called after her.

She turned a little too fast. "Yeah?"

"I…" Regina bit her lip, then reached into her own pocket. "Here." She tossed something at Ellie, who caught it at the last moment.

She squinted at the object in her hands. It was a granola bar. A kidney-shaped sticky note that looked as if it had been stolen from the nurses' station too was attached to it.

Thankfully, Ellie could easily decipher Regina's barely legible doctor's scrawl.

The note said: *Please make sure you eat the five portions of fruit and veggies doctors recommend.*

She stared down at the note, then at the blueberry granola bar and finally at Regina. "This isn't part of a new staff health-care program that hospital admin dragged you into, is it?"

Regina's chuckle sounded embarrassed. "No. This program extends to one nurse only."

Aww. Ellie nearly melted into a puddle of goo. This was Regina's admittedly awkward but super cute way to show her she wasn't just a co-worker to her. Ellie had never wanted to hug someone so much in her life.

"I..." Regina averted her gaze to the documents on her desk. "It's hard for me too," she said very quietly.

Relief slammed into Ellie. So it wasn't only her after all. And Regina was making a real effort to connect and reveal her vulnerabilities. "It'll get easier." She wasn't sure whom she was trying to convince—herself or Regina or possibly both. "We'll figure it out."

Regina nodded.

A sharp rap sounded on the door a second before it swung open, interrupting their eye contact.

Jasmine stood in the doorway. "EMS is coming in with two multi-trauma patients involved in an MVA, one with pelvic injuries and the unrestrained driver with closed head trauma."

Regina's doctor mask slid back into place like a grate rattling down. "ETA?" she asked as she rounded her desk.

"Five minutes."

Ellie's physician-prescribed granola bar would have to wait. She fell into step with Regina as they headed toward trauma bay one.

Chapter 29

"Mom, please," Ellie said for the fifth time. "Would you sit down? It's your day off!"

Her mother shook her head. "It's your sister's birthday, and we're missing a plate."

Vickie rolled her eyes. "No, we aren't. I told you Brandon isn't coming."

Their mother plopped down at the dining room table next to their father but kept shaking her head. "I really don't know why you didn't invite him. We want to meet your new boyfriend!"

"He's not my boyfriend," Vickie said.

Their mom didn't listen. Now she was zeroing in on Ellie. "If you had a new girlfriend, you would bring her home to meet us right away, wouldn't you? Like you did with Chelsea."

Vickie snorted loud enough to outdo an entire herd of trumpeting elephants.

Ellie glared at her. *Great.* Now she was in for an interrogation of epic proportions. "Thanks for throwing me under the bus, Ms. He's Not My Boyfriend; He Just Leaves Hickeys the Size of a Saucer on Me!"

"You're welcome, Ms. We Couldn't Leave the Bedroom Because Regina Had to Keep Her Foot Elevated," Vickie shot back.

Their father looked up from the sugar he was spooning into his coffee. "Regina?" He studied Ellie over the rim of his glasses that he insisted he didn't need. "Is there something you want to tell us, honey?"

Ellie pinched the bridge of her nose. She and Regina really should have had a conversation about what to tell people other than their colleagues, but since Regina rarely talked to her parents and had insisted she had no friends and most of Ellie's were nurses, it hadn't seemed like a priority. Plus the situation between Regina and Vickie was still tense, so Regina would probably run screaming into the night if Ellie even mentioned introducing her to her parents. "I, um, met someone."

"Met?" Vickie echoed. "More like you shelled out a lot of money for her!"

Her mother gasped. "She's a prostitute?"

"It's called sex worker, darling," her father said. "I saw a documentary about that once."

Her dad and his documentaries! Ellie's body temperature shot through the roof. "She's not a sex worker! She's a doctor, for Christ's sake!"

Vickie burst out laughing.

Ellie gritted her teeth. "If you don't stop being such an ass, I'll accidentally forget where I hid your birthday present."

"A doctor?" her father said. "Does she, by any chance, specialize in shoulders?"

"Dad! I told you to make an appointment with an orthopedist to get it X-rayed," Ellie said.

"So she doesn't know a thing about shoulders?" her father asked.

Ellie glared at Vickie before she could open her mouth and tell them that, judging from the sounds coming from Ellie's bedroom, Regina knew a thing or two about a lot of body parts.

"I love you to death, honey," their mother said to their father, "but who cares if she specializes in shoulders? I'm more interested in what she knows about matters of the heart." Then she paled. "Please tell me she's not a cardiologist! One of my cleaning clients is a cardio-something surgeon, and he surgeon-splained the complex process of cleaning toilets to me!"

Ellie and Vickie shared an amused look. They had a couple of cardio-thoracic surgeons like that at CMC.

"No, Mom, she's not a cardiologist or a surgeon." Ellie hesitated but found that she wanted to tell her parents about Regina. She wanted them to understand how wonderful she was, no matter what Vickie might imply. "We actually work together in the emergency department."

"Oh, so you've known her for a while?" her mother asked.

"I thought I did, but it turns out I didn't have a clue. I only really got to know her these past two months."

Their mother put her elbows on the table and leaned her chin on her interlaced fingers to give Ellie her full attention. "So what's she like, your doctor?"

Just hearing her mother refer to Regina as hers made Ellie feel warm all over. "I don't even know where to start." She waved her hands as she searched for the right words to describe Regina. "She's confident and vulnerable, totally no-nonsense at work but surprisingly playful when it's just us, and she has the driest sense of humor, the most amazing cheekbones, and the most beautiful eyes I've ever seen."

An indulgent smile spread across her mother's face. "Either you're dating a supermodel, or you're head over heels for this woman!"

Vickie shrugged. "Well, she *is* hot; I'll give her that."

The doorbell rang.

"I'll go." Ellie jumped up, only too happy to escape her family for a moment.

Regina resisted the urge to shuffle her feet on the porch. She still wasn't sure this had been a bright idea. Maybe she should have called first or at least texted, but she hadn't wanted to appear too needy or overeager to see Ellie on their first day off after three long shifts. This way, she could play it off as an "I just happened to pass by" thing.

The door swung open, and Ellie stood in front of her in stretchy, black leggings and a fuzzy, pink sweater that made Regina wonder if it was as soft as it looked.

"Regina, wow! I mean, hi!" Ellie beamed and grabbed hold of the door as if she would topple over otherwise. "What are you doing here?"

Regina waved her hand toward where she had parked two houses down since all spots at the curb in front of Ellie's place had been taken. "Oh, I was just in the neighborhood, heading over to Swope Park to play a round of disc golf, and when I passed your house, I thought I would drop by and see if you are interested in a lesson."

She congratulated herself on doing a stellar job at sounding totally casual, but judging by Ellie's awed expression, she wasn't fooled for a second. She knew the decision to share other parts of her life was a big deal for Regina.

"I'd really love to, but…" Ellie glanced back over her shoulder. "It's Vickie's birthday, so we're having cake with our parents."

The sharp sting of disappointment surprised Regina. It wasn't that she had wanted to be invited to Vickie's party, but she had looked forward to spending the day with Ellie. "That's okay. Another day, then. Enjoy the time with your family." Quickly, she took a step back.

"Wait!" Ellie leaped after her and wrapped her fingers around Regina's arm, keeping her from retreating farther. "You could come in and meet them."

"I'm not sure that's a good idea." Regina pointed at her golf pants. "I'm not exactly dressed for it, and you barely told me anything about your—"

"Is that Regina?" a female voice hollered from inside. "Ask her in, Ellie! Tell her we want to meet her!"

Regina peered past Ellie into the house.

Ellie's parents, whom she had glimpsed from across the street at the St. Patrick's Day parade, were sitting at the dining room table, craning their necks to see around Ellie and check her out.

"Mom, she can hear you—and so can half the neighborhood." Ellie drew the door all but shut, leaving only a tiny gap and blocking her family's view.

"You told them about me? About us?" Regina wasn't sure how she felt about that.

"I had to. Vickie ratted us out." Ellie studied the porch tiles, then looked back up at Regina. "But also… I wanted to. My parents have always embraced my being a lesbian. I never hid my relationships from them, and I didn't want to start now."

Regina got it. She had never been in the closet either, but for her, that meant letting people assume whatever they wanted, not sharing details about her private life.

"Was that okay?" Ellie asked quietly. "I know I should have discussed it with you first, but I didn't get a chance. My mom's like a dog with a bone when she thinks there's something we're not telling her."

Christ, now she was making Ellie feel insecure. "It's fine." She squeezed Ellie's hand that still rested on her arm. "I want to keep us and work separate, but that doesn't mean I expect you to lie to your parents."

"Oh," Ellie said in a tone as if she hadn't quite known that.

Shit. Regina squeezed her hand harder. She should have talked to her sooner. "You're my girlfriend, Ellie, not my dirty little secret."

"Girlfriend, hmm?" Ellie's eyes shone with happiness, even as her voice shook.

"Hey." Regina ignored the people on the other side of the door and drew Ellie into her arms.

Ellie buried her face against the crook of Regina's neck and hugged her tightly.

Regina's stomach knotted. For the first time in her life, a relationship really mattered to her, and yet she was creating a mess. "I…uh…I'm sorry this—me preferring to keep things separate—is so hard on you," she whispered into Ellie's hair.

Ellie nuzzled closer. "It's okay. I understand."

But to Regina, it wasn't okay at all. She wanted to say she would do better, assure her she would change, anything to not hear that quiver of hurt and insecurity in Ellie's voice anymore, but she wasn't sure it was a promise she could keep.

Someone cleared their throat from a few steps away.

Quickly, Regina ended the embrace but kept one arm loosely wrapped around Ellie, hoping it was the parent-appropriate thing to do.

A short, barrel-chested man of about sixty stood in the doorway. His bald head was slightly sunburned, as if he had worked outside and forgotten to wear a hat. He smoothed a hand over his neatly trimmed beard and regarded her through a pair of dorky glasses. "I've been sent out to lure Regina in with promises of cake."

Regina met his gaze, trying to act as though being introduced to her girlfriend's parents were an everyday occurrence. "What kind of cake?"

A broad smile crinkled his face. "Cheesecake. My mother's recipe."

Damn. Now she couldn't refuse to come in without insulting Ellie's beloved grandmother.

"Could you give us a minute, Dad?" Ellie said.

"You can kiss her inside," her mother called from the dining room. "We don't mind."

"We're not kissing, Mom," Ellie called back. "We're talking." She pushed against her father's sturdy shoulder. Once he had relented and stepped back inside, she turned toward Regina. "I'm sorry. I love my family, but they can be a lot. I'd understand if you don't want to come in."

Ellie kept doing that—offering her an out, and Regina didn't like what it said about herself. She didn't want Ellie to think she would run if she felt cornered. "And miss your grandmother's cheesecake? Never."

"In the interest of full disclosure: It's Grandma's recipe, but my dad made the cake. He's been going through her old cookbook since he cut back on the hours he works for Mom."

So her father was an employee at his wife's company? There was so much she still didn't know about Ellie and her family. Regina shrugged. "I'll take my chances."

Beaming, Ellie took her hand and led her into the house. "They'll probably pester you with a ton of questions, but please don't feel you have to tell them anything you're not comfortable with, okay?" she whispered.

Great. The tension in Regina's muscles increased with every step.

A big, attractive woman in her late fifties rose from the table. She was an inch or two taller than her husband and greeted Regina with a huge smile. The silver parts of her thick, salt-and-pepper hair contrasted with her chocolate-colored eyes that immediately reminded Regina of Ellie's. "You must be Regina. It's so nice to meet you."

Regina let go of Ellie's hand to offer it to her mother. "Nice to meet you too, Mrs. Fisher."

"Oh, please. I'm Lois." She ignored Regina's outstretched hand and pulled her into an embrace.

Regina stood frozen in her exuberant grip for a second. Then she returned it, not wanting her to think Ellie had to make do with a girlfriend who was a bad hugger.

Once Lois let go, Ellie's father shook her hand with as much enthusiasm. "And I'm Clark."

Regina met his handshake with equal pressure. "Nice to— Wait! You are Lois and Clark?"

They nodded with big grins.

"We were obviously meant to be." Lois and her husband gazed at each other as if they were newlyweds.

Ah. No wonder Ellie had a romantic streak a mile wide. Part of Regina's tension eased as she laughed. "Lois and Clark…" She gave Ellie a teasing nudge. "Does that make you Supergirl?"

Ellie leaned against her side. "Only if you are Lena Luthor."

Her closeness and her flirty tone sent a shiver through Regina.

Ellie's parents gave them puzzled looks.

"Sorry," Ellie said. "Lesbian inside joke. They're a popular pairing among *Supergirl* fans."

Her parents chuckled, and it seemed entirely genuine.

So they really were comfortable with Ellie's sexual orientation—unlike Regina's own parents, who had struggled with it the first few years.

Regina finally turned toward Vickie. "Happy birthday." For Ellie's sake, she strove for a friendly tone.

"Thanks," Vickie answered but looked less than enthusiastic to see her.

Well, the feeling was decidedly mutual. "I had no idea it was your birthday, or I wouldn't have shown up empty-handed." Not that she knew what to get Vickie. A muzzle or a gag maybe. She allowed herself to indulge in the fantasy for a moment.

"It's fine," Vickie said. "I didn't expect a present from you. Let's all sit down and have some cake."

Ellie steered Regina to an empty chair next to her, right across from Vickie at the long table, while her parents sat at either end.

Vickie took her time cutting the cake. Her parents studied Regina with the thoroughness of two investigators examining a crime scene.

"Say, Regina, do I know you from somewhere?" Ellie's mom finally asked. "You look familiar. Did we meet at the CMC staff-and-family barbecue last summer?"

CMC had a staff-and-family barbecue? It took all of Regina's considerable self-control not to scrunch up her nose. That sounded like her personal nightmare. "I don't think so. That might have been before I started working at CMC. But you probably saw me at the St. Patrick's Day parade."

"Oh, that's right!" Lois clapped her hands. "You were the one not wearing green."

"What can I say? Really not my color," Regina said.

Ellie energetically shook her head. "I disagree. You looked totally cute with a green lip after our baking class date."

Lois smacked the table with both hands, making the plates rattle. "Wait! You were Bachelorette Number Twelve? So that's why Ellie paid money for you!"

"They thought you were a high-priced call girl," Vickie said with a grin.

Regina shrugged. "I'm not. But it's always good to have career options."

Lois's booming laughter filled the dining room. She reached across the corner of the table to pat Ellie's shoulder. "You were right, honey. She has a wonderful sense of humor."

So they had talked about her before she had shown up. What else had Ellie told her parents about her? Regina took a bite of the cheesecake Vickie deposited on her plate so she wouldn't have to say anything.

"So, Regina," Ellie's father said between forkfuls of cake, "I hear you're an ER doctor."

Regina gripped her fork more tightly. She wasn't eager to discuss the fact that she was working with Ellie. Reluctantly, she nodded.

"Stop it, Dad!" Ellie said. "I know where you are going with this. Regina doesn't want to spend her day off giving you medical advice about your shoulder."

Oh, he wanted medical advice? Regina's grip on the fork loosened. She could do that. Giving medical advice felt a lot safer than being asked about their relationship. "It's fine. I don't mind. So, your shoulder is giving you trouble?"

"It is. When I press here"—he put his fingers on his rotator cuff—"or move my arm, it hurts like hell. It's getting so bad that I can barely lift my arm, and the pain even wakes me up at night. What does that sound like?"

He expected a diagnosis when all he had given her was two sentences, without even letting her examine him? Not that she wanted to. "Well, I could make a guess, but have you asked Ellie what she thinks?"

Everyone's gaze turned to Ellie.

"Because that's the first thing I learned in medical school," Regina continued before he could answer. "The nurses usually know the patient best—and this nurse certainly knows you, so in this case, I'd defer to her."

Ellie's fingers found Regina's leg beneath the table and gently squeezed, nearly making Regina hit her knee as her muscles jerked. "Of course I checked out his shoulder."

"And what was your verdict?" Regina asked.

"My money is on calcific tendonitis." Looking at her father, Ellie added: "Calcium deposits that built up in the tendons of your rotator cuff."

Regina rubbed her chin as if having to think it through even though that had been her best guess too. "Hmm, that sounds plausible. You should make an appointment with an orthopedist to get it X-rayed, Clark."

"Like I told you to," Ellie added.

Clark held up the hand on his good side and regarded her with a proud smile. "All right, you were right. You would have made a fantastic doctor." He turned toward Regina. "Did you know she was admitted to med school?"

Ellie's hand on Regina's leg tensed.

"Yes, I know," Regina said. "Thank God she had the courage to quit."

"Thank God?" Ellie's father echoed.

Her mother grinned. "Oh, you mean because otherwise, her career might have taken her down a different path and you might have never met?"

"No. I mean because I think Ellie is much happier as a nurse and because the world would have missed out on one of the best nurses I've ever worked with."

"One of the best?" Ellie's tone was challenging, but her eyes gleamed as if she was tearing up at Regina's blatant appreciation.

Regina slid her hand beneath the table and covered Ellie's fingers on her leg with her own. "Okay, *the* best." With a nod in Lois's direction, she added, "And, of course, I'm also glad because Ellie and I otherwise might not have met."

Clark toasted them with his coffee mug. "So the hospital is fine with you dating? I know working for your significant other can be tricky."

"Hey!" His wife threw a crumpled-up paper napkin at him, and it bounced off his bald head.

Clark picked it up before Wally could get to it. "Not speaking from personal experience, of course, since my wife is the best boss ever."

"Regina is not my boss, Dad," Ellie said.

He blinked. "She isn't? But isn't that how the hospital hierarchy works? Doctors, then residents, then nurses?"

Ellie sighed. She dug a raisin out of her cheesecake and nudged it around her plate with her fork. "No, Dad. I work *with* Regina, not *for* her. We are part of the same team, but my supervisor is a nurse."

Regina studied her closely. Her father's assumption about nurses being below doctors in the hospital hierarchy bothered her. No, it hurt her. And there was something else in Ellie's expression—something Regina would have missed a few weeks ago, but now she was sure it was there. It looked like an emotion Regina was overly familiar with: guilt.

But before she could be sure, Clark nodded and said, "Oh, so you're considered more like co-workers, and no one can say anything against you two dating?"

"No one can say anything because they don't even know they're dating," Vickie said.

Dammit. That was the last topic Regina had wanted to come up in a conversation with Ellie's parents.

Ellie tossed her fork onto her plate. "They don't know because it's none of their business—just like it's none of yours!"

Vickie's fork clattered onto her plate too. "Like hell it's not! It's my business because I care about you and don't want to see you hurt!"

Their parents looked back and forth between them like spectators at a tennis match.

"If you cared about me, you'd respect my choices." Ellie's voice vibrated with anger. "You don't see me confronting Brandon just because he doesn't declare his love for you in the middle of the ED, do you?"

"That's different!" Vickie shot back. "Brandon and I are on the same page. Neither of us is sure if this is something we want to pursue, so we decided together to just be friends for now. It was a mutual decision, not one of us forcing it on the other!"

Ellie jumped up so fast that her chair screeched across the hardwood floor. "You know what? I think it's time for presents. Why don't I help you bring down the boxes Auntie Helen, Uncle Rob, and the cousins sent?" Not waiting for a reply, she grabbed Vickie's arm and dragged her up.

It dawned on Regina that she would be alone with Ellie's parents in a few seconds. *Hell, no!* She didn't want to find out if Clark had X-ray vision or freeze breath, like his namesake, or would employ other methods to interrogate her. More importantly, Vickie's problem was with her, not with Ellie, so it was on Regina to stop this bullshit once and for all. She got up and blocked their path. "Why don't I help your sister? You stay, finish your cake, and enjoy your time with your parents."

"Um…" Ellie hesitated.

"Let me do this, please." Regina directed Ellie back toward her chair, then strode past Vickie toward the stairs leading to the second floor. "Coming?"

"I don't actually need any help bringing down the boxes," Vickie grumbled.

Regina sent her the kind of look that made even third-year residents come to attention like new recruits. "Oh, yes, you do."

Wally, who had jumped up to follow Ellie and her sister upstairs, scrambled back beneath the table with a low whine as if sensing the tension.

Vickie stomped up the stairs behind her.

Regina sighed. So much for having a discreet discussion. She wrenched open the first door she came to—Ellie's bathroom—dragged Vickie inside, and closed the door behind them.

Okay, not the best choice of locations, but she wanted to get this over with. "If you have a problem with me, why don't you come right out and tell me instead of upsetting Ellie with those passive-aggressive comments?"

"Fine," Vickie snarled back. "I have a problem with you!"

Regina would have loved nothing better than to put Vickie in her place, cut her down with a few acerbic words, but she reined herself in. Vickie wasn't an EMT nosing into her private business; she was Ellie's sister trying to protect her. Intimidating her would only end up hurting

Ellie. "Look," she said, keeping her voice low and controlled with herculean effort, "I get it. I'm a big sister too." She clenched her fists behind her back. *Was* a big sister. But she couldn't bring herself to say it in front of Vickie, so she pushed on. "If someone said what I said and then turned around and dated my sibling, I wouldn't be happy either. But when I acted like I'd never want to date her for real, that had nothing to do with Ellie."

"It had *everything* to do with Ellie!" Vickie's face went crimson. A vein pulsed at her temple. "You basically slept with her, then asked her to call you Dr. Novak and act like it never happened the next day! You're dismissing her as not good enough, like her shitty ex did! How can you pretend that doesn't affect her?"

Cold fury swept through Regina. She grabbed hold of the sink with one hand, not even sure if it was to keep her balance or to stop herself from strangling Vickie. "That's not what—"

"Yes, it is! What do you think it does to Ellie that you deny your relationship as soon as you enter the ED? That she has to lie to her work friends? You're hurting her, you asshole, and you don't even get it! Or maybe you do, and you just don't care."

"I care! I care about her a lot, okay?" Regina hurled the words at her like a spear. "I might even—" She cut herself off at the last second.

Only their harsh breathing interrupted the sudden silence.

"You might even?" Vickie prompted, her voice now very quiet.

Love her. Shit. Regina's knees turned to mush, and she sank onto the closed toilet lid. When had that happened?

"Regina?" Vickie tapped the tiles next to Regina's feet, indicating that she was still waiting for a reply.

No way would Regina finish that sentence. She wasn't ready to admit it, not to Ellie and certainly not to Vickie.

"I care," she repeated. Even that admission felt as if she were trapped in a nightmare in which she showed up at work naked. "And I'm sorry I'm not the kind of partner who can shout it from the rooftops in front of the entire hospital staff. I know she deserves that, but I just… I can't."

Vickie stared at her.

Regina's stomach churned, and for a second, she feared she was going to puke. Two apologies, an admission of failure, and a near love declaration on the same day! What the hell was happening to her?

Vickie gave her a nod, but before she could say something, a staccato of footsteps pounded up the stairs.

"Regina? Vickie?" Ellie sounded alarmed. Maybe the sudden silence from upstairs had scared her.

Regina got up from the toilet lid. "We're here."

Ellie wrenched the door open. Even though she was shorter than either of them, she stood in the doorway like an avenging angel and glared at her sister with fire in her usually gentle eyes. "I swear to God, Vickie, if you don't stop laying into Regina, I'm going to move out and never talk to you again!"

"Whoa!" Vickie held up both hands. "Calm down, sis. We talked and—"

"You mean *shouted*. We could hear it from downstairs."

"We talked and made up, okay?" Vickie said.

Ellie eyed her skeptically. "Really?"

"Really."

Ellie looked at Regina, who tilted her head in confirmation and said, "Really." Not that Vickie had said anything after Regina's near confession, but a nod would do for now.

"All right." Vickie clapped her hands. "Now can we go and get my presents?"

Head still spinning, Regina followed them out of the bathroom.

Once again, they stood on the porch, with the door nearly shut and Ellie's family on the other side.

Ellie reached out and touched Regina's hand. "I'm sorry. I never would have asked you to come in if I'd known it would go like this."

"Um, you think it went badly?" A look of alarm broke through the doctor mask Regina had put on for most of the visit.

Ellie interlaced their fingers. "No, no, it went great. My parents took to you like polar bears to snow. I'm sorry about Vickie being an ass at first."

"It's okay," Regina said. "I have a feeling things will get better from now on. I think we've come to an understanding."

Ellie eyed her. "What happened? You didn't threaten her with sharp medical instruments, did you?"

"No." Regina bent to scratch one of Wally's floppy ears. "I, um, apologized."

"You apologized?" Ellie tugged her back up so Regina would look at her. "What for? She was the one who kept making snide comments!" Her blood still boiled when she thought about it.

"Yes, but I get it. It's a big sister thing."

Ellie sensed there was a lot more Regina wasn't telling her about that conversation, but she wouldn't pressure her. "Are you sure you don't want to come to dinner with us? We're going to Jalapeños."

A grin relaxed the tense muscles of Regina's face. "Tempting, but jalapeño poppers aren't as much fun if I can't show off my sexy tongue skills."

Heat swept up Ellie's neck and into her cheeks. "Shh, my parents are probably straining their ears to listen in." She put one finger against Regina's lips and then—because they were so incredibly soft—took her hand away and pressed a gentle kiss to them instead. "So you're not coming with us?"

"No." Regina returned the whisper of a kiss. "I really need some time on the disc golf course."

Ellie nodded. Obviously, Regina had a lot on her mind, and that was where she went to clear her head, so Ellie wouldn't try to talk her out of it. "Can I call you later?"

"I'd love that." Regina kissed her, more firmly this time, then hurried down the street toward her car.

Ellie craned her neck and watched until Regina disappeared from sight. Even though the situation between Regina and Vickie might improve now, a knot sat in her stomach and wouldn't dissolve.

Something had thrown Regina completely off-balance, and this time, Ellie had a feeling it had nothing to do with Riley.

Chapter 30

Two hours later, Dylan did a victory dance around the last basket of the course. "Yes! Winner!"

Regina rolled her eyes. "You only won because I couldn't focus worth shit."

He studied her in the light of his headlamp as they picked up their backpacks and strolled toward the nearby parking lot. "I noticed. Lots of stress at work?"

She huffed. "I work in an emergency department. What do you think?"

"Yeah, but you always work there, so it can't be that. Is it…Ellie?"

Regina couldn't help tensing. She had called him to come play a glow round with her to escape thinking about her feelings for Ellie, and now they were right back at that topic. "No. Ellie's fine."

"She sure is."

"Hey!"

Dylan laughed. "Don't worry. I was just trying to see if I could get a rise out of you—and I could. So what's up with you two?"

She bristled at him. "Nothing is up. We're just…" She unlocked her car and tossed her backpack onto the passenger seat. With her back to Dylan, she continued as casually as possible, "Dating."

It was quickly becoming so much more than that, but she wasn't ready to admit that. Talking about something so private with a disc golf buddy made her skin itch with unease.

"Yes!" He let out a cheer. "I knew it."

"Calm down," she grumbled and turned to face him. "Nothing to get bent out of shape over."

He looked her in the eyes, probing. "No?"

Shit. Was she getting transparent? "No," she said loudly, as if that would make it true. "Meet me for a glow round tomorrow, and I'll show you who's out of shape."

"All right." He followed her around the car. "Tell Ellie I said hi."

Regina sighed and decided not to protest and say she wouldn't be talking to her tonight because that would be a lie. "Will do." She climbed behind the wheel and pulled the door shut with more force than necessary.

Just as she was about to start the engine, her phone rang in the front pocket of her backpack.

Oh, was that Ellie already?

It took her several seconds to unzip the backpack and pull out the phone. She hurriedly swiped her finger across the screen before the call could go to voice mail.

"Phew. Nearly missed you," she said into the phone. Then she realized her words could be mistaken for an admission of missing Ellie even though they had been separated for only a few hours. "Um, I mean, I nearly missed your call."

Only silence answered.

Shit. Was it not Ellie after all? "Hello?" she asked sharply. "Who's this?"

Just when she was about to check the screen for the caller ID, someone cleared their throat. "Your mother."

Regina's heart slammed against her ribs. She couldn't deal with this. Not when she hadn't prepared a topic to talk about so they could avoid talking about Riley. "Hi, Mom. How are you and Dad doing?"

"We're good. How are you?"

"Good too."

They were a bunch of liars, of course, and suddenly, that was hard to take after spending the day with Ellie's family, who spoke their minds and rarely held back their emotions.

"How's the Dwyer building coming?" Regina asked when the silence stretched too long.

"Um, we finished that in February."

"Oh."

Her father's voice in the background interrupted another awkward silence.

"Your dad wants to know how the weather is in Missouri," her mother said.

Regina opened her mouth to tell them about the sudden drop of temperatures they'd had today. What came out instead was "Did you ever think it was my fault?"

Shit, shit, shit. Why had she asked that? She really didn't want to know the answer to that question. Her fingers hurt as she clenched them around the phone, struggling against the urge to press the *end call* button.

"Um, the weather in Missouri?" her mother asked.

It was tempting to confirm that was what she'd meant, but did she really want to make small talk with her parents for the rest of her life? Maybe it was finally time to face the music and ask the question, no matter what the answer would be. At least then she would know. "No," Regina got out. "Riley's death."

Her mother gasped as if she had touched a live wire. "W-Why would you ask that?"

"Because I need to know." Ellie had planted a tiny kernel of doubt—the possibility that her parents might not have blamed her after all—in her mind, and without her realizing, that tiny seed had grown into a faint hope.

Like a goddamn dandelion seed.

"God, honey, no. Why would we blame you? Just because you were there when he was rushed to the hospital that night doesn't mean it was in your power to save him."

"But that's the thing, Mom. I wasn't there." Again, the words shot out of Regina's mouth beyond her control. "I wasn't there for him all those years before that night. Or the weeks leading up to it when I could have done something about the infection."

"No," her mother said. "Don't put this on yourself. We were there. Every time he relapsed, every time he had to go to court—we were there, lending him money, taking care of his responsibilities... And now I can't help thinking maybe you were right."

"Right about what?" Regina's voice scratched like a needle across an old record.

"You always said we were enabling him. Making things worse," her mother whispered. "And now I can't help thinking you might have been right to blame us."

A tremor ran through Regina's arm that held the phone. "Blame you?" she echoed. "I never blamed you."

"If that's true, why did you cut us out of your life?"

"What? I didn't! I just… I couldn't bear to hear the unspoken accusations in your voice, so I stopped calling."

Her mother's quiet sobs reverberated through the phone, mixed with her father's alarmed voice. "Whatever you thought you heard, it's not true," her mom choked out. "We only ever blamed ourselves."

Regina slumped against the driver's seat. "Maybe we should all stop doing that. Blaming ourselves. Addiction… It's a disease. It's not something we caused or made worse." The doctor in her knew that, at least when it came to her patients struggling with addiction. But now, for the first time, she started to believe that it was true for Riley and them too.

Her mother sniffled. Paper rustled, then she blew her nose. "I know you're right."

"Of course I am. I'm a doctor," Regina said mostly to stop her mother from adding a *but*. There were still too many *buts* swirling through her own mind, and she knew it would take time to silence them all and fully believe she wasn't to blame in any way.

For the first time, she wanted to get there instead of continuing to punish herself.

Her mother's shaky laughter drifted through the phone. Then she sobered. "Come home. For a visit. We want to see you."

Regina hadn't thought she would ever return to California, not even for a visit. "I will. But not yet." She needed the chaos in her head to settle a bit before she felt ready to do that. "Maybe for Dad's birthday this summer."

Perhaps she and Ellie could take a week off and do the touristy thing in San Diego.

The thought gave her pause. Never before had she taken for granted that she and her current girlfriend would still be together in four months, and yet visions of taking Ellie to the beach or strolling through Balboa Park hand in hand danced through her mind.

"We would love that," her mother whispered.

Regina didn't know what else to say. "All right, Mom. I need to go now. I'm in the car."

"Drive safely, honey."

"Will do." She ended the call and sat staring through the windshield into the falling darkness for quite some time.

Ellie sat in her car and stared across the street at the Washington Irving Apartments.

On a whim, she had gotten an order of churros to go before they had left the restaurant. Their heavenly scent filled the car, but she was no longer sure if it was a good idea to deliver them. Maybe she should give Regina some space and call her instead, as she had promised.

She reached for her phone and tapped Regina's contact.

Regina answered on the first ring. "Hey. How was dinner?"

"Hmm, you were right—not as much fun without you there to seduce the lucky jalapeño poppers."

Regina chuckled.

It sounded strange, though. Was she merely tired, or was more going on?

Before Ellie could ask, an ambulance rushed by, its sirens blaring.

"Where are you?" Regina raised her voice to be heard. "I swear I just heard the same siren through the phone and through the window."

Heat climbed up Ellie's neck. "Um, in front of your building."

"What the hell are you doing down there? Come on up!"

Ellie hesitated. "Are you sure? I don't want to—"

"Come on up, or I'll come get you!"

Grinning, Ellie grabbed the bag from the passenger seat and jumped out of the car. She pressed the button on her key fob and glanced back to confirm the car was locked as she hurried across the street.

A minute later, she arrived at Regina's apartment, where Regina leaned against the doorframe in pajama pants and a tank top. "Well, well, well," she drawled. "What a surprise!"

"Good surprise or bad surprise?" Ellie asked.

"Great surprise, considering you come bearing gifts." Regina pointed at the bag in Ellie's hand.

Ellie tried to imitate Regina's characteristic eyebrow arch. "Just because of the churros?"

"No," Regina said, her tone softening. "I'll also never say no to a good-night kiss."

That seemed to be a message—one Ellie was glad to hear. Still, she couldn't help teasing her. "Never? So you accept kisses from random strangers?"

"Only from Ellie Fisher. I'm a picky kisser. Now come in before the churros get cold." Regina hooked her finger behind the belt of Ellie's jeans and pulled her into the apartment.

Ellie followed her into the small kitchen and watched as Regina heated up milk in a saucepan. Her hips swayed and her pajama pants slid lower as she whisked in cocoa powder, chocolate chips, and sugar, revealing several inches of bare skin that drew Ellie's gaze.

Finally, Regina garnished two mugs of hot chocolate with marshmallows—its package as new and unopened as the cocoa powder, as if she had bought the ingredients just in case Ellie came over.

Ellie bit back a grin. If only the ER staff knew prickly Dr. Novak had a core as soft as a marshmallow!

Regina carried the mugs over to the coffee table, while Ellie followed with two plates and the bag.

They sat on the couch, thighs touching, and Ellie instantly decided this was the best part of her day.

Eagerly, Regina dug into the white plastic bag, pulled out a Styrofoam container, and flipped open the lid. "Um, that's not churros."

"I brought you some jalapeño poppers too. Sorry—they don't go with the hot chocolate."

"Says who?" Regina bit off half the fried chili, then washed it down with a sip of hot chocolate before pulling the churros from the bag and wolfing one down.

"Didn't you have dinner?" Ellie asked.

Regina shook her head. "Didn't have an appetite earlier."

"I'm really glad I stopped by, then."

Regina looked up from her food. "Me too."

Aww. Ellie leaned against Regina's shoulder, sipped her hot chocolate, and nibbled on a churro while she watched her eat. "My parents really liked you," Ellie said once she had finished her churro. "They wouldn't shut up about you during dinner."

"Yeah? Despite that shouting match I had with their oldest?"

Ellie laughed. "I think that's what impressed them most." She let go of the mug with one hand to caress Regina's leg. "But you know what impressed me most?"

A grin flashed across Regina's face. "The way my butt looked in my golf pants?"

"That was definitely impressive. But actually, it was the way you deferred to me when my father asked for advice on his shoulder. What you said about me being happier and achieving more as a nurse really made them think." Ellie took a sip of hot chocolate, then added quietly, "They told me how proud of me they are."

Regina paused with a jalapeño popper halfway to her mouth. "They don't normally tell you that?"

"Oh, they do. But it's been a while. Not since I quit med school."

Regina stared at her. "What?"

The outrage in her voice felt good, but she didn't want Regina to judge her parents. "You have to understand where they're coming from. Both of my parents come from very modest backgrounds. My mom started out as a cleaning lady and my dad as a landscaper. They worked hard their entire lives to give me and my sister every opportunity they never had growing up. I've never seen them as happy as when I told them I got into med school. When I dropped out..." Ellie swished her mug and watched the marshmallows swirl around before glancing back up. "I know they were disappointed, and I struggled with feeling guilty for years. If I'm completely honest, I think my parents were the main reason I went into medicine in the first place."

Ellie clutched the mug more tightly. She hadn't meant to reveal that. She had never told anyone—hadn't even fully admitted it to herself.

Regina wiped her hand on a paper napkin, intertwined her fingers with Ellie's, and squeezed gently. "Then I'm really glad you quit and followed your own dream, not your parents'."

"Yeah, but that's what I realized tonight: Me being a doctor wasn't their dream. Me being happy was. They just didn't fully understand that being a nurse is what makes me happy." She glanced into Regina's eyes. "Or at least part of it."

"Hmm." Regina pushed her plate back, even though there was a half-eaten churro on it.

Oh no. Had Ellie's implication that Regina was part of what made her happy been too much, too soon?

"Looks like it was an evening for parental revelations," Regina finally said. "I talked to my mother today."

"Oh my God! You let me ramble on about my parents when you talked to yours?"

Regina firmly shook her head. "You were hardly rambling, and of course I want to know what happened between you and your parents."

But Ellie was much more interested in what had happened between Regina and her parents right now. "What did yours say?"

Regina looked down at their intertwined hands resting on her leg. "That they don't blame me for…for Riley's death. Never did, apparently." Her voice was so low and raw that Ellie had to listen hard to understand. "They thought I stopped calling because I was blaming them."

Ellie rubbed Regina's thigh with the back of her hand. "I'm so glad you finally talked and cleared that up. You already carry a big enough burden, without thinking they are blaming you too. But maybe this can be a start to you letting go of that feeling of guilt. Maybe it can even help you realize your colleagues weren't judging you either."

"Hmm. Maybe." Regina's expression—open and vulnerable so far—shuttered.

Clearly, she wasn't ready to consider it. That would take time, and Ellie was determined to be patient and be there for her, no matter how long it would take.

"Be right back." Regina got up and carried their plates to the kitchen.

Ellie followed with the empty containers. Not that Regina really needed help with the dishes, but Ellie enjoyed every second they spent together.

"You aren't working tomorrow, are you?" Regina asked as they washed their hands side by side.

"No. Thank God. You?"

"I'm not working, but I have to go in to give a lecture for our residents," Regina said.

"Oh." That probably meant she shouldn't overstay her welcome. Ellie tried not to let her disappointment show.

But before she could suggest she leave, Regina pulled her back to the couch and wrapped one arm around her.

Ellie snuggled against her side and let her head sink onto Regina's shoulder.

Regina ran her fingers through Ellie's hair again and again.

Mmm, that felt incredibly good. Ellie's eyes drifted shut.

"Ellie?"

"Hmm?" Ellie opened one eye and peeked up at her.

"Do you want to stay the night?" Regina asked quietly.

Ellie's heart seemed to leap with joy. "I don't have pajamas with me." The words escaped her lips without any involvement from her brain. Why on earth was she finding reasons not to stay when she really, really wanted to?

The tiniest smirk curved Regina's lips. "You won't need them. I was so hungry that I devoured the jalapeño poppers and didn't get a chance to demonstrate my awesome oral skills on them. Want to stay and help me prove them?"

Ellie held back the enthusiastic "yes!" that wanted to pop out. "Um, I never thought I would ever say no to that, but...no."

A look of disbelief spread across Regina's face. "No?"

"You just ate a bunch of jalapeños, so that's probably not a good idea."

"Right." Regina chuckled. "I like spicing things up in the bedroom, but not like that. Hmm, we might have to improvise, especially since I used my hands to eat them. Do you like sex toys?"

"Yes!" Ellie scrambled up from the couch so fast that she nearly hit her shin on the coffee table. It wasn't the promise of hot sex—okay, not *only* that—making her so eager to stay; it was mostly getting to hold Regina all night.

Smiling, Regina took her hand and led her to the bedroom.

Chapter 31

"Any plans for your days off?" Kayla asked once Regina had finished discussing all the patients whose care she was handing over.

Regina shrugged the way she always did when co-workers asked about her private life. "Sleep."

It was the truth. After three twelve-hour shifts in a row, she felt as if she could hibernate for a couple of months. Kayla didn't need to know that she might not be the only one holing up in her bed. If Regina got her wish, Ellie would follow her home instead of heading to her own place to sleep.

Vickie and her partner passed them with an empty gurney. "Regina," she said with a nod.

Regina nodded back. "Vickie."

It was the second time they had seen each other since Vickie's birthday nearly a week ago. Their interactions weren't exactly warm and fuzzy, but the tension and snide remarks were gone.

Kayla's head swiveled back and forth between Regina and Vickie's retreating back. "What was that?"

"What was what?" Regina asked.

"She called you Regina, and you didn't rip her head off!"

"I wouldn't rip it off. Too much energy needed. I would sever it cleanly with a scalpel."

"But you didn't! You called her by her first name too!" Kayla still stared after Vickie. Then she whirled around, her eyes wide. "Oh my God! A week or two ago, she had a giant hickey, and now she's giving you secretive looks and calling you *Regina*! Are you two involved?"

"No! You know I don't..." Regina bit her lip.

"Don't...what?" Kayla prompted.

Shit. Now she had to finish her sentence, but she felt like the lowest scum on earth as she mumbled, "Don't get involved with people I work with." She peered toward exam three, where Ellie was finishing up with her last patient of the shift.

At least the room was at the other end of the ED, where Ellie couldn't overhear, but it barely made Regina feel better. She walked toward the locker room, hoping to shake Kayla, but her colleague followed.

"Why did she give you that conspiratorial look, then?" Kayla asked.

"That wasn't a conspiratorial look. Maybe she has indigestion."

Kayla squinted at her. "Indigestion?"

Regina entered the code for the locker room door into the keypad. Just as she was about to escape, a commotion broke out behind them.

Loud shouts cut through the background noise of beeping monitors and coughing patients. Metal crashed, then sneakers squeaked across the linoleum as two nurses sprinted toward one of the rooms.

Neither of them pushed a crash cart, though, or called for help with a code blue.

"Code gray, ED," a disembodied voice came over the PA system. "Code gray, ED, room three, STAT."

Thoughts raced through Regina's mind at a thousand miles an hour. Code gray meant a combative or violent person. It was a call for security, and they had been dispatched to room three—where Ellie was!

Regina whirled around and hurtled toward exam three in an all-out dash, ignoring the rule she had been taught as a medical student: no running in the ED. Her heart pounded as loudly as her footsteps.

The curtain was already pushed open, so she could see into the room before she came to a stop.

Droplets of blood sprinkled the area around the empty bed. Ellie was sprawled on the floor at the other end of the room, with her back against the wall, clutching her arm.

Regina's first instinct was to rush toward her, but two of the nurses were wrestling with the patient and barely managed to restrain him. He was on the floor, shouting and kicking and trying to punch them.

She hurried over and tackled his legs before he could kick one of the nurses. "Get me two milligrams of lorazepam," she shouted at Kayla, who ran in after her. That would hopefully calm him down.

Two security guards charged in, and one took over Regina's hold on the patient's legs.

Regina used her new freedom to administer the lorazepam. While she impatiently waited for the sedation to kick in, she tried to catch a glimpse of Ellie, but the security guards blocked her view. As soon as the patient's eyelids started to droop, she jumped up on shaky legs. She couldn't wait a second longer to rush to Ellie's side. Her colleagues could handle his transfer from floor to bed and then fix the restraints on him.

Adrenaline pumped through her as she raced to Ellie.

Jasmine had already helped her up. She wrapped an arm around Ellie and led her from the room.

The urge to shoulder Jasmine out of the way and take over gripped Regina, but she reined it in. If she wasn't careful, everyone would start to suspect she had a very personal interest in Ellie's well-being.

Jasmine assisted Ellie to sit on a treatment bed, then waved at their chief resident. "Dr. Collins, would you—?"

"Thanks," Regina said sharply. "I've got this." She jerked the curtain closed and went to Ellie's side with several long strides.

Ellie was pale and her pupils wide, but Regina couldn't tell whether she was hurt or it was from the shock of being attacked.

"What happened?" Regina asked. "Does anything hurt?"

"He became agitated and tried to get out of bed. I was worried he'd rip his IV out, so I told him to stop." Ellie grimaced. "He threw the IV pole at me."

"Jesus!" Regina sharply sucked in air through her gritted teeth. "Did it hit you?"

"No," Ellie said. "I managed to jump back, but I slammed into the wall."

Regina struggled not to let her anger and concern show. She was Ellie's physician right now, not her girlfriend—especially since Jasmine was hovering next to them, watching her every move.

She stared at Regina with the same look on her face her colleagues in LA had sported after Riley's death—as if Regina was two seconds from losing it.

"Did you hit your head?" Under the pretense of palpating her neck and head, Regina cradled Ellie's face. Everything felt normal, but Ellie's pulse was pounding. Or maybe it was her own.

"No, just my elbow." Ellie tapped the arm she'd been clutching earlier.

"Can you move your arm?"

"Yeah." Ellie demonstrated. "Doesn't hurt. I think I just skinned it when I slid down the wall." She turned her arm and craned her neck so she could see her elbow.

Blood stained the long, white sleeve of the shirt Ellie wore beneath her scrub top.

Calm down. It's only a skinned elbow, Regina told herself. This wasn't anything like the night Riley had died. But her heart refused to slow its fast beat.

"Can you take this off so I can check it out?"

Both Regina and Jasmine reached out to help Ellie pull her scrub top over her head at the same time.

Frowning, Regina withdrew her hand and let Jasmine help. It would look weird if she insisted because Jasmine was Ellie's friend, while everyone assumed she was only one of the doctors Ellie worked with.

Regina turned away under the pretense of washing her hands and putting on gloves so Jasmine wouldn't see how hard she was gritting her teeth.

Finally, Jasmine and Ellie managed to free her of both tops.

Regina barely registered the sensible white cotton bra Ellie wore; she was focused on scanning Ellie's arms and back for any injury she might have sustained when she'd hit the wall.

The only thing she could make out was an abrasion on her elbow. Blood oozed from it, but it wasn't spurting or dripping down her arm. Regina saw much worse on a daily basis, and yet her stomach felt queasy. She couldn't stop thinking about what could have happened if Ellie had stood closer to the patient or hadn't jumped out of the way.

"I'm fine." Ellie looked as if she wanted to slide her fingers into Regina's hair to soothe her. "I've been kicked, hit, grabbed, scratched, and spat on before. Most nurses have."

"That doesn't make it right." The words broke out of Regina in an angry burst. "You—any nurse—getting hurt while doing their job is unacceptable. I'll have a word with hospital admin about it."

Jasmine stared at her. Then she shook her head. "Good luck with that."

"So, what's the verdict, Doc?" Ellie asked. "No need for stitches, right?"

"No," Regina said. "You're in luck. I know how much you hate the business end of a needle."

Jasmine's gaze drilled into her.

Shit. She wasn't supposed to know details like that about a co-worker.

"Who doesn't?" Ellie said lightly, saving her butt.

"Not me." Jasmine opened a gauze pad and glanced at Regina. "I can handle this. No need for you to stick around for a simple abrasion. I know you're off the clock already."

Regina didn't back away from the treatment bed. "It's fine. Might look better on the incident report to have a doctor do this."

It was complete bullshit, especially since she had assessed the wound and declared it harmless already, but she didn't wait for Jasmine to protest. She placed a sterile gauze pad over the wound and applied pressure with her palm for a minute to stop the bleeding. "But if you want to leave, feel free," she told Jasmine. "I think your shift ended ten minutes ago too."

Right now, she wanted nothing more than for Jasmine to leave them alone so she could wrap her arms around Ellie and make sure she really was okay.

"No way," Jasmine said. "I'm staying." She winked at Ellie. "In case you need someone to hold your hand."

Ellie laughed. It sounded shaky. "Thanks."

Acid burned behind Regina's sternum. She wanted to be the one to hold Ellie's hand, but she knew she had only herself to blame for the fact that she couldn't.

Carefully, she cleaned the area with a saline solution, just in case there were any fibers from the shirt stuck in the wound, then gently blotted it dry with another piece of gauze. She applied a thin layer of antibiotic ointment before covering it with a non-stick dressing and a self-adherent Coban wrap to hold the dressing in place. "All done."

Ellie put her scrub top back on but didn't bother with the white shirt since its sleeve was blood-soaked. She slid off the treatment bed and sent Regina a smile. "Thanks, Doc."

Regina yanked off her gloves and followed her to the nurses' station, where Ellie filled out an incident report.

Apparently, word about the incident had spread through the hospital like wildfire.

By the time Ellie was done with the report, several nurses, residents, CNAs, and RTs had gathered around her. She got a hug here and a soft squeeze on the shoulder there.

Regina watched it with very mixed feelings. On the one hand, she hated the attention when all she wanted was to slip out of the hospital with Ellie and take her home. On the other hand, it was great to see their colleagues shower Ellie with support and care. No one looked at Ellie as if she were weak just because she still seemed a bit jittery from the scare. There was nothing but compassion on all the faces surrounding Ellie.

Regina didn't want to think about whether her former colleagues in LA had looked at her the same way. Not now.

"I'll go get your bag from the locker," Regina said to Ellie.

But Jasmine held up her hand. "Not necessary, thanks. I'll get it. I need to grab my own before I take Ellie home anyway."

Regina waved her away. "I'll drive her home."

"Nonsense," Jasmine said. "I'm sure it'd be a detour for you. Why would you do that when Ellie's place is practically on my way home?"

Regina shoved her hands into her scrub pants pockets so no one would see her clench her fists. "Because...um...I'm sure I have the better car."

Jasmine put her hands on her hips. "So now we need a luxury limousine to chauffeur someone with an abrasion?"

"Stop it! Both of you!" Ellie waved her hand between their faces, interrupting their heated stare-off. "I didn't hit my head. I can drive myself home."

Jasmine shook her head. "You had quite the scare. I'm not letting you drive, so don't even try." She held Regina's gaze. "I'm her best friend. I'll drive her home."

"And I'm—" Regina bit her lip hard before the words could slip out.

She should just give in and let Jasmine take Ellie home. By the time Regina had showered at home, Jasmine would hopefully be gone, and she could head over and keep an eye on Ellie for the rest of the day.

Ellie gave her the tiniest nod as if sensing her thoughts and telling her it was okay to let Jasmine take her home.

But it wasn't. Why the hell did she keep up this charade when it was hurting Ellie and stopping her from being there for her?

She squared her shoulders and looked Jasmine in the eyes. "I'm her girlfriend, so I'll drive her home. Period."

The emergency department was never a quiet place, but for once, all sound except for the beeping of cardiac monitors and the rush of blood through Regina's ears seemed to stop.

Every nurse, doctor, and staff member of both the day and night shift gaped at her.

Ellie looked even more stunned than their colleagues.

Then Jasmine laughed. "Maybe I'm the one who hit my head. I could have sworn you just said—"

"I did," Regina said.

Jasmine's gaze darted to Ellie. "What the hell, Ellie? Is that true? Dr. Mc…um, Dr. Novak is your girlfriend?" She squeaked out the last word.

A deep flush spread across Ellie's face. Even the tips of her ears took on a bright scarlet hue. "Um, yes," she whispered. Then she glanced at Regina. "Yes, she is," she repeated more loudly.

"See?" one of the nursing assistants whispered to another. "I told you it wasn't just for the auction."

Regina stiffened. Having her personal life out there for everyone to gossip about made her skin crawl, but she would learn to bear it if it meant being there for Ellie.

"How long has this been going on?" Jasmine asked.

Okay, this was going too far! Ellie being her girlfriend was all most of these people needed to know. Regina clapped her hands—just once—but the sound reverberated through the ED. "Don't you have work to do? There are patients to be cared for, people! And if those of you whose shift ended don't want to go home, I'm sure we can find you some work!"

Reluctantly, the staff dispersed until only Jasmine remained. "How long?" she repeated.

Ellie ducked her head. Her ears were still stained crimson. "Two weeks and three days since we finally admitted we wanted to date for real."

"Two weeks…? Christ!" Jasmine tugged on her ponytail, which had come undone, but only created more of a mess. "So all those times when I complained about her stealing our pens or not cleaning up her mess after a lac repair, you just nodded along instead of telling me I'm going on and on about your girlfriend?"

"Jazzy…" Ellie reached out and touched her friend's forearm. "It's not like I didn't want to tell you. I just—"

"I was the one who insisted on keeping it out of the ED," Regina said, not wanting Ellie to be blamed.

Jasmine threw a dark look at Regina. "I can imagine."

"Hey!" Ellie said sharply. "She had her reasons, okay? And if I was okay with it, it's not for you to judge her."

Jasmine regarded her for several seconds, then inflated her cheeks and noisily blew out the air. "This will take some getting used to."

"I know," Ellie said softly. "For all of us. But for the record, you can still complain when she steals our pens or leaves a mess for us nurses to clean up."

Regina stopped herself from telling them that if she didn't clean up after a lac repair, she probably had a very good reason—like being called to an emergency. This wasn't the moment to discuss it. "Come on, ladies. Let's go grab our bags and get out of here."

She kept an eye on Ellie as they went to the locker room. Her gait seemed steady, but Regina stayed by her side anyway, just in case.

When they passed exam room three on their way out, Ellie peeked at the closed curtain. For a second, the panic she must have felt when the patient had attacked her flashed across her face.

Fuck it! Regina reached over and took Ellie's hand, lacing their fingers together in a tight, protective grip.

Ellie's hand went limp in hers as she stared at Regina, then a smile swept away the expression of panic and she squeezed back.

Jasmine's gaze rested on their joined hands as she walked with them to the staff parking lot. "You know, you'd better tell your secret admirer from the cafeteria that you're off the market, Ellie."

Regina frowned at her. "Ellie's got a secret admirer?"

"Seems like you're not the only CMC staff member who can't resist her charms. Why else would someone keep arranging for her to get the good hot chocolate—and pay for it too?"

Ah. That secret admirer. Regina hid a grin.

Ellie tugged Regina closer by their joined hands and leaned her shoulder against hers. "I have a feeling my secret admirer already knows."

An hour later, Ellie was safely tucked into bed—and into Regina's arms—and her mind was finally catching up with the events of the day.

"I can't believe what just happened," she murmured against the bare skin of Regina's shoulder. "I'm still in shock."

Regina trailed her fingertips across Ellie's cheek with a tenderness that none of their colleagues would have ever believed she was capable of. "I can imagine," she whispered. "I bet it was scary. If I were the CEO of CMC, every nurse would have their own security guard following them around. You'd never get a single scratch while at work again." Her passionate growl vibrated through Ellie.

"Um, I didn't mean the attack. That was scary, yeah, but what shocked me even more was you declaring that you're my girlfriend—in front of practically every single staff member!" She tried to lift up on her elbow to study Regina's face, then flinched when pain flared through her arm. "I bet that was scary too."

Regina opened her mouth as if about to deny it, but then her chest lifted and fell beneath a big breath. "It was. But actually not as scary as I thought. Somehow, I had made it into this huge thing in my mind. I was convinced that it would be like that night Riley died all over again… that everyone would look at me differently once they knew this one thing about my private life."

"And I think you were right," Ellie said quietly. "They did."

Regina sighed. "I know. But I don't care."

Ellie slipped her hand beneath the covers and gently poked her. "Liar."

Regina covered her hand with her own, trapping it against her side. "All right, I hate that we are probably the topic of conversation in the break room and around the nurses' station right now. But you know what? I'll learn to deal with it. What I couldn't deal with was letting you out of my sight after you got hurt. Compared to that, our colleagues knowing suddenly seemed insignificant." She stroked Ellie's fingers. "Sorry it took me so long to figure that out."

Ellie stared at her. "A public declaration and an apology from Dr. Regina Novak on the same day?"

Regina's laughter jostled Ellie as if she were lying on a water bed. "I know! But don't get used to it. Since I'm almost always right, I expect I won't have to apologize again for the next decade or so."

Giddiness bubbled up inside Ellie, but she tamped it down. Regina clearly hadn't realized what she had just said or at least she hadn't meant it as a statement that she expected their relationship to last that long.

"But I do," she mumbled against Regina's skin.

Regina lifted her head from the pillow. "You do what?"

"I do expect a certain doctor to apologize if she fails to bring her favorite patient breakfast in bed tomorrow morning."

Regina arched her brows. "Breakfast in bed? I don't think your insurance covers that."

Ellie grinned. "Oh, but you do admit I'm your favorite?"

"Well," Regina drawled, "it was a close call between you and Mrs. Dod—"

Ellie stopped her from finishing the sentence by kissing her.

Chapter 32

Regina kicked the door shut with her heel and followed Ellie into the house.

Wally rushed over from the living room, nose in the air.

Since Ellie had her hands full with the pizza they had picked up on their way home, she couldn't pet him right away.

So he ran to Regina, yipping and yowling as if he hadn't seen her in months even though she had spent every night at Ellie's place since the attack a week ago.

"You know, I could almost become jealous of my dog greeting you first if it weren't so cute," Ellie said.

"He's all right—for a dog." Regina tried to play it cool and pretend to be annoyed at the doggie kisses. She pulled her hand away from Wally's eager tongue. "Ugh! I never thought I would ever say that, but...enough licking!"

A lovely flush swept up Ellie's neck, and she glanced left and right as if making sure her sister wasn't home before she murmured, "That's not what you said last night."

Regina gave her a sensual look. "I wasn't in bed with Wally last night."

Before Ellie could reply, Regina's phone chirped. She pulled it from her pocket as they walked to the kitchen. "Finally! Kayla sent an update!"

Ellie set the pizza box down and turned toward her. "And?"

Regina read the text, which consisted of her three favorite words: *You were right.* She pumped her fist. "I was right! It's pulmonary embolism."

Just before shift change, a woman had come in with acute respiratory distress, tachycardia, and a red, swollen calf. Her GP had insisted it couldn't be a pulmonary embolism because she had IVC filters in place that would catch any blood clots migrating from her leg veins since she had a history of them and couldn't receive blood thinners.

The resident who had assessed her had agreed, but Regina had insisted on a pulmonary CT. The results hadn't been in yet when they had left the hospital.

"But how is that possible?" Ellie asked.

"My hunch was right. The IVC filters had migrated."

"Wow. You're brilliant." Ellie stepped up to her, wrapped her arms around Regina, and pressed a kiss to her jaw.

The brush of Ellie's soft lips made Regina tingle all over, but she resisted the urge to kiss her. There was something she wanted to hear first. "Come on. Say it."

"Say what?" Ellie answered.

"You know what."

"Um, competency is sexy?"

Regina nipped Ellie's ear and slid her hands beneath Ellie's shirt. "That too, but it's not what I want to hear." She dug her fingers into Ellie's bare sides and tickled her, making her squeal with laughter. "Out with them!"

"Out with what?" Ellie gasped out. She tried to squirm away, but her back was to the counter, so there was nowhere to go.

"My favorite three little words." Regina slid her tickling fingers toward Ellie's stomach.

A burst of breathless laughter escaped Ellie. "I love you!" she blurted out.

Regina froze with her fingers against Ellie's warm skin. Of course, she had known what was happening between them wasn't just great sex or casual romance. Ellie had no poker face at all, so it was a miracle they had been able to hide that they were dating from their co-workers for weeks. Every touch, every look revealed her feelings. But hearing it out loud still squeezed the air from Regina's lungs and left her dizzy. "Um, I was talking about *you were right,*" was all she could think of to say.

Panic flashed across Ellie's face. "Oh, crap. I'm sorry. I didn't mean to blurt that out. I mean, it's true, but it's not fair to say it when you might not be ready to—"

"Fair?" Regina said. "It's not like you can help it. After all, I'm smart, sexy, and—"

"Modest."

"Yes, that too, but what I wanted to say is smart, sexy, and completely in love with you too."

For a moment, Ellie looked as if she would burst into tears. Then a beaming smile spread across her face. "You are?"

Regina nodded and tried to pretend the big lump in her throat wasn't there. She wrinkled her nose. "It's almost disgusting how much. I nearly got you flowers yesterday."

Ellie laughed. "No, we definitely can't have that. Instead of flowers, can I...hear it?" she asked in a whisper.

"Hear what?"

"*My* favorite three little words."

Regina swallowed. It wasn't as if she had never said those words to other girlfriends before, but suddenly, she was no longer sure she had ever truly been in love. Whatever she had felt before had been nothing like this. When she looked at Ellie, the emotions that bubbled up made her feel completely defenseless yet at the same time so strong she could take on the entire world.

Ellie looked at her with her big, brown eyes, not even blinking.

Regina slid her hands to Ellie's hips to steady her because Ellie was swaying. Or maybe it was the floor beneath them. "I love you."

Tears gleamed in Ellie's eyes, but she was grinning as if she had won the lottery. Her warm breath washed over Regina as Ellie leaned up and whispered, "I love you too."

With a groan, Regina dipped her head and captured Ellie's lips with her own. She couldn't stop kissing Ellie—her mouth, her cheeks, her throat.

Just when her lips reached the edge of Ellie's V-neck shirt, a key jingled in the lock, and the front door creaked open. "Is that pizza I smell?" Vickie's voice drifted over.

A growl of frustration escaped Regina as she hesitantly lifted her mouth off Ellie's skin and straightened. For an EMT, Vickie really had the worst timing.

Ellie let her head fall to Regina's shoulder and groaned.

"Later," Regina whispered huskily before taking a step back from her.

Vickie appeared in the doorway. Her gaze went from the forgotten pizza box to where they were awkwardly standing in the middle of the kitchen. "Seriously? You can't even keep your hands off each other long enough not to let the pizza get cold?"

Ellie rubbed her earlobe. "No, we were just…um…"

"Brainstorming ideas for how to get out of having to do the auction again next year," Regina threw in.

Vickie opened the cabinet and took out plates. "Did you come up with any bright ideas?"

"Hmm, yes, a really brilliant one." Regina didn't look at her, though. Her full attention was on Ellie. "According to Kayla, being single is a requirement for the bachelors and bachelorettes. So all we have to do to get out of it is to make sure we're still together by the time Valentine's Day comes around."

Ellie let out a dramatic sigh, but her eyes shone with happiness. "I guess I have to keep you, then. After the auction-mandated dates I've been through this year, I really don't want to go through it all again."

"Hey! Are you implying the dates Bachelorette Number Twelve supplied were less than spectacular?"

"Well, the first one ended with a trip to the emergency department, and—"

"True," Regina said before Ellie could mention how the last one had ended. "You'd better keep me, then."

"I will," Ellie said softly.

Vickie rolled her eyes. "Great. You keep each other; I'll keep the pizza." She grabbed the box and raced away with it.

Chaos broke out as Regina and Ellie gave chase, with Wally hot on their heels, barking.

How had her orderly world that consisted of nothing but work and disc golf turned into this?

But as they tackled Vickie to the couch in a show of excellent team work, Regina knew she didn't want to change a thing.

Epilogue

Ten months later

Ellie stood on her tiptoes on top of an orange plastic chair and stretched to the right as far as she could when a pair of sneakers squeaked to a stop behind her.

"What did I tell you about hanging paper hearts?" a cool voice cut through the background noise in the emergency department.

Ellie froze, then dropped to her heels and lowered the string of paper hearts she'd been about to hang. When she looked over her shoulder, a familiar sight greeted her.

Regina stood with her athletic arms folded across her scrub top and glared at Ellie. The tiniest hint of a smile playing around her lips ruined the intimidating effect.

"Yeah, yeah, I know," Ellie said with an affectionate shake of her head. "There's no room in the ED for paper hearts, with it being the least romantic place on earth and all."

"Actually…" Regina scratched her neck and glanced left and right as if to make sure everyone was focused on their own work and not listening in on their conversation. "I changed my mind on that. I was talking about workplace safety. I just read a study that said climbing on chairs is the leading cause of accidents in the workplace."

Ellie turned on the chair to face her. "I disagree."

A frown line appeared between Regina's brows, but Ellie wasn't sure if it was because she had objected to Regina's reasoning or because she had moved around on top of the chair.

"You disagree with a peer-reviewed, scientifically sound study?" Regina asked.

Ellie nodded. "They didn't include all relevant objects in their sample."

Regina arched her brows. "What relevant objects, pray tell, did they fail to include?"

"Me." Ellie tapped her chest, then wavered as she nearly lost her balance.

Cursing under her breath, Regina clutched Ellie's hips and lifted her down.

Ellie's knees went weak as she slid down Regina's body. "See? This is my workplace safety issue number one."

Regina set her down but didn't let go of her hips. "What is?"

"You!"

"Me?" Regina faked innocence, but her smirk revealed that she knew exactly what effect she had on Ellie's knees.

"Yeah, you. You make my legs all wobbly."

Regina's smirk grew. "Well, for the sake of workplace safety, I'd better remove myself from your presence and go back to work."

"Oh, no." Ellie playfully grabbed a handful of Regina's scrub top at her hip and held on so she couldn't move away. "If you don't want me to climb on a chair, I need a tall person to hang the paper hearts."

Regina looked as if Ellie had asked her to lick the hospital floor. "You want *me* to hang paper hearts?"

"Yes, please. For the sake of love…um, workplace safety." She pressed both ends of the string into Regina's hands.

Regina huffed out an overly loud sigh. She turned, lifted up on her tiptoes, reached up as far as she could, and pinned one end of the string to the wall. Then she repeated it with the other end before facing Ellie. "Happy now?"

The paper hearts hung a little lower than last year, but then again, maybe that was only fitting since love had been just out of reach for them back then. Ellie smiled and looked her in the eyes. "Very happy."

Regina's impassive doctor mask wavered. "Me too. But next time—"

"Get a step stool?" Ellie finished for her.

Regina shook her head. "Ask me for help before you climb on the plastic furniture." She pressed a quick kiss to Ellie's cheek—further endangering workplace safety—and strode toward the treatment rooms.

If you enjoyed this book, check out Jae's Fair Oaks Series to read more about the supporting characters you just met.

In book 1, *Perfect Rhythm*, burned-out pop star Leo falls in love with asexual small-town nurse Holly.

In book 2, *Not the Marrying Kind*, bakery owner Sasha falls in love with florist Ashley, thanks to an epic food fight.

Both books can be read as standalone novels.

Other Books from Ylva Publishing

www.ylva-publishing.com

Perfect Rhythm
Jae

ISBN: 978-3-95533-862-6
Length: 298 pages (107,000 words)

Pop star Leontyne Blake is over love and women falling for her image. When she heads home to be near her sick father, she meets small-town nurse Holly, an asexual woman who has no interest in dating, sex, or Leo's fame. Can their tentative friendship develop into something more despite their diverse expectations?

A lesbian romance about finding the perfect rhythm between two very different people.

Not the Marrying Kind
Jae

ISBN: 978-3-96324-194-9
Length: 314 pages (113,000 words)

Small-town florist Ashley loves creating wedding bouquets. Her own love life is far from blossoming since she's stuck in the closet.

Sasha isn't faring much better. Her bakery keeps her too busy for romance anyway.

When the town's first lesbian wedding forces them to work together, Sasha is soon tempting more than just Ash's sweet tooth.

What else is on the menu in this delicious lesbian romance?

L.A. Metro
RJ Nolan

ISBN: 978-3-95533-041-5
Length: 349 pages (97,000 words)

Dr. Kimberly Donovan's life is in shambles. After her medical ethics are questioned, first her family, then her closeted lover, the Chief of the ER, betray her. Determined to make a fresh start, she flees to California and L.A. Metropolitan Hospital. When she meets Jess McKenna, L.A. Metro's Chief of the ER, the attraction is immediate. Can either woman overcome her past to make a future together?

Major Surgery
Lola Keeley

ISBN: 978-3-96324-145-1
Length: 198 pages (69,000 words)

Surgeon and department head Veronica has life perfectly ordered… until the arrival of a new Head of Trauma. Cassie is a brash ex-army surgeon, all action and sharp edges, not interested in rules or playing nice with icy Veronica. However when they're forced to work together to uncover a scandal, things get a little heated in surprising ways.

A lesbian romance about cutting to the heart of matters.

About Jae

Jae grew up amidst the vineyards of southern Germany. She spent her childhood with her nose buried in a book, earning her the nickname "professor." The writing bug bit her at the age of eleven. Since 2006, she has been writing mostly in English.

She used to work as a psychologist but gave up her day job in December 2013 to become a full-time writer and a part-time editor. As far as she's concerned, it's the best job in the world.

When she's not writing, she likes to spend her time reading, indulging her ice cream and office supply addictions, and watching way too many crime shows.

CONNECT WITH JAE
Website: www.jae-fiction.com
E-Mail: jae@jae-fiction.com

Bachelorette Number Twelve
© 2024 by Jae

ISBN: 978-3-96324-862-7

Available in e-book and paperback formats.

Published by Ylva Publishing, legal entity of Ylva Verlag, e.Kfr.

Ylva Verlag, e.Kfr.
Owner: Astrid Ohletz
Am Kirschgarten 2
65830 Kriftel
Germany

www.ylva-publishing.com

First edition: 2024

Credits
Edited by Claire Jarrett
Cover Design and Print Layout by Streetlight Graphics

Printed in Great Britain
by Amazon

36860468R00209